...and it burned twice as hot.

P9-CSV-870

Praise for Christine Feehan's Game novels

PREDATORY GAME

"Feehan's at the top of her game with this explosive, scintillating novel." —*Romantic Times*

DEADLY GAME

"I loved this one and I'll bet you will too." —*Fresh Fiction*

"The fastest-paced, most action-packed, gut-wrenching, adrenaline-driven ride I've ever experienced."
—*Romance Junkies*

CONSPIRACY GAME

"Love and danger are a winning combination in [*Conspiracy Game*]." —*Booklist*

NIGHT GAME

"Suspenseful . . . captivating." —*Publishers Weekly*

"The sensual scenes rival the steaming Bayou. A perfect 10." —*Romance Reviews Today*

SHADOW GAME

"Erotically charged." —*Booklist*

"Christine Feehan delivers action, adventure and passion."
—*Romantic Times*

MIND GAME

"Sultry and suspenseful." —*Publishers Weekly*

"Delightfully unique." —*Midwest Book Review*

BURNING WILD

CHRISTINE FEEHAN

JOVE BOOKS, NEW YORK

THE BERKLEY PUBLISHING GROUP
Published by the Penguin Group
Penguin Group (USA) Inc.
375 Hudson Street, New York, New York 10014, USA
Penguin Group (Canada), 90 Eglinton Avenue East, Suite 700, Toronto, Ontario M4P 2Y3, Canada
(a division of Pearson Penguin Canada Inc.)
Penguin Books Ltd., 80 Strand, London WC2R 0RL, England
Penguin Group Ireland, 25 St. Stephen's Green, Dublin 2, Ireland (a division of Penguin Books Ltd.)
Penguin Group (Australia), 250 Camberwell Road, Camberwell, Victoria 3124, Australia
(a division of Pearson Australia Group Pty. Ltd.)
Penguin Books India Pvt. Ltd., 11 Community Centre, Panchsheel Park, New Delhi—110 017, India
Penguin Group (NZ), 67 Apollo Drive, Rosedale, North Shore 0632, New Zealand
(a division of Pearson New Zealand Ltd.)
Penguin Books (South Africa) (Pty.) Ltd., 24 Sturdee Avenue, Rosebank, Johannesburg 2196,
South Africa

Penguin Books Ltd., Registered Offices: 80 Strand, London WC2R 0RL, England

This is a work of fiction. Names, characters, places, and incidents either are the product of the author's imagination or are used fictitiously, and any resemblance to actual persons, living or dead, business establishments, events, or locales is entirely coincidental. The publisher does not have any control over and does not assume any responsibility for author or third-party websites or their content.

BURNING WILD

A Jove Book / published by arrangement with the author

PRINTING HISTORY
Jove mass-market edition / May 2009

Copyright © 2009 by Christine Feehan.
Excerpt from *Hidden Currents* copyright © 2009 by Christine Feehan.
Cover art by Dan O'Leary.
Cover handlettering by Ron Zinn.
Cover design by George Long.
Text design by Kristin del Rosario.

ISBN: 978-0-515-14623-3

JOVE®
Jove Books are published by The Berkley Publishing Group,
a division of Penguin Group (USA) Inc.,
375 Hudson Street, New York, New York 10014.
JOVE® is a registered trademark of Penguin Group (USA) Inc.
The "J" design is a trademark belonging to Penguin Group (USA) Inc.

PRINTED IN THE UNITED STATES OF AMERICA

10 9 8 7 6 5 4 3 2

For Jack and Lisset,
who know what love is

For My Readers

Be sure to go to http://www.christinefeehan.com/
members/ to sign up for my PRIVATE book announcement list and download the FREE ebook of *Dark Des-
serts*, a book of delicious dessert recipes compiled by
my wonderful readers. Please feel free to e-mail me at
Christine@christinefeehan.com. I would love to hear
from you.

Acknowledgments

Thank you so much, Jack and Lisset, for the hours spent with me teaching me about proper bodyguard procedure. You taught me so much and really added to the realism of the scenes. I can only apologize and acknowledge the creative license taken in the party scene and hope the rest meets with your approval. All mistakes are solely mine.

Thanks to Brian Feehan, for his dedication to detail, and for the hours spent discussing scenes even in the middle of the night when I couldn't put it down. And, of course, thanks to Domini, who gave up a few weekends to help me meet the all-important deadlines. But mostly, thanks to my husband, who always, *always*, sees me through every book. You know what you mean to me.

1

EARLIEST MEMORY

HIS environment was warm and cozy. He wasn't alone. He could hear the other inside him, whispering soft little growls and encouragement. The need for freedom, the promise of a life that had been lived one cycle already and had been incredible. And then the squeezing came, hard shoves, the walls of his cocoon closing around him, twisting in waves to push him out, to expel him from the warmth of his home into cold air and bright lights. At once scents assailed him. He couldn't sort out all the different smells, but the other could. Blood. People. Hospital. The other remembered the smells even when he didn't.

He felt hands on him, shaking him, poking, a sharp prick. He pried open his eyes and looked around this new environment.

"My God, Ryan, he looks like a skinned rat. He's so ugly. He's skinny and useless to us." The voice was resentful, filled with loathing.

He understood the words, or maybe the other did, but

he knew the woman was talking about him. *He* looked like a rat. And rat wasn't good, not if that voice meant anything.

"Shh, Cathy," another voice cautioned. "Someone will hear."

"We can't take it home with us."

"We can't leave it here," the deeper voice said.

"On the way home, I'm finding a Dumpster," the higher-pitched voice hissed. "I'm not getting stuck with that ugly thing."

"Don't be ridiculous, Cathy," Ryan said. "We can't take a chance that we'll be caught. We'll take him home and hire someone to look after him. You'll never have to see him."

"This is your fault. Daddy warned me not to marry you. He said your genes weren't strong enough to produce one of the special ones. I didn't want to get pregnant and have that thing growing in my body, but you insisted I had to carry it. Now *you* deal with it."

"Fine. I'm naming him Jake, after your grandfather." There was malice in Ryan's voice. "Your father never did think I was good enough, and he won't like having my whelp named after his father instead of him."

"Name it any damn thing you want, just keep it away from me."

The hatred and loathing in the cold voice gave the infant—newly named Jake Bannaconni—chills, but he refused to cry.

TWO YEARS

THE sharp pointed shoe caught Jake in the stomach and he doubled over. He should have been faster. He had the reflexes. The other warned him, but he had wanted to be held, had gone looking for her. She was his mother, after all. The mothers on the television and out in the play yard held their sons, but she kicked him hard, her voice screaming for Agnes.

"Get this horrid brat out of my sight. Ugly little rat." Cathy yanked him up by one arm, held him dangling in the air and beat him with her stiletto heel, smashing the shoe into him over and over, his face, his belly, his groin, his thighs, anywhere she could land a blow on his squirming body. Rage and hatred fused together on her cold face.

Deep inside, he felt something wild unfurl, and his fingers curled under, as did his toes. The other hissed to him, cautioned him: *Take it. Let her hit you. Hide what you are. She wants what you are. Hide. Hide.* He breathed away the fire building in his belly and the itch running under his skin.

Mommies weren't like this on television or in the movies. There was no cuddling. There were no hugs and kisses. Slaps and kicks were all he would get from his mother. He watched her on television sometimes, at the parties and fundraisers. She looked so different, smiling for the cameras, clinging to Ryan's arm, stroking his face as if she loved him so much. But behind closed doors there was cruelty and hatred and deceit from both of them. Over time, they taught him to separate fantasy from reality.

FIVE YEARS

"WE absolutely can't keep a governess, or whatever you call that woman, who beats the crap out of our kid. She put out cigarettes on him," Ryan complained. "There are burn marks on his hands. Sooner or later one of the tutors will see and report it."

Jake stayed quiet, very still. He'd perfected the art of sliding silently into a room without their knowledge and listening to the conversation. Most of what they said was still over his head—discussions about business and taking over companies—but he understood the basic truth that lay at the foundation of every meeting. Money was important. Power was important. They had it and he needed it. Agnes wasn't putting cigarettes out on him. Cathy was. Her lovers did sometimes, just to please her. She could make them do anything she wanted no matter how cruel or humiliating. He knew them by sight, by scent, and someday he would ruin them. Money. Power. That was what they had and he needed.

"Nobody cares, Ryan," Cathy said, annoyed with the conversation.

"Someone is going to see those burns and a reporter will get hold of it. We'll be front-page news." Ryan swung around, pointing a finger at her, his voice hardening. "I let you do what you want within reason, Cathy, but you aren't going to ruin us with your senseless little games."

Cathy stabbed her cigarette into the tray. "Really?" Both eyebrows shot up. A crafty expression crossed her face and Jake's stomach tightened. "We might get some great publicity, Ryan, if we can work it right. Our little boy beaten and abused by a trusted member of our household. Tears in front of the camera, me leaning on you. We photograph so well together. A close-up of our child in the hospital looking frail. We could run with that for a long time. I could host a charity event for battered children. It would open more possibilities and get us some great press."

"Agnes will be prosecuted and put in jail. She knows quite a bit about us."

"Don't be stupid. If we do this, Agnes has to disappear."

"Cathy, you can't be serious."

Cathy rolled her eyes. "You're such a sniveling coward, Ryan. Do you think I'm going to let her talk to the police? Or to the press? Hardly."

Ryan turned his head slowly, something feral and predatory in his eyes. Cathy stiffened and lowered her eyes. "We have a very good arrangement, my dear, but perhaps you need another lesson in respecting your husband."

Jake felt his heart hammering loudly. He had never considered his father to be dangerous, but that look, that small movement, just a flexing of muscles, showed that beneath the seeming apathy, Ryan was every bit as cruel as Cathy, or even more so. He'd given himself away.

Cathy pushed a hand through her hair. "No, no, of course not, honey. I'm sorry."

She was genuinely afraid. Jake, hidden as he was, could scent her fear permeating the room.

The tension drained from Ryan and he forced a smile, but his eyes were flat and cold. "How are you going to keep the kid from talking?"

Cathy visibly relaxed, and, even in the shadows, Jake felt the impact of evil. "He won't talk. I can guarantee that. I have to plan this very carefully. We need a few warning signs, some things we can have on record that we discussed with the doctors, expressed our concerns, but no one can substantiate." She rubbed her hands together. "This is good, Ryan. Maybe that skinny little rat will be worth something to us after all."

Instinctively Jake knew he was in for trouble. He had already made up his mind to survive, to beat them at their own game. He could be stronger. He'd seen how to do it. He had to be smarter and faster and more ruthless than any of them. He couldn't stop them yet, but he could endure, and that too would strengthen him.

He opened his hand and looked at the burns there. He had *let* her and her friend put out their cigarettes on him. He had been fast enough to get away, but he hadn't been stupid about it, and he needed to remember this one moment, to mark the occasion so he would know he could be smarter, use his brains to defeat them. Down in his room, when he was certain he was alone, he took out a knife and slowly drew it over his thigh, making the first of many marks to prove to himself, to remind himself, that he had deliberately taken their punishment, that he had *allowed* it.

SIX YEARS

JAKE watched helplessly as Cathy and Ryan killed Agnes. They took tremendous pleasure in it. And they hurt her for a long time before they killed her. He was tied up and forced to watch as they systematically beat to death the woman who had raised him. Agnes had been cruel at times and apathetic at others, but at least she'd taken care of him. He knew what was coming next, because Cathy had told him what would happen to him. She'd smiled as she told him.

When they were through beating him, Jake spent the next two weeks in the hospital, and he never once denied the allegations brought against his former nanny. She'd disappeared after viciously beating their son, Cathy and Ryan claimed.

The police tried to question him, but he was broken, his bones and, even for a time, his spirit. He could only lie in bed, helpless, pain shaking him, cruelty destroying him, remaining absolutely silent, knowing they would kill him if he said anything. He wasn't strong enough yet. He had to push harder. He had to dig deeper. He had so much to learn and, lying in bed while his ribs and arms healed, he had lots of time to formulate a plan.

The reporters came and went. The doctors and nurses felt sorry for Cathy as she quietly and beautifully wept for the cameras and her audience, clinging to her handsome, adoring husband. She played out her role, lavishing attention on the unresponsive boy, her money and her celebrity affording her prime-time coverage. She sought out every possible advantage, leading charities and organizations as long as she could headline and get the television time. Everyone believed her, not because of the evidence of Jake's body, but because of the money and her acting skills. Jake had to admit she was mesmerizing. She could get almost anyone to do what she wanted. He needed those skills now that he knew what he was dealing with.

EIGHT YEARS

CATHY was nervous and upset. Jake Fenton, her grandfather, was coming for another visit. He always insisted on talking alone with Jake, and Cathy didn't like it. She despised her grandfather and even talked about trying to have him killed, but she was afraid of him. Young Jake didn't understand why she was afraid. Fenton lived several states away in Texas, but she always dressed Jake just so and acted completely different, as if she cared about him in front of his grandfather.

She hissed instructions to young Jake, reminding him to mind his manners, to keep his mouth shut, not to answer any questions about Cathy or Ryan or their personal lives. She threatened him with dark punishments if he dared disobey her. Jake found the entire matter of his great-grandfather quite interesting. What did the old man have that frightened Cathy? What did she want from him that made her try to look so respectable and sweet?

Fenton never bought her lies. He smiled and made nice with Cathy and Ryan, but Jake could smell the pretense flowing from one to the other and he could see the contempt in the old man's piercing gaze. Fenton always insisted he talk alone with young Jake, and Jake enjoyed the long conversations, but the aftermath was always hell. Cathy and Ryan used a whip on him to beat him into submission and as an attempt to force every word of the conversation between the old man and their son out of him. Jake became very adept at making up stories and telling them with a straight face, looking the two of them right in the eyes. And then he would go to his room and mark his victory permanently into his skin, the pain clearing the rage and anger from his belly, replacing it with cold resolve.

TEN YEARS

BOOKS. The huge library in his home, which others rarely entered, was a treasure beyond measure. Jake spent most of his time in the library reading in the quiet haven of the room his parents never visited. He read every book on the shelves, regardless of subject, his photographic memory soaking up the knowledge and details and filing them away for future reference.

He learned to stay silent and in the background. He'd slip away from Bridget, the latest nanny, and pad silently through the house, finding each occupant's location. He'd sneak up on them until he was close enough to touch them, but never let them know he was near.

He discovered insider information on stocks. Ryan was extremely intelligent and adept at knowing other people's weaknesses. Jake learned a lot by watching him, the small smile that others took at face value, but that Jake came to know signaled Ryan was about to strike and strike hard. Descended from a powerful family with tremendous banking connections, Ryan's expertise in handling the diversity of companies they owned and his utilization of his political connections were both extremely valuable. Jake's conversations with Grandfather Fenton about stocks and bonds and the financial books he'd read in the library helped him to understand and assimilate the information he gathered when spying on his father.

Today, as Jake crept though the house, he found Cathy with her personal trainer in the exercise room. They rarely used the equipment so much as they used one another. He learned a lot in that room and then further explored the subject with the books he found in the library and the information on the computer. Sex was simply another weapon to be used, like money, to gain power. He resolved to learn everything he could about sex so he could be really good at it. There was no point in having a weapon at his disposal unless he could wield it effectively.

Jake began to work out, to use the powerful muscles running beneath the skin in his thin arms and legs. He used every machine, studying the exercise manuals and VHS tapes carefully and following the instructions, careful never to get caught. Each day, every day, Jake prowled his family's home, observing, listening, reading . . . learning more and more. Everything he filed away, all for one purpose.

One day, when the time was right, he was going to beat his parents at their own game. He would take over every single one of their companies, ruin them financially, expose them to the world for what they were. He would make absolutely certain they knew that the child they had beaten so often, thinking him a victim, was really the strong one, really the predator.

THIRTEEN YEARS

JAKE stood very still as Josiah Trent, his parents' best friend and sometime partner, walked around him, sniffing the air. Deep inside, the other reacted, roaring with rage, raking at Jake, closer to the surface than he'd ever been, demanding to be set free. His skin itched. His muscles ached. His jaw and the inside of his mouth felt small, as if there was no room for his teeth, but he held on grimly, pushing at the other to stay still.

Jake's mind was strong and disciplined now, and instinctively he knew he was in more danger than he'd ever been before. Trent was looking for the other. Those sharp eyes and that bulbous nose wanted to find the beast living inside of Jake. Cathy's breathing was ragged and eager, and her body seemed aroused as Trent walked in circles around Jake.

Jake had made one too many mistakes, moving too fast, jumping too high, showing his emerging skills rather than hiding behind the facade of the weak, useless bookworm his mother always considered him to be. He had known he couldn't ever let them become suspicious, but now he had slipped up and they'd brought in Trent, hoping that Jake was, after all, what they had bred him to be. He would rather die than let them know the truth. That would be allowing them to win.

He clenched his aching teeth and endured the poking and prodding from Trent. The man was a giant, with powerful muscles and glaring eyes. He looked at everyone as if they were beneath him, especially Jake. He made a sound of disgust.

"Useless," he pronounced. "He's useless, Cathy. I told you not to bother having a child with that gutless wonder you married."

"He has money, connections and the right bloodline," she hissed. "And you didn't do any better. I don't see that your daughter has any special talents."

"Better than this disgusting little runt," Trent snapped and shoved at Jake. "At least she can produce a whelp eventually. I'll find her the right man."

Jake allowed himself to stumble, savage triumph nearly

shaking him. Josiah Trent had dismissed him, never once suspecting the other who raged so close to the surface. Trent wasn't nearly as powerful as Cathy and Ryan believed him to be. His was the other family with the "superior" bloodline, yet he could no more sniff out the truth than Cathy and Ryan could with him living right under their roof. It was a huge lesson. Trent was all bluff, his demeanor and act of superiority fooling even the two people Jake viewed as powerful.

"We need a shifter," Trent said. "A true shifter with the nose and the cunning for business, not some scrawny little wimp who everyone will walk on."

A shifter. At last Jake knew what they were after. He had to find the meaning, and if a shifter was that important to them, he had to make certain they never suspected that he was one—if he was. He would spend every hour in the library hunting down the meaning until he knew exactly what he was looking for. He would learn about his other and what he could do, why he was so important to them.

Cathy ran her hand suggestively down Trent's arm. "Maybe we should have tried together." Her voice purred and invited.

Trent looked her up and down, scorn in his eyes, contempt curling his lips. "Not if this is the kind of whelp you produce." Abruptly he spun away and stalked from the room.

Cathy turned on Jake, furious that he'd witnessed her humiliation, furious all over again that he wasn't the child she had set out to create. She swung her open hand at his face. Reflexes made him jump out of the way. Instantly her face darkened. Cathy was furious and Jake could smell her hatred. The fetid scent permeated her entire body, right along with her cloying perfume. He had moved away too fast to allow her to slap his face, his reflexes taking over before he could stop them. Most of the time he stood stoically under her assault, but sometimes he gave himself away without thinking.

Now he knew he had enraged her when he'd dodged her too quickly. Deep inside, the other stretched and unsheathed claws, fighting for supremacy even when they both knew he had to stay hidden. The other was the special prize Cathy had wanted all along. Jake was certain if she ever found out what was inside of him, he'd be locked away with no chance of escaping, ever. He pushed the beast down, willing to take Cathy's fury, her punishment, to look weak and frightened in order to carry out his plan. He wasn't that far away from success. A few more years, a lot more knowledge, and he'd break free.

"What did he say, Cathy?" Ryan stepped quietly into the room and Jake's heart began to pound. There was a look on his face, that small secret smile that terrified Jake now.

"This runt dared to be disrespectful to me," Cathy snarled. "He's useless to us in every way, Ryan."

Jake found himself dragged down to his bedroom in the basement and tied to a pole where first Ryan caned him. And then, in her fury, Cathy took over beating him with the thick cane. The other snarled and fought him for supremacy until Jake was choking on the rumbles backing up in his throat. His skin itched worse than the blinding pain across his back and legs.

"Enough," Ryan eventually decreed. "You're going to kill him and we don't have Agnes to blame this time."

With one last vicious cut, Cathy threw the cane and swept out ahead of her husband, leaving Jake sagging, gasping for breath, unable to control the rising beast. Sliding his bound hands down the pole, he managed to drag the knife from inside his boot and cut the bonds around his wrist, and then he slashed a deep cut across his thigh. He had *allowed* them to beat him. It was *his* choice, not theirs. He was bigger, stronger, smarter, he just chose not to show them. Sobbing, he buried his face in the mattress, desperately trying to breathe through the pain.

His muscles contorted. The itch increased as something live moved under his skin. His fingers ached, his knuckles throbbed. He looked at his hands where knots formed, thick and aching, along the backs of his hands. The pads of his fingers hurt. His body bent forward and he went to the floor. He found himself on all fours, head down, jaw painful. His muscles contracted and locked, and once again his body contorted. His face felt funny, his jaw elongating, his teeth bursting through his gums.

Another sob escaped his throat, but it came out a rumbling growl. Tawny fur burst through the pores of his skin, and darker rosettes sprang along his back and legs. Roped muscles rippled beneath the pelt while his skull widened and thickened. Wildness rose in him and he recognized and embraced the gift, no longer afraid of it. He accepted his other half, opening himself so the other could consume him.

He thought he would disappear until he found he was not wholly human, not wholly leopard, but a separate entity altogether, with the characteristics of both and the ability to use his brain and the leopard's senses. A steel framework of muscles ran through his body and he stretched. His bones ached and cracked in his spine, and then became supple. His body was sore from the beating, from the change, but the strength pouring into him was worth every second of pain.

The leopard lifted his head and scented the air. He could hear the whisper of voices, smelled blood and evil, and he knew in that moment that he was ten times more dangerous than the two upstairs were—that he was capable of killing and that they had created a monster, never realizing what they were unleashing with their hatred and cruelty.

Jake shifted, falling naked to the floor, his back screaming in pain, hot tears flowing down his face, sobbing for the little boy he should have been and never would be. Afraid for what he had become and what he might do. He reached up and gripped the mattress, pulling his fingers across it, leaving long, thin tears from razor-sharp claws.

FIFTEEN YEARS

"IT'S good to see you, Jake," Jake Fenton said and held out his hand.

The smile was genuine. His great-grandfather really was happy to see him. Lies had a distinctive scent Jake had come to recognize. Jake Fenton lied when he smiled at Cathy or Ryan, but he always sought out young Jake and sat down to converse with him. Jake genuinely liked him and in a way it was frightening. The old man was the only person who was kind to him, or who ever seemed to care. And Jake scented death on him. He didn't want to care about Fenton, he didn't trust caring. He didn't trust anyone, but he couldn't help himself. He *liked* the old man. He enjoyed their brief times together even though it always meant a severe beating after he left.

Fenton frowned and turned Jake's hand over, examining his arms before Jake could pull away. "What the hell happened to you? How did you get all these scars, just since the last time I visited? And don't say you're clumsy, Jake. You aren't clumsy." The old man's eyes were shrewd.

Jake glanced around to make certain they were alone. He shouldn't have worried. He would have been able to catch the scent of his enemies had they been close. Cathy despised the old man and Ryan never went near him. There was secret pleasure in knowing his great-grandfather only came to visit him. Fenton lived in Texas and didn't really care for Chicago, but every now and then he'd take a trip to see Jake.

It was Fenton who insisted on the best tutors and it was Fenton who would talk openly about stocks and bonds with him. He insisted Jake learn languages from an early age and usually spoke to Jake in a variety of foreign languages, explaining to him that to do commerce in other countries, one had to know customs and languages. He spoke of his land and how he knew there was oil on it, but they'd been unable to find it. Cathy and Ryan made fun of him, calling the acreage "Fenton's Folly," but Jake loved hearing the excitement in the old man's voice when he spoke of finding the huge resource someday. Fenton wasn't as interested in the money as he was the actual thrill of finding new reserves. And that told Jake that Cathy and Ryan were wrong about the old man—he hadn't thrown his money away; he had so much he didn't need more.

"Jake, the scars? Is it that worthless son of a bitch Ryan? Or my granddaughter? She has a streak of cruelty in her. I never believed that nanny of yours beat you. I can't imagine Cathy not knowing everything that goes on in her household."

"Forget about it, Grandfather," Jake said quietly, his gaze meeting Fenton's. "I'm handling it."

The old man shook his head and dropped down into a chair, looking around the library, his gaze wandering from book to book. Jake already had learned the value of silence and just waited while Fenton obviously made a decision. When he looked up at Jake, he showed every one of his eighty-seven years.

"Have you heard anyone speaking of the leopard people?"

Jake's heart jumped, and he didn't answer right away,

afraid of a trap. He could smell lies and it occurred to him that his great-grandfather might be able to as well. "Tell me."

"You must never reveal any of what I'm about to tell you. Not to anyone. Especially not to your parents or the Trents."

Jake drew in a deep breath, his heart pounding hard. This was it. This was his moment to learn, to become more powerful. "I promise."

Fenton leaned forward and lowered his voice. "The leopard people aren't a myth any more than the oil on my property is. I *know* the oil is there even though I can't find it, just as I know there are shifters in our bloodline even though I can't shift. I met a true shifter once. They're a separate species, not fully human yet not fully animal either. They are both."

Jake moistened his lips. Did the old man know about him? Suspect? Was he looking to trick Jake? He pressed his lips together to keep silent, but his heart raced as his great-grandfather glanced at him sharply.

"There are a few shifters left in the Borneo rain forest, men and women who live with honor, who keep to the old ways. Find them, Jake. Learn from them. They are true to their nature, not the corrupt, twisted beings our bloodlines produce." He sighed heavily. "It's my grandfather's fault. He kidnapped a woman from the forest and forced her to marry him. In those days, women didn't have many rights and no one helped her. He had discovered the secret and knew that with the traits of the species, we could gain wealth and power. And he wanted it. He was ambitious and he wanted it." He hung his head, running his hand over his face. "Our bloodline carries the epitome of cruelty. You don't want to live like them. You must take care to keep yourself decent. The genes are strong in you, and with them come responsibility."

Jake felt his belly knot into tight, hard lumps of protest. "I have to be whatever it takes to get away from them."

Fenton sighed and leaned back in his chair. "Have you ever studied breeding? Breeding anything at all, cattle, dogs, whatever? You can breed good or bad traits into a line. You have to take care, watch what you do, or you end up with very bad blood. Leopards are cunning creatures. You hunt a leopard in the wild and they're one of the few predators that will circle around to stalk and kill their hunter. They can be cruel and fierce and bad-tempered. But they're also cunning, sharp and intelligent. Read up on them, Jake, and then you'll have an idea of what any of us with shifter genetics contends with. We don't have to shift to feel the effects."

"Can you really not shift?" Jake asked. He kept his eyes downcast, his face still, afraid he'd give away his excitement. "I know you said you couldn't, but you know so much."

The old man shook his head. "I really can't. The leopard is there inside me. I reach for it, but shifting eludes me. I traveled to the rain forest when I found the diaries my grandfather kept, and I met some of the people. They aren't like us. We're abominations in comparison. Cathy, my own granddaughter, is a sick, twisted being, cruel beyond measure, and I know I'm responsible. I married a woman to further the bloodline. Don't do that. Don't continue this experiment. It's dangerous and the people we create are dangerous."

"Like me," Jake said quietly.

Fenton stared at him.

"You know what they're like behind closed doors, yet you left me here with them," Jake accused, voicing the reason he didn't trust the old man. "They would have let me go."

"Never. They would have fought to keep you because they have to present a certain picture to the outside world."

"They hate me."

"They fear you."

Jake's golden gaze jumped to his great-grandfather's face and burned there, a fixed focus, while his heart pounded. It was true. They feared him. And they should, because someday he was going to be stronger, faster, smarter and much, much crueler than they'd ever dreamt of being—and he was going to tear their world apart.

EIGHTEEN YEARS

JAKE Fenton was dead and young Jake felt as if he were the only one mourning the man. Cathy and Ryan hadn't bothered to go to the funeral, but they sat in the lawyer's office, waiting hopefully for an inheritance, although both had loudly speculated that Fenton had used up every penny on acquiring more and more worthless land. When the news came, Ryan and Cathy were stunned and pleased. Fenton owned several companies and even more stocks. They inherited two construction companies outright and, between the two of them, what appeared to be the majority of stock in a chain of major hotels.

Young Jake was given three companies, a mediocre plastics plant that barely kept its head above water, a company called Uni-Diversified Holdings and a corporation that was a parent company for several smaller businesses. He also inherited Fenton's Folly, which was a huge tract of land in Texas no one wanted, two corn farms and several tracts in other states that appeared to be swampland. Stocks were in his name as well as a sizable cash inheritance, although Cathy and Ryan received the bulk of the money.

The lawyer went on to explain that there were a couple of absolute conditions that had to be met. No one could contest the will or they would forfeit their portions immediately. Cathy and Ryan could not inherit from Jake, even if he should die, nor could Jake ever sell to them or give them anything of Fenton's. If he did die before his fiftieth birthday and he had no children, the land, money and stocks would be put in a trust for a list of charities and an immediate investigation into Jake's death would take place. At that time, two letters that Jake Fenton wrote would be opened that might aid the investigators.

Young Jake noted that Cathy looked quite pale, but she didn't say a word. The tension in the room was palpable. They had lost their whipping boy. He had a place to go, he had money and he was of age. There was little they could do about it. Fenton had outmaneuvered them. Without a word to him, his enemies left the lawyer's office.

Jake remained, accepting the letter Fenton had left that carefully detailed his future plans for his cornfields and how he meant to use them for plastic. He had specific business plans for the little plastics company. And there was one more thing: Uni-Diversified Holdings held enough stocks that, when coupled with Jake's personal stock, Jake became the majority stockholder in the companies his parents owned. The corporation was an umbrella for several foreign businesses that were proving to be strong moneymakers. Jake was instantly a multimillionaire and well on his way to his first billion.

NINETEEN YEARS

JAKE found the Texas ranch to be a kind of paradise. The leopard could run free through the numerous trees and wild foliage his grandfather had encouraged to grow. The house was enormous, a mansion by even Texas standards, with a library most cities would envy. He continued his studies in languages as well as business, hiring his own tutors, studying each company he owned and listening carefully to those Fenton had trusted to run them.

He went out each night, running in his leopard form, the acres of land protecting his secrets from outsiders. For the first time he tasted freedom and he smelled—*oil*. The scent was strong beneath the land in numerous places, and he knew when he told the drillers where to dig, they would strike black gold.

Jake wasn't content with others handling his business. He studied his grandfather's plans for each business and where he expected to take the companies in the years to come. He found that if he attended the board meetings his ability to scent lies and fear came in handy. Very quickly Jake made a name for himself as a man to contend with. He rarely spoke; mainly he listened. But when he wanted something done, nothing stood in his way.

His developing magnetic personality and his ability to mesmerize individuals soon allowed him access to every kind of information he could want. When he couldn't talk his way into a circle, he could buy his way in. He found he was irresistible to women and he fostered that, making certain he knew every way of keeping a woman wanting him, willing to do anything for him.

TWENTY-THREE YEARS

THE first oil well hit immediately. At the same time, his venture into plastics took off, making him a huge player in the industry. If anyone underestimated him because of his age, they quickly revised their opinion. He was ruthless and calculating and not afraid to make enemies, although he was careful to cultivate friendships and alliances.

He continued with his great-grandfather's tradition of acquiring land, always inspecting the entire acreage first, using his leopard to scent oil or natural gas. He picked up large tracts in North Dakota, where he suspected oil, and miles of land in the Appalachians, where he scented natural gas reserves. It mattered little that everyone around thought he made bad investments; he knew the oil and gas were there for discovery, and when the time was right, he would find it.

He added to the ranch, picking up more and more land to give his leopard a sanctuary. He ran as a leopard almost nightly, needing the release, finding he felt caged. Always he studied, building his bank of knowledge, always toward the same end. Power. Money. Becoming so strong no one could ever make him a victim again. Waiting for the right moment to take down his enemies.

TWENTY-FIVE YEARS

"HELLO, Alice," Jake said softly—too softly.

She gasped and spun around. His secretary. Bitch spy. He smelled his father all over her. She sat at his desk, trying to get into his computer. He'd known the moment he'd recruited her, Ryan's stench permeating her body.

"I needed to get the Kalwaski file," she said hastily, her face flaming red. "You asked for the reports and I accidentally ruined my copy."

"And you didn't think to call me?" He sniffed the air, scenting the lie. He'd been more than careful not to give her anything at all damaging or important. He trusted no one, and she was relatively new. Now she'd proved to be in the enemy camp as he'd suspected. He stalked her around the desk.

Alice tried to hit the power button to turn off his computer, but he was faster, and far stronger. "Bad, bad girl, Alice. Industrial espionage is such a nasty and dangerous business."

She burst into tears and threw herself forward, into his arms, running her hands down his chest to the zipper of his slacks. "I'll do anything you want."

He slapped her hands away, disgusted. "I'm sure you would. Your kind usually do, but you don't tempt me in the least, not with another man's stench all over you."

She went white, her eyes widening in horror. "What are you going to do?"

He knew he looked murderous. He *felt* murderous. Not at her; she was a pawn manipulated by a master. Ryan and Cathy used sex to control others, and in truth, Jake wasn't above doing so himself, but not with her, not with someone so deceitful and under his father's thumb. No, there were other ways.

"I'm going to turn you over to the police." He let that sink in.

Her sobbing grew louder. Time stretched out while Alice became more desperate. "Please, Mr. Bannaconni, please don't do that. I'm sorry. Really sorry. Your father—"

"Ryan, or Bannaconni, but never my father," he interrupted, his voice a merciless whip.

She flinched visibly. "I couldn't say no."

He knew how his father mesmerized people, especially women, using a combination of sex and cruelty to keep them hypnotized. No, she probably couldn't say no. Ryan was shrewd and cunning, a shark with his handsome face and abundance of money. Jake's little secretary would have been overwhelmed by his attentions. She would have done anything for him.

"I don't suppose you could have," he murmured.

Alice collapsed into a chair. "I've never done anything like this before in my life, Mr. Bannaconni. I swear I haven't, and I'll never do it again."

That smelled like the truth. "Ryan manipulates women," Jake said softly, tilting her chin so she looked into his eyes.

He stared at her without blinking, focusing on her completely, dropping his voice to a low, soothing note. "He preys on young, vulnerable women, so many of them, using sex to get his way."

She wiped at the tears still streaming down her face. "He's married. He told me he could never leave her, but he was so unhappy."

"Of course he did. He tells them all that. And then he gets them to spy for him."

"On his own son?"

"We don't claim the relationship." He leaned his hip against the desk. "Maybe you should pass him information."

"Mr. Bannaconni!" Alice gasped, shaking her head. "I'm sorry. I really am."

He tapped his finger on the desk as if considering the idea. "I know you are. I'm not going to have you prosecuted, but maybe we can find a way to save your job and your reputation as well. Maybe we can feed Ryan a few things that won't harm us and yet will satisfy him. Although"— he looked at her sternly—"you might want to quit sleeping with him and ask for a good sum of money instead."

He allowed a small smile to touch his mouth. Alice never noticed that it didn't reach his eyes. She was the first of many such recruits.

TWENTY-EIGHT YEARS

JAKE took his first trip to the Borneo rain forest to find his heritage. The rain forest overpowered him, a seductive mistress, beckoning him with mystery and promise. He never expected to feel peace or solace, but the network of tree branches in the canopy formed a highway where he could run and perfect his skills as a leopard. Trees competed for every inch of space. The floor was surprisingly open, yet vines and flowers draped every tree branch, and brightly colored birds were in constant motion.

There in the forest he could barely contain the wildness raging within him. The change swept through him before he had a chance to think, the dangerous animal bursting free, stretching the roped muscles and leaping onto the limbs overhead. Bands of sunshine poured like gold from the sky down through the trees to light up the foliage and cages of roots. There was no silence in the jungle, as he first thought. The rain forest was alive with sound, rustles and chirps and loud calls. The other creatures knew he was there, a stranger walking their land, and almost immediately he was joined by the keepers of the forest.

The leopard people were secretive and territorial, but they recognized him as one of their own. One of them—a man named Drake Donovon, who had been recently injured and walked with the help of crutches—watched over him. Jake didn't kid himself that it was friendship. Drake was a powerfully built man, as the others were, carrying most of his strength in his chest, shoulders and arms, and he had piercing eyes that could look through a man and judge him. Jake didn't want him seeing to his soul. Drake wouldn't find it like the others in his village. Jake was flawed, a child shaped and molded into a monster.

He had long since perfected the art of subjugation, and he pushed down his dominant personality in order to gain the knowledge he needed from the others. The leopard people had a code they lived by, even with their animal traits ingrained so deep. In spite of himself, Jake found he admired them. They had quick tempers and could be very jealous, so much so that Jake rarely saw one of their children or females, but they were also men who risked their lives to rescue kidnap victims along the waterways and return them safely to their homes.

Jake found he was reluctant to leave. He wanted to establish ties to the community so, in the end, he helped to fund their cause, pouring his money into their network of businesses, strengthening their abilities to purchase up-to-date weapons and much-needed medical supplies. Money was the only thing he had to offer, and he was more than willing to part with it in order to keep the door held open for his return.

THIRTY YEARS

HE had it all—and he had nothing. *Nothing*. Everything he wanted was finally in place. He could take down the companies of his enemies, sell them off piece by piece and make another fortune. Jake sat in his private jet and looked around at the luxuries his money had bought him, and he knew it was all worthless. He was alone. He would always be alone. He could have nearly any woman he wanted, but he wanted none of them—not permanently. His life was empty. Yes. He could avenge his childhood and he could ruin his enemies, but once that goal was achieved, what would he have left? Absolutely nothing.

The pull of the rain forest was irresistible and Jake found that even with nightly runs on his Texas ranch, he was becoming an insomniac. He spent most of the night working in his office or pacing the floors of his home after running free. He knew he needed something more in his life, but he didn't know what. And even if he had known, he didn't know how to get the things he'd talked about with Drake Donovon. So here he was, back in Borneo, to talk to a total stranger about what life really meant.

He took a trip down the Amazon into the interior of the rain forest, and the moment he stepped out of the boat, he inhaled deeply. Already the animals and birds were announcing his presence to the others, but . . . there was something wrong.

Jake tossed his backpack aside and took off running deeper into the forest, leaping over fallen trunks, avoiding vines and the grasping flowers roping the trees. He stripped as he ran, as he'd learned from many years of practice. His muscles moved like molten steel, flowing beneath his skin, the wild beast already breaking free. He wanted the other's senses, welcomed them, embracing the change as he kicked off his shoes and paused only to toss his jeans aside.

His body bent, bones and sinew popping, lengthening, shifting until his other burst free, going to all fours, still running, sheer adrenaline and joy pouring into him. The lure of staying in his leopard form was tremendous. He didn't have to worry about life or his decisions or what kind of monster he was. He only had to run free and lead a simple, full existence surrounded by the beauty of the forest. He could lose himself in the other.

The scent of blood and smoke and death assailed his nostrils as he ran. His whiskers were radar antennae, bouncing information to him so that his brain flooded with stimuli. *Drake Donovon.* If there was fear, it wasn't coming from Drake. Only defiance, fury, rage pouring from him and filling the night around him. The sounds of taunting laughter, hard fists hitting flesh, fresh blood bursting into the air so that the forest erupted into more shrieks of alarm.

Jake raced along the forest highway, high above in the trees, ignoring the screaming monkeys and the cries of the birds. He coughed once, twice, warning Drake of his arrival. In his life, Jake had never once stood for another. He fought his own battles and never asked for or expected help. He didn't have friendships or trust any other being. Drake had given him information, but he hadn't offered friendship, nor would Jake have accepted it, yet Jake didn't hesitate any more than the leopard rushing toward three men with guns.

One stood over Drake's bloody form, beating him methodically with a thick cane.

"Where are they? Tell me where they are!"

The man kicked at Drake's injured leg and for the first time Drake screamed. Something ugly and deep burst free in Jake and he launched himself at Drake's assailant, going instinctively for the kill, raking at the jugular with sharp claws as he knocked the man flat.

Gunfire erupted, kissing the leopard's shoulder, but Jake was already in motion, as fluid as water, using the dead body as a springboard to take the second man from the side, sinking teeth deep into the throat. The third man stumbled backward as another leopard rushed him from the trees. A third landed on his back, slashing and tearing.

Jake shifted to his human form and knelt beside Drake, running a hand over his damaged, bloody body. For the first time he knew someone other than himself mattered to him, but he still didn't understand why, only that he was grateful he was capable of the feeling.

2

TWO YEARS LATER

JAKE Bannaconni swore viciously as he swerved the sleek, purring Ferrari just in time to miss the Buick pulling out right in front of him. Downshifting, he was around the car and gone, the Ferrari a silver streak on the treacherous mountain road. Ahead of him, on the switchbacks, he caught glimpses of the Porsche he was pursuing. The low, sporty car was veering all over the road, traveling insanely fast on the steep, narrow ribbon of a highway. Thanks to his "other," Jake had amazing reflexes and vision, and that advantage allowed him to push his car to the limit in an attempt to catch his quarry, even on the narrow, twisting mountain road.

A quick glance in the rearview mirror revealed his face was a granite mask, hard lines etched deep, his golden eyes twin chips of ice, glittering menacingly. It didn't matter that he could scare anyone with his look; he felt murderous in that moment. He didn't care about the two occupants of that car, both falling down drunk, pawing each other obscenely in front of everyone at the senator's party, but he damn well wasn't going to let them destroy his child.

Shaina Trent, society's darling, jet-setter, life of the party and precious do-anything-for-daddy daughter of Josiah Trent, was carrying his son. How could he have been so damned careless? He had known exactly what she was when he'd bedded her. He had known both his family and hers had wanted the alliance. Each family suspected that he was the very thing they'd been seeking all along—a shifter—and they wanted his powerful blood to boost their fading abilities. Most of all, they wanted to regain control of him. He should have suspected something when Shaina had thrown herself at him—after all, she'd never looked at him before, always acting so superior and barely acknowledging him at the parties he'd attended in the past. Her daddy must have commanded his little girl to seduce Jake to get what they wanted—a baby.

He downshifted and put on a burst of speed as he caught another glimpse of the Porsche sliding sideways around a turn. His heart went to his throat. Shaina's boyfriend was so drunk he stayed in the wrong lane through the entire turn. He doubted either even realized Jake was in pursuit.

Jake cursed himself for being such an idiot to ever allow himself to get in such a predicament. Desperate to find a way to shackle him, the two families had made an alliance and, like an idiot, he had fallen into their trap. A part of him even felt guilty and thought he deserved exactly what he got.

He had deliberately slept with Shaina, despising her father, yet all along she'd been using him just as he had been using her. He hadn't been stupid enough to believe her when she told him she was on birth control, but he had been an idiot to use the condoms she'd produced. What none of them had figured out yet was he would gladly burn in hell before he would accommodate them. The treacherous bitch.

Planned pregnancy was the oldest snare in the book. It was too late now; he had to live with the consequences—and so did the rest of them. Both families—and Shaina—had seriously underestimated him. He had planned his revenge for years. He had everything in place. It wouldn't take much to ruin either family financially and he wasn't above using any means available to buy freedom for his child.

Jake slammed his open palm on the steering wheel. He should have stayed away from Shaina. He didn't love her, didn't even like her, but he just hadn't been able resist thumbing his nose at Josiah.

He'd carelessly given them the baby they wanted, but he'd be damned if they'd keep him. Jake didn't care whether the boy was a shifter or not. He would find a nurse, a decent one, to come in and raise him right. He couldn't love the boy—the last vestige of anything as soft as love had been beaten out of him long ago—but eventually he'd find someone who could.

A muscle jerked along his jaw. He'd always been savage, clawing and fighting his way out of the cage his family tried to keep him in. There was no way in hell they were going to cage his child. His son would never know that unnatural, deceitful life. A nurse wasn't a perfect solution, but it was the best Jake could do.

Careless, self-absorbed Shaina was doing nothing to protect the health of her unborn child, so here Jake was in California, chasing her down. He had the jet standing by to take her back to his ranch in Texas where his guards would keep her out of trouble and away from drugs and alcohol until the baby was born. He had a team of doctors at his disposal, the best his money could buy, and he was going to make certain the kid had the best possible start.

Jake swore viciously again. Shaina could drive off a cliff for all he cared, but he made it clear that he owned her father's company, had bought up the stock, and he would ruin them all if they dared cross him. The child was his, bought and paid for. Shaina damn well was not going to endanger it. He had turned the tables neatly, ruthlessly, finding a bitter pleasure in all their shocked faces.

Shaina, damn her, had no right to drink herself silly and poison the unborn baby. She had no right to go off with a drunken fool when she was so close to delivery. She had thought herself safe, a thousand miles away from his home state, never dreaming he would be concerned enough about the baby to track her down.

With each passing mile, he shortened the distance between the Ferrari and Porsche, closing the gap steadily, relentlessly. He could see the convertible now, weaving all over the highway, crossing the center line, changing lanes, tires squealing a protest around every sharp curve. He was right above them, looking down, and he saw Shaina move her hand to caress the driver's lap. The Porsche swerved again into the other lane.

His heart jumped, and an icy shiver feathered down his spine. He caught a glimpse of a little Volkswagen Bug puttering along, two turns ahead, right in the path of the oncoming car. Jake actually called out a warning, totally helpless to stop the inevitable.

The collision rocked the ground, shattering the peace of the night, a cacophony of terrible noises he would never forget. Grinding metal, the scream of brakes, the force of the vehicles coming together, folding like accordions. The sight and sounds sent chills down his spine. Sparks flew, the convertible tumbled over and over, spilling gas everywhere. The Volkswagen, a compacted scrap of twisted metal, slammed into the mountain, flames licking along its length and up along the dried grass.

The smell of gas and flames and blood hit him hard. Jake hesitated long enough to report the accident from his cell phone. Leaping from the Ferrari, he sprinted toward the closest car, the crushed Volkswagen. The road was strewn with shattered glass and metal fragments. Shaina and her new boyfriend lay motionless on the ground in the distance, blood running from them in streams. Neither had been wearing a seat belt and both had been thrown several feet from the car. He doubted if anyone could have lived through the force of that head-on collision, but something propelled him forward in spite of the flames moving quickly along the road.

Gas was everywhere, even splashed along the mountain-side where the Volkswagen had tumbled end over end. Inside the Volkswagen, two occupants were hanging upside down, held by their seat belts, heads and arms dangling limply. He pulled at the nearest door. It was already hot with the flames licking at it from the flaming grass on the mountain. With superhuman strength he tore it open and reached inside to unsnap the passenger's seat belt. The body fell into his arms.

It was a woman, covered in glass and blood but alive. The burning gas left him no time to examine her first. He lifted her out of the crumpled vehicle, closing his ears to her cry of pain. He ran a distance from the cars to deposit her on the grass. Blood was pumping from a terrible gash in her leg and he yanked off his belt and wrapped it tightly around her thigh, just above the gash.

When he turned back, the Volkswagen was already engulfed in flames. He had no hope of bringing out the other victim. He hoped the occupant had been killed instantly. Resolutely he turned toward the convertible. He had covered half the distance when an agonized cry froze him in a fragment of time that would remain etched in his mind forever.

"Andy!"

The woman he had rescued had somehow managed to get to her feet, which was a miracle, considering her injuries. She stumbled back toward the Volkswagen. For a moment he could only stare incredulously. She had broken bones, was covered in deep, ragged gashes, her face was a mask of blood, yet she was running back, right into a wall of flames, and she moved with astonishing speed.

For a split second, pure shock held Jake frozen to the spot. The gasoline on the road had ignited. The flames actually licked at her legs, yet she continued to race toward the fiercely burning vehicle. The woman had to have known the car was going to explode at any moment, yet still she ran toward it.

Jake cut her off just a few feet from the car, snatching her up into his arms, sprinting away from the intense heat and building conflagration. She fought like a wildcat, kicking, scratching, the blood making her so slippery he lost his hold more than once. Each time he dropped her, she didn't hesitate to turn back, her eyes on the burning car as she tried to run and then crawl back toward it.

"It's too late," he cried harshly, "he's already dead!" Ruthlessly he flung her to the ground, covering her body with his own, pinning her down while the earth beneath them rocked with the force of the explosion.

"Andy." She whispered the name, a lost, forlorn sound wrenched straight from the heart.

In an instant, all the fight went out of her. She lay motionless in Jake's arms, small, completely vulnerable and broken, her eyes staring up at him, unseeing. Again, time seemed to stand still. Everything tunneled until he was focused wholly on her eyes. Enormous, tilted like a cat's, aquamarine with dark orbs, unusual and mesmerizing, now haunted. She seemed familiar—too familiar. He knew her, and yet he didn't.

For the first time in his life he felt a strong protective urge welling up out of nowhere. He became aware of the gathering crowd staring down at the woman as others leaving the party came upon the scene. Instinctively he shielded her, barking orders to check the overturned convertible, to ensure an ambulance and the police were on the way.

He worked furiously at stemming the flow of blood pouring from the woman's temple and from her leg. A part of him knew he should be thinking instead of Shaina and the child she was carrying, but his mind was consumed with the woman he protected. All he could do was vow silently not to allow her to slip away as she so clearly wanted to do.

Her grief-stricken green eyes begged him to let her go. Where had he seen those eyes before? He looked into them again, drawn by some unseen force. Almond shape, pupils round and black, the irises a rare aquamarine, the blue-green surrounded by a golden circle. Unusual. And yet somehow familiar.

"Let me go."

Jake found himself leaning close to her, his breath warm against her skin. He held her gaze with ruthless command, letting her know he refused to allow her to slip away, that he would hold her to him through sheer will alone. "No." He said the word implacably. "Did you hear me? No." He denied her a second time, his teeth snapping together in finality as he applied more pressure to the pumping wound in her leg.

She closed her eyes and turned her face away from him as if she had no fight left in her. The ambulance was there, paramedics pushing him aside to work on her. A short distance away, firefighters draped a blanket over Shaina's friend. It occurred to Jake with grim satisfaction that this was one accident Shaina's father could not make go away with his money.

More paramedics were working desperately at Shaina's side. It took him a minute to realize they were taking the baby—his son. His heart in his throat, he waited until he heard the triumphant cheers. The child was alive, which was more than they could say for the mother. He waited to feel emotion—any emotion—at Shaina's death or at the birth of his son. He felt nothing at all, only a sense of contempt for the way Shaina had lived and died. Silently cursing his own cold nature, he looked down at the woman lying so still, her dark eyes staring past the paramedic to the burned car. He shifted slightly while they worked on her, to block her view.

Jake followed the ambulances carrying his son and the woman to a small hospital. Although the place seemed a little primitive by Jake's standards, the overworked staff seemed to know their jobs.

"I'm Officer Nate Peterson." A young highway patrolman thrust a cup of coffee into his bloody hands.

Her blood. The woman with the mesmerizing eyes. Her blood was all over him. Jake's shoulders sagged and all at once he was immensely tired, but he needed to find out if she was still alive.

"Can you tell me what happened, sir?" the officer asked. The young patrolman was shaking so badly he could hardly hold his pen. "Andy and I were good friends," the man admitted, choking back emotion.

"Tell me about him," Jake said, curious about the man who inspired such loyalty that a woman would run through fire to save him, even with her own terrible injuries. A man who could make a patrolman shake and hold back real tears. Jake could *feel* the genuine emotion pouring from the other man. He looked around the hospital and found others looking just as distressed.

"His name was Andrew Reynolds and he was twenty-five, best mechanic in town. He could fix anything with an engine. I was best man at his wedding only five months ago. He was so happy that Emma married him. *They* were so happy."

Emma. That was her name. "Is she still alive?" He held his breath.

The patrolman nodded. "As far as I know. She's in surgery. Did you see the accident?"

Jake crumpled up the paper coffee cup and threw it in the trash can. "Shaina and her friend were drunk. I followed them from Senator Hindman's party. Shaina Trent, the woman, was carrying my child. I'm sorry, I don't know the man."

He gave the rest of his statement as clearly as possible, knowing the skidmarks would bear him out.

Jake overheard a young nurse crying in the hall and he walked over to her on the pretext of comforting her. "Are you all right?" He used his voice shamelessly, the tone that was both mesmerizing as well as commanding, designed to put everyone at ease.

She sniffed several times, her eyes bright and a little interested when she saw him. Jake stuck out his hand and patted her shoulder. "I'm Jake Bannaconni." He knew the name would be recognizable, and when her eyes widened, satisfaction settled in his belly. "Can you tell me about the woman? Is she alive?" He looked at the nurse's name tag. Chelsey Harden.

Chelsey nodded. "She's in surgery. She's only twenty-one. I can't believe this happened. She called me earlier today and said she'd just found out she was pregnant. She was so happy. She was telling Andy tonight at dinner. I bet she didn't even have a chance to tell him." She covered her face for a moment and broke into sobs.

Jake patted her shoulder again. "I take it you two were friends."

Chelsey hiccupped and blew her nose. "Very good

friends. I went to school with Andrew and he introduced us. Now she has no one. Andrew's parents died last year in a car crash and Emma told me her parents had died when she was a teen. They only had each other. It seems like some kind of curse or something, all these car wrecks." Her face whitened and she covered her mouth with her hand. "I'm sorry. Your wife was killed as well. I'm so sorry."

Jake shook his head. "We weren't married, but we were having a child."

"He's going to be fine. He's a little early, but he's very healthy," Chelsey hastened to assure him.

"How long will he have to stay here?"

Meaning how much time did he have to set things in motion. He had a vague idea what he wanted to do, but no real plan. It was obvious the staff felt sorry for him. His pregnant girlfriend had run off with another man. Shaina was the paparazzi's dream. She loved the spotlight, and her exploits kept many gossip magazines in print.

The world believed that she'd left Jake brokenhearted, and it suited them both to let that assumption go unchallenged. Now that Shaina was dead, sympathy would surround Jake, and he could use that to his advantage.

"You'll have to talk to the doctor, but for a preemie, he's healthy. Maybe a week, but I honestly couldn't tell you." Chelsey let out a soft sigh. "Emma really wanted a family. It was so important to her and to Andy, because they didn't have anyone at all, so they kept saying they would have a big family."

Jake raked a hand through his hair. He should have his son transported immediately back to a hospital in Texas and return home. This wasn't his mess to clean up. But he knew he wouldn't. He had looked into Emma Reynolds's blue-green eyes and something had opened up in him, something nameless he didn't understand. Whatever it was, he couldn't just walk away.

A man approached, and beside Jake, Chelsey straightened, immediately changing her demeanor to a very professional face. The newcomer must be a hospital administrator. Someone had probably recognized Jake and they were sending the big guns to make certain he was comfortable with his son's treatment.

"You're burned, Mr. Bannaconni, on your hands and arms. You need to have that taken care of."

"I didn't even notice," Jake said truthfully, but he allowed the hospital staff lead him away to an examination room.

He sized up the hospital administrator as his burns were treated. Dignified. Sincere. He was fiercely proud of his hospital—Jake could tell that the moment the doctor began showing him around—yet clearly the hospital had little money to bring in modern equipment.

Jake seized the moment, murmuring about a sizable donation for the care his son had received, asking questions about his child, about how long he'd have to stay, about the repercussions of an early birth and what he could do to better help the hospital care for him. And then he managed to turn the conversation to Emma Reynolds and how terrible he felt for her situation. What were her injuries? Did she need special doctors? He would be more than happy to fly in who or what they needed to help.

Dr. John Grogan, head of the hospital, tried to convince Jake that Emma Reynolds wasn't his responsibility.

Jake looked very grave. "I'm well aware that the rest of the world might think that, but the mother of my child was responsible for Emma's injuries and the death of her husband. Since apparently Emma has no one else, taking care of bills and making certain she has anything she needs is the least that I can do for her." He glanced around and lowered his voice. "I'd prefer that no reporters know I'm here or that my son is still here."

Grogan nodded. "We're a small hospital, Mr. Banna-conni, but we're very discreet."

Jake let out a relieved sigh and slumped a little to show how tired and upset he was. "Please let Emma's doctors know I'm willing to help out. I need to see my son now, if that's possible."

The first step toward inserting himself into Emma's life was accomplished. He let himself be led to the nursery where he donned a gown, mask and gloves to stare down at the wrinkled little boy who lay naked in the small incubator beneath the glare of the hospital lights.

"HOW is she today, Chelsey?" Jake asked as the young nurse came down the hallway toward him. "I've just come back from seeing my son and thought I'd peek in on her."

Emma's room was the first room closest to the nursery. She was pregnant and the OB doctor wanted her nearby in case she began to miscarry after her traumatic ordeal. It was easy enough for Jake to use the excuse that she was so close to his son to look in on her. Though conscious, Emma had been listless and unresponsive to the doctors and nurses. But when he walked in, her blue-green gaze would jump to his face and stay there.

Chelsey sighed. "She doesn't talk to anyone, Mr. Ban-naconni. We're all a little afraid for her. But I heard your son was doing better. He's breathing on his own now and it's been only three days."

"Yes, he seems much better, although he should be gaining more weight, they tell me." Jake paused with his hand on Emma's door. So far no one had ever stopped him from going in. Today he wanted Emma to give the staff her permission to allow him to help her. "I'm going to try to give Emma a reason to live today. You gave me the idea the other day when we talked."

Chelsey patted his shoulder and this time her smile was flirtatious. "I hope you can find a way to get through to her."

Jake smiled back, letting his gaze slide over her with a man's interest. Chelsey's breath caught in her throat and she gave him a little wave as she sauntered off, her hips swaying more than usual. Jake pushed open the door to Emma's room and slipped inside.

As he entered he heard Chelsey giggle. "He's so hot, Anna. My God, when he smiles I think I'm going to orgasm on the spot."

He glanced at Emma and knew she'd heard Chelsey's comment. He closed the doors on the laughing nurses and crossed to her side.

Emma held her breath. He was back. She could go far away from the others and not have to face the reality of being completely alone again, not have to think of her beloved Andrew as dead, not have to deal with losing his baby, but then this man would come in and sit down, filling the room, filling her head with the scent and sight of him, compelling her to live again. He forced her back to the surface every time, where there was no escape from the terrible grief that overwhelmed her.

Silently she pleaded for him to go, to just let her be in the fuzzy, disconnected state that protected her from feeling—but once his gaze focused on her, it didn't leave.

"How are you today, Emma?" He always sounded intimate, talking to her as if they were best friends—more than friends. Closer. He used the pads of his fingertips to stroke back her hair. "Are you feeling any better?"

Each time he touched her, no matter how light, she felt as if electricity arced between them, zapping her alive again, so that the fears and the sorrow were closer than ever. And he held her there, gently but firmly, forcing her to look at her empty life while unimaginable grief poured into her, holding her prisoner.

She didn't answer him. She never did, just looked up at him mutely, begging him to let her drift back into her safe little cocoon.

Jake dragged a chair to the side of the bed, spun it around and straddled it. "I named the baby this morning. I didn't ever think much about what to call him, but I wanted to give him a good name, something that he'd be happy with even as an adult. I found a baby book on names in the waiting room."

She couldn't look away from his face. His tone was soft and low and very intense, but there was something that was a little off. She couldn't tell what it was. His eyes never left her face. He reminded her of a leopard with his golden-green eyes and his unblinking, piercing stare, so focused on her there was nowhere to hide.

He leaned forward. "He's so little, Emma. I swear I could fit him in the palm of my hand. It scares me to think of taking him home when I don't know the first thing about taking care of a baby. Does it scare you? You're going to have a baby. Did they tell you that? That the baby is still alive with only you to protect it?"

Her breath caught in her throat and her hands moved to cover her stomach. Was it true? She could feel her heart pound, hear it thundering in her ears. She'd willed herself to die, she'd *wanted* to die, and she would have taken her baby—Andy's baby—with her. She closed her eyes briefly, afraid she'd heard wrong.

Jake sighed softly and ran his fingers through his hair as if in agitation. "That's what scares me. There's only me to parent, to give the baby a good home, and I'm so far from the real deal." That admission slipped out and his voice rang with truth.

She swallowed—hard. Her throat convulsed. It took effort to part her dried lips and she had to reach for her voice. When it came it was thin and shaky and nearly unrecognizable. "Are you certain? About my baby? Are you certain I didn't lose it?"

He leaned closer to her. Jake Bannaconni. She'd heard his name spoken in hushed, awed whispers, but she still couldn't figure out why she knew him. What was there that was so familiar, and why did she feel as if his will held hers?

"Your baby is fine, Emma. The doctor said even with the blood loss, the baby appears to be healthy." Jake covered her hand with his. "There are no signs that the pregnancy will terminate. You're going to be a mother."

Tears burned behind her eyes again. Her baby. Her precious baby was safe. She wasn't entirely alone and there was a small piece of Andy growing inside of her. "Thank you for telling me about the baby. I was afraid to ask and no one thought to tell me. They only told me about my head, my leg, a million other injuries, and . . ." She trailed off and stared up at the ceiling, blinking, tears welling in her eyes.

"Andrew," he supplied gently. "I'm sorry, Emma. We both have to live with what happened. And we both have babies to raise by ourselves." He flashed a small smile. "I have the feeling you'll be much better at the parenting part of it than I will."

"You'll be a good father," she reassured him absently. "Don't worry so much." How in the world was she going to take care of a baby?

Jake picked up Emma's hand from where it lay quietly under his, his thumb moving along the back of it. His touch was achingly familiar. "Have they said when you can get out of here?"

Emma shook her head. "Where would I go?" The thought of her apartment, her home with Andrew, was too much for her to contemplate. She couldn't face going back to their home and trying to pack up Andy's things.

"We'll deal with it later, when you're feeling stronger," he assured. "I called my lawyer and asked him to look into insurance for you and a settlement of some sort. I hope you don't mind, but I at least wanted to get the ball rolling for you. I know you don't want to think about money, but it will be important when you have the baby."

Emma lifted her lashes, allowing her gaze to drift over his face. There was something about him that haunted her, commanded her, drew her like a magnet when she wanted to be left alone, to simply disappear. No one else compelled her as he did. She could simply go inside her mind and stay there, not face life without her beloved Andy. But once this man entered the room, he seemed to steal her will. She knew him. The memory of him nagged at her, yet she couldn't place him.

She could remember the events leading up to the accident, sitting in the car, so excited, the news of her pregnancy on the tip of her tongue. But she was holding back, determined to wait until they were at the restaurant and she could see Andy's expression, watch his eyes and his mouth when she revealed they were going to have their first child. He'd died without ever knowing. She hated that. Her gaze flicked again to Jake's face.

She didn't remember the crash. She remembered after, when there was pain and fire and Jake staring at her, stopping her from following Andy. His eyes fascinated her, pulled at her, a predator searching for prey. His focused stare made her uncomfortable, yet in some strange way comforted her. Maybe if her head ever stopped throbbing and the doctors backed off the pain medication she could think more clearly, but right now his personality was too strong and she couldn't think.

"How do I know you? I can't recall that we've ever met, but when I look into your eyes, I feel like I know you."

"I'm the man who pulled you out of the car." He looked

down and withdrew his hand from hers to rub at his temples, as if he had the same headache she did. "I'm sorry I couldn't get to your husband. The fire was everywhere."

She saw burns on his hands and her heart jumped. She reached out and caught his wrists, turning the scorched palms over. "Is this from pulling me out of the car?"

Jake drew back, something inside him shaken from the touch of fingers on his skin. It wasn't sexual. He responded to women in a sexual way as a rule and he didn't mind relating to them in a physical way. He controlled women easily when they had a mutual attraction, but this was something altogether different and he didn't trust the feeling at all. "Yes." His voice came out gruffer than he intended.

She let out a small sigh. "I'm sorry you were hurt."

"Emma," Jake said softly, "what matters is that you and the baby are safe." He regretted pulling away from her when she'd voluntarily reached out to him.

Chelsey popped her head in the door. "You need anything, Emma?" she asked, but her gaze devoured Jake.

Emma's face closed down, her eyes going vague. When she didn't respond, Chelsey frowned and looked at Jake. He rose and patted Emma's limp hand.

"I'll get you a few things from your apartment, Emma," he said deliberately. "I'll be back this evening." He nodded toward the hallway and Chelsey followed him out. "I'll need her key and the address," he told the nurse.

"I don't want to get into trouble," Chelsey said.

Jake stepped closer, leaning down as if to keep their conversation totally private. His voice was low and compelling, but he knew the heat of his body and the scent of his cologne enveloped her. She inhaled and a small shiver of awareness went through her. "I wouldn't let you get into trouble. Emma has to snap out of this, and if she has a few things familiar to her, it may help. You're just helping your friend and you saw she didn't object."

Chelsey nodded and hurried away, to return with the key and a small piece of paper with the address on it.

"You're a good friend to Emma," Jake said as he pocketed the key and quickly walked away before she could change her mind.

JAKE found Emma's apartment building with little problem. He stood in the doorway and surveyed the small living space. Small? Hell, it was tiny. The furniture was old and worn with use, the china was chipped and cracked. The couple had nothing. He stalked through the four rooms. This entire apartment would fit into his master bedroom. Frustration grew with each step and he paced back and forth, prowling like the caged cat he was. There was something here he couldn't quite put his finger on. Something he needed to understand, *had* to understand. It was a burning drive in his gut.

Everything was very neat and clean, so much so he found himself throwing out the dead roses in the little vase. They seemed an obscenity in the atmosphere of the apartment. He paced restlessly again, quick, fluid steps of sheer power. There was a key but he was missing it. He halted abruptly. Pictures were everywhere, on the walls, the desk, a small bureau, and there was an album sitting on a coffee table.

He studied one of the photos. The couple was looking at each other, as they seemed to be in every other picture, as if they only had eyes for each other. Their expressions were genuine, love shining brightly between them until it was almost tangible.

He traced Emma's lips with a gentle fingertip. He had never seen two people who looked so happy. It was in their eyes, it was in their faces. Emma took his breath away. In most of the pictures she wore little or no makeup.

She was very small, almost too slender, with an abundance of flaming red hair framing her fragile heart-shaped face. He had never had the slightest attraction to skinny women—he preferred lush curves—but he couldn't stop staring at her face, her eyes. He touched her picture again, tracing the outline of her face, his other hand gripping the cheap frame until his knuckles were white. He put it down abruptly.

The kitchen was filled with baked goods, including a hardened loaf of bread that had obviously been baked from scratch. The bathroom held two toothbrushes, one white, one blue, side by side in a container. There was a pregnancy test kit right next to the small soap dish. In the corner of the mirror, someone had written "Yes!" with lipstick.

In the bedroom, without a qualm, he went through their clothes. Andrew's shirts were a bit threadbare, but every button was in place, every tear neatly repaired. Every shirt was clean and ironed. He found a jacket with tiny embroidered stitches on the inside seam. *Someone loves you.* He stared at the words, feeling a yawning chasm of emptiness welling up inside him.

Jake Bannaconni was elite. He had superior intelligence, strength, vision and sense of smell. Muscles rippled beneath his skin, flowing like water, fluid and controlled. He was one of the youngest billionaires ever reported by *Forbes*, and he wielded vast political power. He had the savage, animalistic magnetism of his species and the ruthless logic required to strategize and plan boardroom battles. He could mesmerize people with the sheer strength of his personality; he could attract and seduce the most beautiful women in the world, and frequently did so; but he could not make them love him. Yet this . . . this *mechanic* had commanded love from all those around him. It made no sense.

What had made Andrew Reynolds so damned special

that he could inspire that kind of love? That kind of loyalty? Hell, Jake couldn't claim love or loyalty from his own parents, let alone anyone else. As far as he could see, Reynolds hadn't given his wife a damned thing, yet everywhere he looked he could see evidence of their happiness.

He touched Emma's brush, strands of red hair gleaming at him like spun silk. His gut clenched. Longing nearly overwhelmed him. More than longing. Black jealousy assailed him. He'd heard his kind had that dangerous trait, but never once in his life had he experienced it. The emotion, so strong, was so intense it left a bitter taste in his mouth, knotted his gut and gave a killing edge to his already volatile temper. Andrew and Emma's life was a fairy tale. A fucking fairy tale. It wasn't real. It couldn't be real. She didn't have decent clothes. Every pair of her jeans was faded and worn. There were only two dresses hanging in the closet.

He found books on birds everywhere, an amateur design for a greenhouse aviary drafted by a feminine hand. He folded the drawings carefully and slipped them inside his coat pocket. He found a notebook that fascinated him. Every charcoal drawing was of leopards in various poses, some half sketched, some highly detailed. The pad was older and well worn, as if someone had looked at it often.

He spent another hour in the apartment, not really understanding why, but he couldn't pull himself away. He was a man who needed freedom and open space. He was intensely sexual, drawing women and bedding them whenever, wherever he wanted. He'd never considered having a woman of his own, yet looking around that tiny nothing apartment made him feel as if all the money in the world, all the political clout, all the secrets of what he was and who he was, all of it was nothing compared to what Andrew Reynolds had had.

Jake closed and locked the door. Someone had to look

at him that way—not just someone. Emma. He couldn't walk away and leave her. The thought of another man finding her, possessing her, sent rage careening through his mind. Inside, he roared a protest. Emma should have been nothing to him, but he couldn't get the sight or scent of her from his mind.

He wanted the damned fairy tale. He could be patient. He was methodical and completely ruthless. Once set on a course of action he was implacable, unswerving. No one, nothing, stayed in his way for long. A grim smile touched the slightly cruel edges of his mouth. He played to win, and he always did. It never mattered how long it took. He always won. He wanted what Andrew had. He wanted Emma Reynolds—not some other woman; Emma—and he would have her. Nothing, and no one, would stand in his way.

3

"I'M thirty-three years old today, Emma," Jake announced as he walked into her hospital room. He placed the items he'd brought from her apartment on the small table near her bed. He'd deliberately waited three days before visiting, although he made certain she heard his voice in the hall. Chelsey had expressed concern several times that Emma wasn't eating and seemed very upset.

Emma's gaze jumped to his face, her fingers plucking at the sheet covering her.

"It's a hell of a thing to be my age and have a baby I don't know how to take care of. I've studied all kinds of things and speak several languages, but I never thought to learn how to change a baby's diapers. They're going to release him in another few days and then what am I going to do?"

Jake picked up her brush and crossed the room to her side. "You look a little pale to me. Are they still giving you pain medication?"

Emma moistened her dry lips, drawing his attention to her mouth. He dug through his pocket and held the lip balm out to her, expecting her to take it. "I found this in your bathroom and figured you might want it."

Emma took the tube from him, her fingers brushing his palm. She was trembling. He waited for her to coat her cracked lips before he spoke again. "Can you scoot up or do you need for me to help you?"

Emma looked startled, frowning at him. "Why?"

"I'm going to brush your hair. I'm probably not any better at that than changing diapers, but it might make you feel human again." Jake poured authority into his voice, acting very matter-of-fact, as if he brushed her hair every day.

She swallowed and looked around a little helplessly, as if she didn't quite know what to do. He gave her no choice and reached across the bed to gently lift her body into a sitting position before he slid in behind her and seated himself on the bed. His thighs wrapped around her hips. A sense of haunting familiarity washed over him, as if he'd done this a million times. His fingers slid into the mass of tangled hair and that too felt familiar.

Jake took a breath and drew the scent of her into his lungs, the woman—who belonged to another man—that he meant to keep for himself, to steal. "Emma?" His voice took on an inquiring tone. "Are you all right?" He dropped his hands to her shoulders.

Emma shook her head.

"Tell me." He ran the brush through her long hair, careful not to pull. He'd never brushed a woman's hair in his life, yet it felt as if he had. Instinctively he held the silken strands above the knots so it wouldn't pull on her scalp as he brushed. He knew she had a tender scalp, and for a moment he heard her laughing explanation, as if she had spoken aloud, that the curls made her sensitive. They'd never once talked about brushing hair, but the memory was in his mind, clear and vivid.

Emma felt his hands in her hair and she closed her eyes,

realizing she'd been waiting for him, needing him, needing his strength. It upset her that she needed anyone, and she was ashamed that she couldn't seem to cope on her own. She couldn't get out of bed, couldn't face her apartment without Andy, and now . . . Her chest ached. Her heart felt so heavy she was afraid she'd choke with the need for air.

"Emma." His voice held an edge, a command. "Tell me."

"The doctor said the baby is at risk and I have to be on bed rest."

There. She'd said it aloud. Finally faced the terrible news because he was there. A complete stranger. Why had she been waiting for him? She'd been angry and hurt that he'd stayed away so long. She'd barely been aware of the doctors and nurses bustling around her, trying to be cheerful, but she'd been acutely aware of him each time he'd been in the hallway outside the nursery looking at his baby. And she'd overheard the nurses gossiping endlessly about how sexy and hot he was.

She didn't want to cry anymore. She wasn't even certain she could. All day long, all night, all she could do was think of Andy, miss him, pray he'd died quickly, without pain. Now she was terrified of losing his child, of not having a way to take care of herself or the baby. She had no one to help her. She was completely and utterly alone in the world.

"What are they saying is wrong?"

His voice was calm and the sound of it steadied her. His hands moved through her hair with the tug of the brush and somehow even that motion soothed her. She took a gulp of air and found she could think better with him close to her.

"I have some internal injuries and they think my body won't hold the baby as it grows. I'll have to be on complete bed rest by my fourth month."

The brush stroked through her hair a few more times before he put it down and divided her hair into three strands. "We can get a second opinion, Emma. It's not hard to fly someone in. If he agrees, then you'll just do whatever it takes."

"How?" She turned to look at him over her shoulder. "I don't have Andy to help me. They operated on my leg; I can't walk, I can't work. I don't have a clue what to do." She detested sounding so pathetic.

He tugged on her hair until she turned back away from him, her shoulders sagging. "We'll do just what we're doing now. Help each other. I've got money and a big house if you need it."

She stiffened. "I don't need a handout." She did, though. That was what was so humiliating. She was practically begging for a stranger to settle her life. She knew she was doing it, but she couldn't stop herself, not with this man. Who was he? Why did he feel so familiar and strong?

She covered her face with one hand. He'd suffered a loss as well. Shaina. The name tasted bitter in her mouth. Shaina and her drunken friend had killed Andy. Strange, she could see pain in Jake's eyes sometimes but never feel it, while it coursed through her veins along with grief, carrying her on a tide of sorrow so strong she was afraid she could never feel happiness again.

"You know there will be a settlement," Jake said. "You'll have plenty of money. I can get my lawyers to continue working on it for you. Once you have that, you won't have to worry about money for a while. There should be plenty to take care of you and the baby."

"Blood money. Money can't replace Andrew." She jerked forward, away from the comfort of his touch.

His hands tightened in her hair, tugging at her scalp, and she gave a little squeak.

"Settle down. I'm not the one you're mad at," Jake pointed out. "And whatever the reason, the money will help with the baby. And you're going to need it, so if you don't mind, I'll just take care of that little detail for you until you can come to terms with it."

"Whatever."

Her voice was low, but triumph shot through Jake at her acceptance of his help. He wanted to take away her sorrow, yet a part of him was amazed and gratified that she could actually feel sorrow. He had been upset over his great-grandfather's death, but not half as upset as she was over her husband's. It fascinated him that she was capable of loving someone so deeply that her life was shattered when he was gone. Try as he might, Jake could not feel sorrow over Shaina's death.

He found himself not liking that side of him, that cold, unemotional part of him that would take advantage of a woman as genuine as Emma. From the little information he'd gleaned from the hospital staff and the apartment, he'd discovered Emma was an independent woman with strong opinions and a sense of fun. But right now she seemed vulnerable and fragile, weighed down by grief and loss. The harsh realities of his world had long ago taught him no one could be so genuine, but though he kept thinking he would find a way to trip her up, he had not been able to. If she was an actress, she deserved an Oscar.

Beneath his hands he felt her stiffen, go on alert, turning her head toward the door.

"The baby's crying," she said. "Can you bring him in here?"

Jake frowned. He had the ability to hear and sort sounds due to his "other," and he instantly recognized the cry of his son. He was leopard, his brain automatically recording sounds and conversations, sorting through data and registering facts around him, yet Emma had heard the cry and instinctively turned toward it before it had registered with him.

His chest suddenly felt heavy, and in his ears, his blood thundered. His mother never once had responded to his cries, not when he'd been an infant, and certainly not when he'd been a toddler. This woman, this stranger, had more regard for his infant son than Jake did. He felt shame and guilt and confusion—something that happened a lot in her presence.

"If that's what you want," he murmured, sliding off the bed, away from her warmth.

"Yes, please."

How could anyone who suffered such losses, who was reeling from so many blows, respond to the son of the woman who had caused the accident? Jake couldn't make sense of her. In some ways she scared him—something very hard to do. Jake wasn't afraid of pain or much of anything, really, but Emma shook him up in places he hadn't known existed. He didn't trust anyone, least of all anyone he didn't understand.

As he gingerly carried the boy back to Emma's room, he tried to figure out what possible angle she could have other than genuine warmth. *He* had a motive for bringing the child to her. He wanted her in his life, loving him and the boy. If he could use her interest in the infant to trap her into coming home with him, he would do it. But what *was* her interest? Certainly not in him as a male. Hell, she didn't even seem to notice he was a man. Not his money. Nothing. He simply didn't interest her.

When he pushed open her door, her gaze jumped to his face and he revised his opinion. There was something between them—strength, power. He mesmerized her. She was vulnerable and needed someone stronger to take over until she could face her life without Andrew. She saw the strength and power of his leopard, the steel in Jake, and because she needed those qualities, he drew her to him, and that was a start.

Her gaze drifted down to the baby he was holding awkwardly, out and away from his body. He flashed a small, baffled grin at her. "He needs changing. I tried to get the nurses to do it, but they said I needed the practice. It's scary stuff holding a wiggling baby in the palm of my hand."

"That's not the right way to hold him, Jake," she counseled gently. "You want to keep his body close up against yours so he feels safe."

"He's wet." Jake made a face.

"He's the baby, not you. Put him on the bed so you can change him."

Jake couldn't get the diaper on to save his life. He put the boy down on the bed beside Emma as he worked, all thumbs, to get the diaper to stay on. The moment he lifted the infant, the covering would slip off and fall to the bed. The baby wailed in protest, little arms flailing about in the air while Jake made a production of raking his hands through his hair and breathing hard.

"You aren't doing it right." Emma's voice was tinged with amusement.

Jake felt triumph burst through him, but he kept an agitated, helpless frown on his face. "I can see that," he admitted, gritting his teeth. "There seems to be some secret eluding me." He kept one hand on the baby's stomach to prevent him from falling off the edge of the bed and glanced at Emma.

The louder the baby cried and the more he squirmed, the more color seemed to come into her pale face. Jake could see she was getting distressed watching his apparent ineptness.

She leaned toward the baby. "Let me."

Jake allowed himself to sink down onto the bed beside

her. "I don't know if you should be moving around too much."

"It's just my leg," Emma said. She winced as she tried to shift her injured limb beneath the blankets, stretching out to sit up straighter.

Jake sighed. "Here. You take the wet boy and I'll move your leg for you."

He practically dumped the baby into her arms, sagging diaper and all, before reaching under the covers and half lifting her to pull her into a more comfortable position. "How's that?"

Emma nodded without answering Jake, looking down instead into the baby's face. He looked like his father. His eyes. Not the normal fuzzy blue color of most newborn's but rather serious golden eyes that didn't smile. That was what bothered her about Jake. His voice was expressive, and sometimes his mouth smiled or frowned, but there was no emotion in his eyes. And there was little in his son's eyes. As if the boy already had suffered too much pain and sorrow. She knew about that and didn't want the infant to start out his life in sadness.

"It's all right, little one," she murmured softly. "No one's ever going to hurt you."

Jake's head jerked around. "Don't promise him that. Don't tell him lies." His voice was harsh, and he reached for the infant, dragging him out of her arms.

Emma studied his face. There was something there. Finally. Real emotion. In his eyes. A dark, twisted pain that she glimpsed briefly before he blinked and it was gone, as if it had never been. Deep. Wrong. Glittering with menace. Making her heart pound with dread. Jake Bannaconni was a very dangerous man.

Jake looked down as the little boy squirmed in his hands and for the first time Jake actually *saw* him. The boy had his eyes and a wild tuft of dark hair. There was intelligence in those antique-gold eyes, so much that Jake found himself running his fingers over the boy's hands, searching for evidence of anything unusual beneath that soft baby skin. The tiny bones felt perfect, although birdlike. The baby stopped crying to watch him with those unblinking cat's eyes.

"People lie," he said gruffly. "I'll do my best to protect you, but people can't be trusted."

"Jake." Emma's voice was soft with compassion. "He doesn't need to be taught that right now. He just needs to feel safe and secure, to have his diapers changed and food in his tummy. Most of all he needs to be surrounded with love."

Jake's belly knotted at that word. Everyone made claims of loving everything and everybody, but in reality it was all about what they could get. At least he was honest with himself. He wanted Emma to look at him the way she had looked at Andrew. He was willing to use any weapon in his vast arsenal to get what he wanted. He looked down at his son, knowing right at that moment that the infant was his best choice, better even than money.

Jake forced a smile as he laid the child down directly in front of Emma. "Who knew changing diapers could be so difficult?" He handed her the diaper. "I named him Kyle," he added.

"Is that a family name?" Emma asked.

"No," he responded tersely, took a breath and tried to soften it. "No, I just liked the name."

Emma's lashes fluttered. "Well, it's a beautiful name." She put her finger in the tiny hand of the baby and Kyle instantly closed his hand around hers. "*He's* beautiful."

"Yes, he is." Jake really looked at his son, a little in awe. The tiny, perfect face, his legs kicking with such force. Before, he'd thought of him as wriggling and red, but now he took note of the boy's features, the catlike eyes, the bowed mouth and the tuft of dark hair. He found himself smiling. "He really is, isn't he? But he's so little, he scares me." There was some truth in that as well. "I've never held a baby, let alone been responsible for one. I feel like I'm all thumbs."

Emma carefully fit the diaper to him and watched as Jake awkwardly tried to pick the boy up. Again he held him out away from his body.

"The nurses say I have to learn to feed him, but he doesn't like the way I'm doing it and he isn't eating very much," Jake admitted in a low voice, as if it pained him to admit he couldn't do something perfectly. "I can find oil in ground that no one suspects is there, but I can't feed or diaper a baby." He wiped his hand across his forehead.

Emma held out her arms. "Let me show you."

Jake held his breath as Emma took Kyle into her arms, cradling him against her breasts. She enfolded him, surrounding him with her warmth and the softness of her body.

"You want to hold a baby very close so they feel safe." She smiled down at the small, upturned face. "Give me the bottle and I'll show you how to feed him." She held one hand out.

Jake put a supporting hand under the baby's bottom. "Don't drop him." He remembered the countless falls to the floor, the feel of a shoe hitting his body, the toe of a boot in his stomach. He hadn't thought about it for years. He was no father—he sure as hell didn't know what he was doing— but no kid of his was going to be bounced on a hard floor.

"I'm not going to drop him," she assured.

Jake hesitated, studying her face. She seemed so damned genuine, but no one was really like her. No one. Watching her closely, he handed her the small bottle, bending his head close to see how she teased the baby's mouth until he opened. At once he began suckling. Kyle didn't turn his head from side to side as he'd done earlier when the nurse had tried to show Jake what to do. Jake had been impatient and annoyed, feeling as if he was wasting his time. Watching Emma with Kyle made him feel different.

"Emma, do you remember what happened?"

Her gaze flicked to his face and her arms tightened around the baby. She nodded. "Not how it happened, only you holding me down and fire all around us." She swallowed hard, her eyes shimmering with tears. "Andy . . ."

He put his arm around her as if she belonged there—with him. "I know, Emma. I'm sorry. I couldn't get him out. It was too late."

"Don't blame yourself." She looked up at him again and her eyes looked like two deep pools. For a moment he thought he was falling forward. "Did he suffer?"

His fingers went to the nape of her neck, massaging the tension in an effort to comfort her. "No. He died immediately. He never felt the fire."

She bit down hard on her lip and stared into Kyle's face. "The people in the other car? They both died, didn't they?" She swallowed visibly, trying to remember everything she'd overhead. "You knew them both?"

Jake reached out and took Kyle's little hand. "His mother died, as well as the driver. The medics delivered my son and saved his life. I was lucky they could get the baby out in time."

"I'm sorry about your wife."

"We weren't married," Jake admitted in a low voice.

Again her gaze flicked to his face. "I'm sorry," she said again. She turned her attention to Kyle, cradling him close to her, ducking her head so that her face was hidden.

Jake realized she felt bad for him, that the tears shimmering in her eyes were for him, for Kyle—not for herself. It was to his advantage to allow her to think he'd been crazy about Shaina—that he felt the same sorrow at losing a loved one as she did. It gave them another bond. He considered letting her believe it, but something inside, something strong, welled up in him, refusing to let him lie to her about that. Not even by omission.

"Emma," Jake said softly and waited until she looked up at him. "I didn't love Shaina. I don't have the same emotions as you do." Maybe he really wanted to warn her. All the advantages were on his side. Maybe there was a shred of decency left in him and he believed she deserved it. Or, God help him, Drake Donovon, his semi-friend and now part-time counselor, with his constant set of rules and talk of honor, was getting to him. Whatever, Jake knew he had to tell her the truth.

"I despised her. She deliberately got pregnant to blackmail me into marriage. And then when it didn't work, she drank and did drugs while she was pregnant. I had to have someone watching her all the time. I came here to bring her back to my ranch, to keep the baby safe until he was born. You lost someone you loved. Shaina was . . ." *Like me.* He couldn't bring himself to say it and he just trailed off.

Emma stared up at his face, her eyes wide and unblinking, completely focused on him so that he went still, feeling threatened—feeling as though she could see all the way to his soul, to the cold monster living there, waiting to strike. She shook her head slowly. "Not like you." As if he'd spoken the words aloud and she'd heard them. "You aren't who you think you are."

He knew exactly who and what he was. He never spared himself by trying to whitewash his character. He'd embraced the cold monster, refusing to fall victim ever again. He would be stronger, more cunning, faster, more ruthless, than every enemy he had. And he would never be vulnerable again—not to anyone. They would find him an implacable enemy who pulled no punches and had no mercy when he struck at them—at any of them. And this one, this young, fragile woman who looked at the world through rose-colored glasses, she was going to belong to him and he was taking her, whether she wanted it or not. No, he was *exactly* like his enemies, only worse.

He paced away from the bed, away from her intent gaze. He was the one in control, not her. He wasn't falling prey to her sweetness, or to the way she made him feel guilty. He controlled everyone in his world. He didn't need others. They needed him. She wasn't going to turn the tables on him by looking into his soul and seeing something he kept hidden from the world.

Vulnerable. For a moment she made him feel that way, as if she could hurt him, as if she had some power over him he didn't understand. Jake rejected the feeling immediately. He would never be vulnerable again. And neither would his son. He glanced at the baby in her arms. He didn't want or love the kid, but he was going to do right by him. He would see to it that Kyle had every advantage, and just looking at the baby in Emma's arms, he knew this woman was the one he wanted for his son.

The hell with it all. He had a plan and he was going to carry it out. Emma would benefit and so would her child. Jake would be fair about it. Eventually she would grow to love him, even if he couldn't love her back. Hell, he could even be faithful if he had to. He would give her a home, Kyle would have someone who would be good to him, and she would be well cared for. He had no doubt that he could satisfy her in bed and teach her to satisfy his every need. It would work out for both of them—for all of them. He shoved down whatever humanity still lay within him and hardened his heart.

He was taking her over. One small piece at a time, starting here, starting now, just the way he went after the companies he wanted. He studied his prey, assessed the weaknesses and vulnerabilities. Emma needed a home and money while she was pregnant. His lawyers would be the ones working for a settlement, and just like contracts for businesses could be misplaced, "lost," or bought off, his lawyers could delay every procedure to ensure she needed him. Yeah, he was a bastard, cold and cruel and calculating, but he let himself off the hook by reminding himself he would take good care of her as he did all his possessions.

And make no mistake, Emma Reynolds. You will be my possession.

Emma would be no different from Kyle. He would see to everything for them and just keep emotionally distant. No one ever took what he owned.

As she fed the baby, Emma watched Jake pace the length of her room. His eyes shone with a power that both terrified and intrigued her. His body moved with a fluid grace that suggested danger. She knew she was mesmerized by his strength and confidence, by his very arrogance, yet there was something eluding her, something about him that was so familiar to her that drew her more than her need for someone to take charge. And right now she didn't care all that much about living, other than to save her baby. If Jake Bannaconni wanted to take charge, she was going to let him—at least for a while.

He didn't know her, only that she was young and lost and helpless right now. Once she could think without hurting, without being so afraid of taking a breath, she would be all right. At the moment, she couldn't make decisions and be certain of what she was doing. Jake seemed to know exactly what he was doing. And whether he thought of himself as a good man or not, a part of her reached for him, wanted—no, even *needed*—to do as he asked her. Wanted to reach beyond the emptiness in his eyes and the blankness of his expression and see who he really was. And that had never happened before, not even with her beloved Andrew.

She kissed Kyle's forehead and leaned down to whisper in his ear. "It will be all right. You'll see. Don't be afraid." Because she was there and she needed the baby to focus her attention on, to give her something to cling to. She looked up at Jake's face and caught a hint of satisfaction there. She filed it away. He wanted her attached to his son. Maybe he feared bringing the child home on his own, and she couldn't blame him, although it was rumored he had enough money to hire an army of nurses. Whatever his reason, it didn't really matter to her, not right then.

"How long before Kyle can go home with you?" Emma asked, nuzzling the baby's head.

"A few more days, the doctors are saying. They want his weight up a little bit. What are they saying about you?"

She shrugged. "Pretty much the same thing."

"Do you have any family?"

Emma instinctively knew he already had the answer, but for some reason he wanted to force her to admit the truth out loud. "No." The moment she told him, she understood. It left her with nothing—and no one—and that shook her even more. She looked up at him, trying to see beyond her grief to care that she was putting herself in the hands of a complete stranger.

"Are you all right with Kyle? I'll put a call in to my lawyers and get them started again on the settlement for you with the insurance company. And I need to make certain I have doctors lined up to care for you and Kyle once we're home. You are coming with us, aren't you, Emma? Because honestly, I really need your help."

"What's home?" Her voice shook a little.

"I have a ranch in Texas. I own property in quite a few

places, but the ranch is my primary home and where I'd like you to stay. I can hire help while you're on bed rest to take care of Kyle."

She shook her head. "I don't want you spending money on me."

He shrugged his broad shoulders. "I think I have enough to take care of you without worrying too much about going hungry."

She knew the name Bannaconni. She'd heard the whispers around the hospital. Private jets, exotic cars, men rushing to bring him papers to sign and rumors of a new wing for the hospital and lots of very up-to-date equipment. "Just because you have money doesn't mean people should take advantage of you." She shook her head. "I don't want that."

Then she was the only one on the planet. Was she really too good to be true? Everyone wanted something. His fingers itched to shake her. He needed to get a private investigator to find out everything he could about little Ms. Reynolds. The more information he had on her, the better equipped he would be to control her.

"You won't be taking advantage of me. If you prefer, we can keep an accounting of any expenses I incur and you can pay me back when you get your settlement. I don't want you to be misled, though. The ranch is very secluded, very remote. We don't get or encourage many visitors, although I have ranch hands who work regularly for me and live on the property, so you won't be alone when I have to go away on business. We can also get a temporary housekeeper to keep you company. If you want the job when you're stronger, looking after the house and Kyle and your baby, then of course you can have it."

She frowned and nuzzled the baby again. "You're offering me a job as a housekeeper, looking after your home and child?"

He shrugged. "I don't know the first thing about babies, or what to do with them. You can get the diaper on him, which makes you one step ahead of me already."

"Jake," Emma said gently, "you can't be so desperate you'd hire a perfect stranger to take care of your son. I don't want to talk myself out of a job, but . . ."

"And a home," he added.

"And a home," she agreed, "especially when I'm in such a bad situation. But you don't know me. How can you trust me with your child?"

"I don't."

The two softly spoken words were uttered with complete honesty. Emma's head snapped up and her gaze collided with his. A chill went down her spine.

"I'm hiring a private investigator. And I'll warn you, I don't want to ever see or hear or find evidence of physical, psychological or emotional abuse toward my son. I would destroy anyone who harmed him."

For the first time, she smiled—a genuine smile. It was small, but it was there. "At least you have some sense."

"I knew I'd be hiring someone. I need a housekeeper and someone to look after Kyle. If that works for you after you have your baby and you enjoy Texas, then we'll work that out. By that time you'll probably have more money than me and won't want to stay." He shrugged, careful not to allow any expression on his face.

She didn't have a prayer of escaping once he had her on the ranch. He'd find ways to keep her there. Even if she didn't fall for him at first, there was Kyle. And then he'd make certain her child was crazy about him. And the clincher was sex. Hot, demanding sex. If there was one thing he was damned good at, it was sex and his ability to make a woman come crawling back for more.

Jake let his gaze move over her. She was beautiful in a wild, exotic way. Not the polished sophistication he was used to, but certainly she looked sexy with her unusual eyes and her flawless skin. Her mouth was the thing of fantasies. He had absolute confidence in himself when it came to tying her to him with sex. Even Shaina, who ultimately despised him, had kept coming back, begging him for more.

Sex was his ultimate weapon over a woman like Emma. She was sweet and innocent and very young in spite of having been married and experiencing a tragic loss. There was brightness in her, and a purity that made her easy prey for a skilled hunter—and he was skilled. By sundown he'd know everything about her, including her favorite flowers, favorite color, and every dark secret and hidden wish.

"I can't hire a detective to investigate you," Emma pointed out. "So it hardly seems fair."

He caught her chin, the pad of his thumb sliding over her lips. "You need more moisturizer. Your lower lip is splitting. And you can read all about me in the tabloids. Would you like me to bring you back a few magazines? Most of the junk is pure bullshit, but there might be a word or two of truth in them."

"Tempting. Very tempting. Reading and believing gossip is so me."

He took the lip balm from the nightstand and ran his index finger through it, applying it to her sore mouth. "Kyle's asleep. How'd you do that? When I hold him after he eats, he squirms around and usually spits up everywhere." He said it more to distract her than to find out the information. He didn't intend to be feeding the kid, let alone holding him after he ate, but he couldn't imagine that she'd let him get away with applying lip balm.

Jake wanted her used to his touch. He had seven months—maybe even longer, after her baby was born—to get her accustomed to his close proximity. He didn't want her thinking about it, or being at all aware of him until it was too late. He made certain no touch seemed sexual, only comforting. The more she accepted his touch and got used to him, the more she relied on him, the easier it would be to take over her life. He would teach her to accept him without her knowing what was happening. By the time she was ready to accept another relationship, her life would be tightly, irrevocably bound to his.

"I told you," Emma's soft voice sounded faintly amused. "His tummy will get upset and he'll never go to sleep if you hold him out away from your body. You have to hold him close to you, up against your chest." Her eyes went soft and more green than blue. "Are you afraid to hold him close?"

If it was possible, he might have flushed a deep red. He wanted to shake her again. He wasn't afraid. The kid was just small. Jake was enormously strong. If he closed his fingers too tightly, he might injure the baby—that was all. It wasn't fear. He wasn't afraid of anything.

Emma extended her arms toward Jake, holding out the baby to him. Jake let out his breath and reached for the boy, intending to leave, to hand him over to a nurse.

"Don't go yet," Emma said and patted the bed beside her as she slid back down, wincing as she moved her injured leg. "Stay with me for just a little while so I don't get paranoid about going with you to Texas."

He rarely stayed with anyone longer than absolutely necessary, and Emma got under his skin with her haunted eyes and fragile vulnerability. On top of that, his son was sleeping peacefully in the palm of his hand. If he sat on the bed, he would be trapped by the two of them, by their vulnerability and need for protection. The wildness in him stirred every time he got close to Emma, rising up like the untamed creature it was, recognizing her in some mysterious way he didn't understand or trust. Swearing under his breath, he sank down beside the small, broken woman.

She pushed at his arms, forcing him to bring Kyle close to his chest so that infant lay nestled tightly against his heart. "Like that. Babies sometimes get a sense of falling and they fling out their arms, frightened. When the blanket is tight around them or they are in close to your body, they feel safe. He can hear your heart beat and feel your warmth." She raised her guileless gaze to his. "When you hold someone, don't you feel safe and warm?"

His gaze shifted from hers. Hell. No one asked him those kinds of questions, not in all of his thirty-three years. He looked down at his son. The baby's face was relaxed, tiny, so pink and naked. He slept peacefully, his breath so light Jake could barely feel his chest rise and fall.

Jake swallowed hard and slipped his finger against the tiny palm. The boy had paper-thin fingernails, so small they were barely there. A lump rose in his throat, threatening to choke him. The little hands were perfect, all the fingers, lines and whorls, knuckles, everything. The small fingers wrapped around his bigger one and Jake held up his other, much larger hand to study the two together. "Look at that, Emma. I swear, my hands must have looked like that when I was a baby."

"You should get his handprints now and then again each year to compare them. Put yours right next to his. It will be fun for you to watch him grow. I planned on doing that when my baby was born."

"Plan," Jake corrected gently.

She kept her head down.

"Emma. Look at me." He used his velvet no nonsense voice.

Her head jerked up, her gaze meeting his, tears turning the aquamarine eyes to a deep, vivid, shimmering green. He slid his hand under her chin to hold her captive, his thumb feathering along her trembling mouth. "When your baby is born, you plan on keeping records of handprints," he repeated.

She swallowed hard. Tears tracked down her face.

Jake wiped them away with the pad of his thumb. "Say it, Emma. When the baby is born. You aren't going to lose it. Say it out loud."

She swallowed again and nodded. "When the baby's born." Her voice came out in a whisper.

He smiled and leaned in to brush his mouth over the top of her head. "That's my girl. You're tired. Go to sleep and forget about everything. Thanks for helping me figure out how to hold him."

He resisted the urge to stay with her, the silent plea in her eyes. She was having more of an effect on him than he had counted on. Sighing, he closed the door behind him.

OVER the next few days, Jake brought Kyle to Emma's room and set up a command post on the small desk by her bedside. The hospital's IT administrator installed a network drop for his laptop, and he ran his business from her room while she grew stronger and the baby put on more weight. Jake occasionally fell asleep in the chair, but most of the time he rarely slept.

He learned to awkwardly change Kyle's diapers and give him a bottle, surprised that the boy seemed to recognize him. Kyle obviously preferred Emma, with her soothing voice and gentle rocking. Jake placed the child into her arms the moment she asked for him, wanting the bond to grow strong. When the hospital began to make noises about Emma being discharged, he brought up the subject of traveling with him to Texas again.

"Emma. You are coming home with us, aren't you?" He kept his voice very gentle and matter-of-fact, as if it didn't matter and it was wholly up to her. In reality, she had nowhere else to go and no money, and she desperately needed care. He had sprung the trap and she was well and truly caught.

Emma looked very confused and somewhat ashamed, but a little helpless. He knew he had won the moment he saw her face. He patted her shoulder and gave her a smile. "I'll arrange everything."

He had won the first battle just as he had known he would. And he would win the entire war. He was a master strategist; Emma Reynolds had no hope of defeating him.

He made the necessary calls to the lawyer, ensuring she would have no finances available to her for several months, knowing things could be delayed much longer, if necessary. He made the calls to the ranch, setting up a nursery and a room for her. He personally supervised the movers, hating to save reminders of Andrew Reynolds, but knowing he had to. The doctors were on his side and helped him arrange for an ambulance to take Emma to his waiting private jet. Weak, pregnant and penniless, with no family to aid her, and already attached to his son, Emma Reynolds allowed Jake Bannaconni to take over her life.

4

FOUR MONTHS LATER

AFTER seventy-two hours without sleep, Jake moved wearily through the kitchen when he spotted the light on the coffeepot and the plate of food with a lid over it.

"Damn it, Emma," he snapped through clenched teeth, but he stalked to the long granite countertop and lifted the lid over the plate.

It was still hot. She had no business getting out of bed, going down the stairs and cooking a meal. He employed a cook. Damned if he ever saw her cook. Emma was already running his house from her bed, and the moment he went off to attend to business, she made her way downstairs. She claimed she stayed on the sofa, or sat in the plush kitchen chairs, but mostly she lied her little ass off and did what she wanted to do. Like now, having made certain he had a hot meal waiting when he came home.

He was used to coming home to a silent house. It was rarely silent now. She loved music and almost always had it on throughout the house. He'd become used to hearing her laughter, soft and inviting, the low murmur of her voice when she talked to Kyle. The nurse he'd hired told him she might as well not be there, because Emma wanted Kyle with her all the time.

The house itself was different. Everything was different. He hadn't expected that. Candles. Scents. Cookies and fresh bread. The low sound of her voice. The knowledge of her presence. Emma was everywhere when he'd thought he'd confined her to a single room. The last doctor visit had been a disaster. The doctor had warned that the pregnancy and birth might be even more difficult than first suspected and that Emma was at risk as much as the baby. She'd been adamant against terminating the pregnancy and now he lived in fear of losing her. Sometimes, if he thought about it too much, he could barely breathe.

Most nights when he came home he went to her room and spent the evening with her and the baby. She wasn't supposed to lift the infant, so he would place Kyle in her arms and watch her stare down at the boy's face with that look. The one he wanted for himself. One month and she was already crazy about the boy. She always looked up at Jake with a welcoming smile, pleased to see him, but he found he wanted more—he wanted *that* look. *The* look.

He was drawn to her room, the pull so strong he was beginning to grow alarmed over it. Not tonight. Tonight he'd eat alone in the kitchen and pull back a little until he found his balance. It was essential that he remain in control, and somehow Emma always made him feel a little out of control.

In spite of his resolve, he found himself on the stairs, and he paused, looking at the life-sized bronzed leopard statue at the base of the atrium where plants grew, stretching toward the skylight. "I really need more willpower," he muttered aloud to it, then carried the plate up the stairs and walked to her room, cursing every step of the way.

A small nightlight was the only beacon, but he stepped inside the spacious room and moved unerringly to the chair. He could smell her scent. All Emma. There was a wildness to her fragrance he could never quite figure out, the outdoor air, clear and crisp after a summer rain, the faint scent of peaches mingling with an exotic spice. But it was the strange, honeyed, very elusive wild flavor he could almost taste that drove him crazy.

Emma sat up on the bed, her eyes lighting up, a quick welcoming smile on her face that made his heart stumble.

"You look so tired," she greeted softly, running her fingertips over his arm. "You work too hard, Jake."

His belly knotted. It did that a lot around her. The sound of her voice wreaked havoc on his senses, yet there was a strange peace he found in her presence.

He took a bite and regarded her sternly over the plate. "You aren't supposed to be up. What am I going to have to do to keep you in bed?"

"You worry about everyone but yourself."

His gut clenched hotly at that. A protest. He worried about himself first, always moving pawns around on a chessboard to suit him, directing lives—directing *her* life. Yet she believed his "great dad and loving provider" act. He got up at night with Kyle and brought him to her, staying in the room while she fed the boy. She thought it was because he loved his son so much. And afterward she always put the infant in his arms, expecting him to rock Kyle back to sleep. And he did, but not because he wanted to do it. Not because he enjoyed holding a baby in his arms, although sometimes he questioned whether he secretly was beginning to look forward to that time with his son. *No way.* He almost shook his head violently at his thoughts. He wanted Emma to see him showering Kyle with attention; that was his only reason.

"I want you to do as your doctor says, Emma. Stay in

bed. You have to think of your baby, not whether or not I have dinner. We have a cook for that."

Emma studied the lines in Jake's face. He looked far more tired than usual. Something wasn't right. "The cook goes home after four. You always work late and some of the boys get hungry so I like to have something ready on the stove. And the doctor hasn't put me on full bed rest yet, Jake, so stop worrying so much. All I do is lounge around."

Jake's strange golden eyes blazed down at her. He reached across to capture her chin and hold her facing him, his grip strong, fingers biting a little at her. "I know exactly what you do, Emma, and I wouldn't call it lounging. Would you like to tell me why I employ a nurse and a cook, when you do all the work?"

He was chastising her. She pushed down a smile, knowing he wouldn't appreciate her strange sense of humor. Everyone seemed afraid of Jake with his gruff manner and hard, piercing eyes, but she found him compelling and at times even tender, taking care of those who lived on his ranch with a fierce protectiveness. Even his men. There was his crew of roughnecks that occasionally came to the house, the oil drillers that scattered to the four winds when they weren't working and the cowboys who took care of his cattle and fields who lived on the ranch in houses or the bunkhouse. They often came up to the main house to talk to Jake, and she got into the habit of making fresh bread and pastries for them.

"I have no idea why you hired them. I told you that if I was going to take the housekeeping job and look after Kyle, I didn't want anyone else running the house."

She tilted her chin at him, refusing to be intimidated by the warning glitter in his eyes. As much as she worried about him, and as much as she wanted to smooth the lines in his face, she refused to cater to his temper or his bossiness. The man didn't know how to talk without giving an order. She often found herself wanting to please him, telling herself it was to ease the constant strain he was under, but more likely it was her terrible penchant for wounded creatures. And he was wounded, whether anyone else could see it or not. She knew he'd be horrified at her assessment of him. Jake was the most independent man she'd ever met.

He leaned closer to her. "No one will run the house after you've recovered from having the baby. In the meantime, let them wait on you."

"I'm not staying in bed until I absolutely have to. Partial bed rest means I can get up a bit. And Kyle prefers me to the nurse."

"Well of course he prefers you to the old bat. She never cracks a smile, at least not around me. Not that I hired her for her ability to smile."

"Why did you hire her?"

"Her credentials are impeccable."

"She doesn't know a thing about babies; not really. Some people have a natural ability. She doesn't," Emma insisted.

The nurse specialized in difficult pregnancies, not babies. He shrugged and set the empty plate aside. "She doesn't approve of my lifestyle." He shot her a sheepish grin. "I don't think my considerable charm works on her."

Emma felt the first stirrings of protectiveness toward Jake. And more than a little anger toward the absent nurse. "Who is she to judge your lifestyle? What's wrong with it?"

Jake shrugged again. "You're protected here, Emma, but there are a lot of people interested in my life. When they can't find any details to talk about, they make it up."

She turned his matter-of-fact statement over and over in her mind. "Me." She met his golden gaze. "They're speculating about me and who I am and why I'm here."

"The accident was in California four months ago. Everyone thought Shaina broke my heart. And now I've got the mystery woman living with me, but no one sees her. The rumor is she's pregnant as well."

"And the nurse—Miss Hacker thinks the baby is yours?"

"I haven't said any different," he admitted.

"Why?"

He looked away from her briefly, then reached over and took her hand, his thumb sliding up and down the back of her hand. "I can't. We can't. We have to think about protecting the baby. We need to let everyone think it's mine."

"No!" Emma pulled her hand away. "It's Andrew's baby, the last part of him."

"Emma, honey, you aren't thinking. We both know the baby is Andrew's, but what happens if something goes wrong? I think like that, plan ahead. It's what I do. I take apart companies and sell them piece by piece, but in order to take over in the first place, I have to look ahead and determine the things that might happen and plan for them. I'm not leaving your baby homeless or to the authorities. Be angry with me for it, but I know what's it's like to be raised—"

Abruptly he snapped his mouth closed, leapt to his feet and stalked out.

Emma sat in the dark for a long time, her heart pounding, as she faced the very real possibility that her baby might live and she might not. The doctors had discussed the possibility with her, but she'd dismissed it. Evidently Jake hadn't, and he was already preparing to save her child, when she hadn't even thought about what might happen. She got up, pulled on her robe and padded barefoot down the hall to the nursery. He was there, just as she knew he would be, standing guard over his son.

"Jake." He didn't turn and she knew he had been aware of her coming in. "I'm sorry. You're right about this, but I don't want you to think I expect . . ."

He flicked her a warning glance over his shoulder. "Go

to bed, Emma. I'm not myself tonight and you're the last person I want to fight with."

"I just wanted to say I was sorry."

He swung around in that fluid, predatory way of his and swept her up into his arms, as if she were a child, cradling her close the way she'd taught him to hold Kyle. "What part of 'bed' don't you understand?"

He sounded rough and exasperated, but his hands were gentle as he carried her to her bed and pulled the sheet up to her chin. He even dropped a kiss on top of her head, just as she'd seen him do with Kyle. "Go to sleep. We have all the time in the world to figure it out."

God help him, he hoped it was true.

ONE MONTH LATER

JAKE tossed his pen onto his desk and heaved an exaggerated sigh. If there'd been someone to yell at, he would have done so, but instead there was only him, locked in the silence of his office. He'd created this wing of the house to be attached but separate. Soundproof. He found his acute hearing could be a distraction when he was trying to study the various companies he was interested in acquiring—especially lately. There were small alarms scattered through the various rooms to alert him to intruders because his office was doubly soundproofed. He always had liked silence. He'd *needed* silence, the peace of it. Silence was one of the few things that calmed his mind, like running free late at night in his other form.

He sighed again and laced his fingers behind his head. Silence wasn't working so well with him at the moment and he didn't understand why. His home was so different now. Emma and Kyle had been here five months and already the place was transformed. There was a warmth now, and he felt peace when he sat in the nursery or when he entered Emma's room. Now his office seemed cold and distant. The silence distracted him. He found himself listening for the low murmur of Emma's voice and the soft little sounds his son made.

Jake sat up straight, alarm shooting through him. His son. He never thought in those terms. Emma often referred to Kyle that way, but Jake thought of him as the infant, the baby, even the kid—*not* his son. What the hell was happening to him? What was she doing? Turning his life upside down. This wasn't how it was supposed to work. His life was supposed to be unaffected, maybe easier, but certainly not more difficult.

Emma never listened to him. Well, she listened, she just didn't do what he told her to do. She always gave him that little mysterious smile of hers and—and *nothing*. She simply did what she wanted. No one ever did that around him. The world was afraid of him, and rightly so. It didn't matter how stern he got with her, or how ugly his temper got. She maintained that small smile and just did whatever she wanted. It was frustrating and arousing, and made him want to use other methods to control her little rebellions.

He raked his hands through his hair. He liked the sound of her voice, the scent of her skin, the candles she burned, the way she always had something for him to eat. He loved the look on her face when she held Kyle and when she rubbed her hands protectively over the small mound of her stomach. He had the feeling he was a little obsessed with Emma. He kept waiting for her true nature to emerge, but she remained generous and kind and so gentle. The shadows in her eyes were slowly receding. She still had nightmares and he spent most nights in her room with her, but she didn't burst into tears as often.

A tingle of awareness crept down his spine and he was on his feet before he even realized what he was reacting to.

There was no other warning, only that weird sense the other gave him, but he knew something was wrong. He sprinted through the spacious hall to the connecting door that led from the business wing to the main part of the house, his heart pounding.

He could hear Kyle screaming, Emma's usually calm voice raised and another woman shrieking. With a sinking heart, he recognized the other woman's vicious voice. For one moment he was disoriented, thrown back in time to the small, helpless child he'd been. The scars on his thigh throbbed in tune to his pounding pulse.

"Emma?" He called her name as he took the stairs two at a time, leaping, using his leopard's agility to clear the banister when he was close to the top.

He hit the hallway floor running, streaking fast, fear clogging his throat. Cathy Bannaconni was more than capable of harming Emma. She would immediately sense Emma's vulnerability and go for the jugular, battering her emotionally and physically. Worse, Emma might admit that the child she was carrying was Andrew's, and everything he planned could be lost.

"You money-hungry, conniving little whore, you will never be mistress here. You're nothing. An opportunist. Some little tart who lost her husband and hops in bed with my son the next day to trap him with your mongrel of a child. Give me my grandson immediately or I'll have you thrown out on your whoring ass."

As Jake entered the nursery, he could see Emma, pale and defiant, her chin up, aquamarine eyes shimmering with fire, as she held Kyle to her with a protective fury. Blood surged to his cock, heated, unexpected, inappropriate. She looked glorious, a spitting wildcat protecting her cub, quite capable of biting off a hand if it came too close.

"Don't you touch him," Emma said. "Jake's down in his office and he can decide whether or not you're going to take Kyle out of the house. No one takes him without Jake's permission, not even you. And you don't get to come into our home and bully our nurse or our cook, and you certainly don't drag the baby out of his crib when he's asleep and scare him like that. I don't care who you are."

"*Your* nurse?" Cathy screamed. "*Nothing* in this house is yours and it never will be." She stepped closer, thrusting her twisted, angry face close to Emma's. "You can count on that. I'll see you in hell before I ever see such a tramp attached to my family."

"Cathy." Jake said her name, his voice low, rumbling with menace.

Both women whirled to face him. Instantly the room went silent. Kyle abruptly stopped crying, as if the sound of Jake's voice reassured him. Emma dropped her face protectively over the baby, but not before Jake saw the sudden sheen of tears. He walked to her, breathing deep, stilling the raging monster rising to the surface in a fury of temper, wanting to rend and tear and destroy. Very gently he rested his hands on Emma's shoulders, deliberately dropping a kiss on top of her head.

"Take Kyle and go to your room, Emma. Let me deal with this person."

"Jake!" Cathy wailed his name. "This—your *mistress* was so rude to me."

Emma shook her head. "Jake, I wasn't."

"Go, honey." He stroked a hand down the length of her hair. "You aren't supposed to be out of bed. Take Kyle. He doesn't need to be in here."

Emma didn't look at Cathy, but caught up Kyle's favorite blanket and walked out, her bare feet padding down the hall toward her room.

Jake took another calming breath and let it out. "What are you doing here?"

"I came to see my grandson." Cathy's eyes narrowed.

"And I've heard the rumors; we all have. I can see that nothing's changed. You're still the same, Jake. Irresponsible and foolish. You're a womanizer and you don't seem to realize that there are women who are clever and manipulative who will trap you in any way that they can. I'm your mother—"

"Get out." He bit out the words, his fingers curling involuntarily, knuckles aching, bones cracking. He felt sharpened claws ripping into the palm of his hand, tearing at his own flesh. He opened his hands and flexed, holding the rapidly forming paws out away from his body where she could see the long, wicked claws protruding from his fingers as the change threatened to consume him. "Get out now." The scent of something wild, something feral, permeated the room.

Cathy backed away from him, stinking of fear. He could hear her heart racing, beckoning the predator. She gasped as she saw Jake's eyes go completely golden, the orbs darkening into the focused stare of the leopard. She turned and ran, a small wail of absolute terror escaping. She pushed past the nurse who stood at the foot of the stairs and bolted out the front door.

Jake managed to make it to the nursery door, slamming it closed, leaning against it as the change swept through him, clothes ripping at the seams, his back bending, spine stretching, bones popping. He dropped to all fours, breathing deep, trying to hold back the tidal wave of fury consuming him. Other than his first change, the leopard had only come out when he summoned him. But the animal was furious now, clawing for freedom, determined to hunt the enemy.

He ducked his head, breathing hard, panting, his sides heaving as his skin itched and a wave of fur slid over his back and down his legs and spine. His mouth filled with teeth, and his knuckles turned, curling under, the razor-sharp claws tearing long strips in the floor as he dug deep and raked, desperate to hold back the beast.

"Jake?" Emma's voice called out to him. A breath of air, fresh and clean, driving the stench of his enemy from his nostrils.

He drew her into his lungs, into his mind, shaking with the effort to keep the leopard under control. Slowly—too slowly—his human form reasserted itself. "I'll be right there," he called when he could speak. His voice sounded different, rumbling with a velvet growl, even to his own ears.

He sank back against the door and dropped his face into his hands. He scented blood, and the leopard tried to come out again. He pushed back hard against the door, just in case, forcing the leopard—and himself—back under control. Very slowly, he dragged himself to his feet. His shirt was in tatters, but his jeans were intact. There was little he could do for the floor. He wiped his face with the remains of his shirt and was surprised when he found smears of blood. Curious, he turned his hands over. His claws had burst from his fingers and torn his palms when he'd made a fist.

"Tell me you're all right," Emma insisted.

He took another breath and let it out, realizing that he wanted to be with Emma and Kyle more than he wanted to disappear in the change, to run free of his past in his other form, to wreak vengeance on his enemies. Jake didn't let himself think too hard about why. He stood up and went to them just as he was, tattered shirt, bloody hands and bare feet.

Emma gasped when she saw him, standing immediately, putting Kyle on the bed while she reached for him. "What happened? What did she do to you?"

He caught her and pulled her tight against him, holding her close, breathing her in, allowing the memories to recede until he could push the door shut on them. He caught her face in his hands and pressed kisses along her eyes, feathered more down her chin, barely resisting her upturned mouth—that fantasy mouth. His heart beat too loud and he feared she would push him away, but she didn't. Instead she slid her arms around his waist and she rested her face against his chest, just letting him hold her.

"I'm sorry," she said gently. "She was angry at me, not you."

"She's evil," Jake said. "Thank you for not letting her touch my son." Very gently, he put Emma aside, not trusting himself in his present unfamiliar state. He felt vulnerable and shaky. He didn't trust his temper, the leopard, or his need of her. Already his body was responding to the softness of hers, to her scent and the silk of her hair. He couldn't afford to blow everything he'd done by letting her see how she affected him.

He lifted Kyle into his arms and held the boy close. "She kept you safe, just like she said she would," he murmured, astonished that it was true. *Emma.* She wielded some kind of magic he didn't understand. His heart felt soft and alien as he looked down at his son. "She kept you safe," he repeated and kissed the little forehead. Jake's entire body trembled. He actually felt weak.

"Jake." Emma's voice was soft. "Sit down. I want to look at your hands."

He looked at her over the top of the baby's head. She looked small and fragile, so pale and thin, without makeup, her wealth of hair curling in every direction, but she was made of steel. "You're an amazing woman, Emma."

"You need to sit down, Jake," Emma coaxed softly.

She tugged at his arm, her gaze searching his face. For the first time she realized Jake Bannaconni—the man with everything, the man who could buy and sell the world—needed someone. Needed her. For all his gruff ways and arrogant orders, he had no idea how to feel emotion, and when his feelings overwhelmed him, like now, he was lost, or he turned to anger or ran from it. She didn't think anyone needed help quite as much as Jake did. Right now he was looking at his son with a stunned, confused expression, as if he never expected to love the boy. She could have told him that first day, when he'd fumbled to change his diaper, that love grew in spite of a person, and that someday Kyle would take over his life.

Jake's gaze collided with hers and for a moment something hot sizzled and burned between them, but he blinked and that smooth, arrogant mask slid into place. "I know the doctor said complete bed rest, Emma. The next time I find you up, you'll be in trouble."

Emma wanted to laugh. He sounded so serious. So in charge. He probably thought he was. "Then give me Kyle and you go get the things I need to clean those scratches on your hands. I'll be so good."

He scowled at her. "No, you won't." He waited until she settled back into the bed and he handed her the baby. "You exasperate the hell out of me."

"I know I do." Emma just smiled up at him. In that moment she realized that in spite of his bossy ways, and the sense of danger that sometimes sent a shiver down her spine, she liked him. "Go get the antiseptic. Kyle and I will wait right here for you." She nearly laughed at the confused male look that crept across his face before he turned and stalked out.

TWO MONTHS LATER

"IT'S too soon, Jake," Emma sobbed, squeezing his hand as they carried her from the helicopter. "Don't let anything happen to the baby. No matter what. You promised me. If anything goes wrong, you know I want you to take her."

"Don't talk like that," Jake snapped back. "You're going to be fine, Emma. And so will the baby. Just relax and let the doctors do their job."

He had assembled the best team of experts he could find and flown her to the best hospital, and he wasn't leaving without Emma and the baby. He tasted fear in his mouth. His heart hammered too fast, too hard, but he refused to even consider that something could happen to her.

"Thank God you hired this old bat," the nurse said with a quick wink and a grin at Emma. "Otherwise we might not have known until it was too late." She patted Emma's shoulder.

Jake couldn't find it in him to smile at the joke. Over the last few months he'd come to know Brenda Hacker—the old bat, as he often referred to her. She'd gotten over her aversion to him, mostly he thought because she liked Emma. Who didn't like Emma? Even the cowboys had come up to the main house when the helicopter had landed to take her to the hospital. All of them had looked as somber and upset as he felt. He'd tightened the security at the ranch and left the cook and a bodyguard in charge of Kyle and orders that no one come or leave while he was gone.

Once he'd finished giving everyone he could think of every order possible, he was left with the feeling that he had no more control. It was a frightening feeling. Emma caught his hand, holding it tight as they put her on a gurney and rushed her to a preparation room.

"Promise me, Jake. Whatever it takes. Say it."

"Damn it, Emma. Nothing will happen to you." He crouched beside her head, his lips against her ear. Even he could see the bright red blood dripping from the table as they slid lines into her arms, racing against the clock, preparing to take her to surgery.

"They have to take her now, Jake," Brenda said. "Let them go."

"No! He has to promise," Emma said.

Jake caught her face in his hands and kissed her. Right on her mouth. Uncaring that she might not want it, or that she would be angry later. His eyes burned and his throat felt clogged with a million regrets. "I give you my word. But you live, damn it. Do you hear me, Emma? You live."

Brenda took his arm and tugged gently. Jake shook her off, taking a step after the departing gurney, noticing that they were practically running as they took her away from him. He swore softly under his breath and stepped to the window, looking out, wanting to be alone. The nurse moved away and he breathed a sigh of relief.

He had no idea how to handle his life anymore without Emma in it. His carefully laid plans didn't matter as much as making certain she was alive, somewhere in the world, preferably in his home. She was sunshine and laughter and she just plain made him feel good. She was the most exasperating woman in the world, but he found every day filled with her.

When he worked in his office, she intruded on his thoughts continually. When he ran free as the leopard, she ran with him in his mind. When he rode horses and checked cattle down in the steep ravine, she was there. Even in the oil fields she intruded, so that he craved the sight and sound and scent of her. At night, tired and exhausted, he looked forward to going home to her.

How many nights had he sat on her bed, nudging her to scoot over so he could stretch out while they talked together in the dark? She was small and soft beside him, her hair like silk on the pillow. Sometimes he rubbed the strands between his fingers as she told him about her day. When the baby kicked, she would grab his hand and put it on her stomach, and he'd feel the tiny little thud and wonder would spread through him like a warm tide.

He didn't want to lose that small life growing inside of

her any more than he wanted to lose Emma. Jake frowned and shook his head, trying to deny his anxiety. Surely the baby didn't matter to him so much, but the loss would devastate Emma. She couldn't take another death. He couldn't let himself think too much. He had to trust in his preparations. The teams of doctors, both for Emma and her unborn child. The blood he made certain was on hand.

"Jake?"

Jake swung around and nodded to the man who'd entered, his lawyer, John Stillman. He'd done a background check on Stillman long before he ever approached the man to represent his personal interests. Stillman was a man his great-grandfather had casually mentioned, an up-and-coming lawyer who was impressive. If the man had impressed his great-grandfather, Jake was willing to meet him. During the interview Jake had asked questions, lots of questions, designed to make the man uncomfortable, but not once had he smelled a lie.

"The nurse called me the minute there was a problem, just as you instructed. Emma signed the papers on the helicopter ride over, giving formal consent for you to adopt the baby. Ms. Hacker witnessed her signature. The rest is a formality. I'll take it to the judge."

"Tonight, John," Jake said. "I want it done the moment the child is born."

If the baby lived, it would bear his name. He had promised Emma he would give the child his name and raise it, and he had every intention of keeping his word to her. One more tie to her. If Emma died . . . He slammed the door shut on that thought, his heart contracting painfully.

"She's in surgery?"

Jake nodded, unable to find his voice. Activity in the halls sent him striding past the lawyer. He turned as a doctor approached.

"Emma?" He bit her name out, fear skittering through his body like a lethal snake.

"I'm sorry, Mr. Bannaconni, she's still in surgery."

He couldn't breathe. He stood there, head down, not looking at any of them, and thought he was going to choke on his own fear. It was silly, really. He'd been beaten nearly to death as a child and he hadn't experienced such a wave of terror. How had she done that? How had she snuck into his head and wrapped herself so tightly around him, he didn't know how to live without her in his life?

The doctor cleared his throat. "Your little girl is underweight, of course, and will have to be in a radiant warmer. She's unable to keep her body temperature, but we did expect that, with her being so early. She's having a little trouble breathing on her own and we have her on a ventilator. There are a few problems . . ."

Jake swung around, meeting the doctor's gaze. "You do whatever it takes to make my daughter live and be healthy. That's why you're here. We both knew it wouldn't be easy, but I was told you were the best at what you do. So you do it."

"I'll do my best." The doctor knew better than to promise something he wasn't certain he could deliver to a grief-stricken parent.

"Her name is Andraya Emma Bannaconni."

"Yes, sir. The nurses will bring the paperwork."

"I want it immediately. I want her to have an official name immediately."

"Would you like to see her?"

Jake forced air through his lungs. "Not until Emma is safe." He turned his back again, dismissing the man. His fingers curled, nails digging into his palm. It had been years since he felt the slice of a knife in his thigh, but he wanted to feel it now, to score another victory. His daughter was alive. Now he needed Emma to live.

He waited until he heard the doctor's retreating footsteps before glancing over his shoulder at his lawyer and then turning back to the window, not daring to show his face while he was vulnerable. "As soon as we take care of the paperwork here, you leave and take care of the adoption. I want it filed immediately."

"Jake, with your name on the birth certificate, she's safe for the time being."

Jake's voice went low, threatening. "I want it filed today," he repeated, "whatever it costs. And make certain the ruling is sealed and doesn't become a media event. I mean that, John. You make certain anyone seeing those papers understands there will be severe repercussions if it comes out that I'm not her biological father." He looked over his shoulder, pinning Stillman with a hard gaze. "I'll make it my business to destroy them if they fuck this up. You let them know who they're dealing with."

Stillman stood behind him for a long time, then went to sit down, waiting for the nurse to bring the papers to fill out. He wasn't surprised when an administrator brought the paper immediately. Jake took his time, penning neatly, making certain the child would be safe should anything happen to the mother. Stillman stayed quiet in a corner, feeling as though he couldn't leave Jake alone, although the man so obviously wanted to be.

Jake began to pace like a dangerous animal. He felt dangerous, scattered, out of control—all things that brought the leopard close to the surface. His skin itched and his temper smoldered. He found himself angry with Emma for continuing a pregnancy that could kill her. He was angry with himself for allowing her to get close enough to him to make him feel so lost without her. He didn't honestly know how it had happened when *he'd* set out to entrap *her*.

He rested his hand on the window, spreading his fingers wide, his throat raw, his belly in tight, protesting knots.

The glass fogged from his breath and he traced letters in the mist. *Let her live.* Three words. That was all. A lifetime of nothing and finally Emma. Let her live. He leaned forward and rested his forehead against the pane. He didn't know why he couldn't stop thinking about her, but he knew if she made it through this, he would have to distance himself enough to regain the control between them. *Please, God, if you exist, let her live.*

He closed his eyes and breathed deep, turning his will to find her. *Emma. I won't let you leave me. You can't go. Do you hear me? I'm giving you an order. Hang on to life. The children need you. Kyle. Andraya.*

He wouldn't use himself as a bargaining chip. She didn't look at him with that look. The one she reserved for Kyle. Or Andrew. That bastard Andrew, who'd had it all. *We have a baby girl. A beautiful little girl. Live for her.*

For me. Live for me.

Why couldn't anyone love him? He pulled back and stared at his own reflection. Cold. Unfeeling. The eyes of a predator. Yet right then he wasn't unfeeling. His lungs heaved and his eyes burned. The leopard leapt and roared, clawed for freedom to protect him from too much feeling.

He smelled Emma's blood long before the doctor made his way down the hall to where he waited, his pulse pounding, afraid to move, to turn, to see the look on the man's face.

"Mr. Bannaconni?"

"Just tell me." Jake kept his back to the man, his shoulders stiff, his spine straight.

"Your fiancée is in recovery. We had to give her a great deal of blood, but she made it through the surgery. We've done our best to correct the damage that occurred at the time of the accident, so it's possible she could carry another child sometime in the future, but she has to get through tonight. She's weak, Mr. Bannaconni. I won't lie to you. We aren't out of the woods yet."

Jake swung around, golden eyes glittering, so that the doctor sucked in his breath and stepped back a pace. "I want to see her now. Take me to her."

"She's in recovery. You'll have to wait until she's out and in her room."

Jake's eyes narrowed and he took a step forward. A low, warning growl rumbled in his throat. Stillman leapt up and stepped between the two men.

"I suggest, Doctor, that you take Mr. Bannaconni to his fiancée immediately. If anyone can ensure that she doesn't die, it will be him. He won't be in your way." The lawyer's voice was smooth, but left little to argue with.

The doctor reached behind him and slid his card through the mechanism to disengage the lock. "This way, sir."

Jake followed the man to the recovery room. Emma looked small and lost, her face white, her eyes closed. There was blood in one bag and a clear liquid in another. Brenda Hacker shot him a quick, reassuring smile as she toed a chair in his direction. Jake straddled it up near Emma's head, facing her, and settled in for a long night. He had no intentions of losing Emma at this point, and if sheer will meant anything, she would be staying right with him.

5

"YOU keep it up, boss man, and we're not going to have any crew left," Drake Donovon said. He leaned forward in the saddle and spat on the ground. "You've always been as mean as a snake, Jake, but now you're getting downright ugly."

"You think I give a damn whether they like me or not?" Jake snarled. "And don't call me 'boss man.' You only do it when you're pissed."

Drake shrugged. "You lose me any more of my crew and I'll be walking myself." His probing gaze slid over Jake, clearly assessing him. "You brought me here to educate you about your heritage, but you don't listen to me." He looked around, his face suddenly etched with something close to sorrow. "I have a hard time breathing here. If I can't be of help to you, I need to go back to the forest where I belong."

"No way, Drake. I need you here." Jake cursed the fact that he'd been so moody, so edgy, everything and everyone around him making him want to fight, to rip and tear at anything. The mood swings didn't seem to let up, not for a moment, and the black temper rode him so hard that he actually felt uncomfortable even in his own skin. He knew he had a cruel side to him, he just hadn't been so aware of it slipping out before he could get control. He despised that part of him, so like his parents, so cutting and cold. He'd sworn he would never be like that, yet here he was, the master of cruelty.

What the hell had Emma said to him the other night while he lay on her bed, his blood pounding with need in his veins. *Power corrupts.* It had been another night where neither could sleep and they'd engaged in one of their common "we don't know what the hell we're talking about" conversations, but that little phrase stuck in his head. His parents were corrupted by the need for money and power. Was it possible he was just as corrupted? He hated admitting to Emma he had a sense of entitlement.

"I listen to you, Drake," Jake said. Drake Donovon was not a man to be pushed around. Danger lurked just beneath the surface. He was a good man to have on one's side, but would definitely make a bitter, unrelenting enemy. Jake raked his fingers through his hair, wanting to jump out of his skin. If he ever needed anyone in his life right then, it was Drake.

Drake shook his head. He was built along the same lines as Jake, broad shoulders; thick, muscular chest; ropes of muscles along his arms and thighs. An enormously strong man, yet lithe and fluid, moving silently, like water flowing over rock. It wasn't difficult to notice the pronounced limp he had when he moved. When he was still, everything stopped. He became so still he was nearly a part of his surroundings. His blond hair was shaggy and untamed, his eyes a little strange, piercing and focused, a brilliant golden green.

"You need a woman. I told you, you can't go that long and let the tension build up."

"I've had women, sometimes twice in a day. A few times more, damn it. It doesn't do any good. I'm still as hard as a rock and feel meaner than ever. It claws at me day and night until I think I'm going insane. I haven't slept in weeks. I can barely walk half the time, and if a man comes near the house, I want to rip his fucking head off." Not to mention, when he lay beside Emma on her bed, he felt guilty, as though he'd betrayed her. And worse, he wanted to attack her. He was afraid he might actually lose control one day and just roll her under him and bury himself deep and hard, the way he wanted.

Drake blinked, his eyes suddenly narrowing, one eyebrow shooting up. "Near the house?" he echoed. "And what claws at you?"

"I need sex every minute, but when a woman touches me, I end up despising them. My skin crawls and I find myself doing things, saying things . . ." He broke off, his lips tightening. "I'm not very proud of myself. I act like a bastard—and they just come back for more. Then I walk into the house and it starts all over again."

"You have a woman there. Emma."

Drake's voice irritated Jake when he said her name. Smooth. Like velvet. Knots formed in his belly. "What about her?"

"She takes care of your son. Your house. Does all the things a man's woman does for him. But you don't have sex."

"That's right." Jake's voice rumbled with a low, warning growl. He didn't want Drake, with his good looks and charm, going up to the house with Emma. That would push Jake right over the edge. "Not with Emma."

Drake frowned at the sound of Jake's voice. He took a good long look at Jake's eyes and body language. "I thought

this woman was just your housekeeper, but you're pretty
wound up about her, Jake." Now there was curiosity in
Drake's voice.

Jake didn't want Drake or anyone else curious about
Emma. He hadn't expected to want to be with her. To feel
a sense of peace even with his body raging out of control.
She was supposed to want to be with him, not the other
way around. She'd turned his entire life upside down and
he couldn't do a damned thing about it. She had him *suffering*, physically, emotionally, in every way possible and
his temper was getting shorter and shorter.

"I'm wound up, but not because of her," Jake lied. And it
was a lie. Blatant. Stupid. Hell, he was obsessive over Emma
and getting worse every day.

He used every excuse to go into her room at night. He
was pathetically grateful for the nightmares she sometimes
had, and for the fact that she'd gotten used to him stretching out beside her while they talked in hushed, intimate
voices. Of course she didn't know his body was as hard as
a rock, and that the moment he left her, he jerked off like
some silly teenage boy with no control.

"I want to meet her again."

Instantly the air thickened with tension. Murderous
rage swept through Jake, a tidal wave that shook him.
Thunder crashed in his ears, his blood boiled and fire
burned in his belly. He actually saw red. Beneath his
skin, something wild broke free and ran, itching uncon-
trollably. His jaw filled with teeth; his lips drew back in a
snarl. Jake turned his head away from Drake, knowing
his eyes glowed a feral red. He took several deep breaths
to try to control the rampaging leopard clawing to break
free.

As the wild animal in him wrestled for supremacy, his
horse reared, screaming in fear, then suddenly lunged and

bucked, trying to dislodge him. Jake dug his knees in harder and controlled the animal, murmuring soothing words, grateful for the distraction.

When the horse was calm, he glanced warily at Drake. "You've met Emma several times." Drake wasn't like the other men, flocking around her, looking for handouts of fresh coffee, baked bread and cookies. Drake had a tendency to be a loner, keeping to himself, living in one of the smaller cabins on the property.

Drake shrugged. "If she's affecting you like this . . ."

Jake frowned. "I didn't say she was having any effect on me at all. I'm restless and bored, but women don't get under my skin."

Drake snorted derisively. If it had been any other man, Jake would have been tempted to knock him off his horse. But Drake was different. He held a certain respect for Drake, so he kept his vicious temper under check.

"I'll tell you straight up, Jake," Drake said, gathering the reins. "You're acting a hell of a lot like a man who has a mate going into heat." He pushed back his hat and turned his horse away. "If that's the case, the symptoms only get worse."

"I don't have a mate. And women don't go into heat."

Drake nodded. "So you say." He dug his heels into the horse's side and trotted away, leaving Jake staring after him.

"WHEN will he be here?" Susan Hindman hopped up and down excitedly, leaping from one foot to the other. "Honestly, Emma, how can you stay so calm?"

Emma smiled one of her slow smiles and continued kneading the bread dough. "He'll be here soon enough, if he's radioed in. Don't worry, you'll have plenty of time to

be with him. After all, you'll be here another four weeks."
Susan was Senator Hindman's daughter, and he'd called
and asked if they could watch her while the senator was
out of the country. She was good company and Emma
really liked her, but she had a terrible crush on Jake.

"Four weeks," Susan echoed, dramatically clasping her
hands to her heart. "It's probably just as well he was gone
when I arrived, I don't know how I'll stand it."

Emma laughed, a soft, pleasant sound that sounded
melodic to Susan. "You're so silly, Susie. He's no different
than other men." A dimple appeared along the right corner
of her mouth, melting when she added, "Perhaps a little
more of a tyrant."

"Oh, Emma." Exasperated that Emma didn't share her
latest heartthrob, Susan shook her head. "I don't understand you. He's gorgeous. All those incredible muscles."
She hugged herself ecstatically. "Muscles everywhere.
Wide shoulders. And that tan and those eyes. He's to die
for. You must be blind."

"It's a definite possibility," Emma agreed, laughing at
Susan's drama.

"And he's richer than rich. He gets invited to the best
parties, he's on the cover of magazines, in the newspaper.
He knows movie stars and the president and, well, everybody. He knows everybody."

At sixteen, Susan was tall and lanky, without curves but
with a coltish grace promising well for the future. Her
hair was dark and curly, she had laughing hazel eyes with
a generous spray of freckles across her nose. Jake wasn't
aware of her visit yet, and Susan was anxious that he hurry
home. He had called Emma three times a day, impressing
Susan to no end, but Emma only seemed to find Jake very
amusing and mildly exasperating instead of incredibly romantic.

"Your father has a great deal of money," Emma reminded mildly, "and he's always in the news. He certainly knows the president and more than his share of influential people."

"Oh." Susan dismissed her father with a wave of her hand. "Dad's just . . . well, Dad. Jake is different. He's so exciting."

Emma hid a smile, one inquisitive eyebrow going up. "Exciting?"

"Handsome. And all the rumors about him. People are afraid of him, you know. Daddy says he's one of the most powerful men in the world."

"Money and power aren't everything, Susie." It was a gentle reprimand. "And looks aren't everything either."

"Well, I know that. Daddy says he has such a brilliant mind and it's totally wasted on this ranch. He should be in politics, not just dabbling." She frowned. "But of course, he's got lots of enemies. Daddy says his kind always do. He says Jake is a barracuda in the boardroom and no one's business is safe from him. Better to be his friend than his enemy. Jake's just so fabulous and women chase him all the time."

"I'll bet your father didn't know your big ears were around when he said all that either," Emma said good-naturedly. She gave a last pat to the dough and went to the sink, shoving rather unsuccessfully at the unruly red hair spilling down her back in spiraling wisps, not to mention around her face and into her large eyes.

It bothered her that Jake was everything Susan's father had said he was. He did make enemies easily, and he seemed ruthless in his business dealings with others. Emma didn't fully understand the concept of buying and taking apart other companies, but she knew Jake was considered merciless when he conducted business.

She took another look at the birthday cake she'd decorated earlier, hoping Jake really would make it home this time before the weather brought another disaster. She wanted to surprise him with a small celebration.

"Just last month I saw Linda Rawlins and Jake get into a huge fight over you."

Emma swung around, her eyes enormous. "Me? Why me?"

Susan immediately felt contrite. Emma was very small and slender with flawless skin; well, almost flawless. She had two very faint scars marring the perfection of her face, both on the left side, one up near her eye, the other a long, thin crescent ending near the corner of her mouth. Susan had never gotten up the courage to ask her about those scars and Emma had never volunteered the information. Emma's past remained something of a mystery. Even her father didn't talk about Emma.

Jake had brought her from somewhere on the West Coast to be his housekeeper. That was all anyone ever said. Susan adored her ever since their first meeting, when her father had gone to Jake's house seeking campaign funds. She'd discovered Emma in the kitchen, laughing with the two toddlers. Immediately she'd pitched in to help and they had become good friends.

Her most secret desire was to have Emma's incredibly large green eyes and silky red-gold hair curving around her own face and cascading down her back to her waist in waves. Emma was sweet and understanding; she was always ready to listen to anyone, whether it was one of the ranch hands, Susan, or one of the children. Yet Emma always looked very vulnerable. Even at sixteen, Susan felt protective toward her.

"I was just kidding," Susan lied baldly, not liking the flicker of pain in the depths of Emma's eyes.

"You may as well tell me." Emma sighed, pulling a large barrette from the pocket of her faded blue jeans. She caught at the thick mass of hair and clipped it at the nape of her neck. The pulled-back style emphasized her high cheekbones.

Susan looked uneasy. "It's only gossip, Emma, I didn't believe it."

"Believe what? Come on, Susie, you've gone this far."

"Well." Susan scuffed at the Mediterranean tiles with her foot uncomfortably. "I was in the hall, it wasn't like I was eavesdropping on purpose or anything."

"Susie."

"All right, but I wasn't listening on purpose. Linda way-laid Jake at this party and asked him to take her to the Bingleys' party, which you probably know is the big event of the season."

Emma didn't, but she nodded anyway, trying not to wince when she heard the other woman's name.

Susan grinned suddenly. "Can you believe it? I wished I'd had a tape recorder. The great Linda Rawlins actually having to ask a man to escort her. I could have made thousands selling that information to the tabloids. Little shipping heiress shunned by the oil king."

"You read too many gossip magazines," Emma scolded determinedly.

"Yeah, probably." Susan was unrepentant. "But they're so much fun."

"Get on with it."

"Jake was cool and very polite in that distant way he has, but you know, with that sort of bored, *totally* hot look he gets. He told Linda he was taking you and she blew up. Like, big time. Sky high. She was shrieking at him at the top of her lungs. She told him nobody in society would ever accept you, and that his own parents thought it laughable that he was with you and that he was only doing it to spite them. Then she called you a domestic servant. Jake looked down at her with that sort of contempt thing he does and then she really got nasty."

Emma twisted her fingers together. Lately she'd been emotional and upset, and for some strange reason Susan's gossip really upset her. She knew everyone gossiped about Jake; he just took it in stride. But she was always out of sight on the ranch where no one saw her and she saw no one. She rarely even left the ranch. Linda had come by to see her already and said very ugly things in spite of the fact that Emma had tried to reassure her she was just the housekeeper.

"Linda said everyone knew Jake was Andraya's father and he got both you and Shaina pregnant at the same time and he only kept you around because of his illegitimate brats." Susan was outraged all over again, her fists clenched at her sides. She was definitely loyal to Emma.

Emma paled beneath her golden tan. "What did Jake say?" It was one thing to say it to her, here at the house, but to publicly scream it to Jake at a party was something altogether different.

"He didn't deny it. He just looked Linda up and down sort of like she was a loathsome bug and he stalked off in that cool way he walks. He was so gorgeous. And Linda looked pathetic and jealous."

Emma passed a shaking hand over her face and sat down rather abruptly. She didn't want people using her or Andraya to get at Jake.

"Oh, Emma," Susan wailed. "I'm sorry. I didn't mean to upset you. Linda's jealous. It's just that Jake is so different with you. You never seem to notice, but he's"—she hesitated, searching for the right word—"indifferent toward women. He brushes them off like flies; he has no time for them. You never go to parties but you should see him.

Honestly, I'd die if he looked at me the way he does at those women, with such contempt, as if they're so far beneath him."

In spite of herself, Emma had to laugh. "He can't be that bad or they wouldn't be falling all over him."

"Other people aren't like you, Emma," Susan felt compelled to point out. "They'd sell their souls for all that money and power. And he's so hot. Women would put up with a lot for that. Plus, I think there's something about taming the bad boy."

"That's insane. You've been reading too many novels, Susan. In real life, if the man is bossy and arrogant, he isn't all that easy to live with. And I doubt if women throw themselves at Jake just because of his bank account."

"Sure they do," Susan insisted. "Dad's a senator, and a widower. Believe me, I've seen the women go after him and know all the signs." She wrinkled her nose. "You met Dana when she brought me. My governess. Ha. What a crock. She's so after Dad, and you saw how stuck-up she was with you. She treats me like that, as if I'm so far beneath her, yet she thinks I'm going to let her be my stepmom."

Emma hadn't cared for Dana, although she wasn't going to admit it aloud to Susan. The woman was too cold and made too many cutting remarks to Susan for Emma's liking.

"Jake is different with you and it shows," Susan continued, warmed to her theme. "He's gentle and he laughs around you. He calls you three times a day and he kisses you. You just don't believe me because you don't see him away from here."

"Oh, for heaven's sake. I run his house. Of course he calls me. I have to give him his messages. And just for your information, he doesn't kiss me, he just sort of pecks me. We've lived here two years together. We're affectionate, that's all."

"Daddy said you nearly died when Andraya was born and Jake didn't leave your side once," Susan pointed out. "And he named Andraya while you were unconscious. And Andraya and Kyle look alike."

Susan was fishing for information, but Emma didn't take the bait. "Poor Jake. How awful of Linda to throw all of that in his face."

"Look alive, Emma." A short, stocky man with laughing blue eyes and a shock of sun-bleached hair stuck his head in the door. "Boss is on the way in, landed ten minutes ago." He grinned at Susan, letting out a slow, appreciative wolf whistle making the young girl blush wildly.

"Thanks, Joshua," Emma acknowledged dryly. "I'll have fresh coffee on."

Joshua saluted, winked at Susan and ducked back outside. Emma stood in the center of the room for a moment, staring out the huge picture window. Such an innocent conversation on Susan's part, yet it brought back a flood of memories Emma dared not think about. She shivered, remembering the feel of hard hands gripping her with incredible strength, the smell of gasoline, the loud roar of flames, the emptiness that never quite went away. It had been a long while since she'd allowed herself to think about that day.

"Emma?" Susan's concern was evident in her voice, drawing Emma back to the present. "Are you all right?"

"Yes, of course, honey. Run along and check those kids for me, will you? They were playing horses in Kyle's room but they're being very quiet. There're some things I need to do."

"You're sure I didn't upset you? Linda's just jealous, nothing more, Emma."

Emma forced herself to smile. "Linda doesn't bother me; it isn't the first time she's called me a domestic servant. I should have known she couldn't resist spreading gossip." She measured coffee into the filter with the casual ease of long practice.

"She called you that? To your face? How inexcusably rude."

"Check Kyle and Andraya," Emma reminded. "And don't be too upset, Susie. Linda is a close friend of Jake's parents, and they remind me every chance they get that I am a domestic servant. It doesn't bother me a bit to be called one. I'm certain Linda got that from them, and she thinks working for a living is something awful, but I certainly don't. I'm very good at running this house."

"You aren't a servant." Susan was horrified.

Emma spun around and hurried from the kitchen, down the hall, through the large family room and right out the front door. For once she wouldn't be greeting Jake when he came in. She wanted to be alone for a while. After two years of peace, she felt like she was waking up. She loved her life, the ranch that had become her home, and the two children. Kyle was as much hers as Andraya was. The problem was she thought of Jake as hers as well. Lately she'd become restless and moody, and just thinking of Jake could make her body come alive in ways it hadn't for the last two years.

Dear Jake, it was so like him to take the brunt of the gossip on his wide shoulders—to protect her and never say a word about the rumors. If she complained about anything at all, just a mere mention, whatever it was disappeared, was fixed or managed without a word.

She couldn't face him right now. She felt confused when she was near Jake—her body growing more and more uncomfortable in his presence. Every sense heightened when he came near. His scent, masculine and forbidden, tantalized her. The drawling sound of his voice was like a caress over her skin. Maybe it had happened so gradually she hadn't been aware of her attraction to him, but she'd lived comfortably with him for two years, and to her it seemed as if, all of a sudden, when he was near, her body reacted by coming alive. And when he was gone, she couldn't stop thinking about him.

She hurried across the driveway, running down the path to the stables. What a mess they would all be in if she made the mistake of allowing him to know she was sexually attracted to him. Kyle called her Mommy, believed she was his mother, and for all intents and purposes she was. She loved him as if he were her flesh and blood. Kyle and Andraya loved each other as brother and sister. And Jake was equally wonderful to both of them. And she loved Jake. Really loved him. She had loved him long before she was attracted sexually. And falling for him that way would only ruin everything.

Emma laughed softly to herself, remembering Jake getting up night after night to help her with Kyle, to change wet diapers and feed him. Now, with Andraya, he still got up, even if Kyle stayed asleep. When he was home, he fixed her tea or chocolate and sat with her while she rocked the baby to sleep. He never seemed to actually go to bed, spending most nights in her room. Sometimes he stretched out on the bed beside her, and those nights had become a kind of private hell. She wanted him there, yet the temptation of his body was becoming dangerous.

He would have had sex with her. He was nearly always hard, always ready. It wasn't that difficult to see the impressive bulge in the front of his jeans, and he never bothered to hide it or appeared embarrassed or ashamed. But she didn't want to become one of his women. He treated them with total indifference, contempt even, and she couldn't live with that.

Emma caught up a bridle, running a practiced eye over the horses standing patiently in the stalls. She wanted one with stored-up, restless energy. Maybe if she took a long ride, she would be able to calm her body down and figure out why she was so restless and edgy and desperate for a man's body. Not just any man—Jake.

"Emma." A quiet, menacing voice made her stiffen. Powerful fingers bit into her shoulder, spinning her around. "What the hell's going on here?" Jake demanded. Diamond-hard eyes raked her pale features, noting the shadows lurking in her dark eyes, dwelling on the pulse beating frantically in her throat, touching on her soft, trembling mouth.

The sight of him always robbed her of breath. Jake was formidable, overpowering, dangerous. A rock for all of them, yet he moved silently, like a cat in the night. "I'm going riding, Jake," she answered, straining to keep her voice even. She loved looking at him, all that flowing power, the swift impatience, the way the corners of his eyes crinkled right before he smiled. But he could be very overwhelming when he chose to be intimidating—as he was doing now.

He swore, pulling her soft body right up against his tough, well-muscled one. He had a day's growth of beard, and up this close she could smell his outdoorsy, masculine scent. "Like hell you are. I haven't seen you in two long weeks. What's up?"

With an effort, Emma managed a faint smile. "Nothing, Jake. I was shirking duties, that's all. How was your trip?"

Swift annoyance spread across his sensual features. She could feel the tension in his large frame. "Come on," he snapped impatiently, whirling around, taking her with him. "If we're going to spar, we may as well be comfortable."

He moved with the lithe, flowing grace of a prowling jungle cat, power and coordination combined. Emma, with her shorter legs, was forced to run to match his lazy, long stride. He glanced down at her bent head, his eyes a glittering gold, and deliberately slowed his pace to accommodate her. Casually retaining possession of her arm, he dropped his flat-brimmed hat on a chair as they went through the family room.

"Was that Susan Hindman I saw upstairs?" he demanded abruptly, releasing her as they entered the kitchen. "She was peeking over the banister and making eyes at me."

Emma nodded, rubbing absently at the marks of his fingers on her arm. "She's staying with us while her father's away in London. He asked me right after you left. I didn't think you'd object. Her governess, Dana Anderson, brought her along with a gentleman they said was her tutor, a Harold Givens." Jake didn't like strangers on the ranch.

"What's she been saying to you?" Jake's handsome features were set and hard. He looked very formidable. Even so, he reached out to take her arm in the palm of his hand, his touch gentle as he examined her skin for finger marks. The pads of his fingers stroked caresses over the marks, his touch lingering, sending tingles of arousal along her nerve endings to spread through her body.

She pulled her hand away because he looked as if he might kiss her better, and her pulse began to hammer hard, first in her throat, then in her breasts, and finally in her most feminine core. Color swept up her neck. It was so humiliating to be out of control of her body when it had never happened before. He couldn't know. She couldn't give herself away to his sharp, probing gaze.

"Sorry, you have such fair skin, honey. I always forget that. What did Susan have to say?" he persisted.

She shrugged lightly, ignoring the strange sensations his nearness produced in her. "Only girl talk." She kept her voice even but his touch had disturbed her so much she couldn't meet his gaze.

He sighed, his golden eyes never leaving her face. "God, I'm tired. It's been a long two weeks. You have any coffee made?"

She flashed him a quick smile. "Of course, you know I do. Want to eat?" She handed him a steaming mug. He did look tired, his hair tousled and unruly, just the way she liked it best.

He shook his head. "Coffee's great. I've been dreaming about your coffee. Where are the little monsters?"

"Upstairs playing. I'm surprised they're not down here already. They must not have heard you come in." She watched him toss his coat aside and sink into one of the kitchen chairs. Without conscious thought, Emma reached out and pushed an unruly lock of hair from his forehead.

He tilted the chair, golden eyes on the pulse beating at the hollow of her throat. She moved with a curious, delicately feminine retreat. A crooked smile touched his mouth. He deliberately allowed his eyes a lazy exploration of her soft, curving body. "Have the kids been good?"

"They're always good, although they missed you, if that's what you're asking." Emma poured herself a cup of coffee and leaned against the sink, a small but relatively safe distance from him.

"And what about you? Did you miss me?" His voice was a soft whisper, like fingers skimming along her skin.

Faint color stole into her face. She loved the sound of his voice. "Of course I missed you. I always miss you." And she did, as arrogant and bossy as he was. "I was hoping you'd come home today."

"Why today?" He took another sip of coffee with an appreciative smile. "This is better than gold. I really miss your coffee when I'm away."

"It's your birthday."

Jake narrowed his eyes, sitting up straighter, watching Emma cross the room to the overhead cupboards. She had to reach high, stand on her toes, but she managed to pull a large, flat package down. He tried not to react, to stiffen, to get up and walk out. It was a birthday present, no big deal, and he couldn't very well tell her he didn't want it, wouldn't know what to do with it. Little kindnesses were too hard to accept. She had a look on her face that was a birthday present in itself, and more than he could ever want.

Emma had made his house a home. She always went that extra mile, always showing him in so many ways that he mattered to her. Like now. He set his coffee mug on the table, afraid his hands might tremble and give him away. He should have realized she would remember from two years earlier when she'd been in the hospital and he'd told her. She'd been barely conscious of anything, grieving and frightened, yet she remembered a trivial detail like his birthday.

She had insisted on celebrating Kyle's birthdays, but that was different—far different with the spotlight on him. He stood up, the leopard in him restless at his sudden edgy mood swing—at the adrenaline surging through his veins.

"I made this for you."

Her trip to town Joshua had reported. He'd scrambled to send bodyguards with her, men she wouldn't realize were there to protect her. This was why. This package she held out to him. He took it from her hand, surprised at the weight of it. She looked anxious.

"The big question," she teased, shifting from one foot

to the other. "What does one get for the man who has everything?"

He set the package on the table, running his hand over the thin paper, the pads of his fingers absorbing the texture. His first ever birthday present. Some part of him still didn't trust the feeling and wanted to run, but another part wanted to savor the moment, to draw out the anticipation of seeing what she got just for him.

He took a breath, let it out and tore off the paper. His own face stared up at him, half man, half leopard. The power of the leopard was in the eyes, golden and focused and staring at him from any angle. The painting was amazing, and captured stillness and a wild, untamed mystery. More than that, the painter seemed to know the subject, every line, every curve, the strength and remoteness, although each stroke of the brush conveyed a caress, a loving hand.

He couldn't speak, his vocal cords paralyzed. Did she know? It wasn't a capture of the change itself, more a picture of a dual personality. This was not the work of an amateur, although there was a certain rawness to the painting. She was good. Better than good.

"You don't have to hang it if you don't like it, Jake. You love leopards so much. I always notice you touching the bronze statue you have beside the stairway. And your office has amazing sculptures and paintings of leopards. I thought you'd like . . ."

His fingers settled around the nape of her neck, pulling her to him, his thumb under her chin, forcing her face upward toward his descending mouth.

Emma panicked, watching his brooding eyes go golden right before she felt his breath. Her heart stammered. His lips were velvet soft, firm, so warm and insistent. Butterfly wings fluttered in her stomach. His tongue stroked across the seam of her mouth and she couldn't stop the sigh that escaped. His other hand fisted in her hair, controlling her head, turning to the perfect angle to give him access.

Jake couldn't have stopped himself had his life depended on it. He had waited so long to taste her, to feel the velvet-soft lips crushed under his, to seek the warm, moist paradise of her mouth. The trouble was, once he started, he couldn't seem to stop. He lost all control, losing himself in the fiery heat and amazing, unique taste that was Emma.

She stayed very still for a moment, allowing his invasion. But as his demands grew, she began to respond, so that he breathed for both of them, tangling his tongue with hers in an erotic dance that sent lightning streaking through his body, making the blood pound in his shaft and every cell in his body leap to life. The leopard prowled close to the surface, demanding a mate, raking and clawing at his belly with need.

He had no choice but to lift his head for self-preservation. If he went any further, if he touched her as he ached to do, he would never stop. He took a breath, staring down at her face, memorizing every detail.

Emma stepped back, her eyes a little glazed. "What was that?" she asked, struggling for breath.

"That was a thank-you. I love the painting." He flashed a smile at her. "I've never actually had a birthday present before. This is my first."

She frowned. "Never? Why would—"

His look stopped her midsentence.

The tension drained out of her, although she still had a wary expression on her face. "Then I'm very glad I painted it for you. It wasn't easy keeping it a secret, but you're gone a lot these days and that gave me the extra time."

He frowned. He had an excellent sense of smell and it

was odd that he hadn't noticed the scent of paint. "Where did you work on it?"

Emma fairly beamed at him, making him want to gather her back into his arms.

"Joshua built me a small room in the barn. It's not like you go there often, so we thought it the best possible place to keep a secret."

Every muscle in his body contracted. The leopard leapt, raking at him, snarling in protest. Even his cock tightened, a hard, pulsing weapon threatening to wreak vengeance. "I'm sorry," he said softly. "What did you say?"

Emma flashed another grin. "Can you believe it? We managed to actually keep the painting a secret. It was really difficult to get the lighting right. Poor Joshua had to change it about a hundred times before I was satisfied. I hadn't painted in a long while, so I was nervous about doing it for you. He was great, though, when I told him how important it was to me."

Her voice faded in and out as hot blood surged and retreated, ebbing and flowing like a series of tidal waves. Thunder crashed in his ears and he breathed down the black jealousy that threatened to break free. He tried not to picture Joshua alone with Emma, their two heads together, so close, a breath apart. He curled his fingers into a tight fist.

He'd never been a jealous man. This horrific emotion shaking him was ugly and destructive. He fought for control, shocked at his inability to stop the rising tide of anger. He wanted to feel Joshua's neck beneath his fingers, feel the man choking, the breath leaving his body. He wanted to rake open the belly, the fierce need primitive and strong.

"Just how great was he?" His voice was a growl, a threat rumbling in his throat.

He turned on Emma, his much larger frame looming over hers, backing her against the sink, trapping her body against the counter, one arm coming down on either side of her to form a cage. "How great, Emma?"

Danger hummed in the air. Emma felt the tension in the room heighten but wasn't certain why. What it did to her body was frightening. Her breasts tightened, nipples peaking. Arousal teased at her stomach and thighs. Hot liquid pooled and her womb spasmed. Her breath came in a ragged rush. She was all too aware of the heat of his body, of every muscle moving beneath his skin. His eyes glittered like old gold, and his mouth put erotic fantasies in her head.

In all her life she'd never felt so achy, so in need, and she could see why women threw themselves at Jake. It was a little humiliating to be among them, a woman wanting to beg for his attention. She lowered her gaze, not wanting him to see what was happening to her. Even her skin felt him, an electric tingle that sizzled across her nerve endings.

"Damn it, Emma, fucking answer me."

Okay. Now she was really sick. His harsh demand only sent a surge of fire through the liquid heat. Her tight inner muscles convulsed. She took a deep breath and let it out, determined not to allow her acute sexual awareness of him to affect her. "Are you angry with me for something, Jake?" Her skin itched, and for a moment she swore something moved inside of her, unfurling and wild. Her clothes actually hurt, pressing against her sensitive skin. She ached to turn her face up to Jake's and devour his mouth, to shred his clothes and feast on his body.

Emma's throat closed and she shrank back against the counter, horrified at her thoughts. What was wrong with her? She'd never behaved like that. Never felt wanton and needy and desperate for sex. And with Jake? She'd never be able to live with herself afterward. After she became one of his discarded women. She'd have to leave Kyle. Take Andraya away from everything she knew. She had to get away from him.

In desperation, Emma lifted both hands and shoved hard at the wall of Jake's chest.

6

JAKE trapped Emma's hands against the wall of his chest and held her there. The hard push hadn't even rocked him. "I'm not angry with you, honey. I'm sorry I'm acting like such a bastard. There's no excuse." And there wasn't. Hell, she'd wanted to surprise him. She had surprised him. Not one other person in the world had thought to acknowledge his birthday. Only Emma. And he was snarling at her.

She looked up at him, her eyes searching his face. He did his best to look reassuring when he just wanted to kiss her again, this time making certain she felt the possession, so that she would know just whom she belonged to. Jake rubbed at his shadowed jaw, irritated by his thoughts. He'd put a lot of effort into his plan and Joshua wasn't going to sneak in and take Emma out from under him when he wasn't looking.

"Was it really bad out there?" Emma asked, trying to guess at the reason for his bad mood.

"We had to shift the entire herd until the men can get the fences back up and clear out the debris. I lost more than

I'd first thought in that freak storm. Water backed up the canyon, causing a land shift."

"I'm sorry." She spoke quietly, sympathetically, picturing the dead and bloated cattle lying half buried in the mud.

He was watching her expressive face. "You're too soft," he drawled lazily, allowing her hands to slip away from his chest. His thumb slid over her skin, savoring the feel of her. "It's a cattle ranch, honey. We're going to have a few disasters."

"So you keep telling me." The tension in the room was slowly dissipating and Emma felt herself beginning to relax. Jake stepped away from her and she instantly felt the loss of his body heat, but it allowed her blood to cool and the terrible aching need to fade a bit. She took another deep breath, thankful she was regaining control.

Having a physical relationship with Jake would be total personal suicide. He didn't keep women for long. He used them, let them use him, and then he discarded them. He wasn't even nice about it, although she'd noticed most of the women kept coming back for more. She'd always felt sorry for his women as they called and left messages he never returned. She thought them a little sick to want such a twisted relationship, but here she was, her body melting into a pool of need at his feet. It was humiliating.

Just one time having sex with him and she would jeopardize the home she'd come to love. She would have to leave Kyle and take Andraya from Jake.

Jake legally adopted Andraya. The thought leapt unbidden into her head.

The one thing she knew about Jake was that he made a bitter, relentless enemy. He used every means possible to destroy his enemies. If she left, would he try to take Andraya from her? Not only was it a possibility, it was a probability.

Jake sprawled in a chair, feet out in front of him, his

gaze once again on her face. "Never play poker, Emma," he advised. He kicked at a chair, spinning it around in invitation. "I'm not in the mood for cat-and-mouse games, so sit down for a minute and tell me what's gotten you so upset."

"Let's leave it, Jake," Emma suggested softly, not meeting his focused stare. He could unnerve anyone with that look. Why did he have to be so darned perceptive, noticing the slightest differences about her? He noticed everything about everyone, the tiniest details, and she needed time to think about things and come up with a plan just in case.

He reached out a long, powerful arm and gently tapped her cheek. "Not when it bothers you. You know I'm not going to let you get out of here until you tell me, so spill it."

She rubbed the palm of her hand nervously along her jean-clad thigh. "I've been thinking about our situation."

"Well, don't," he snapped abruptly, his rugged features hardening. His eyes glittered dangerously at her, daring her to continue the conversation.

Emma scowled at him, ignoring the chair and leaning back against the counter to regard him with troubled eyes. "I thought you wanted me to tell you what I was worried about. Just because you don't like something doesn't mean it just goes away."

A brief flash of amusement slipped through his bad temper. "Sure it does. If I tell you to quit worrying about something, it's because I have it handled."

She rolled her eyes. "Really, Jake? Sometimes you make me want to be a twelve-year-old and stick my finger down my throat to gag myself. Do you honestly think you can order me not to worry and I'll just stop?"

"Sure. Have you ever known me not to handle a problem, especially one you were worried about?" He shrugged his shoulders.

Emma planted her hands on the counter behind her and lifted herself up to sit. He did take care of any problem.

Even if she mentioned it casually, he immediately fixed the least little thing. He did it so smoothly she often didn't even notice. "This isn't that kind of thing."

"All right. Spit it out."

Now that she had his attention, she wished she'd let him divert the conversation. She tried to choose each word carefully. "I've just been thinking about the future. I've been drifting along without any real plan. It's so comfortable here and I'm not really looking forward to leaving."

Something dangerous crossed his face and she paused. He had gone very still, his lids dropping so that he'd narrowed his gaze. His eyes had gone completely golden, slipping into the absolute, single-minded concentration that she found unnerving.

"Andraya and Kyle are as close as blood siblings. They love each other and they love both of us. If you found someone you wanted—"

"Emma, this is such bullshit. You aren't going anywhere. And I'm not finding anyone else." He waved his hand dismissively.

"We have to think about it. We do, Jake, whether you want to face it or not. The longer the children are together, the harder it's going to be to break them up. The thought of losing Kyle is already more than I can bear."

"You're not losing him because you aren't leaving. What the hell has Susan Hindman been saying to you that's gotten you all upset?"

"It isn't Susan, Jake. You're legally Andraya's father. I'm not Kyle's mother. If something happened, I'd be the one to lose out, possibly on both of them."

He was on his feet, tall, enormously strong, towering over her, looking suddenly ruthless and a little cruel. Temper was riding him hard. "Okay, now you're just pissing me off on purpose. What the fuck does that mean, Emma? Tell me what you mean by that."

She held out a hand to ward him off, but he kept coming, wedging his hips between her legs and catching both of her upper arms to give her a little shake. His fingers dug deep. His eyes looked like glittering jewels, hot and angry, his body giving off a blazing heat.

"You're the one who's always telling me to think about the future instead of the past. It's not like we can stay here like this forever. And then what happens to me? Don't pretend you wouldn't demand your rights to visit with Andraya."

Without visibly moving, his hand snaked out, hard fingers spanning her throat, allowing her to feel his immense strength. His thumb tipped her chin up so she was forced to look up at him. He was enormously strong, and it showed in his well-defined, rippling muscles and the powerful grip of his hands.

"You aren't leaving me," he growled very softly. His gaze dropped to her trembling mouth and he made an effort to soften his voice. "If you're so damned worried about your rights, let's get John here tonight, now, and have him draw up adoption papers. You never brought it up, so I just assumed you knew you were his mother and that was the end of it. But if you need the legality of a formal adoption, then just do it."

"You still have the advantage, Jake. You know every judge."

A muscle ticked along his jaw. For a moment her heart nearly stopped. He looked more like a leopard than a man, a predator about to leap on and devour prey.

"If you fucking want to get married, just say so and we'll get it done along with the adoption. Whatever it takes to stop this bullshit about leaving. As my wife you'll have the same playing field and I can pretty much guarantee that judges will like you better than they will me. And don't give me crap about me finding someone else. If I was going to find someone, I would have already done it. For Christ's sake, Emma."

"Well, what if I find someone else?"

"How are you going to do that, locked in this house with two kids and still pining away for someone who's never coming back? You don't even look at men, Emma, so no, you're sure as hell not going to find someone else."

Fury swept through Emma, her temper rising up out of nowhere, something rare but lethal once she got going. She was tempted to slap his face, but it wasn't her style. She reached behind her to keep her itching palms away from him and came in contact with the sprayer on the sink. Without thought she turned on the faucet and blasted him with cold water right in his arrogant, handsome face.

"Maybe you ought to stop being such a hothead, Jake."

Emma released the trigger and dropped the sprayer in the sink, torn between horror at what she'd done, anger at his callous proposal and the implication that *she* might never find someone else, and laughter as water ran down his face over his shocked expression and dripped onto his very expensive soaked shirt.

There was complete silence. A heartbeat. Two. Hard hands seized her, swinging her smaller body over his shoulder as if she were a sack of potatoes. One hand came down hard on her wriggling butt, a stinging blow that made her yelp as he strode to the door and carried her outside down the long drive.

Heat flashed across her bottom and spread deep inside, the swat triggering a different memory, or maybe it had been an erotic dream, lying across his lap, his hand coming down hard and then rubbing sensually as he was doing now.

Her heart jumped. Where had that come from? Lately she'd been having dreams of Jake, dreams of things she'd never consciously thought about. Emma drummed at his broad back with her fists, fuming, embarrassed, not at being upside down but at the heat rising in her body and the blood surging so hotly.

Jake delivered a second smack, this time a little harder than the first, and once again rubbed at her bottom to take the sting away, sending fire shooting through her veins. "Stop it, Emma. You so deserve this and you know it."

The deep growl of his voice sent an illicit thrill coursing through her bloodstream. She wished her jeans weren't so tight or her panties so skimpy. She could feel his hand burning right through the thin material as he rubbed to ease the sting.

She caught a glimpse of Joshua's startled face as Jake stalked past him. She looked around quickly, seeing the direction in which they were heading, and knew instantly what he intended. "Don't you dare, Jake." Emma caught at the back of his shirt with both fists, realizing what he planned. "I mean it. Don't you dare."

He kept walking at the same pace, with long, purposeful, ground-eating strides. Emma clutched him harder, trying desperately not to laugh at the ridiculous situation. She should have known Jake would retaliate. What ever had possessed her to spray him with the kitchen sprayer? She'd been too angry to think clearly, but it hadn't occurred to her that Jake might ever do this. "Stop. Don't do it." She couldn't help it that her voice turned to pleading. Or that laughter played around the edges. She'd always had the worst sense of humor.

Jake swung her from his shoulder, cradling her for a moment, then held her out from his body and dropped her unceremoniously into the large horse trough. She came up sputtering, splashing water ferociously at his face, laughing so hard she could barely stand.

Jake stood over the horse trough, water cascading over him as she used the flat of her hand to send a huge wave into the air. Time slowed down so that the droplets of water glistened like diamonds and the sun seemed to surround her head, turning her red hair into a bright halo of light and gleaming off her pearly teeth. Her laughter was infectious, melodic, irresistible, and he found himself laughing with her. *Laughing.* Deep inside, happiness blossomed and spread. He'd never thought much about being happy. Not like this—something simple. Something not revenge, or dark and ugly. Something not about making money. Just laughing at the absurdity of their argument.

He reached into the trough and hauled her out, swinging her easily to the ground, one arm locked around her waist, holding her wet body against his. The air was crisp and cold and she shivered, but her laughing face was turned up toward his and—God help him—he was tempted almost beyond all control. He was beginning to understand the story of Adam and Eve.

"You're crazy, Emma. You know that?" His voice was gruff. Husky. He could hear the need almost as much as he felt the ache, not in his groin—although he was as hard as a rock—but in his chest. He actually pressed a hand over his heart. "Let's get you back inside. I didn't realize it was so cold out here."

She slipped under his shoulder naturally, as if she belonged there, her arm curling around his waist, still laughing up at him.

Snickers broke out behind them and she ducked beneath Jake's arm to peer at the ranch hands. They stood with wide grins on their faces, doubled over laughing.

"Having a little trouble, boss?" Joshua called.

"Need a hand there?" Darrin, another hand, yelled.

"Hey!" Emma objected. "No cookies for either of you for a month."

The leopard in Jake scented genuine camaraderie, an honest shock at his out-of-character behavior and real laughter. He didn't know how to react. A part of him wanted to join in the laughter, to share in the moment the way Emma did, to have fun. Hell. This silliness was fun. He didn't know how to react, or even what to say, so he just grinned, waved them back to work and kept her walking toward the house, slightly uncomfortable that his work crew had seen him acting so childish, but still feeling a small glow.

"I'm never living that one down," Emma said, smacking his chest. "I can't believe you dumped me in the horse trough." She smacked him again. "And you spanked me. Sheesh, I'm not two, you know."

His palm immediately dropped to the enticing curve of her bottom, rubbing caresses. "I couldn't resist."

She made a face. "I don't think that was an apology."

"No? Imagine that."

She reached behind her and removed his hand. "And now you're just being a perv."

He bent his head until his lips brushed her ear. "Not a perv, Emma, an opportunist."

Emma kept her head bent. He kissed her often, touched her often, but never with that lingering, possessive hint to his touch. Was it her imagination because she was suddenly so aware of him? Because he'd kissed her senseless with his birthday thank-you? She had to get a grip. She was so out of sorts, so restless and moody lately.

She told herself as she lay in bed at night, unable to sleep, that she missed a man's touch, the feel of his body. She definitely missed Andy. He'd been nothing like Jake, so different it was nearly impossible to find any common ground with the two of them.

Andy had been fun loving and uncomplicated. He didn't harbor obviously painful secrets. There was no intrigue about Andy at all. He was exactly what you saw—open and honest and ready to help anyone. Not closed off emotionally, as Jake was. He trusted people, and always thought the best of everyone. Jake trusted no one and expected people to double-cross him at every turn. Andy had boyish good looks and charm, where Jake was all hard edges, a brooding, dangerous man who exuded sex from every pore, a man in every sense of the word.

Jake rarely smiled, he barked orders and he was so protective the children could barely move without bodyguards getting under their feet. She doubted if Andy would have noticed danger even if it hit him in the face, let alone simply imagined it or suspected something or someone was out to hurt them. Andy took it as his right that she would cook and bake and do all the little things she loved doing for him, where Jake always seemed shocked and even a little wary of any kindnesses done for him. He noticed everything she did, and often didn't seem to know what to say or do in return—but he noticed.

Jake's hand wrapped around the nape of her neck. "You've gone away again, Emma. You've been doing that a lot lately."

She managed a quick, reassuring smile. "I know you've got work to do this evening, Jake. You always do. But I made you a cake. I thought after dinner you could do the birthday thing with the kids. They'll make a terrible mess, but they'll love it."

She couldn't keep the anxiety from her upturned face. She shouldn't have told the children they were going to have a birthday party with him, but she'd been planning his surprise for days and they'd seen the preparations. She held her breath.

"Emma, do I let you and the children down often?"

She hesitated, unsure how to reply. He did everything for her and for the children. "Of course not, Jake. You take care of everything." That at least was honest.

He moved closer to her, trying to surround her shivering body with heat as they stood together just outside the kitchen. "I'm not talking about things like that. You have a look on your face, like you think I might ignore the party you planned. Do I do that? Not be there for you and the kids emotionally? I don't mean to. If something is important, you need to let me know. I'm not very good at the family thing. I don't really know what I'm doing half the time, so I follow your lead."

Emma took a breath and let it out, suddenly wanting to cry for him. He could do that in one heartbeat, with one revelation of his past, make her feel his vulnerability, his absolute, single-minded resolve to learn how to live in a family. She hated hurting Jake. He really did try with them, and maybe it was only with them, but every evening he was home, he tucked the kids in their beds and definitely seemed to enjoy the family dinners. He just wasn't home often. He always asked about the children when he called, always wanted every detail, but he didn't participate that much in actual hands-on parenting.

"Emma." He said her name quietly, his hand on the doorknob. "If blowing out candles and watching Kyle and Andraya make a mess is important to you, or to them, then of course I'll be there."

"Thanks, Jake," Emma said. "I think Kyle and Andraya will have fun."

Jake opened the door and allowed her through. "You'd better grab a hot shower. Susan can watch the little ones while you get cleaned up. I do have some work to do in my office before dinner, but if I get tied up, just come get me."

Emma glanced at her watch. "I've got a telephone repairman coming any minute, Jake, and we needed to fix the phones in your office as well. I'm sorry, I didn't think you were going to be home until this evening."

"What's wrong with the phones?"

Emma frowned. "I don't know. There's an echo I don't

like. Joshua thought the squirrels might have chewed on the lines, so I'm having everything checked, starting in the house and working backward. He shouldn't be in your office long. I'll get him out as soon as possible."

"Have Joshua do a security sweep as soon as he leaves," Jake cautioned. "And have him stay with the man at all times."

She stuck her chin in the air. "*I'll* stay with him at all times. I'm perfectly capable of looking after the house."

"Joshua isn't looking after the house," Jake snapped, his eyebrows drawing together. "He's looking after you."

"We've had this conversation a million times, Jake. I'm not two. I don't need looking after. It's my job, not Joshua's."

Jake opened his mouth and closed it. She had the most sexy, stubborn look on her face he'd ever seen. His body reacted with a hot flair of need, a need to conquer, a drive to change that look to submission, compliance, hunger even. Few people ever argued with him or stood up to him, but Emma had no problem at all giving him her opinion.

He tasted her in his mouth. His body ached. He pushed a towel into her hands. "If you get any strange vibes, call me or Joshua immediately." He stepped away from her, frowned and turned back. "And I want Josh in the house. That's nonnegotiable."

Emma drew herself up to her full height. "Absolutely not. I take care of the house, not Joshua. If I don't like something, I'll let you know."

A hint of a smile flickered across his face. She had the little bite in her voice he loved to hear. It didn't matter how often he offered to rehire a cook or a nanny, she refused and he was grateful. He had come to enjoy the way she ran the house, the scent of cookies and freshly baked bread in his kitchen and the sound of laughter echoing often through the halls. She considered the house her domain and she guarded it jealously.

"Joshua stays in the house, Emma. You're too trusting."

Emma made a face at him, shivering, her teeth chattering as she reached for another kitchen towel. "I am not. Just because I like people doesn't mean I'm trusting. I'm well aware you're worried about Kyle's and Andraya's safety. I agree totally with you that they should have bodyguards. I've never once objected to that."

Jake walked back to her, his body crowding hers until she could feel his heat. She backed up until her bottom hit the edge of the table and she had to stop abruptly. Jake took the towels from her as he deftly removed her barrette with the other hand and slipped it into his pocket where so many others had disappeared before it. Emma found it impossible not to notice the way his muscles rippled beneath his soaked shirt, how wide his shoulders were and how strong his arms seemed.

Her body reacted again, blood surging hotly, something wild inside of her reaching for him. She breathed away the need, her breasts rising and falling, aching to be touched, her nipples tightening into hard peaks she was desperate to hide. He began to rub at the silky strands of wet hair in an attempt to dry them. His arm brushed her breast and her womb clenched and pulsed. She caught her breath and counted in her head, trying to think of anything but how his waist tapered into his narrow hips and how the front of his jeans had an impressive bulge.

For a moment, just one moment, an image rose in her head: Jake's strong hands on her shoulders, pushing slightly until she obeyed his silent command and she was kneeling, reaching for him, wanting the familiar shape and texture of him, already anticipating his masculine taste and the way he'd make her feel, as if only she could bring him exquisite ecstasy. She'd love looking up at him, meeting his eyes while she took control, driving him past all sanity until he was truly helpless under her erotic onslaught.

Her breath caught in her throat and her heart slammed hard inside her chest. She'd been a virgin when she'd married Andrew. They'd only been married five short months when the accident happened. She didn't know the first thing about sex, not sex like the images in her head. Her attempts to please him had been funny and not very successful.

"Hey." Jake tugged at her hair. "Are you listening to me?"

Had he been talking? Color rushed into her face. "Only when you make sense."

Jake tugged a little harder on her hair until he tilted her head back, forcing her to look into his eyes. "Don't ignore me when I'm talking about safety, Emma. You can object to having someone in the house with you, but sadly, honey, when it comes to your safety, I get the last word whether you like it or not." He dropped a kiss on the tip of her nose and left the towel draped over her head. "I don't want Susan to be a problem for you. If she causes you more work, or any trouble . . ."

"She won't. She's watching the children for me. She's very good with them."

Jake inclined his head. "I'm heading for the shower. I suggest you do the same. If you feel like conserving water, you can shower with me."

Shower with him? Had he actually said that, or was her imagination running wild? What in the world was wrong with her? Emma stood speechless, the idea of being naked in a shower with Jake sending her already hot blood erupting into a fiery conflagration she could barely comprehend. She needed a shower, all right. An icy-cold one would be best.

Dragging the towel from her head, she took the back staircase, wanting to avoid Susan and the children until she was cleaned up and centered once again. Jake had managed to rattle her when she was already feeling so moody. She sighed, stripping off wet clothes and flinging them into the laundry basket before stepping under the spray. She was simply missing being close to a man. It had been two years. Maybe Jake was right and she was hiding away on the ranch, rarely venturing out other than to buy groceries and things for the children. Jake took care of everything for her.

She sighed. She needed to make a change. Jake had kept her safe in a little cocoon. She'd relied on him and he'd simply shouldered the burden, just as he took on everything else in his life. He barked orders but he was rarely angry, not with her and certainly not with the children. She wanted to stay where she was. She liked her life, liked cooking for Jake and some of the ranch hands, liked taking care of the children. She'd always wanted a home and she couldn't ask for a better one. She couldn't ruin it by having an affair with Jake. And if she was ever stupid enough to give Jake control over her . . . She shuddered at the thought. Jake could take full advantage.

She shampooed her hair, closing her eyes to absorb the sensation of soap and water running in rivulets over her skin. Her skin felt too tight, too sensitive. Everywhere she touched she felt fingers of arousal pulsing through her body. She leaned against the shower wall, frowning, trying to understand what was happening to her. Her breasts felt full and heavy, aching with the need to be touched. She felt empty inside, her body flushed, almost feverish. The water actually hurt her skin.

Emma stepped out of the tiled stall and wrapped herself in a towel, looking in the mirror and feeling a little dazed. The need to be touched was growing, not lessening, and it had come on slowly, so slowly she hadn't realized what was happening until the last week. Everything seemed different to her, as if all her senses were heightened.

A thump on the door had her whirling around with a small gasp.

"Hey! Emma, look alive. The phone repairman is here."

Emma took a deep breath and let it out. She had to pull herself together and stop all the silly nonsense that could threaten their very comfortable world. She dressed briskly and once again quickly caught her hair in a barrette, pulling it back away from her face, making a mental note to have it cut soon. She wore it up far more often than down anyway. Running after the two small children made it impossible to style.

Joshua waited on the stairs for her. "I'm supposed to stay with you."

"You're supposed to stay in the house." Emma pushed past him, her hand brushing his chest. She felt a shudder of awareness go through him and she turned her head to look at him. Joshua had always—*always*—acted like an older brother. Now he was looking at her with speculative eyes. She frowned at him. "Go away, Joshua."

"You smell good."

"You smell like horses. Where is our guest and why did you leave him alone?" Her voice was tinged with exasperation. Everyone was losing their minds lately, not just her. Joshua stared at her with hot eyes, making her uncomfortable.

She ran lightly down the stairs into the entryway to find a young man standing awkwardly, staring around him with a slightly awed expression on his face. "Hello, I'm Emma Reynolds, the housekeeper. I'll show you all the phones."

"Greg Patterson."

"The housekeeper?" Joshua snorted.

Emma glared at him. "Thank you so much, Joshua. I'll show him the phones. If you'd like, I made fresh bread. It's in the bread basket on the counter."

Joshua frowned at her. "Emma . . ."

She smiled serenely. "It's your favorite. I know you're

on a break, so I made fresh coffee for you as well." There. She'd given him a good reason to stay in the house and not make it look like they didn't trust the phone man. She kept her smile, willing Joshua to follow her lead.

"The kids?"

"Taken care of," she answered, grimly hanging on to her smile. Did he think she was an idiot? Of course she'd made certain Susan knew to keep Andraya and Kyle locked away in the nursery while they had company in the house. He was almost as bad as Jake. She'd lived with the security for two years, understood it and accepted it, but *she* didn't need a babysitter. She was not going to be humiliated by having Joshua follow them from room to room. He could sit in the kitchen and listen for screams if he was as paranoid as Jake. Jake had said in the house, not necessarily in the room.

The scent of fresh-baked bread permeated the house, and after a brief hesitation and quick warning glare at the telecommunications man, Joshua abruptly turned on his heel and headed for the kitchen.

Emma turned her attention to the workman. He was short and stocky, with wavy brown hair and warm, smiling eyes. He looked so familiar Emma found herself frowning, trying to place him. "Do I know you?"

"Sort of." He followed her down the hall, staring, a little awed at the massive, beautiful rooms they passed. "We've bumped into each other in the grocery store, in the produce section. You helped me pick up my apples when I dropped them."

Emma laughed. "I remember, of course. You enjoy juggling."

His gaze flickered downward to her left hand, noted the absence of a ring as she waved him into a room. "Quite a house you've got here."

"Thank you." Emma loved the house, and appreciated anyone who recognized its beauty. "It takes quite a bit of care, but I love working here."

"I always wanted to see this estate. No one can actually get on the property without an escort. The grounds are incredible and the house even more so."

"It is a working cattle ranch," Emma explained.

"Is Mr. Bannaconni here much?"

Emma tossed a small smile over her shoulder, but didn't answer the query. Her loyalty was solidly with Jake, and as such, she never gave information about him to anyone. The smallest remark could end up in a tabloid, and Jake had enough people hounding him. In truth, he flew often out of the country as well as to the many states where he owned properties, but he always returned home to the ranch.

They passed the long, wide, sweeping staircase and the high ceiling where the bronze leopard sat amid climbing plants. She was pleased at Patterson's swift intake of breath. "This house is amazing. You must love it here."

"Yes, I do." And she took great pride in making certain it was clean. Jake insisted on cleaners coming twice a week, but she managed every day and it made her feel possessive and proud of their home.

She gestured toward the phone in the den. "This is where I notice the noise the most. The other phones have just a tinge, but this one is more pronounced."

Greg set his equipment down and watched as she perched on the arm of a chair across the room from him. "This may take a while."

"That's fine. I expected it to," she answered, her voice pleasant.

Greg snuck another quick look at her before returning his gaze to the phone cradled in his hand. "Are you and Mr. Bannaconni together? I didn't notice a ring, but that doesn't seem to make much of a difference these days."

Emma stiffened. Was he looking for information for the tabloids? She tried to keep her voice light and casual. "I work here."

Greg shot her a quick, shy smile. "Well, in that case, there's a great movie opening at the theater tomorrow night that I was hoping to see. I don't suppose you'd want to go with me?" He couldn't make himself look at her when he asked her, rubbing at an imaginary fleck of dirt on the telephone instead.

Emma sucked in her breath. She'd never dated anyone, not really. Not before Andrew. But Jake had just taunted her, made fun of her actually, by telling her she'd never find another man because she didn't pay attention to men. Jake, Greg seemed young and uncomplicated, even tame. He certainly didn't stir her sexually, but she needed something, a change, a way to deal with the way Jake made her feel.

"If you don't mind me meeting you there, and it would have to be the late show," Emma found herself agreeing. She held her breath, suddenly hoping he would say no.

"Great!" An enthusiastic smile lit his eyes. "Tomorrow night, then."

Emma's heart thudded in alarm. What had she done? Jake had hurt her ego, and in a small spurt of defiance she had made a decision she wasn't really ready for. And it wasn't fair to Greg. She had no real interest in him. Her decision was really about being afraid of herself, of the aching needs she couldn't quite get free of. She wasn't herself lately at all, and her dreams were downright humiliating. Every single one of them was about Jake and things she had no real knowledge of and wasn't certain she really wanted to learn.

"Greg, I'll go with you as a friend. Nothing more. If that's not what you want, then I'll have to back out. I should have made that clear." She kept her voice gentle, low, sorry she might be hurting him, angry with herself for getting into such a position because of pride and fear. It wasn't Greg's fault that he'd happened along at precisely the moment she would agree.

"I understand. It's all good," he said. "I'd like to go with you."

He sent her another brief grin, one that was strangely reminiscent of Andy's. Sweet. Not asking for anything. Friendly. Maybe he was just what she needed. Jake's personality was overwhelming, swamping her, chipping away at her resistance. Everything about Jake tore at her continually. His intense needs. His dark, brooding manner. His pain. His arousal. His orders and flashes of temper. The way he softened when he was with her. The way he lay next to her when he couldn't sleep and idly played with strands of her hair, sometimes touching her soft skin and sliding his fingers over her warmth as if she belonged to him.

Just thinking about his touch made her slick with damp heat. She took a breath, let it out and forced a smile, trying to understand what Greg was saying to her.

Greg explained every detail as he worked, his voice droning on and on, until she felt desperate. It was impossible not to think about Jake when she wasn't in the least bit interested in how the phone worked. She heard him call her name and looked up expectantly, embarrassed that she'd drifted off a second time.

Greg frowned as he looked at the phone. "What exactly are you hearing? Because the line appears clean."

"I don't hear it until I actually talk, or someone else is talking to me. If I'm quiet, it's not there. I had a couple of the ranch hands listen and only Joshua could hear it, but it really bothers me." It made her uneasy. The phone in Jake's office didn't seem to have the same problem on it. She'd gone into his sanctuary and checked herself, relieved when his private line appeared to be clear. She just had a bad feeling.

"Do you hear voices?"

Emma burst out laughing. Greg looked up, a little startled, realized how his question might sound and then joined her.

"The line appears to be clear. My equipment is showing a strong signal, but if you only hear it when you are actually speaking, we could be dealing with something like spy equipment." His eyes brightened and he grinned at her much like a small boy. "That would be cool. Could someone be spying on you?"

"I think you've been watching too many movies," Emma said, forcing another laugh, suddenly quite uncomfortable. Even the paparazzi were known to bug houses, and someone like Jake had all kinds of enemies.

Greg laughed again. "Well, it would certainly be a first if I ran across spy equipment."

7

JAKE stood just outside the open door, his heart beating in his throat as he breathed away the need for the leopard to rise. In that moment, with Emma's innocent laughter ringing in his ears and the scent of her arousal filling his senses, he recognized that he was becoming dangerous. Something was very wrong. He should be in his office, locked away from all noise, never overhearing the play between a man and woman. He could hear the male interest in the man's voice, the innocence in Emma's tone. Yet she was definitely aroused, and that maddened him. He felt cruel, capable of viciousness. He hated that ugly part of him, the one that rose when he felt things too deeply, telling him, showing him that he carried the legacy of evil in his blood.

He knew he needed help. He would have to talk to Drake, find a way to combat the intense jealousy sweeping through him at the mere thought of any man around Emma. She had become an obsession, invading his thoughts every moment of the day, torturing his body with a permanent hard-on, massive and thick and so damned painful he could barely walk at times. Nothing he did helped, no woman sated him—he burned for Emma. Somehow she'd managed to turn the tables on his plan. She was supposed to be obsessed with him, but somehow it hadn't turned out that way.

He stood, leaning one hip casually against the doorjamb, waiting for her to look up, watching her face, the way her eyes shone, the way her mouth was so expressive. She stayed across the room from the man, which was the only thing allowing Jake to keep his sanity. The leopard was so close. His chest rumbled with growls, his throat ached with the need to roar. His teeth hurt from trying to hold back the change, the need to leap upon his enemy—his rival—and rip him open. And Emma. What he wanted to do to Emma.

His body, so hard, every muscle taut, skin too hot to touch, his cock so full and sensitive that every step he took was painful. He needed to . . . He just *needed*.

Emma looked up and her eyes met his. For a moment time seemed to stand still. Her gaze softened, warmed, and in that moment his heart squeezed hard and his stomach tightened. His fingers curled into his palm. He remained silent, afraid his voice would come out more leopard than human.

"Greg can't hear that hum I told you about on the phone line."

Greg? Who the hell was Greg to be called by his first name? Did she know him? The man was staring at him with that slightly awed look people often got in his presence. He showed his teeth without actually smiling. Maybe it came out a snarl. He didn't know and he sure as hell didn't care. Greg froze, so he must have snarled. He felt with his tongue for his canines. Did they feel sharper? He breathed to keep his leopard at bay.

"Joshua told me he heard it as well," Jake managed. He

kept his voice low, but even so, he saw Emma flick him a worried look. He wasn't in any state to reassure her.

"Greg mentioned if the line was clear and we heard something it could be spy equipment, and you know how the paparazzi are always trying to get into the house."

"I can check the phone jacks for chips or recorders," Greg offered.

"Don't bother, my security can take it from here," he said, dismissing the man, and stalking away. He wanted the man the hell out of his house.

Jake didn't want to go. He *had* to go. He had to find Drake, to run, let the leopard loose where it couldn't do any harm. Breathing hard, he turned away from them, striding through the kitchen, stopping abruptly when he saw Joshua with his feet up on a chair, drinking coffee and eating a slice of freshly baked bread.

"I thought I told you to stay with Emma," he snapped.

Joshua jumped up so fast he knocked the chair over. "You said stay in the house and I'm here."

"That's bullshit and you know it. You've got some man in my home staring at Emma like she's the candy in a store, while you're fucking feeding your face. Throw the son of a bitch out of here and have security check the phone jacks again, not just with equipment, but visually. If they can't do their job, get rid of them."

"Fine, it's done," Joshua tried to soothe him.

Jake was pacing, swinging his head in agitation. His face had gone dark, his eyes clouding, going almost completely gold as his vision shifted from human to animal.

Grabbing the radio hanging at his side, Joshua spoke into it quickly before moving to put the table between him and his boss, barking out the orders for security to check the phone jacks visually and then calling to Drake for backup.

"Jake. Listen to me. Concentrate. You're in a thrall. A

fit of madness. You have to fight hard against it. Come with me now. Let's get you out of here before it's too late." Joshua's own voice roughened, his vision changing to bands of colored heat. All senses immediately sharpened, heightened.

Jake heard him as if from a distance, the voice fading in and out. His muscles ached. His back bent. He wanted Emma underneath him, screaming his name. The image filled his vision and then his sight went red as he scented other males.

"Damn it, Drake. Hurry," Joshua called again into the radio. "I'm not going to be able to hold him by myself." He held his palm out toward Jake. "You brought me to your ranch to help you, Jake. I'm trying to do that. Go run. Let your leopard loose."

Thunder crashed in Jake's ears. His blood surged hotly, the need to claim his mate so strong he shook with it. The animal consumed him bit by bit.

"Your other is riding you hard. We don't want a fight in your kitchen." Joshua's own leopard rose to meet the aggression of Jake's. This was going to be a disaster.

The door burst open and Drake limped in. He hissed a command in the language of their species, one Jake couldn't understand, but the leopard did. "Jake. Go to the truck. We have to go now." His tone left no room for argument. The situation was going to turn ugly fast.

Jake glanced toward the room where Emma's voice could be heard, still murmuring softly to the repairman.

"Evan's coming to escort him off the property," Joshua assured.

Jake recognized he had little control and struggled to rein in the leopard, fighting for supremacy at least until he could make certain Emma and the children were safe. It was going to take both Joshua and Drake to control the snarling cat clawing and fighting for a kill. He tried to speak, but mostly what came out was a rumble of madness. "Emma." He couldn't—wouldn't leave until he knew someone was watching over her.

As if that one growling word made sense, Drake snapped an order at Joshua. "Get Darrin in here. Tell him to call up two other hands and guard the house with the kids and Emma until one of the three of us gets back." Even as he spoke, he ushered Jake out of the house.

Jake could barely walk, his body so heavy and throbbing, so aroused that every step was painful. The leopard fought him every inch of the way, trying to get back, to circle around Drake, snarling menacingly, using mock charges to threaten. Drake snarled back, his own leopard shepherding Jake. Joshua helped the moment he was able, careful to keep a distance as Jake paced back and forth, the growls rumbling louder and more ferocious, but, in effect, herding him toward the truck.

The biggest danger would occur in the close confines of the truck. Drake and Joshua had to rely on Jake to stay focused and hold his leopard at bay until they could get him to the far side of the ranch where they could let him run free.

Drake slammed the door once they had him caged inside the cab and leapt into the driver's seat. "What the hell is going on, Joshua? I'm not around the house, but this is definitely a thrall. Is there a female close?"

Joshua shrugged. "Only Emma. I've been around her dozens of times and she's never triggered my leopard. Although . . ." He trailed off, glancing at his boss.

Jake breathed harshly, his chest rising and falling in an effort to hold back the change. His skin hurt, shrinking, far too small to cover his frame. He tore his shirt off as the itch spread and something alive ran just under the surface. His brain was filled with a red haze, a dark-edged rage and fierce hunger for one woman. He was consumed with Emma, with the desire for her body, with the need to make her his. He hated every male, desperate to destroy them, understanding the cruelties of his parents as the cat enflamed him beyond sanity.

Fighting it, he hung his head, panting, his mouth full of teeth, his heart savage, his body in lust. He broke out in a sweat, wanting to caution Drake to hurry, but he couldn't speak, didn't dare open his mouth for fear his muzzle would be completed. They were miles from safety, barreling over the track to take them to his hidden sanctuary, and Drake and Joshua, the two men he could call friends, were trapped in the small cab of the truck with him, risking their lives to save everyone on the ranch.

Trees and lush foliage resembled a cool, exotic forest where his leopard was free to run in safety without the threat of killing cattle, harming cowboys or being seen. Drake watched over him there, helping him learn to shift on the run, as well as learn the way of the leopard people and how to cache clothes and supplies every few miles just in case.

The atmosphere in the truck remained tense while fur rippled over Jake's body and claws burst from his fingertips. He shuddered with the effort to hold back the change.

"Fight it," Drake snapped, his words a command. "You have a strong will, Jake. To be leopard, you have to be strong, to be in control at all times, whether you're in human form or leopard form. You're responsible for all actions in both forms."

Joshua swore under his breath. "We were taught from the time we were young. We had the benefit of the elders at all times. How could he possibly be prepared for the thrall? Most of us can barely hold back our leopard, and we've trained for years. He's going to kill someone."

"No, he isn't," Drake said, his voice firm. "Do you hear me, Jake? Fight for control. When you shift, you'll think he's stronger, but he's still *you*. The core of *you*. You dictate to him. He'll want to kill any male within miles of his female. That's natural, very normal, but the feeling will be stronger than anything you've ever known, any hatred, any rage, a murderous need that rakes at your gut and roars in your belly. You have to control it. If this happens and you're near your woman, it's a thousand times worse, and you have to be careful what you do to her. The instinct to conquer and dominate is overwhelming. Control is everything. Do you understand me? Nod your head if you can hear me and comprehend what I'm saying."

Jake shredded the leather on the seat, the rumbling in his chest deepening. He nodded his head, trying to absorb the importance of Drake's statement when every bone in his body seemed to be cracking and splintering, every muscle tearing and every cell screaming in demand for Emma. He knew it was Emma triggering this violent storm of fury. She filled his mouth with her taste; he felt her flesh next to his, was desperate to bury his cock deep inside her. To pound mercilessly. To sink his teeth in her neck and force her to submit completely to him. To admit she belonged to him and only him. Emma.

Oh God, Emma, where are you? Are you safe? Be safe. I need you. He took a breath, fighting for sanity, fighting to keep her safe in spite of his every need. *No! Stay away from me. What the hell is happening to me?*

His eyes burned. Fear beat in his veins. He wasn't going to live through this without killing someone. The need rose up like a tidal wave, swamping him, shaking him—worse, the need to cause pain, to hurt someone, as this hurt, this terrible, driving obsession. His stomach lurched, roiled, wanted to heave at the idea that he could be so twisted, so disgusting as to want to torture someone, that he could perhaps derive any kind of pleasure or satisfaction from another's pain. He may as well be dead. He would be dead before he allowed himself to harm Emma or the children, before he became like his parents.

His sides heaving, his body bent, taking him to the floor of the truck. The walls were too close, the cab too small. He fought to keep the leopard at bay. A few more miles. What was Drake doing?

"His eyes are completely gone," Joshua reported. "I don't know how the hell he's holding on. We've got to get him out of the truck."

Drake stomped down harder on the gas pedal. He was going far too fast for the road conditions, but risking an accident was a better choice than finding himself locked in a small area with a fully grown, enraged male leopard in the midst of a thrall. Drake's own leopard was fighting for supremacy, ripping and clawing in an effort to protect him. Twice, his stiletto-sharp claws emerged and retracted. He hadn't shifted since he'd been shot and the doctors had reconstructed his leg, leaving in a metal plate. There was no freedom for him or his leopard.

He jerked the wheel around and slid into the stand of trees just inside the preserve. He yanked a tranquilizing rifle from the rack at the back window and bailed out, Joshua following suit on the opposite side of the truck.

Inside the truck, Jake's body contorted as he tried desperately to shed his jeans, his claws tearing them into strips. He kicked the torn material away as the change took him, the ropes of muscles doubling, tripling beneath the thick rosette fur.

Drake backed off from the rocking truck, moving out and away from the trees. The hope was that Jake would force his leopard into the forested area. If he allowed the leopard free rein, the male would go for his mate, and they'd have no choice but to tranquilize him to keep him from killing any human males in close proximity to Emma.

Drake hoped it didn't come to that. To dart a leopard was no easy task, and it came with consequences. Often the heart of a big cat simply couldn't take the drugs and shut down completely.

The large male leopard went crazy, throwing itself against the walls of the truck, ripping at the seats and slamming into the windows until spiderweb cracks appeared in the windshield.

"He's gone, Drake," Joshua warned. "Out of his mind. You'll have to take him when he tries to bolt."

Drake stubbornly shook his head. "He's strong."

"If Emma is his mate and she's starting into the Han Vol Don, and they've been mated at least once before in another cycle, the thrall will be too strong for a novice. You don't know what's inside him, Drake. You said yourself his parents were bred from a corrupt bloodline. He's dangerous. There could be a massacre."

"He'll do this."

"He's never heard of the Han Vol Don. How can he understand what's happening to him?"

"He'll do this," Drake repeated. "I know him. His strength. His determination. He'll control his leopard."

"Damn it, man. You're betting your life."

The truck rocked again and the leopard stuck his head out the open door. It went eerily silent. Still. The fur was dark with sweat. As if sensing a threat, birds fell silent and insects ceased all sound. The leopard lowered his head, golden eyes staring at Drake with focused intent.

"He's locked on you, he's locked on you," Joshua warned, tearing at his own shirt and tossing it aside. He yanked off both boots, keeping his eyes on the leopard.

The leopard leapt from its still-standing position, clearing a good six feet or more, touched the ground and sprang a second time.

"Shoot him," Joshua implored, tearing off his jeans and kicking them away. He took two running steps and began shifting as he sprinted toward Drake and the leopard.

The leopard hit Drake with the force of a freight train, slamming into his chest and knocking him backward. Drake used the rifle to ward off the powerful cat, although it was a flimsy defense, and the raking claws streaked fire across his chest, just missing his throat.

"Jake. Fight!" He looked straight into the golden eyes.

Joshua's leopard came in from the side. Jake leapt, spinning in midair to avoid the attack. His mind red with rage, the call for blood filling his thoughts, he barely heard Drake's voice. He respected Drake. Liked him. Yet he could barely distinguish Drake from his mortal enemies.

Faced with the scent of a human male blocking his way back to his mate, with a male leopard rushing toward him and with a murderous rage in his heart, Jake tried to concentrate on Drake's voice. He needed something to drown out the roaring of his leopard.

Joshua's leopard leapt the remaining distance, determined to keep him off Drake. Jake spun, his flexible spine nearly folding double as he whirled to meet the new threat. The slash of the stiletto claws sent pain flashing along Jake's thigh. For a moment his lungs burned with agony and he drew a deep, shuddering breath. Victory. Victory in pain. Pain was his life, and it steadied him as nothing else could have.

He took hold of his snarling leopard and forced his iron will on the cat. Murmuring soothing words, he promised they'd have their mate soon. He backed the snarling cat up, inch by inch. His leopard fought him every step of the way, instincts warring with his human mind. Jake was strong—stronger than the leopard when it came to his determination—and the leopard abruptly gave in, spinning around and running into the trees.

The leopard ran, putting on a burst of speed to take him deep into the woods. The need for his mate bordered on desperation, and Jake wanted the leopard as far from the ranch and Emma as possible. He had no idea what was happening to him as a leopard—or as a man—but he had to learn to control it before he could possibly make any demands on Emma.

The wind rose and howled through the trees, warning of a coming storm. Darkness spread and with it came the rain. The drops poured down as if the very skies wept for him, wept with him for the vicious cruelty running in his veins. The large pads allowed him to be silent as he moved fast, going deeper into the protection of the woods, trying to outrun himself and his ugly, brutal nature. He had feared his entire life that he would be like them—the enemies— and a part of him had tried to convince himself it wasn't so, but the way his body and his mind burned obsessively for Emma, the way he reacted each time he saw her, the violent emotions swirling in his belly all told a different story.

The leopard turned his face up to the rain and wind, allowing it to sweep over him, hoping it would cleanse him. The storm increased in strength, the wind whipping through the trees, bending samplings, tearing off leaves and cracking smaller boughs so that debris rained down on him. The wind on his fur felt right, the storm adding to the leopard's edgy mood. He was free. He could lose himself here, where the trees and the water drowned out the noise of the city. Where no one could stop him from taking his prey as he was meant to do. There was music in the wind and leaves, kinship with the animals and birds. He belonged somewhere. He ran free, going for miles even when his heart felt as though it was bursting and his breath came in great puffs of vapor.

He came to a swollen stream and plunged in without

hesitation, uncaring that the current caught at him, buffeting the large cat and sweeping him down toward a bend. Branches hit him hard, rolling him under, and he came up snarling and spitting, using his heavy, roped muscles to power him to the edge where he could drag himself onto land.

He stood, head down, sides heaving, fighting for breath, fighting himself. What the hell was he doing? He had set himself on a course of revenge and somewhere along the line that course had altered. He didn't understand emotion and he didn't trust it. His emotions were too violent, too intense, and he was too capable of hurting others.

The pain from the claw rakes on his side reminded him of every single victory of his childhood, every time he exerted control, every time he built his determination to survive and grow strong. The leopard lay down under a large tree, the umbrella of leaves and branches swaying wildly with the turbulent wind, allowing the rain to continually pour down on him, cooling the heat of his body and the wildness of his mind.

Drake had been with him for two years. Joshua had followed, leaving the rain forest to try a different life. He was more easygoing than Drake, laughed more, but behind his green eyes were dark shadows. Jake hadn't pried when Joshua had asked for a job. Jake knew he was leopard, a friend of Drake's, and although a part of him was envious at the easy relationship between the two men who had grown up together—leaving him to be an outsider looking in—he was still grateful to have a second leopard to help instruct him. Neither had ever said he would feel like this—complete meltdown.

He admired Drake's strength. The leopard was every bit a part of them as breathing was, yet Drake couldn't shift. He'd taken a bullet that had shattered his leg, and the metal plate holding him together prevented him from shifting.

Something had to be done about that soon. Drake couldn't live without his leopard forever.

Deep inside the leopard, Jake went on alert. He was on the verge of an important discovery. *Drake couldn't live without his leopard forever.* Drake wasn't a leopard. He wasn't a man. He was both. Together. The man needed the leopard and the leopard needed the man. One couldn't survive long without the other. Drake's leopard lived inside him, but he couldn't run free. Couldn't run and breathe and feel the joy of the leopard as it raced in open territory or leapt leisurely from one branch to the next. What was the leopard doing? Thinking? Feeling? He couldn't survive long in such a state, and neither would Drake.

So what of his own leopard? What had he given to it? What had he done for it? He had closed himself off from that part, careful to protect himself. He feared the leopard would make him into his parents and allow the animalistic qualities in his nature free rein. But running free night after night had calmed his rage, allowed him to escape the pain of his nightmarish childhood. All along, even as a toddler, way before the leopard had emerged, the leopard had given him the strength to endure.

Drake had traveled thousands of miles with him on faith alone, willing to give up part of his life, his own need and love of the rain forest, in order to instruct Jake in his heritage. Money meant little to Drake. It was merely a means to an end, a tool with which to do the things he felt necessary. He had come to Texas only to aid Jake. As always, Jake had distrusted every kindness. And he distrusted the leopard—his other half. The leopard had waited for him, for his acceptance, rising only when Jake needed his strength, when something—or someone—triggered his instincts or when Jake needed to disappear and run free. Not once had Jake shared himself as Drake had told him was necessary for full development.

He was afraid. The realization stunned him. He had thought himself long past fear. He had survived when others would never have made it, and he'd survived through sheer guts and determination, in the midst of a wild storm, his sides heaving, sweat darkening his fear, panting with horror when he'd known all along what lay within him. Jake didn't want to give himself to anyone, not to the children, not to the leopard and certainly not to Emma. They were to be his. Controlled by him. Dictated to in his perfect world that he built and ruled.

All along, Drake had told him he had to let go. With his heart pounding, he tasted terror in his mouth. If he let go and the leopard swallowed him, he was lost. If he loved his children and something happened to them, his heart would be torn out. If he gave himself to Emma and she threw him away, he would not survive.

The leopard put his head down on his paws and wept, tears mingling with the raindrops as the storm begin to abate. He had always refused to think of himself as a victim. He had survived because he was strong and it had been *his* choice not to fight back. He hadn't allowed the leopard to leap upon his enemies and rend and tear until they were no more, although more than once he had raged inside to do so. His control had always been his proof to himself that he was different. To let that go, to trust, to give, was truly terrifying.

For the first time in Jake's life, he realized he might not be strong enough to overcome the trauma of his childhood. He had never acknowledged to himself that he had been abused. It had been a way of life and he had learned lessons, very hard lessons, but they shaped him into a successful man—and an even more successful businessman. He thought of himself as untouchable, and in most ways he was. He had the reputation of being too rich, too politically connected, too ruthless and too dangerous to mess with.

But he was afraid of himself. His biggest enemy was inside of him. Drake had said he couldn't live separate from his leopard, and if he didn't embrace the beast, welcome it and learn to use what he considered failings as strengths, he would never really be alive. And eventually the leopard would fight him every inch of the way. He didn't want to chance it. Everything in him rebelled, but he was dangerously close to hurting Emma, to destroying his home—the only home he'd ever known.

The leopard stretched out his paws and raked deep into the earth. Night settled in, bringing the sounds of insects and owls hunting prey. He lay quiet, listening to the endless cycle of life, knowing he couldn't give Emma up. She was supposed to need him. The children were supposed to need him. He could accept that and he'd be an incredible partner, seeing to everything for them, but he didn't want to feel that attachment himself. He couldn't have that.

He argued with himself for hours before he finally knew he had no choice. He couldn't risk turning himself over to something as cruel and bad-tempered as his enemies. Their blood ran in his veins. Their leopards may not have emerged fully, as his had, but the traits were bred into them and they lacked the control he had learned over the years. He had managed to turn the leopard from Drake, even in the midst of its enraged madness, and he would not give it even a small amount of control. He wouldn't risk losing Emma and the children—or himself.

Jake emerged from the woods barefoot, shirtless and still buttoning the jeans Drake and Joshua had thoughtfully left hanging in the branch of a tree for him. Drake sat out in the rain, in the bed of the pickup, and as Jake approached, his head went up, alert, and he immediately jumped down. In spite of his leg injury, he still moved with a fluid grace that often caught Jake off guard.

"Are you all right? I thought about sending Joshua to find you, but . . ." Drake trailed off.

Jake shrugged his shoulders. "You thought I might try to tear him to pieces."

Drake's answering smile was faint. "Something like that."

Jake shook his head as he approached his friend. Drake's shirt was slashed to ribbons and there were bloodstains on his chest. "Are you hurt?"

Shame burned through Jake. He prided himself on his control, but he'd barely managed to stop the beast as it attacked Drake. He was grateful he hadn't attempted to turn himself over to the leopard. Drake and Joshua were from different bloodlines, they clearly didn't have the madness that ran in his veins.

"Just a few scratches," Drake answered casually. "I've had far worse playing around with friends in leopard form."

Jake stretched his tired muscles. The rain had slowed to a fine drizzle. "I'm sorry, Drake. I could have hurt you."

Drake sent him another small grin. "I knew you wouldn't."

"Then you knew more than I did. Where's Joshua?"

The grin widened. "Sleeping like a baby. He wasn't worried about you."

"He does a good job of pretending," Jake said. "He worries. Why do you suppose he left the rain forest? He isn't all that happy here, but he doesn't want to go back."

"Joshua is Joshua. He doesn't share much about his life. Whatever happened must have been bad or he never would have left. No one leaves because they want to."

"You did," Jake pointed out.

"I couldn't stay in the forest without letting my leopard run, and I can't shift. It became . . . difficult."

"Did the doctors try grafting your own bone?"

Drake nodded. "It didn't work. I didn't understand the

entire process, but some of us have the ability to regenerate bones and others don't. I apparently don't."

"Did you try using someone else's bone?"

"Like a cadaver?" Drake made a face. "We incinerate our dead immediately. It's the only way for our species to survive, to keep our existence secret. And it doesn't make much sense that if I can't use a piece of my bone, then someone else's would work, now does it?"

"They can do all sorts of things now, Drake. You just have to find the right man." Jake opened the door to the pickup and paused to look around.

He owned everything for miles. He'd patiently acquired acre after acre, adding on to the land his great-grandfather had given him until he had a sanctuary. He'd turned miles of that into a shaded, wooded area for his leopard. He had built a cattle empire. Step by step, patiently. And he had slowly begun drilling for the oil he knew was on other tracts of land he'd inherited. Recently he had acquired several large pieces of property he was certain concealed natural gas just waiting to be developed. Looking at Drake—his friend—the one person who had stood for him, he realized that all of his accomplishments stacked up to very little. Billions of dollars maybe, but the money was a tool for him. And he knew what he had to do with it.

Drake needed a solution. In comparison to his friend's problem, the years Jake had put into his plan to take down his enemies seemed a waste when a man as good as Drake was suffering.

Jake cleared his throat. He found it strange to think about another person, to worry about them. Emma's influence. She was doing something to him with her presence that he couldn't quite understand, but he knew she had changed him somehow in the brief two years she'd lived in his home. He didn't know when the change had occurred, but he knew Drake was more important than any revenge possible.

Jake pulled open the door. "Do you want me to drive?"

Drake shook his head. "I've got it. Just shove Joshua over."

Jake gave the other man a good-natured push and Joshua lifted his head and growled a warning. "Get in the back," Jake said. "You can sleep there."

Joshua snarled but complied, curling up to go back to sleep even before Jake slid into the passenger side. "Who did your surgery? Are there doctors in your village?"

"We have one doctor for our people, but no specialist like I needed, and my bones won't graft and shift."

Drake sounded matter-of-fact on the surface, but Jake listened with heightened senses. Drake didn't show by his expression that he was depressed, but Jake caught the heavy note in his voice and looked at him sharply. "I need you here, Drake." He kept his voice low, the admission churning his gut. He hated that feeling, the sudden clawing fear at the idea of losing his friend. He wasn't supposed to need anyone. It made him feel vulnerable and small.

He took a breath. No. It wasn't really fear of losing Drake. He had asked Drake to come to him, to leave the rain forest and help him. Drake was his responsibility. That was all. The way Emma and the children and even Joshua were his responsibility. He needed to find a way to help the man, to save him, because there were few good men left in the world.

Drake didn't pretend to misunderstand what they were talking about. "You're going to find out soon enough that a leopard can't be suppressed forever. I don't have a lot of time left, Jake. And frankly, what the hell is there left for me?"

"Surgery. Don't be an idiot. You don't give up until you've tried everything, and you haven't even begun to scratch the surface. Your bone won't work. We don't have a cadaver, but you have me. Or Joshua. One of us might have the ability to regenerate and if we don't, we'll find someone who does have it."

Drake shot him a look out of the corner of his eye. "I doubt it's that easy."

"Nothing worthwhile ever is." Jake's mind was already working at a fast pace. He could easily set several of his staff searching for the best team of orthopedic surgeons. With enough money, anyone could be bought. And the one thing he had was money. "I'll set it in motion tomorrow. If neither Joshua or I can be used, we'll keep looking for a donor until we find one."

Drake moistened his suddenly dry lips. "You think someone could really fix me? That I could go without the plate? I thought about having them amputate the leg."

"Why shouldn't they be able to fix it? We just need the right surgeon and the right donor." He glanced out the window. "You forgot to turn on the headlights. You're using your leopard's night vision."

He'd noticed both Joshua and Drake did that a lot, interchanged the leopard's senses with their own. Maybe their leopards weren't as destructive as his and were more easily controlled. He'd studied the animal quite a bit. They had bad tempers. Jealous rages. They were highly intelligent and cunning, and were secretive creatures. He was all of those, amplified a million times.

Drake didn't bother with the headlights. Instead, he changed the subject. They were driving over the trail back toward the ranch house. "You need to tell me everything you know about Emma's background. I know you must have had her investigated before you ever hired her."

"I've got her file, but there's not much in it. Where she went to school. Her parents." Jake gave another casual shrug.

"Have you read about or spoken about the Han Vol Don with anyone?" Drake asked.

"I've heard you use the term. What is it?"

"Females are very different from males in our species. No one knows what triggers the Han Vol Don. It isn't puberty or sexual activity. We have no idea, and believe me, we've tried to figure it out. For males the leopards shift when the leopard is strong enough or the boy is undergoing extreme stress. Maybe a combination of the two. It is very different for our women."

"And the Han Vol Don is . . ." Jake looked at Drake expectantly, a hint of impatience in his eyes. He knew about being male.

"Dangerous. To everyone. A female will suddenly go into a combined heat, both woman and leopard merging together. She throws off an alluring scent, and when in close proximity, her presence can trigger a thrall—the madness you experienced—in a mate. Mates find and recognize one another lifetime after lifetime. I think Emma may be leopard."

The moment he heard the word *mate*, the leopard in him leapt and the man in him recoiled. He wasn't anyone's mate, least of all Emma's. She was *his*. She belonged to him, but he belonged with no one. His life was a carefully built sham.

"That's impossible. There's nothing whatsoever in her past to make me think that. And she was married to someone else." The last came out too much like an accusation, and Jake kept his eyes fixed on the fences as they raced by them.

"That doesn't mean she wasn't your mate in a previous life. Are there ever times when she seems familiar to you? Do you have memories of her that you shouldn't have?"

Jake took a breath. "How could she be leopard and not know?"

"The heat comes on slowly and in small stops and starts. One day she's fine, the next she can be moody, with a heightened sexual stimulation throwing off the allure to any male in the vicinity. Even the leopard can't scent her when the heat is in the diminished phase, but races to her when it rises."

"What happens to her if she's leopard?"

"Eventually her leopard will emerge, but it is always in the midst of a sexual heat. The leopard will affect the woman. She'll be as needy as her cat."

Jake's body responded to the thought of Emma in need. He could take care of her needs as no one else could. He had complete faith in himself that he could bind her to him with sex. He had learned a long time ago how to make a woman beg for him. Maybe he'd been taking the wrong tack with her all along.

Drake pulled the pickup down the long, winding drive and around to the back of the ranch house where the kitchen door was. "One more thing, Jake. While you were running, security radioed us. They found a microchip recording data, a voice-activated chip in the phone jack in the den. They've removed the chip and have it for you. We haven't had visitors other than the two who brought Susan to the ranch. I had security check their names. Dana Anderson is the governess, and Harold Givens is the tutor. We're running checks on them now."

"Thanks, Drake. For everything." Jake leapt out, but held on to the door, preventing Drake from driving away. "I meant what I said about the surgery. I'll put some people on it immediately." He forced himself to look at the claw marks on Drake's chest. "Make certain you take care of that. You don't want to get infected."

"Okay, Mom," Drake answered. "Good night." He tossed Jake his wallet and cell phone.

Jake caught the two items, slammed the door closed and stepped back, watching as Drake continued along the road toward the smaller cabins where several of the hands stayed. Then he turned and walked up the walk to the door of the kitchen. He paused a moment to text his lawyers with instructions to put adoption on a fast track for Emma, before going into the house.

He stopped immediately. Even in the dark he saw the cake and he knew he was meant to see it. Emma always cleaned up, but she had left the cake in the middle of the table, along with his painting and two other brightly wrapped gifts. He picked them up. One card said *Kyle* with green crayon scribbled over it, and the other said *From Andraya*, covered in messy purple.

His heart contracted. He'd screwed up big-time. He wasn't cut out for the father or husband thing. Even as he thought it he climbed the stairs and went into the children's room to kiss them good night before turning resolutely to Emma's room. He frowned, standing in front of it. The door was closed. As long as he'd known her, she'd never slept with the door closed all the way because she wanted to be certain of hearing the children. He put his hand on the doorknob and turned it. It was locked.

Fury swept through him, instant and ferocious, his temper ugly and black. She was angry with him and she dared to lock her door against him? He'd be damned if she started that.

8

EMMA pressed her face into the pillow to muffle the sound of her weeping. Although Susan was downstairs in one of the guest rooms, she didn't want to chance her overhearing. She especially didn't want the children to hear. She had thought herself all cried out after Andrew, but here she was, falling apart, feeling confused and alone and so upset without any real reason other than she'd accepted a date. Why had she done that? She didn't want to go out with Greg Patterson.

For pride's sake, of course. Jake had so casually dismissed her ability to be attractive to a man. So maybe no man had approached her since Andrew's death, but she hadn't really wanted them to. She'd been busy. Mourning Andy. Taking care of Kyle. Having babies. Keeping a large house. It had only been two years. Was she supposed to fling herself at the nearest man?

She turned over and wiped at her burning eyes. She hadn't cried like this in months. Life with Andrew had been straightforward and easy. With Jake it seemed so complicated. She was in a world she didn't always understand. As long as she stayed protected on the estate, far from people, she felt wrapped in a cocoon of safety. Jake had a strong personality, but she could deal with him if she just stayed on an equal footing. His acquaintances were another matter altogether.

His associates treated her like a piece of the furniture, or a servant—and technically, she *was* a servant. She was the housekeeper, not the mistress of the house. Jake gave her such free rein, she had grown complacent, believing that this house was her home. The petty meanness and raised eyebrows had never hurt until now—until she realized the precarious position she'd put not only herself in, but Andraya and Kyle as well.

She wouldn't call the men and women who came to the house Jake's friends. They were business associates, people looking for favors—or trying to get close to him. She could have told them, after watching him for two years, that Jake didn't let anyone close. There was always a distance between him and everyone else—including the children.

Was that why she was weeping? She had waited as long as she could for Jake, and when it was apparent he wasn't coming to his own birthday party, she'd let the children blow out the candles and eat. Quite a bit ended up in their hair and all over their clothes so she'd whisked them to their baths. As she washed the cake from their hair and skin she finally realized how alone she was—how alone they all were. They lived in the shadow of Jake's presence, day in and day out, yet he hadn't really made them a part of his life.

Jake listened when she told him of the children's progress and related all the cute things they did as they grew and began discovering the world around them, but his face didn't light up; he didn't laugh the way he should. He held himself back from them—apart from them. She'd felt sad-

ness for Kyle and Andraya as well as for herself. In that
moment she'd realized there was no real hope for her and
Jake. As much as she loved and respected him, as much as
her body craved his, she would need much, much more
than he was capable of or willing to give her. She'd put the
children to bed and come to her room, locking the door so
they wouldn't walk in on her if they heard her unrestrained
sobbing.

Now she had the added humiliation of her body burning
day and night, desperate for Jake's touch. She could barely
face herself, remembering how she'd practically thrown
herself at Jake, kissing him—*kissing* him. She touched her
mouth, her lips, remembering the feel and shape of him,
his taste and texture. She wanted to crawl into him, devour
him, the urges so strong and overwhelming she didn't trust
herself near him. She was going to ruin everything she had.
Or maybe she really didn't have anything at all.

Great sobs wracked her body, tightened her chest and
tore at her throat.

"Why the hell did you lock me out?"

Emma nearly jumped off the bed, her eyes going wide
with shock, her heart slamming hard in her chest, then
pounding fast as adrenaline poured into her body.

"Are you crazy?" she demanded. "Jake, you scared me."
She threw her pillow in the direction of his voice, unable to
stop the aggression surging through her. "Get out."

The missile didn't slow him down. He stalked across the
room to tower over her. She should have been intimidated,
as was obviously his intent, but his behavior only made her
angrier.

She shoved her hair back to glare at him. "You are such
an ass. Don't you have any boundaries? My door was
locked. *Locked.* That clearly means don't come in."

Jake's anger melted the moment he saw her sitting in the
middle of her bed with her long hair tousled and unkempt

as if she'd just been made love to. Her eyes were large, framed with thick lashes, staring up at him with sparks of fire radiating from them. She looked kissable, too kissable. He could barely resist leaning down and taking possession of her mouth. It was only then that he noted her face, pale with red splotches and traces of tears.

His gut clenched. He caught her chin and tipped her face up to his. "You've been crying."

She jerked back, turning her face away from him. "Hence the locked door and the need for privacy. Now please go and leave me to it." She wiggled her fingers toward the door dismissively.

"No."

Her head snapped back around, hair flying in all directions. "Jake. I'm clearly upset. Could you just for once have a little respect and let me be tonight?"

"I'm not leaving you alone when you're upset." He sank down onto the bed, forcing her to scoot over a little to give him sufficient room. "I'm sorry about the birthday party. My absence was unavoidable."

"Don't flatter yourself."

He could see it made her even angrier that she had automatically moved over for him. So often in the past two years he'd come to her room and they'd lain side by side, talking when neither could sleep, and he counted on that familiar closeness.

"I'm not crying because of you or the fact that you didn't show up to your own birthday party. Although selfish, it wasn't entirely unexpected."

He winced at her accurately delivered punch. Emma sat with her knees drawn up, rocking back and forth in obvious distress. He doubted if she even knew how upset she was. She was curled up as small as she could make herself, her eyes drowning in tears. Jake reached over and scooped her up easily, cradling her against his body, holding her close to him.

"If it wasn't me that upset you so badly, what was it? I'll take care of it, but you have to tell me what's wrong first." He brushed a trail of kisses from her temple to the corner of her mouth and back up, stealing every tear with his lips.

Emma buried her face against his chest. She couldn't look at him. The moment his mouth slid over her skin, electrical charges raced from her breasts to her belly. She didn't dare look up—she might start kissing him, and then what would happen? She had no doubt that Jake would be willing to have sex with her. He was always willing to have sex with someone. She could feel him, hard as a rock, against the backs of her thighs, but she wasn't made for one-night stands or passionate flings that burned out fast. She had two children she loved and a home she wanted to stay in. Giving in to sexual desire would momentarily satisfy her, but would ultimately cost her everything. Jake just couldn't—or wouldn't—make an emotional commitment.

"Talk to me, honey. You can tell me anything, Emma."

His hands ran up and down her arms, over her scorching skin, driving her temperature up even more.

"I'm just having a bad day, Jake. I have them sometimes. Everyone does." Her skin was so sensitive it almost hurt to have him touching her. The sensation had faded for a while earlier in the evening, but now it seemed to be returning with more force than ever. "I have to lie down. And the light has to be off. And I need to be alone."

Jake frowned and rubbed his face over hers, almost like a cat. "Maybe I should call a doctor, Emma. You feel a little feverish to me."

In spite of everything, she felt the urge to smile. Jake probably had never used the word feverish in his life before Kyle was born, and now he was throwing it around like an old pro. "I'm fine. Crying always makes a person hot and sweaty." She was too. And he smelled so good, fresh from a shower; she could always tell. His hair was damp and he smelled clean with a faint, elusive tang of wild.

"That's not good enough, Emma. Some women may just cry for no reason, but not you. Someone or something upset you. I intend to know what it was before I leave this room tonight." He allowed her to slip out of his arms.

She closed her eyes against the feel of the pads of his fingers sliding over her skin as she stretched out on the bed, giving him plenty of room so he wouldn't have to touch her. "I guess you really don't understand the concept of a locked door."

He shrugged, there in the near dark, rolling his broad shoulders in the casual way he always had. She was instantly aware of every muscle sliding under his skin. Emma squeezed her eyelids closed tighter. She drew in a breath and took him into her lungs.

"Locked doors are for everyone else, honey." He leaned over, brushed a kiss across her forehead and stretched out beside her.

She realized how completely natural it felt. She'd been married to Andrew five months. She'd been with Jake for two years. He'd been coming to her room every single night, from the very first day she'd moved to his home. He'd held her that first night when she'd awakened with a terrible nightmare, the stench of fire and the heat of flames still so raw and vivid. His every gesture was more familiar to her than Andrew's. When she remembered a man's touch, it was Jake's touch. When she burned at night for a man's body, it was Jake's body. When had that all started to happen? And why now? Why was she waking up now? She was terrified of the change, afraid she would lose everything.

"Tell me about your parents. You don't talk much about them," Jake said.

"My parents?" Emma echoed, startled. Her heart fluttered.

His hand slid against hers, his fingers tangling with hers. She ached inside as he brought their joined hands to his chest, right over his heart. He always did that—tied them together. She was tied to him by far more than the children.

"You do have parents, don't you?"

The rare amusement in his voice tugged at her heartstrings. She could feel his body, solid and warm right beside hers. She could count his steady heartbeats. "Of course I have parents. Do you think I crawled out from under a rock?"

He brought her fingers up to his lips and bit down on the ends. His mouth was hot and moist and his teeth strong, although the bite was gentle and sent little tingles of arousal teasing along her thighs and belly. "I think you don't want to tell me about your parents. Did you have a happy childhood?" He turned his head to look at her. "I just assumed that you did because you're such a happy person."

She found herself smiling at him. "I did. My parents were very loving. We traveled a lot. My father had a difficult time settling down and we moved often. He was always restless. I'd come home from a friend's house and we'd be packed up with everything already in the car. I rarely had time to say good-bye. We'd just leave."

"That must have been difficult."

"I wanted a home, you know, the traditional house with a yard like everyone else, and a regular school . . ."

"You didn't attend school?"

Her gaze jumped to his face. His voice had been carefully neutral and he was looking at her fingers, absently bringing them to his mouth, nipping at the tips. "I'm very well educated, thank you," she said, frowning, wary now.

Her frown was wasted on him. He bit at the ends of her

fingers, his teeth scraping back and forth. The sensation was intensely seductive, sending lightning lashing through her bloodstream. Her breasts ached. It didn't help that she was ready for bed, without a bra, and the thin material of her pajama top rubbed against her nipples as they hardened into tight peaks. The look on his face was sensual but remote, as if sensuality was so inherent in his character that even when he wasn't paying attention, women couldn't help but feel his sexual heat.

He suddenly turned his head to look at her and her heart quickened, pounding hard, her breath catching in her lungs. His golden eyes held possession, mesmerizing her, robbing her of speech. Her mouth opened, but absolutely nothing came out.

"I know you're educated. I just always imagined you in school with other kids. I had private tutors. I always wondered what it was like to go to a school with other children."

Emma pressed her lips together, feeling them tingle. He was just so focused when he looked at her, so completely concentrated on her, that she felt threatened in some ways and completely exhilarated in others. "So did I," she managed to get out.

"Emma." His voice went soft, melting her. "You're so tense. Something happened tonight and I want to know what it is."

His thigh rubbed against hers as he turned onto his side, propping himself up on one elbow, his body curling around hers protectively. He was closer to her than ever, so close she could exchange breath with him. He was the most beautiful man she'd ever encountered, in a raw, sexual way. Each time he moved, ropes of muscles rippled and slid beneath his skin, a powerful, fluid, very sensual movement that heated her blood no matter how hard she tried not to notice.

His palm cupped the side of her face, his thumb sliding gently over her cheek to the corner of her mouth. "Honey, I swear to you, I had every intention of being home tonight. Something came up that was unavoidable. I'll make it up to the kids. I'm trying to be better about being involved with them. Believe me, I know I leave them with you more than I should." He was stabbing in the dark, trying to get her to open up. He wished it was just the party she was upset about. He could make up for that. But no, there was something far deeper, and he had a bad feeling about the direction her thoughts were taking her.

Emma closed her eyes to block out the sight of him, but her other senses immediately became heightened. Liquid heat rushed, dampening between her legs, her blood pounding with need. She had always secretly condemned Jake for his sexual exploits with women. He never hid the fact that women found him attractive. She knew they visited him at his office in the city and she knew why. Maybe all along she'd been jealous and had never identified her own attraction to him. But it was horrible to feel like one of those women.

She didn't want to be one more woman standing in line, vying for his attention, begging to be noticed, discarded the moment she serviced his needs. How could she tell him that she couldn't have him in her bed anymore because all she thought about was climbing on top of him? Why did everything he do seem so sexual right now, when he'd been doing the same exact thing for the past two years and she'd never once reacted? She must have been the one who had changed. A fresh wave of tears flooded her eyes.

"That's it," Jake snapped, his hands framing her face, thumbs under her chin, brushing seductively. He bent his head to hers and stole her breath. "You have to stop. Do you hear me, Emma? You have to stop or I'm going to do something neither of us will ever be able to take back."

She pressed her forehead to his. "I don't know what's wrong with me, Jake, but I hate it. I feel like I'm climbing out of my skin."

He stroked his hand down her face. "You've gone through a lot in two years. Losing a husband, bed rest, taking care of a baby, having another one, taking over the reins of this house—which, if I haven't told you, you've done an amazing job with. I think you're entitled to a meltdown. You've only left the ranch to do a little shopping, and even then, most things are delivered. You never take time off for yourself."

Mothers didn't take time off. She didn't think of herself as the housekeeper; she was Kyle's and Andraya's mother. But this wasn't really her home. Kyle wasn't her son. She had a job. It was a *job*. "We've never talked about time off." Is that how he saw what she did? A job?

She felt numb inside, and thank God, the burning inferno was cooling, the sensitivity of her skin lessening. The craving for him didn't lessen, but at least it wasn't so raw and biting that she was afraid of attacking him.

He blinked. The golden eyes nearly glowed. A faint rumble, much like a growl, emanated from deep in his chest. "You want time off?"

She frowned. "Isn't that what you just said? That I don't take time off?"

"I made a statement. I didn't ask a question."

Emma thumped her head against the pillow. "What did you mean? I thought you meant I should go on vacation or have a night or two off."

"If you went on vacation or took a few nights off, I'd have to hire a stranger to take your place. I don't want strangers running around in my home or around the children. And we'd need more bodyguards. I meant read a book. I told you I bought a horse for you. I'll take you riding. Those are the sorts of things I meant."

"You didn't say you bought me my own horse."

He scowled at her. "A vacation? You want to go on a vacation? You have to tell me these things in advance, Emma, so I can take the time off. We'll have to find a place where it will be easy to look after the children. I can have one of the secretaries start researching for us. And I did tell you that I bought a horse."

She had the beginnings of a headache. It might have been from all the tears, but more likely it was Jake driving her crazy. He wasn't making any sense. "You told me you bought the horse," she admitted, using her most patient voice, "but you forgot to say you bought it for me. It was during one of the short, informative calls in the middle of the night."

"I always call you late. I don't sleep like other people."

She knew that was true. He was in her room every night, pacing or stretching out beside her on her bed, in the dark, plying her with questions. "When was the last time you slept?"

He rolled back over onto his back and laced his fingers behind his head. "I don't remember. A few days ago. I sleep better when I'm home."

She didn't know when. Most nights he stayed in her room until two or three in the morning. Sometimes he paced back and forth in the children's rooms like a caged animal. Jake was so complicated, and he just plain wore her out sometimes. She kept trying to figure him out when he never talked about his childhood. She'd only met his mother the one time and it hadn't been pleasant. She knew there was a standing order to keep his parents from the property, and Kyle and Andraya were guarded at all times.

As if reading her mind, Jake turned the tables on her. "Tell me about your parents."

She glanced at him. "Like what?"

"Did you ever travel outside the States? Where were

they from originally? What did your father do for a living?"

She frowned up at the ceiling. "We always had money, but you know, I don't know what my father did in terms of a job. We didn't have tons of money, not like you—but then you own just about half of the United States. Still, we never wanted for anything."

"You never asked your father what he did for a living?"

"No. I don't know why. I wasn't around a lot of other children so I guess it never came up. The last couple of years before he died, he spent a great deal of time on his laptop, and I know he often went to Internet cafés when he traveled. I assumed he needed to do so for work."

"And your mother?"

"She looked after us. She painted. She was a wonderful artist." Emma kept her answers brief, and worked to keep wariness from her voice. She'd been taught *never* to discuss her parents, and although they were dead, the rule still held.

"So that's where you get your talent."

Emma was pleased that he thought her talented and pointed out something in her that was like her mother. "She drew all the time on sketchpads and I did the same in the car. We used to pass the charcoals back and forth, and when we stayed at a place for any length of time, almost the first thing she did was set up a room we could paint in."

"When I went to your apartment the first time, I found an old sketchpad. I thought it looked important so I brought it to you. Your mother's?"

She swallowed the sudden lump clogging her throat and nodded.

He shifted enough to tug at strands of her long hair, wrapping them around his finger as he talked. "The movers packed some paintings. Why don't you have them up in your room?"

She was silent for a few moments, turning the question

over and over in her mind. He wasn't going to like the answer, and when he didn't like something he could be very unpredictable. "At first I was grieving and not paying too much attention to anything. When I thought about the paintings and wanted to see them, maybe for comfort, I was on bed rest and couldn't go rummaging through boxes."

He tugged hard enough on her hair for her to give a little yelp. "You should have told me. I would have gotten them put up for you. After the bed rest?"

She shot him a small scowl but he wasn't looking at her and it was completely wasted. "Stop pulling my hair." He didn't let go, but began rubbing the strands back and forth between his fingers almost absently. She sighed and let it go, knowing she was stalling. "After Andraya was born I was tired all the time, adjusting to two babies and a house to run. By the time I got to bed at night I was exhausted."

"You had a lot of nightmares," he pointed out.

She couldn't deny it. He'd often sprinted to her room to make certain she was all right and stayed to talk until she fell asleep again. "That's true," she admitted. "After that, I just wasn't certain if I was going to stay or not. I thought I'd give it some time while I figured out what I was going to do after the money came in from the settlement."

Beside her, Jake went very still. "You think about leaving me quite a bit, don't you?"

Was there hurt in his voice? She was usually quite adept at reading the emotional nuances in people's voices, but Jake was different. He always sounded casual, his voice soft and mesmerizing no matter the subject. Even when he was angry, he lowered his voice rather than raise it. "I don't think about leaving you." It was absurd—the way they were talking, they might have been in a relationship. "I didn't know if the job was going to work out. Things would change if you married someone. You can't pretend they wouldn't."

"You can put your mind at ease about my getting married. The women I know are treacherous bitches and I wouldn't allow them anywhere near my money, my home or you. Certainly not my children. So I think I can safely say that marriage to any of them is out."

"You just let them near your body."

She pressed her lips together, hating the mixture of emotion in her voice that made him turn his head to look at her, his gaze suddenly speculative. She hadn't realized until that moment that she was angry with him. She hadn't even known that she was jealous. She didn't want Jake as her lover or anything else. Any kind of relationship other than the platonic one they had would be a disaster. Jake wasn't easy to live with as a boss. As a lover or a husband, he'd rule with an iron fist.

"We can't all be perfect little saints, never enjoying the pleasures of the flesh."

She curled her nails into her palm, hard enough to hurt. The tips of her fingers ached. "Get out of my room. I mean it. You're being insulting and I've had a bad enough day without putting up with a lot of crap from you. Get out."

He didn't budge. "Why is that an insult? Basically you pointed out that I was a sinner. What's wrong with me pointing out that you're a saint?"

"You're being deliberately insulting and you know it." She flung her arm across her eyes. "I'm so tired, Jake. I wanted today to be a good day for you. I looked forward to you coming home and tried to make things special for your birthday. I don't know what went wrong, but I just want to crawl under the blankets and try again tomorrow." Her throat clogged with tears again and that made her want to weep just for being such an idiot. What was wrong with her lately?

Jake turned on his side, one hand sliding through her hair. "You did make my birthday special, Emma. I've never had a present or a cake before. I'm never going to forget what you did for me. And tomorrow morning I'll open the presents with Kyle and Andraya. We can have cake for breakfast."

She tried not to laugh. "No, you won't. They can't have cake for breakfast."

"Why not?"

He sounded innocent enough, but she knew him better than that. The moment he'd had a son, he'd probably researched every fact he could find about nutrition and health care. More than likely he'd consulted every leading authority he could find. He had a mind for facts and details, and she doubted if he ever forgot anything he read.

"You know very well why not. We can't take a chance on spoiling them too much, Jake. Andraya is already showing signs of being a little princess."

"She is a princess."

"In her own mind."

Jake wrapped a length of her hair around his hand and brought the silken strands to his face. "In my mind as well. But if you say no cake for breakfast, no cake it is. You're the boss."

She nearly snorted. "Since when? No one ever bosses you, Jake." He ran his home and the ranch in the same way he ran his business. He didn't trust anyone enough to give them much room. Drake, Joshua and perhaps her, were the few he gave a little leeway to, but not much. He would be hell to live with. He would want complete control. Why that made her want to cry all over again, she didn't know. But tears burned on the ends of her lashes, further humiliating her.

"I'm sorry, Jake. I honestly don't know what's wrong

with me. I don't. It isn't you. I'm just falling apart. I wasn't even like this when I was pregnant."

His hand slipped over her shoulder and down her arm to nudge under the hem of her shirt and splay across her belly as if he could feel a child growing there. "I think you just need to have someone hold you while you fall asleep. Remember when you had your nightmares." He bent his head to hers and brushed a kiss along her temple. "I held you and you went to sleep."

That was true, but her body hadn't been on fire. He'd been hard then too, just like he was now, and completely unashamed of it. But now was different because she was too aware of him, lying hard and thick, burning against her thigh like a brand.

"Do you want more children?"

Her gaze jumped to his face. "Why do you ask?"

"I've been thinking about it lately. Wondering how you felt about it. With Kyle and Andraya so close in age I thought you might feel they were more than enough." He pulled his hand from her stomach, the pads of his fingers sliding across her ribs while his knuckles brushed the undersides of her breasts.

She was looking right into his eyes and couldn't tell if it was an accident or if he'd meant to touch her so intimately. Before she could ask, he added in that same low tone, "I've asked John to prepare the adoption papers for you to adopt Kyle."

She felt a quick burst of pleasure that he not only remembered, but that he'd already instructed his lawyer. She had no idea when he could have found the time, but that was so like Jake, making the adoption a priority when they'd barely mentioned it.

"Thank you. I feel as if I'm Kyle's mother already. Making it legal takes a huge load off my mind."

"You didn't answer. Will you want more children?"

"I don't know. With the right person." She didn't want to leave. She didn't want to break up Andraya and Kyle.

He rubbed the pad of his finger back and forth over her eyebrow, in the now familiar stroke he often used to help her fall asleep. The gesture soothed her for some unknown reason, almost as if he was petting her. The palm of his hand covered her eyes as he stroked, and she lowered her lashes and let the tension drain from her body.

"What about you, Jake?"

Jake drew in a deep breath. He was going to have more children and he was going to have them with Emma. "In another year or two, before Kyle and Andraya get too much older." Because it would keep Emma close to him.

He didn't know much about love, but he knew how to seduce a woman. Whether or not Drake was right about Emma, she was the one he was keeping. He would tie her to him in as many ways as possible, including with more children. He could afford them, and he could hire help. If his other children were at all like Kyle and Andraya, then he could learn to care for them in his way.

"Were you an only child?" His finger traced across her closed eyelid, along her high cheekbone and down to her full lips.

"That's another thing we have in common. I don't have any other siblings. I lost my parents in a car accident just before I turned nineteen. I had no one else, no other relatives."

"What happened? Were you in the car?"

He felt the small shudder that went through her. "No, but I found the car."

He stroked her hair to soothe her. "I didn't mean to bring up bad memories." He wasn't certain which was worse—having monsters for parents or losing parents you loved right in front of you. He didn't know that kind of loss. He couldn't imagine losing Emma. The idea left him without air, with a blank, numb mind, and he wasn't even in love. He didn't know the meaning of the word. He wasn't capable of love, but he knew she was.

"I'm sorry, honey, that was thoughtless of me to bring up your parents and the accident before you went to sleep. I had no idea." He bent his head the scant few inches to brush a kiss over each eye and then he resumed stroking her face with the pads of his fingers.

"It was a difficult time when I lost them," she admitted, her voice drowsy. She turned onto her side, facing him, but she didn't open her eyes. "We always had a plan in place if we were separated and something went wrong." She was so sleepy and warm. Jake made her feel safe, otherwise she never would have told him anything, yet she couldn't stop the words pouring out of her. It was almost a relief. "I waited for an hour at the library for them, but they didn't come. So I went to the rendezvous point. We weren't supposed to call on the cell phone. I waited there for another hour and then I knew something was really wrong."

Jake tightened his arms around her and brushed kisses along her temple. "That must have been so frightening."

"I was terrified. My parents were my entire life. There was a cache of money and papers and I took it, but instead of going to the next spot, the final meeting place before I was supposed to disappear, I stole a bike and rode outside of town, along the road they would have been driving. The road was very winding and steep. I had to walk in places and I knew if they ever found out, they'd be furious with me, but I couldn't help myself."

She was silent so long he prompted her. "You found them."

Her breath hissed out between her teeth. "Yes, I found them." Her voice was strained and very low. He could barely catch the thread of sound even with his acute hearing. "Their car had gone off the road. My mother had died right away;

at least, I think—I hope she did. But my father . . ." She trailed off and buried her tear-wet face against his chest.

"Emma?"

She shook her head.

"Honey. Just tell me."

Emma was silent for a long time, but then her lashes lifted and she looked into his eyes, searching for something there, some reassurance. "My father had been alive, but someone had tortured him. There were small cuts all over his body. Whoever had done it had started a fire and left the bodies to burn. I could see tracks leading away from the car."

"What kind of tracks?" He could barely breathe, knowing she'd been through such a thing, knowing how close she'd been to killers. What had her father been into?

"Big cat tracks."

His mouth went dry at the revelation. Leopard tracks? Was Drake right about her, then? Everything pointed to it, yet how could that be? He had to gather more information on her. Now was certainly not the time to mention that he could shift into a cat.

"I'd given my word to them that if anything went wrong, I'd leave, go thousands of miles away. And I did. I made my way to California, because I promised them I would."

If Emma gave her word, there was no question she would carry it out. If Emma married him, there would be no cheating, no leaving, no breaking of her vows.

"You met Andrew and married him." Changing her last name, making her more difficult to trace. "I'm sorry, Emma, that must have been so difficult." He transferred his hand to her hair, sliding over the silky strands. The action soothed him almost as much as it did her. He felt tension slipping from his body. "Did your mother always like leopards? Is that where you got your love of sketching leopards as well?" He wanted her to remember her mother that way, something beautiful they shared together.

"Yes, but she never did one like the painting I did for you, the half man and half leopard. She loved big cats. She painted amazing lifelike pictures of them, but none with a half-human, half-cat face. I just think sometimes you have a stillness about you, and the way you move, like water over sand, fluid and silent—that reminds me of a leopard."

"Not a tiger?" he asked curiously. Emma's insights were one of the things he admired in her. She had amazing instincts. He was beginning to think Drake might be right about Emma, and it if was true, he didn't know if that would help his cause or make it more difficult.

"Leopards are more unpredictable." Her lashes lifted. Fluttered. He could see amusement in her green eyes. Cat's eyes. "And have bad tempers."

He heard the smile in her voice and bent closer to inhale her fragrance. Sometimes he wanted to take her happiness into his lungs, to fill his body, his bloodstream, to keep for his own. He didn't know how to be happy. He was fiercely protective, maybe too much so to be happy. He had built an empire, and he guarded it ferociously, but he was always aware his enemies were circling. Emma had gone through a terrible ordeal, yet she still had the capacity to love, to tease, to find happiness and fun.

"I don't have a bad temper. I just like things done a certain way."

She made a little moue with her lips and his heart lurched. His blood surged hotly and his cock jerked, hot and hard and fully awakened. Jake took a breath and let it out, sliding his palm down her arm to tangle his fingers with hers so he wouldn't cup the temptation of her breast. He had to go slow, let her get used to the idea of a man in her life again. She hadn't been ready, but he'd planted the seed and hopefully she'd let go of Andrew, and Jake would be there for her.

Truthfully, he'd been with her much longer than Andrew.

She'd known her husband only a couple of months before they'd married, and she'd been with him five months before his death. Emma had shared Jake's life for more than two years. Andrew had been a boy, not a man, and as sweet as he'd been to Emma, she needed a man.

Jake could tell she was fairly inexperienced when it came to sex. He'd bet his life that she'd been a virgin when she met Andrew. The things he wanted to do to her would probably shock her. He brought her hand up to his mouth and chewed on the tips of her fingers.

"You're very oral," she whispered, amusement in her voice.

She sounded sleepy, and he knew she was drifting or she never would have made the uncensored comment, and she sure wouldn't have told him about the way her parents had died.

"You have no idea, honey," he whispered, deliberately wicked, and leaned in close to tease at the soft, vulnerable spot where her shoulder met her neck. His tongue licked at her warm skin, filling him with her taste so that he couldn't resist rubbing his lips over the spot.

She lifted her shoulder slightly, but she had already drifted too far into sleep to do more than that slight protest. Jake allowed his teeth to scrape back and forth before biting down gently. The leopard in him urged him to do more, to leave his mark on her, to proclaim ownership, but Jake lifted his head enough to give himself breathing room.

"Sleep well, honey," he whispered. "I'll see you in the morning."

9

"DADDY, what's illoment mean?" Kyle asked.

Jake frowned and looked up at Emma for an interpretation. She seemed to always know exactly what the children were saying. She was leaning in the doorway, watching him unwrap the small presents from the squealing children while he sat on Kyle's bed with them. Andraya threw herself into his lap and wrapped her arms around his neck, clinging like a monkey, while Kyle stared earnestly up at his face.

Emma looked good enough to eat, and since he'd lain awake most of the night thinking of her lying on her bed clothed in her thin pajamas with nothing else beneath them, he found himself very hungry. She stirred and looked uncomfortable, shrugging her shoulders and giving him a small shake of her head.

"Is everyone ready for breakfast?" She sounded cheerful—too cheerful.

Jake's gaze narrowed on her face. She knew exactly what Kyle had asked. She didn't want to answer. He turned back to Kyle. "Who said that word to you?"

"The bad lady."

Jake jerked his head up again and glared at Emma. "The bad lady," he echoed, looking at Emma instead of his son. "What bad lady?"

"Kyle," Emma intervened.

Jake held up his hand, signaling Emma to silence as he slowly stood with Andraya still in his arms, his large frame dominating the room. "What bad lady, Kyle?" Jake asked, his voice deceptively gentle.

"The one that makes Mommy cry."

There was dead silence in the room. No one moved, not even Andraya. Jake fought down the volcano that threatened to explode. He took a breath, counted to ten and let it out. "Susan?" He raised his voice, calling out into the hall, never once taking his eyes from Emma's pale face.

The teenage girl came running, her face glowing with near worship, eager to help him. "I'm sorry, am I late for breakfast?"

"Not at all," Jake said pleasantly. "I didn't get a chance to tell you we're glad you've come for a visit. I'd like you to take Andraya and Kyle down to the kitchen and feed them."

Susan looked a bit flustered, opening her mouth several times to respond, but nothing came out. She held her hands out to the children. Kyle slipped his hand in hers, but Andraya clung to Jake.

Emma turned away, but Jake's hand snaked out, fingers settling around her wrist like a bracelet. "Oh, no, you don't. You're not going anywhere." With one hand he removed Andraya. "Go with Susan. There's a good girl," he murmured.

Andraya studied his face for a moment to determine if a temper tantrum would do any good, but when she saw the inflexible set of his jaw, she went willingly with Susan. Jake waited until the children had gone down the stairs.

"I have a standing order in this house. We don't have visitors unless I okay them first. I said Senator Hindman and his daughter were welcome to come occasionally, I don't recall ever giving permission for anyone else. Unless Susan is considered the 'bad lady' and has made you cry, that means someone else has been on my property and in my home."

Each word was distinct, bit out between his teeth, his voice lower than normal and rumbling with menace.

Emma stepped back—she couldn't help herself—but he followed, step for step, like a macabre dance, until her back hit the wall and she couldn't go any farther. Jake planted his hands against the wall on either side of her head, effectively caging her in. Up close he was quite large and intimidating and he knew it, and he didn't mind this time that she looked up at him with a touch of fear in her eyes. A good scare might do some good.

"Right after you left on this last trip, Jerico was on duty at the gate and he called the house and told me your girlfriend was here."

His eyebrow shot up. "My girlfriend? I don't have girlfriends and you know it."

Impatience crossed her expressive face. "Fine, then—the woman you sleep with."

"I don't sleep with women either—unless it's you. Who is this woman who claimed to be my girlfriend? Did she actually use that silly phrase?"

Impatience went to pure exasperation. "*Jerico* used that phrase. He said your girlfriend, Linda Rawlins, was at the gate and needed to come up to the house."

"And you fell for that?"

"I thought you were dating her. And sleeping with her."

He allowed utter derision mixed with contempt to show in his eyes. "I don't date and I don't sleep. She came to my office in town and blew me a couple of times. I fucked her, pure and simple, because I hurt like hell and wanted it to stop. She knew there were no strings and never would be. My girlfriend." He shook his head. "I thought you knew better than that. What the hell did she want?"

He pulled out his radio and spoke into it. "Drake, I want Jerico waiting in my office immediately." He glanced down at Emma. "I know you instructed a bodyguard to come into the house with her. Give me a name."

"Jake." She tilted her chin at him.

"Don't make me any angrier than I already am."

Emma blew out her breath, dropped her eyes and shrugged. "Joshua." Emma curled her fingers curled into two tight fists.

Jake stared down at her, deliberately goading her, angry that she'd put herself in the line of fire when he'd gone to so much trouble to protect her. In another minute, if she didn't get her temper under control, she was going to take a swing at him. He spoke into the radio a second time. "Have Joshua join me there as well." He caught Emma's chin and forced her to look at him. "A slut is a slut no matter where she comes from, Emma, and you should know that. How could you let her trick you and invade my home?"

"If she's a slut, what does that make you?" Emma demanded, almost spitting mad. "She isn't the only woman you have falling all over herself to have sex with you."

Her eyes were beautiful, almost glowing, like two dazzling emerald jewels. He wouldn't have been surprised if sparks flew at him at any moment. "The difference is, Linda would sell her soul to the highest bidder and she uses sex to try to get what she wants."

"And you don't?"

"Not yet. But believe me, honey, that's going to happen soon. Now tell me what the hell went on and how the children got involved."

"Go to hell." Her temper rose to meet his.

His gaze narrowed, focused, burned into hers. His body went still, aggressive, dominating, as he surrounded her with power and heat.

She took a breath. He had moved closer, and that single inhalation pushed her breasts against his chest so that he felt the rise and fall, felt the slide of her hard nipples against him. Lightning streaked from chest to groin. He wanted to press against her body and rub himself on her like a cat. He was instantly, fiercely aroused, and got the image of her dropping to her knees and sliding her perfect fantasy mouth tightly around his thick, pulsing cock.

Anger arced between them, right along with heightened sexual awareness. He could smell their combined scents, a heady, potent mixture of sexual scents that acted like an aphrodisiac on him. He bent his head lower until his mouth was against her ear. "Watch what you say to me or you're going to find out just what happens when you push me too far."

"I don't intimidate so easily, Jake. And I refuse to jump through hoops like everyone else around you does."

His hand slid around her throat, tipping her head back, forcing her face up to his. "You really want to play power games with me, Emma? Because I can feel your body responding to mine. Do you think I can't tell when a woman wants me?" He pushed into her, nearly lifting her body onto his so that his heavy erection was snuggled into her hot mound.

"So I can be another one of your many cast-off sluts you can feel superior to? So you can get that look of contempt on your face every time you mention my name? Nice invitation, but really, no thanks." She didn't move away from him, or look away, matching him temper for temper. "My body may respond to yours—I'm not dead; and you're very sexy, which you well know—but believe me when I tell you, my head is absolutely screaming 'no way in hell.'"

All he heard were the words "no way in hell." Fury
burned in his eyes and he caught her by her upper arms,
yanking her onto her toes, dropping his head to hers, his
lips crushing hers, grinding them into her teeth. There was
nothing sweet about Jake in that moment. He took what he
wanted, making a statement, demanding her response, conquering her, branding her, the hot pressure forcing her
mouth open so he could own her.

Heat and flames streaked through his bloodstream and
what was meant as a punishment became something else
altogether. Her body fought him, but her mouth didn't, instead fusing with his, devouring hungrily, their tongues
dueling wildly while her body struggled against his sudden
weight. He pinned her against the wall, sliding one hand to
her breast, finding her tight nipple and stroking and tugging as he'd wanted to do for the past two long years.

Emotion poured into him as if a dam had broken, shaking him, flooding his system with unexpected and unwanted . . . what? Not love. It couldn't be love. The thought,
the feeling, terrified him, but he couldn't deny touching
her, kissing her, feeling her body melting into his was unlike anything he'd ever come close to experiencing when
he'd thought he'd known passion and great sex. Something
about Emma brought out every male instinct he had—even
tenderness—when he'd never known it for himself. He
hadn't expected the waves of feeling that came rushing
over him, the joy bursting through him, sweeping him up
with every bit of the intensity and adding to the strength of
his physical need of her.

The jackhammers drilling into his head increased their
tempo while his leopard leapt and roared for supremacy.
She gasped for breath, going boneless under the onslaught
of his hands and mouth. His knee slid between her legs,
grinding into her, the junction like a furnace, inciting him
all the more. He dragged her thin top down, exposing her

breasts, his mouth never leaving hers, still feeding ferociously while his hands found bare flesh.

He jerked at her bra, desperate to feel the soft, creamy mounds spilling into his palms. The feel of the soft weight in his bare hands nearly made him weep. He wanted to know every single inch of her, needed to find a way to slow down to savor the taste of her. His mouth left hers and he blazed a trail of fire down her throat to her breast.

Emma gasped and arched to him as he took her in his mouth, suckling strongly, his tongue flicking the hard peak, his teeth biting down, sending shock waves through her body.

Emma heard her own keening wail and knew she was in terrible trouble. The chemistry between them was explosive, her skin so sensitive she could barely stand the touch of her clothing. She couldn't stop herself from rubbing back and forth against his knee. Her mouth felt empty, just as her body did. She wanted him to fill her up, to relieve the terrible ache that was building and building until she needed to scream and plead for him to be inside her. This was Jake, the man she loved desperately, and she wanted him with every cell in her body.

He lifted her with one strong arm. "Wrap your legs around me." He needed to be closer, needed to be inside of her, sharing the same skin.

Emma did as he asked, opening herself to him. A strange purring sound came from her as he rocked against her, and she rubbed her body hard against his thick bulge. The thin material between them frustrated her and she glanced down. She could see herself, her full breasts spilling out, her body flushed and needy, her hips bucking against him while her legs wrapped around him tightly. She'd lost her mind. *She* was attacking *him*.

"Stop." It came out a whisper, a hoarse, needy whisper, her breath coming in ragged gasps. "We have to stop."

"We have to get our clothes off," he countered, his mouth greedy at her breast.

Her body nearly convulsed with pleasure. She was building to an orgasm, something she'd rarely had with Andrew, yet Jake hadn't even penetrated her. "Jake, please." She didn't know if she was begging him to take her right there in the hallway or if she was looking for freedom. She'd never in her life felt so desperate to have a man inside of her.

She felt his hands tugging at the drawstring of her pants while his mouth continued to suckle at her breast. His teeth tugged and nipped while his tongue flicked back and forth. She felt each touch deep in her womb, so that her inner muscles gripped at nothing. She was empty and needy, aching for him. She needed to push him away but she couldn't find the strength. "I wouldn't be able to live with myself," she whispered. "Or with you."

He went utterly still. He even seemed to stop breathing for a moment, and she knew he was struggling for control. He held her tight against him, so tight she could feel his heavy shaft pulsing against her mound. His mouth reluctantly left her aching breast and he buried his face between her neck and shoulder. They stayed that way a long time, neither moving, fighting for breath, for a way to pull back, for a way to defuse what had just happened between them.

Jake moved first, slowly lowering her legs back to the floor, his hands framing her face. "I'm sorry, Emma. There's no excuse and I'm not going to try to find one for you."

She couldn't blame the entire thing on him; she'd more than responded. She didn't know what had come over her. She stood there, the wall holding her up, looking at his face, her breasts spilling out of her bra, wild and wanton, with the strawberry marks from his teeth and mouth all over them. She couldn't find her voice, or her will.

Jake pulled her top up, but the material rubbed against

her hard nipples, sending streaks of arousal lashing from her breasts to her spasming womb. "I'm sorry too," was all she could manage.

"I need to know what Linda said to you," Jake said, "whether you want to tell me or not. It's important, Emma. It isn't just about my ego and my being a control freak. I know you think I'm paranoid about you and the children, but I have good reason."

The last thing she wanted to do was talk and make sense. She needed to take a cold shower and then hide her head under the blankets for the rest of her life. Jake seemed to be able to switch off intense arousal with little problem. His body was still hard, but she rarely saw him any other way. He still was close to her, nearly skin to skin, the heat of his body warming her and his masculine scent enveloping her. She didn't push him away because her legs were so weak she was afraid she'd fall if he stepped back.

She fought to control her breathing and tried to make sense, tried to be as nonchalant as he managed. "Linda said she needed to talk to me, that it was important. Although she never said it outright, she implied she had a message for me from you."

He frowned down at her, shaking his head as if disappointed in her. "I would have called you myself if that were the case."

"I know that. I do. I don't know what I was thinking." Which wasn't entirely true. She'd been curious to see what Jake's "girlfriend" looked like. Emma had an acute sense of smell, and all too often she scented another woman when Jake came through the door in the evening after he'd been to his downtown office. Curiosity and maybe a little jealousy had gotten the best of her and she told Jerico to have Linda escorted up to the house.

"What did Linda have to say?"

Emma tried to keep color from spreading up her neck

and into her face. Linda had said a lot of things, most of which had been downright insulting. It had only taken a minute in Linda's company to realize that the message she'd come to deliver wasn't from Jake but from Linda herself. The gist of it was: Emma would never have Jake because Linda had staked her claim. Kyle had unfortunately heard Linda screaming at her that no matter how many illegitimate bastard children she had with Jake, he would never stoop to marrying someone so far beneath him.

"Emma." Jake said her name in warning.

Emma tilted her chin at him. "She was insulting. I handled it. It was unfortunate that Kyle overheard her yelling at me. He's never really heard yelling before, so I think it was disturbing and he remembered it. Don't worry, Jake. I learned my lesson. It was quite uncomfortable, and Kyle was upset afterward. I rocked him to sleep for a couple of nights before he got over it."

"You cried." His throat closed unexpectedly. He hadn't been there to comfort her when she went to sleep.

"A little. I'm not used to people yelling at me or being insulting either. She said some pretty ugly things, but I realized she thinks we're living together. Obviously she believes you're Andraya's father . . ."

"I *am* Andraya's father," he said in a low tone.

"Of course. I meant birth father. She feels threatened by that, and evidently so do your parents."

Every muscle in his body contracted. His head came up, eyes glittering dangerously, and he had to suppress the rumbling growl rising in his chest. "How did they get into the conversation?" He had never been able to acknowledge them as his parents, let alone refer to them as his mother and father. To him, they would always be his enemies.

Emma shrugged. "Linda is apparently good friends with them and they don't want to see you brought down by a nobody like me. They want to make certain I know that my children will never be welcome into their circle. As I wasn't planning on joining any circles, I wasn't too upset by it."

She was lying. Jake could always smell a lie. The things Linda had said had hurt. No one wanted to be told they weren't good enough to be part of a family. Jake cupped the nape of her neck, his thumb sliding along her soft skin. "You aren't anything like those people, Emma. You're so far above them you can't even imagine. They're all cruel and vicious. I don't want you anywhere near them, unless I'm standing right beside you. And I don't want the children exposed to them—ever."

"I can take care of myself."

"They would eat you alive. You have no idea what they're capable of and I don't want you ever to find out. I protect you all for a reason. I employ bodyguards for a reason. No one comes onto the property without my permission."

"I understand, Jake. I really do, and I'm sorry. I should have protected the children better. It never occurred to me that Linda Rawlins would be involved in anything that could harm either of them. I don't know her, but I've read about her in newspapers and magazines numerous times. She seemed a little haughty maybe, and frivolous, running from one party to another, but I honestly never thought of her as dangerous."

"Anyone who runs in the same crowd, anyone connected at all to the people who gave birth to me, is extremely dangerous. Given the chance, they would harm either of the children, and certainly you."

"I understand. It won't happen again. I'm sorry it happened this time. I really am."

Jake bent his head and brushed his mouth across her temple. "I should have made the situation much clearer to you. Joshua should have stayed in that room with you every moment and Jerico should never have allowed her onto the property in the first place."

"Wait." Emma caught at his arm as he turned away. "I told Jerico to send her up and Joshua was protecting the children. You told me I ran this household when you were away. If either of them gets in trouble for doing what I asked, I'll have no authority at all. It's my fault, not theirs."

He kept his expression blank. Yes, the men were to do what she said, unless it involved her safety. Joshua acted as Emma's bodyguard, not the children's, although she had no idea. Drake looked after the children. Both men should have been present. He had a lot to say to both Jerico and Joshua, whether Emma liked it or not. But she had that anxious look that made him want to kiss her until the look disappeared.

"Don't worry. I won't do anything to undermine your authority." He was just going to make it very plain that if anyone ever got through security again, he was going to beat both of them within an inch of their lives. And he would make them very aware that Emma was to be protected at all times. He forced a smile. "I won't be home for dinner. I have an important meeting tonight. A few investors are very interested in acquiring one of my companies. The company hasn't made any money, and they're offering way more money than the company is worth, so they have something up their sleeves. I need to meet with them face-to-face to figure out what it is. Don't expect me until late." He also suspected that the company manager was on his enemies' payroll, and he intended to find out for certain.

Emma nodded. She had planned to call Greg Patterson and cancel her date with him, but after what had happened between her and Jake, she wanted to see if she reacted to Greg. If she did, then her problem was simply that she'd gone too long without a man. *Let that be it.*

Jake turned back to her, a slight frown on his face. "What did you say?"

She blinked in surprise. "I didn't say anything."

He stood there in the hall, tall, as sexy as sin, remote, his golden eyes drifting over her body with a little too much possession in his gaze, until Emma pressed herself back against the wall to keep from sliding down it. His stare came back up to her face, to her mouth, and his hand moved to the front of his jeans, his palm sliding over the hard bulge.

"Sometimes you make me wish I was a decent man, Emma."

Emma's breath caught in her throat as he turned away from her, an oath slipping out from between his clenched teeth as he strode away. She held on to the wall, trembling, shocked at the way she reacted to him, to his crudeness and his blatant sensuality, when she'd always been attracted to gentle, kind souls. There was little gentle or kind about Jake.

She retreated to her room to pull herself back together before facing Susan and the children. She could hear them in the distance, laughing, and the sound allowed her to breathe again. She just needed to go back to what she did best. The children were her first priority. She loved them and she provided a home for them.

Jake needed someone, whether he knew it or not. Not sexually—not in the usual way he related to women—but on a more emotional, intimate level. He needed someone to make a difference in his life and make his house a home. Emma had been happy in her role as his housekeeper, but she had to begin slowly separating herself from the close and very strange relationship she'd formed with him over the past two years.

In her room, Emma pulled a thick sweater over her thin T-shirt and tried to put Jake out of her mind. Tonight she was going on a date with Greg Patterson, a nice, uncomplicated man, and she intended to enjoy herself. She needed to get out and breathe. She'd allowed the ranch to consume her and she had to think about making a life for herself outside of it.

For now, however, she was going to be the mommy and make certain her children and her houseguest were happy.

She hurried down the wide, curving staircase and paused halfway down to look at the bronze statue of a crouched leopard. It was snarling, lips drawn back to expose sharp teeth, eyes fierce with ropes of muscle rippling beneath the rosette-dotted fur. The bronze leopard stood in the midst of several plants and appeared lifelike, a fierce wild predator, still and focused, hunting prey and all too reminiscent of Jake when he looked at her.

Her head went up when she heard Andraya shriek and Kyle laugh. Susan shouted something and Andraya and Kyle let out another round of high-pitched glee. She ran to the kitchen, only to stop in the doorway and see cake all over the floor and the table. Kyle and Andraya sat in their high chairs covered in frosting, and what remained of the birthday cake was a mass of crumbs and frosting between them. She could see the marks of fingers in the cake where the children had scooped out handfuls and eaten them, thrown them and dumped them on their heads.

"Susan?" she asked, raising an eyebrow at the teenager.

Susan opened and closed her mouth several times. "They said you fed them cake for breakfast. I have no idea how to cook, or what babies eat."

Kyle glared at her. "I'm not a baby. 'Draya is."

"Kyle, don't talk like that to Susan," Emma said gently. She removed what was left of the cake from the table and tugged Susan over to the sink. "Children are not fed cake for breakfast."

"They both threw it at me and then at each other."

Emma fixed a stern eye on the children. "They both will have a time-out and then apologize," she said.

Andraya's lower lip came out in a pout, but Emma ignored her while she removed as much cake as possible from Susan's hair and clothes. "I think you'd better go take a shower while I clean up the little munchkins."

"I want to hear all about Jake," Susan protested. "What did he say about me staying here for a couple of weeks? Do you think he likes my hair?" She patted the sophisticated weave she'd gotten just before coming to stay at the Bannaconni estate.

"Jake doesn't comment on appearances as a rule," Emma said, trying to let Susan down easy. The teen had a major crush on the man, and it wasn't as if Emma could blame her. She turned to Kyle and began cleaning him up. He was going to need a bath to get his hair clean, but judging from the bright eyes, huge dimples and baby grin stretching from ear to ear, he looked as if he'd thoroughly enjoyed the morning.

Susan raced upstairs to shower while Emma cleaned the kitchen and children and then took them upstairs for a bath. By the time she was back down with them, Jake was pacing in the kitchen again like a caged cat, and Susan looked pale and wide-eyed, as if she might faint—or cry—any moment.

The children ran to Jake, who bent immediately to pick them up. "Susan made the coffee," he announced grimly.

Emma turned her back, hiding a smile. Susan's hero had feet of clay. He was a coffee drinker and he tended to be grumpy in the morning without it. Most of the men who worked close to the house were in the habit of dropping in to fill their travel mugs with coffee as well.

"I'm on it," she said, biting down hard on her amusement. Susan sniffed and Emma put her arm around the girl. "Would you take the kids to the play yard? I think Evan's here this morning to watch over them. He can help you."

Susan perked up immediately. Evan was fairly young, looked like a "hot" cowboy in his jeans and boots and hat, and didn't mind flirting with her even though she was a teenager. Although he rarely spoke, he gave off the impression of being the strong, silent type, which made him mysterious to Susan. "Of course, Emma," she agreed, to show Jake she wasn't as useless as he thought she was.

"Speak French to them. Only French," Emma added deliberately, shooting Jake a clear reprimand over her shoulder. "Today is French day."

Susan stuck her chin in the air as she reached for the two children, giving Jake her haughtiest look.

When Andraya protested, holding on to Jake's neck tightly, he gently pried her loose, speaking in fluent French, telling her to go with Susan and play. Andraya sulked, but she always minded Jake and she went outside where Evan waited to escort them to the play yard.

"That girl can't even make coffee," Jake said.

"That girl has a name. It's Susan. She has a housekeeper, three maids, a cook and no mother, Jake. Her governess, that horrible Dana Anderson woman, couldn't care less about her and belittles her at every opportunity. Susan speaks three languages and happens to be studying at college level already. And you can't make coffee either."

Jake came up behind her, bending over her shoulder as she ground the fresh coffee beans. "What makes you think I can't make coffee?"

"Because without coffee you're a total grump and if you're up before me, you still don't make it."

"Only because your coffee is so much better."

"Susan made coffee this morning for you, you just didn't like it."

"I wouldn't call what she made coffee."

She drove her elbow back, hard, into his side. "Go away. You're annoying me more than usual this morning."

"I don't like strangers in my house."

"Jake. Really. Seriously. Susan is a teenage girl without a mother and her father is never home. Have a little compassion. She's got a crush on you and you're just mean." She spun around, her back to the counter, and glared at him. "It's just mean."

Jake straightened his tall body, catching her at the waist with both hands to lift her, placing her on the countertop beside the coffeepot so she faced him. "I'll be better with her. I'll make an effort."

"Do you promise?" Once Jake gave his word, he always followed through.

He hesitated. She'd known him long enough to know what he was thinking. "Don't you dare use this as a bargaining chip. You should make an effort with Susan because she's young and without much of a family. She's a nice girl and she needs a little help right now, and not just so you can get your way."

"You sound so sexy when you get bossy, Emma," he teased. "I said I'll make an effort with her and I will. I forgot to tell you I hired a new man. He's a friend of Drake's and Joshua's and he's been ill. He doesn't talk much, but he's a good man. Work your magic on him, will you? But don't flirt."

"I don't flirt." She glared at him. "Go to your office and get out of my kitchen. I'm liable to bake something for you and put arsenic in it if you keep this up."

"I'm just edgy lately when it comes to you, so don't hang out too much with the new guy. I don't know him and he doesn't know me."

"You aren't making any sense. If he's Drake's friend and you're hiring him, I take it he's been thoroughly investigated and you're not worried he'll cause any of us harm. What are you going on about?"

Jake lifted her from the counter and set her away from

him, his hand sliding over her hip and along her bottom, his palm lingering, even rubbing. "Having to beat the living daylights out of a man I respect, or doing even worse than that. Just behave yourself."

"Jake." She spun around, pushing at the wall of his chest. "What was that?"

"What?"

"You just groped me on the butt. I'm not two, you know."

"I wouldn't be groping you if you were two."

She put both hands on her hips and gave him her sternest look. "Are you aware that little feel you copped could be interpreted as sexual harassment in the workplace?"

"You wouldn't take any money, remember, so technically you don't work for me. You're the mother of my children and you make the best damn coffee I've ever had in my life." He flashed an unrepentant grin at her. "If I want more children, sooner or later I'm going to have to do more than grope your butt. You might as well get used to it."

She tried to stay annoyed with him and not feel the flush of pleasure at being called the mother of his children, or feel happy that he thought of her that way. She'd refused to take money for running the household when he'd taken such great care of her, and then the settlement his lawyers had arranged for her and Andraya had been more money than she ever heard of. He had set up trust funds for both Andraya and Kyle, so money wasn't going to be a problem. Truthfully, Jake had never really treated her like an employee—more like a pampered pet, indulged but still under his rule. Not taking his money always made her feel more on par with him. She didn't have to obey his orders.

She sighed. He was so complicated, so difficult to be around all the time, with his edgy moods and his brooding silences. She knew him better than most people did, but she still found him difficult to read, particularly when he was in the kind of mood he was now.

She pointed to the door. "Get out. You're outrageous this morning. I've got things to do."

Perversely, he straddled a chair. "I'm starving. Feed me."

"I thought you had things to do," she objected, but she was already at the refrigerator, pulling out eggs, bacon and orange juice. "Didn't you have some big meeting you had to prepare for? I figured you must have tons of lawyers to hand you documents so you can make an informed, knowledgeable decision."

"Not on this one. They'll give me the documents and everything I read will tell me the best thing to do is to sell the company. It's a small real estate business and it seems to be losing large amounts of money. It acquires land and rarely sells it. The manager has brought me several deals in the last few months, advising me to sell. The lawyers agree with him."

"But you're not going to sell."

"No, I'm not. We've acquired several pieces of land adjacent to the property I inherited from my great-grandfather in North Dakota, as well as land running from Pennsylvania to New York. I'm working on adding to that acreage, and suddenly I've got someone very interested in acquiring the business and all of its properties. Someone has been snooping around my properties and they've been bribing my manager."

She glanced at him over her shoulder. Disloyalty was Jake's biggest hot button. He could be ruthless and vindictive when he caught an employee spying or cheating. She'd seen his cold anger and she'd never wanted that brutal, merciless side of Jake ever directed toward her. He paid his employees very well and they had excellent benefits and retirement and vacation plans. In return, he expected their best work and absolute loyalty.

"Jake." She kept her voice low. Emma was certain he

felt hurt when someone betrayed him, but he wasn't aware that he did. He let intense anger and contempt rule him to keep from feeling any gentler emotion. "I'm sorry. This manager . . . did you consider him a friend?"

Jake stood there a long moment, studying her eyes, her emotions chasing across her face. She was so different from him. "I don't have friends, Emma. Except for you. Maybe Drake and Joshua." Although he couldn't bring himself to trust any of them completely.

Emma's lips curved and her smile warmed the inner part of him where sometimes he felt there was nothing but rage or the need for revenge. "I *am* your friend, and that's why you should always listen to me. I give great advice."

She was teasing him again, her voice mischievous, inviting. He'd heard her use that same exact tone with the children. She made them feel loved, made them feel important to her and precious, and somehow she did the same with him. Was he in the least bit special to her? Or did she make everyone around her feel that way?

"Jake?" The smile faded from Emma's face, concern creeping into her expression. "Are you really upset about this meeting?"

He shrugged. Hell no, he wasn't upset. Let the bastards come at him. He was ready for them. He welcomed ferreting out traitors, and his manager was taking someone else's money. He'd find the reason soon enough and he'd set things right in his own way. He just liked that look on her face. He studied her expression, the look in her eyes. His heart contracted. He didn't know what love looked like. He knew she was capable of great self-sacrifice and loyalty, and maybe that was what love was. If so, she was looking at him with something close to it.

She stepped closer, close enough that he could feel the heat of her body. In that moment, as his body reacted to her nearness, he realized she was the reason he couldn't sleep at night. She was the reason no matter how many women serviced him, he couldn't stop the aching hardness. Emma. His body demanded Emma and no one else would do. She was the reason he felt disgust with himself—and guilt—when he touched other women.

He backed away from her, the revelation shaking him. His heart pounded in his chest, his lungs burning for air. She was supposed to be captivated by *him*, not the other way around. He wasn't about to give anyone that kind of power over him.

"Jake?" she said again.

He shook his head. "I'm heading for the office. I'll catch breakfast in town." He turned and went out the door without a backward glance, leaving her staring after him.

10

EMMA knew she had to stop obsessing over Jake. If she'd still been considering cancelling her date, Jake's strange behavior all morning proved to her that he was far too complicated of a man for a woman like her. She wasn't sophisticated and she didn't have the ability to be a jet-setter or even be part of that side of his life. They thought differently. Jake thought differently. One moment he blew hot and the next cold. He was far too complicated for her and he was the type of man to break a woman's heart if she let him.

Since Jake wasn't having breakfast, she quickly turned off the stove and finished cleaning before going outside to join Susan and the children. If the children were outdoors, Jake required a bodyguard present, even on the property. If she took them off the property to the doctor's office or any-where else, he sent at least two of the men with them, some-times three. Although she thought his precautions a little excessive, she decided to trust his judgment. If he had en-emies, she didn't want them getting to the children.

Evan smiled and waved at her as she approached. He

was a big man, muscular, a former prizefighter, fast on his feet with tremendous upper body strength and quick reflexes, but he had a major speech impediment. Often he signed rather than spoke, and both Andraya and Kyle were learning to sign. They liked their "secret" language with him. He seemed to genuinely care for the children and never tired of pushing them on the swings or catching them sliding down the winding tube slide.

Emma watched him for a minute as Susan chattered away in French, which he clearly didn't understand. He smiled a lot, flashing a ready grin, but his attention was clearly on his surroundings. He dressed like an authentic cowboy and he probably could ride, but he wasn't babysitting and he wasn't working the ranch. He was watching over his charges and taking his job very seriously.

She crossed her arms, a sudden shiver going down her spine. What did Jake know that she didn't? Who was he afraid of?

"Ma'am?"

She spun around so quickly she tripped and nearly fell. Hard hands caught at her arm, fingers biting deep to prevent her from falling. Ordinarily she had acute hearing and a heightened sense of smell, but she hadn't realized anyone was near her.

"I'm sorry, Miss Emma." The man released her immediately. "Jake told me to introduce myself when you came out. I'm Conner Vega."

The man stood straight, his large frame too thin, his hair shaggy and thick, one half of his face quite beautiful and the other covered in four deep scars that ran from his hairline to the side of his jaw, as if something had tried to rake his face from his skull. She forced herself to look at him, at the masculine beauty on one side of his face and the horrendous damage done to the other. He was quite pale and gaunt, as if he'd been ill for a long time. He didn't look like a cowboy or a bodyguard, and he certainly wasn't a businessman, not with the merciless slash of his mouth, yet Jake had hired him.

Emma held out her hand. Her arm hurt where he'd grabbed her, and she knew she'd have bruises. He was enormously strong for someone so gaunt. "It's good to meet you. Are you hungry? There's always coffee ready in the kitchen and I usually have fresh bread baked or cookies to grab on the run."

"Jake gave me one of the cabins with a kitchen. I brought a few things with me so I'm good, thanks."

"He keeps food supplies for the men in the common pantry. Did he show you where? When you take anything from there, just check it off the list. It makes it easier for me to replace the supplies so we keep them from running low."

He nodded, then stepped back and lifted his hand slightly. "I just wanted to introduce myself to you so you wouldn't think a stranger was hanging around the children."

"Thank you, I appreciate that," Emma said.

She watched him walk away and rubbed at her arm again. Along with the bruises there was a long scratch, as if his nail had caught her when he'd pulled her upright. She sighed, realizing the latest addition was just like everyone else on the ranch. Drake with his bum leg; Joshua with his pretend smile and the pain in his eyes; Evan with his speech problem; Conner with his scars; and of course, Jake's biggest rescue—Emma, with her lost husband and difficult pregnancy. Jake collected strays whether he knew it or not. She'd met several of the people who worked for him. One was an older couple, intensely loyal to him, and she'd heard Jake on the phone with them on several occasions, sorting out some fund for them and getting back a house that had been repossessed.

Jake had so many personalities. He could be difficult and at times even cruel, yet he was so generous. She spent far too much time thinking about him. As hard as she tried not to, throughout the rest of day she found herself daydreaming about Jake, puzzling, worried, annoyed, frustrated—so many emotions. At least her body wasn't going up in flames at his mere scent as she cleaned the house and played with the children. There was some relief in that.

Susan was a big help, although she talked a lot, mostly about Jake and Evan. At the end of the day, after Emma had listened to Susan for hours and put the children to bed, she really wanted to just sit back with her feet up, but she made herself take a shower and do her hair. She wore it down her back, the way Jake liked it most. She'd always had great hair, the one attribute she loved about herself. Most of the time she wore it up out of the way, but Jake often took her hair out of the clip so that the silky strands would cascade down her back to her waist. She found a long-forgotten short silk blouse that dressed up her favorite swingy skirt and walked down the stairs.

"You look beautiful," Susan greeted her in the hallway. "Where are you going tonight?"

"Just to a movie, but I go out so rarely"—*make that never*—"that I thought I'd make the most of it." Was a part of her angry at Jake for making it so impossible to be with him? She paused, afraid she was more upset with him than she'd realized. She'd been honest with Greg, telling him she wanted to go out only as a friend, but maybe even that wasn't the truth.

"That's so cool that Jake is taking you to a movie."

Emma stiffened. "I'm not going with Jake. He's at a business meeting tonight."

Susan frowned. "Are you going by yourself? I thought you said it was a date."

"Sort of a date. He's a friend."

Susan's eyebrow shot up. "*He?* Does Jake know?"

Emma's stomach knotted. Fear curled inside her, making her more annoyed and determined than ever. "It isn't Jake's business what I do."

Susan looked shocked. "Okay, Emma. You're teasing the tiger."

"I've told you, Jake and I are not like that."

"Maybe you're not like that, but I've seen him with you. He definitely has the hots for you. No joke, Emma. If you don't know it, you're the only person on this ranch that doesn't."

Emma closed her eyes, briefly wishing there was more to it than that. "He has the hots for all women, Susan." She pulled on a short black cardigan and caught up her purse. It was quite cold, but she figured the theater would be warm enough. "Don't wait up."

"Don't you worry about that. I don't want to be up when Jake comes home and finds you gone," Susan said. "He's the type that might kill the messenger, and I was on my way to bed anyway."

Emma rolled her eyes. "You're so dramatic. Jake doesn't care what I do off this ranch." She started down the hall.

"You keep believing that," Susan said.

Emma hurried into the kitchen, glancing at her watch. "One of the men will stay in the house, so if you need help, just call out." She picked up the phone and punched the intercom button to the main cabin. "Joshua, send one of the bodyguards up to the house for the rest of the evening. I'm heading out."

There was a stunned silence and then Joshua gave a croak. "Out?"

She wasn't going to explain herself. Just that tone had irritated her. It was obvious she'd waited far too long to assert herself. "Just send someone now."

She hurried out to the Jeep that was kept parked near the house for her use on the property.

"Wait!" A figure came flying toward the Jeep, out of the darkness. Joshua leaned into the vehicle through the open window and actually took the keys right out of the ignition. "Where are you going? It's eight thirty." He stared at her. "You're dressed up. What are you doing, Emma?" He sounded shocked.

"I'm going on a date, Joshua," she answered quietly, fighting the mixture of indignation and amusement.

"A date?" he echoed, his voice hitting a high note. "With a man?"

She smiled at him sweetly. "That is fairly standard, isn't it, or have I gotten it wrong after all this time?"

"Nobody told me." Joshua's mind raced frantically. Emma never went anywhere off the ranch without an escort. Who would dare ask her out? Who would be so crazy as to take his life in his hands? Who was off that evening? He tried to remain calm.

"I wasn't aware I had to tell you," Emma replied mildly. She held out her hand for the keys. "I'm late. Hand them over."

He backed up a step, little dots of sweat forming on his forehead. "Does Jake know about this?"

"Jake is at a business meeting, Susan is watching the children and I'm taking the night off. It's the first time in two years. I deserve it, don't you think?"

Joshua raked a nervous hand through his hair. "Yeah, well, just who is this guy?"

"No one you know." Emma leaned out through the window of the Jeep and took the keys from his hand. "Don't worry, Joshua. You're acting like a father. I'll come home at a reasonable hour."

"But you never go out," he protested. "You never wear a

skirt." He passed a hand over his face and blinked at her. "You never look like this."

She laughed ruefully. "I'm not sure that's actually a compliment. I'll see you tomorrow, Joshua."

"Oh, God, Emma." He nearly wailed it. "You aren't thinking of spending the night with this guy, are you? I'll get killed for this. I'm dead. Boiled in oil."

Emma scowled at him with exasperation. It was clear she needed to leave the ranch more often. Did they all think she wasn't date-worthy? "Will you stop? It has nothing to do with you. I'm just going to a movie, maybe out for coffee afterward. Don't wait up."

"Skip the coffee." He glanced at his watch. "It's too late for the early show. Call the guy and cancel."

"Joshua." Exasperated, Emma started the Jeep.

"Wait! I'll drive you in," he said desperately.

She patted his arm. "Not on your life. Stop worrying. I'm following Jake's orders."

Joshua stared at her with his mouth open, clearly at a loss for words. Then he cleared his throat. "You sure?"

"Absolutely. Why do you think I'm doing this? Jake told me to."

"He did?" Joshua echoed. "That doesn't sound like him."

She nodded solemnly, gave a cheery little wave and roared off, leaving Joshua frowning after her in a swirling cloud of dust.

"Drake!" Joshua bellowed at the top of his lungs as he sprinted toward Drake's truck.

Drake beat him to the driver's seat, gun in hand, looking wildly around and then after the Jeep. "That wasn't . . ." He'd already started the vehicle and reversed, wheeling the truck around to follow the fast-moving vehicle. "Who's in the Jeep?"

"Emma." Joshua sounded like doom.

"Emma?" Drake echoed, barely able to believe his ears. "Where the hell is she going this time of night, and why aren't a couple of bodyguards with her?"

"The movies." Joshua grimaced. "Emma's going out. On a date."

"A what?"

Few things shocked Drake, and Joshua was pleased to see he was shaking at the news.

"Date—a date—with a man. Someone I don't know. Someone you don't know."

Together they groaned and said simultaneously, "Someone *Jake* doesn't know."

Drake called the main gate. "Emma's coming through, Jerico. Let her go. We're on it." He turned to Joshua with a raised eyebrow. "What movie are we going to see?"

"Hell, I don't know, but I'm definitely getting too old for this kind of thing. Don't get too close to her. If she spots us, we're dead. She has a mean streak in her. She'll pull our coffee privileges."

"We're probably already dead. You couldn't stop her? She's a sweet little thing," Drake said. "And you should never have allowed her to go without a bodyguard."

"Ha! You try it. She smiles at you sweetly, nods her head a lot and does whatever the hell she wants to do. You can't stop that woman short of tying her up. And believe me, I considered it."

"Jake's going to go up like a volcano," Drake announced grimly. "You should have tied her up."

"Hell, Drake, you gave the order to let her off the property. I'm going to make sure Jake knows that when he pulls off our fingernails." He brightened as he settled against the seat. "We could murder the guy while she's in the ladies' room."

They followed her right to the theater, Drake keeping a

few cars between them at all times. "The movie better not be some sloppy love story," Joshua hissed as they crept through the parking lot, hiding behind cars, keeping pace with her.

"Uh-oh," Drake said. "I think lover boy is waiting. There he is, he's taking both her hands in his, gazing into her eyes. You recognize him?"

"I think he's the telephone guy. I've seen him around. Jake isn't going to like this," Joshua pointed out with a little groan.

"Neither is Emma if she catches us. I wish we could just get rid of this guy somehow. Got any ideas?" Drake asked hopefully.

"Maybe we should call Jake right now and just let him handle it," Joshua suggested.

"Are you crazy?" Drake pushed money at the woman at the ticket counter. "Whatever movie they're going into," he added, nodding toward Emma and her date as they went inside.

"Hey, we're in luck," Joshua exclaimed gleefully. "It's a comedy. I hope we get good seats."

"Joshua!" Drake smacked the younger man with his hat. "We're here to keep an eye on lover boy. How the hell did he slip by us that we haven't checked him out?"

"I hope you've got more money. I don't have a cent. This is great. I really did want to see this movie." Joshua was patting his pockets. "I need popcorn."

Drake shoved him, scowling darkly. "Will you keep your mind on the job? You keep it up and I'll leave you out here."

"Quick! They're going in," Joshua pointed out hastily. "We'll lose them. Get in line, will you?"

"Shh," Drake admonished, allowing several couples to go in front of them. "And I'm not getting you popcorn. We're working."

"Don't be such a cheapskate. I'd like popcorn. You just can't watch a good movie without popcorn. If he doesn't stop at the snack bar, you follow them and I'll catch up after I get us some popcorn. I'll need money though."

"Forget the damned popcorn," Drake ordered.

"You just don't know how to have a good time," Joshua sulked.

"Just keep your eye on her. What got into her anyway? Is she mad at the boss? They have a fight?"

"She said he told her to go out," Joshua said. "And if I know anything at all about Emma, it's that she doesn't lie."

"The man's a damned idiot."

"Either that or he was a misunderstood idiot." Joshua ducked behind a pillar. "They're getting popcorn. It smells so good. Come on, Drake, buy some popcorn."

"Will it shut you up?" Drake demanded furiously.

"I promise." Joshua folded his arms complacently over his chest.

They hung back, waiting for Emma and her date to be seated in the darkened theater, before finding a space two rows behind her.

Joshua was enthralled with the comedy, laughing so heartily the girls seated next to him kept giggling together.

Drake dug elbows into Joshua's ribs. "He's making his move."

"Who is?" Joshua's eyes were glued to the screen.

"The guy, her date. He put his arm around the back of her seat."

Joshua sat up, glaring daggers. "Wanna break his arm? We could make it look like an accident."

"Oh, shut up. You're no help. Just watch the damn movie." Drake sounded totally exasperated.

"Fine." Joshua managed to look hurt for all of five minutes, until the movie had him doubling over with shoulder-shaking chuckles.

They had a few bad minutes when the lights went up, finding themselves trapped by the people leaving. They had to pretend they were looking for something on the floor to allow Emma and her escort to pass. Drake sent up a silent prayer that Emma would go straight home, but it wasn't answered. They were forced to follow her to the Chateau, a very expensive French restaurant.

Drake looked down at their work clothes and boots. "She'll spot us for certain. Maybe we should wait outside."

"If we wait outside, and we have to tell Jake about this evening, he'll beat the crap out of us. And I don't feel like taking a beating because Emma is feeling frisky."

JAKE allowed the talk to flow around him. The scent of conspiracy was heavy in his nostrils and betrayal reeked at the table, but everyone there smiled and played their high-stakes games. Dean Hopkins, the manager for his small, seemingly failing business, was all for the sale, laying the advantages out carefully while the circle of investors nodded their heads and tried to convince him they were helping him out. Jake kept his face expressionless, watching them all closely, wanting to sniff out the underlying reason they were so set on buying a failing business.

The man who interested him the most was Bernard Williams, a lawyer for the firm known to represent his old enemy, Josiah Trent. Williams knew Jake was poised to take over Trent's business. One false move and everything would come tumbling down. Yet here the man sat, prepared to sell Jake out and make him an enemy for life, over what? What did they know that he didn't?

The small real estate chain hadn't turned a profit in three years. Jake intended to keep it that way. He could afford the loss, but it shouldn't have garnered any real attention, not from men like those seated around him, and certainly not the kind of offer they'd made. Hopkins must have discovered his plans and sold him out, or maybe he was a pawn. That was the question. Who had betrayed him? To find out, he would endure sitting through this boring charade, because once he found the man, he would destroy him . . .

Slightly bored, he glanced around the beautiful, elegant restaurant. A couple came through the door, catching his eye. For a moment time actually stood still, every muscle in his body paralyzed so that he was completely motionless. His heart seemed to stop beating. His breath stilled in his lungs until he couldn't breathe.

Emma. His Emma. For two long years, he'd waited patiently for her to come alive. And now she had, but for another man. Not for him. Emma dressed up for another man; not for him. Emma smiling up at a perfect stranger and draping her sweater over the back of her chair. There was no possible way to concentrate on what was being said at his all-important meeting, so Jake didn't bother to try. Who gave a damn about a few million dollars and a traitor when his life had just gone up in flames?

Emma looked beautiful. When he wrapped his hands around her throat, he'd be sure to tell her that. He'd come to catch a traitor, and the biggest one of all was the person he'd come to trust above all others.

He was going to fire every damn bodyguard he had working for him. How dared they allow her off the ranch without a guard? Who was the son of a bitch who was trespassing on his territory anyway? Jake recognized the bastard as the man who'd come to his ranch and worked on the phones. He'd probably seduced Emma in Jake's own office. The image of her on his desk—naked—rose up to taunt him, and he felt the shift inside, the leopard snarling and fighting for supremacy. For one terrible moment he wanted to give the leopard freedom, wanted him to feel his enemy's throat torn and bleeding beneath the crush of his jaws.

He rose, a fluid rippling of muscles, causing a sudden hush among his business associates. Without a word of explanation, he stalked across the room, carelessly loosening his tie, his eyes glittering gold, fixed on his prey. Emma glanced up, and her velvet eyes widened in surprise. Jake couldn't detect the littlest bit of guilt. His fingers itched to punish her. Instead, he toed a chair around and very deliberately wedged it between theirs.

With casual ease he bent his dark head to her silky red one to brush a lingering and very possessive kiss on her shocked mouth. He made certain he used tongue, lots of tongue, one hand anchoring in her hair, forcing her head up so he could take his time making his statement. A blatant brand of ownership.

Color rose in Emma's face and her eyes went emerald green, but she had sense enough not to pull away from him or fight. He let her feel the edge of his teeth on her soft lower lip before dropping into the chair, his mouth smiling, his amber eyes diamond hard. He extended his hand to the man. "Jake Bannaconni. I don't believe we've met." He remembered everyone, but he wasn't about to let a rival believe himself memorable.

"Greg Patterson." The man was totally flabbergasted, his face pale beneath his tan. "We met the other day in your office."

Jake leaned back, stretched his arm casually around Emma's chair. His fingers found the nape of her neck, began a slow, intimate massage. "So who's at home with the kids, baby?" He spoke to Emma but his eyes were measuring the width of Greg Patterson's hands against the marks on her skin.

"Susan." Involuntarily, Emma placed her hand over the smudges on her arm. Damn, the man saw everything. And his fingers were inducing a spreading heat in her body, one that she couldn't possibly ignore.

"You think she's old enough to handle them?" There was a soft intimacy in his voice, one that excluded all others and wrapped them together.

"She's sixteen, Jake," Emma reminded.

Jake rubbed his knuckles along her jaw before turning his attention to Greg. "Where'd you two go tonight?" Jake's voice was perfectly pitched, friendly, interested, filled with urban sophistication. The golden eyes were merciless, slashing, a cold, bleak, brilliant challenge as they settled in an unblinking stare on Patterson's face.

Patterson squirmed uncomfortably. "The movies."

Jake threaded his fingers through Emma's, brought her palm to the warmth of his mouth, his eyes meeting hers. "Did you enjoy it, honey? You know you never should have left the ranch unescorted." With absolute deliberation he bit down into the center of the palm. His eyes dared her to make a scene. She gasped, but he refused to relinquish her hand when she tugged. Instead, his tongue swirled over the bite, soothing the sting.

Retaining possession of her hand, he tucked their laced fingers comfortably, intimately, under his chin, and turned his attention back to Patterson. "It isn't safe for Emma to be out without a bodyguard. I have enemies and they know they can get to me through her."

He rubbed her knuckles along his blue-shadowed jaw, back and forth, a lazy, sexy movement. Every now and then, he brought her hand to the warmth of his mouth to nibble almost seductively at her fingertips.

"Of course, I'd kill anyone who tried to take her away from me." He made the statement matter-of-factly in a low, velvet-soft voice, looking Patterson directly in the eye, meaning every word.

Greg paled visibly and a shiver of apprehension went down Emma's spine. Her gaze jumped to Jake's face. He smiled at her but his eyes glittered with promise until she looked down.

"Don't worry," Emma murmured. "We weren't exactly alone." She could barely stammer the words out.

Jake was doing all kinds of things to her body with his absentminded ministrations. Although he was acting so seductive and loving, she knew he was angry with her. Jake was at his most dangerous, acting possessive and skimming far too close to the edge of his control. She'd never been on the receiving end of his anger. Her pulse had skyrocketed and every nerve ending sizzled with heat. A little desperately, she tried to pull her hand away, but Jake didn't seem to notice. If anything he tightened his hold. Her heart began to beat faster.

"We weren't?" Greg sat up straight, aware he was in deadly peril. No one could call Bannaconni subtle, and he had the kind of power that could make men disappear.

"Drake and Joshua were seated two rows behind us. Joshua really enjoyed the film. That was him laughing his head off," she explained to Greg, trying to ignore the way Jake's fingers bit into her wrist.

"Emma's very precious to me," Jake murmured, nuzzling her hand again. "It's nice to know I don't have to commit murder tonight."

Emma closed her eyes briefly. He was so angry. Had she deliberately set out to make him that way? She had a sinking feeling she might have.

Patterson cleared his throat. "Were you considering murder?" He tried to smile, make it a joke.

The golden eyes slashed at him. "Very seriously considering it." There was nothing humorous in those glittering eyes.

"Jake." Josiah Trent's lawyer, Bernard, stood over them frowning at each one of them. "Is something wrong?"

"Nothing I can't handle." Jake barely glanced up.

"We haven't got this thing settled," Bernard objected.

"As far as I'm concerned we have," Jake answered with deceptive laziness. His arm curled around Emma's shoulders, his hand sliding down, his fingers absently playing with her hair. "I gave you an answer."

"You didn't listen to the proposal."

"We'll take it up again later."

A swift look of annoyance crossed Bernard's face. "This is so important?"

The golden eyes flickered over the lawyer. Jake brought Emma's fingers to his mouth. "More important than anything else, Bernard. Now go away." Deliberately, and quite rudely, he dismissed the lawyer.

Bernard Williams stalked angrily away.

Jake glanced at the gold watch on his wrist. "You finished with your coffee, baby? It's getting late." He stood up, one hand drawing her up with him, clamping her to his side, refusing to give her any other choice, the other hand extending to Greg. "It was a pleasure meeting you. I appreciate your taking Emma to the movies." Carelessly he dropped several bills on the table, paying for the coffee and dessert they hadn't touched. "We can't be out late, Patterson. You never know when a little one is going to have nightmares. Right, honey?"

Emma didn't know whether to laugh or cry. Surely he could see the impression he was giving her date. Talking about the children, who was watching them, for heaven's sake. Kissing her very publicly, practically shoving his tongue down her throat. No wonder people talked about them. Greg already looked as if he might faint. She barely had time to whisper a quick good night before Jake drew her across the room.

"Slow down. Jake, it's a little undignified running after you in high heels. Your step makes three of mine."

"You shouldn't be wearing the damned things," he snapped, but he did slow a fraction. He glanced down at the top of her silky head, his rough features etched in granite. "You can ride home with me. Joshua will drive the Jeep."

"They probably left," she pointed out logically.

"They damn well better not have."

She put a small, placating hand on his arm. "Are you angry with me?"

"Angry? What the hell would I have to be angry about?" He nodded curtly to several of his business associates. Most of them stared at Emma in open curiosity.

She glanced back to see Greg Patterson standing by their table, looking as if he'd been run over by a truck.

Jake jerked her around when he caught her looking back. "Finding my woman out with another man, dressed the way you are? Why the hell would I be angry about that? I hope you weren't expecting him to kiss you good night." There was an audible snap of Jake's white teeth.

"What is wrong with you?" Emma's temper began to rise. Something alive ran under her skin, creating a wave of heat that itched as it spread through her body. "I'm not your woman."

"Like hell, you're not." His fingers were an iron band around her arm as he dragged her out to the parking lot.

Jake spotted her two bodyguards immediately. They were lounging against their truck, waiting just as he knew they'd be. Jake held out his hand for the keys to the Jeep, and scowled at Emma when she hesitated.

"I'm perfectly capable of driving myself home," she protested.

"Don't," he hissed. "Just give me the fucking keys."

Emma dropped the keys into his hand. Jake tossed them to Joshua. "I heard you enjoyed the movie."

"I don't appreciate you two following me," Emma felt compelled to point out.

"You'd better appreciate it," Jake snarled. "They're the only reason I haven't strangled you." His hands caught her shoulders in a firm grip, gave her a little shake. "You never, ever, leave the ranch without a bodyguard. Not ever. Do you have any idea the kind of danger you put yourself in?"

"I refuse to argue with you over it," Emma said. "It's cold out here. And I'm not riding home with you, Jake. Give me back the keys, Joshua."

"Do you really want to make a scene here in the parking lot, Emma? Because I can throw your ass over my shoulder and toss you in the car, if that's the way you want it. You're going home with me."

She stood toe-to-toe with him, but the anger coming off him in waves changed her mind. He was quite capable of a public scene and he wouldn't mind in the least. Jake shrugged out of his coat, bundled her in it and stalked to the Ferrari, taking her with him, waiting at her door until she got in. Emma nervously swept a hand through her hair as Jake slid in beside her. He reached across her to lock the seat belt around her. For some inexplicable reason she felt trapped. "Jake?" She said his name softly, gently, wanting reassurance.

"Don't say anything, Emma." He didn't look at her. With controlled violence, he spun the wheel and fell in behind Drake's truck, with Joshua directly following them in the Jeep.

Emma closed her eyes and lay back in the seat. The tension in the interior of the car could be cut with a knife. He was actually trembling with rage. Seething with it. She could feel it swirling inside of him, dark and ugly and violent. She sighed, wishing she could share the humor of the evening with him, the way Joshua and Drake had acted in the show, the look on Greg's face when Jake had come over and sat between them. If Jake had been the least bit like Andrew, they would be laughing together.

Once they arrived at the ranch, Jake's fingers bit into her upper arm and he hauled her right out of the car. Emma went with him into the house just for the sake of peace. But he didn't release her. He continued on down the hall toward his office.

Emma struggled. "Let go of me, Jake. You're hurting me." He wasn't, but she was suddenly tired, the beginnings of a headache coming on. He was in a foul mood and she didn't particularly feel like dealing with it.

"I want to talk to you," he bit out between clenched teeth, thrusting her into the room. "I think it's been a long time coming."

Emma stumbled and had to catch at the back of a chair to keep from falling. She kicked off her high heels. "What is it, Jake? I'm really very tired and I don't particularly care for your mood."

"My mood?" An eyebrow went up, his fist clenched. "You don't care for my mood?" His eyes burned with fury.

"No, not really. You're angry and I can't understand why." She hung on to her patience; one of them had to show good sense.

"All the way home I told myself I wouldn't lose my temper, I'd be perfectly reasonable when we talked. You don't even know why I'm angry?" His eyes were glittering, a golden menace.

"Not really, no."

"I hate it when you're so damned calm. Do you ever lose control, Emma?" He took a step closer, his temper barely held in check. He wanted to kiss that look right off of her face. Two long years of waiting. She was his, made for him. Belonged to him. He wanted to rake his claws over Patterson's belly and tear out his guts, watch him die a slow, terrible death.

"Who the hell is Greg Patterson? When did he ask you out and why the hell did you go with him?"

Emma tried to fight down her own anger, knowing she could lose everything if she got into a fight with Jake. He owned her home and everything in it, but she couldn't let him talk to her the way he was. She tried to be reasonable, but there was a part of her that knew she had deliberately precipitated the crisis, and she couldn't stop herself from pushing him even more.

"If anyone should be angry here, it should be me. After the way you acted, do you think he'd ask me out again? You made it sound as if we had children together, as if we lived together. He probably thought you caught me stepping out on you."

"Another date!" He caught her shoulders, his fingers biting into her soft skin, hauling her very close to his large, masculine frame. She could feel the heat from his body enveloping her. "You go out on another date and I'll break his neck. And just so you have it straight, Emma, we do have children together. You do live with me."

She scowled at him. "You know very well we're not like that. And you're the one who said I needed a man."

"And just what the hell am I?"

She stared at him, blinking rapidly. "You are not the least bit interested in me."

"I fucking asked you to marry me," he pointed out, furious beyond anything he'd ever known. "What the hell more do you want?" He swore aloud, too angry to say another word.

Jake jerked her into his arms, crushing her body right up against his. One hand twisted in her hair, the other held her chin so he could claim her mouth. There was nothing gentle or sweet about his kiss. The touch of his lips sent an electric shock running through her. He bit down on her lower lip just hard enough to cause her to gasp and then he was pure male domination, invading her softness, tasting, punishing.

11

EMMA couldn't move, didn't dare to struggle, recognizing in that moment how dangerous Jake really was. His strength was enormous, his hunger stark and raw. Fully aroused, he seemed capable of anything. He growled low in his throat, his kiss deepening until he was almost eating at her mouth in an effort to devour her. He drove her backward until she was against the wall, never lifting his mouth from hers. Emma ran her tongue along the edge of his teeth, feeling a sharpness, tasting his desire as he cupped the back of her head and held her there, his mouth moving over hers, turning her body to liquid fire.

Jake captured both her hands in his and drew them over her head, holding her pinned there, his body rubbing along hers like a cat. Something wild in her responded, her body burning with unnatural heat. He was a primitive male claiming his mate, and her bones melted until she was living, pliant silk, and every nerve ending was alive from their combined fiery heat. She shaped her body to his, pressing close, her mouth moving mindlessly beneath his, tongues twining, stroking, his taste bursting through her like erotic champagne bubbles.

She couldn't think, could only feel, her body going up in flames, needing his. If he was growling, she was moaning, breathless and hungry and so needy she couldn't stand the weight of her clothes on her skin.

There was nothing unsure about Jake; he made love the way he did everything—ruthlessly, decisively, in total command. At the same time, he was wild, out of control, sweeping her with him in a storm of intensity. His mouth left hers to travel along her vulnerable throat, deliberately biting, suckling, leaving marks of possession on her soft skin. He grasped the front of her blouse and pulled, ripping the thin material down the front, then dragged her skirt from her as if he found anything keeping her body from his touch and sight offensive to him.

As such, he couldn't seem to wait long enough to even rid himself of her bra. His mouth tracked burning kisses down to the lacy material covering her breasts. Emma heard the low, raw sound escaping her throat as his mouth closed over her breast, right through the lace, teeth scraping, his tongue hot and wicked, swirling over the hard bud of her nipple. His arms, thick with roped muscles, dragged her closer, his mouth pulling with strong, urgent hunger.

He wasn't gentle—he was hungry, feasting at her, claiming her, small, feral growls rumbling in his chest and throat. "Mine," he snarled and drew her into the hot inferno of his mouth. "Mine," he reiterated, his teeth biting down until she cried out and his tongue immediately laved and soothed.

Her body was a furnace, and she arched against him, trying to get as much of her skin in contact with his as possible. His hands moved over her possessively, stroked along her narrow rib cage and small waist, and bit into the curve of her hip. All the while he tugged and pulled at her nip-

ples, teeth scraping, until the line between pain and pleasure blurred and she was crying with need.

Jake yanked her leg up around his, his hand finding her
calf, traveling upward, shaping the perfection of her bone
structure, moving along her inner thigh. Emma's hands
tightened around his neck, clinging to him, while the world
faded away so that there were only his hands and his mouth
and the ravenous hunger raging between them. Arousal sent
flames teasing at her thighs until her shaking legs threatened to give out.

Emma tried to find enough breath to speak, to make her
brain function properly. "Jake. We have to think about
what we're doing." But she couldn't think. There was no
thinking, only the feel of his hands and mouth and the heat
of his body.

Jake's response was a low growl, rough, achingly sensual. His fingers pressed along her thigh, and she felt the
bite of his nails, another mark on her body. Then he grasped
her lace panties and yanked, ripping them away to push his
palm against her welcoming moist heat, sweeping away
every objection she might have thought of.

Emma gasped, her body fragmenting, rippling with life,
with pleasure, at his touch. He was everywhere, hard and
strong, his mouth hot, right through the lace of her bra. His
lips left her breast to travel back up her throat, her chin,
finding her mouth, brutal with need, and she wrapped her
arms tightly around him, holding him closer, matching him
desire for desire.

"Jake, slow down," she whispered, afraid of her own
passion, afraid of the sheer intensity and violence neither
seemed to be able to control. She looked up at his face,
lines harsh with lust, his eyes hooded and sensual, the
irises gone, replaced by burning gold.

Jake felt the leopard pushing close to the surface, rising
with the ferocity of his need, and he fought to maintain a

semblance of control when there was none to have. His cock raged to be inside her, desperate for the hot, wet silk of her sheath and the pleasure and relief only she could bring to his body.

"I fucking have to be inside you," he whispered crudely into her mouth, unable to stop himself, while he drove one finger into her fire. He groaned as her muscles clenched tightly around him. Deliberately he pushed deeper, inserting two fingers into her hot, slick channel to test her readiness.

He wanted her there on the floor of his office, where there was no give, where he could hold her down and drive himself deep, taking what was rightfully his. He grasped her buttocks and urged her more firmly against his hand, his fingers sliding deep, gliding in and out of her, while his tongue claimed possession of her mouth. His body was on fire, a strange roaring in his ears. He was heavy and full, beyond aching.

It wasn't enough. He needed her touching him, needing her wanting him with the same wild frenzy of torment. He caught at his belt buckle, dragged his trousers open, so that he felt some measure of relief.

"I need you to touch me, baby. Right now, damn it." His voice was a ragged snarl that he tried to gentle but couldn't. "Emma, I need you, honey. Touch me. Please, just fucking touch me." Desperate for the feel of her hands on him, he gave her no choice. He bunched one hand in her hair and guided her hand to his cock with the other.

His body trembled at the first touch of her fingers against his pulsing flesh, at the way her fingers shaped him, stroked and caressed. He shuddered, pushing into her hand, while he gripped her hair and forced her to her knees. "Put your mouth on me," he commanded harshly. It was as if his cock had a life of its own, was on fire, so thick he felt he would burst.

He wasn't going to live another moment unless she complied. His cock leaked into her palm and she rubbed the sensitive head with the tip of her thumb, looking up at him, her eyes slumberous, sexy. She looked impossibly sensual kneeling at his feet, her body bare except for her lacy bra, droplets of moisture caught in the fiery curls at the junction of her legs, her breasts spilling out, his marks of possession down her throat and over the soft mounds. He was fully clothed, his cock thick and hard and hurting like a son of a bitch.

"Fucking put your mouth on me now," he hissed between clenched teeth as her tongue slipped out to curl around the broad, flared head, to taste the pearly drops there.

Emma bent forward and he lost his breath, his mind, his entire being, as she began to suckle him. She consumed him with her passion, with hot, terrible pleasure. Her mouth was a tube of fire burning him, scorching him, tight like a fist, milking at him, her tongue sliding over and under, lapping greedily at his base, along his sac and back up to once again engulf him.

The leopard roared and he felt his claws stretching, felt his bones snapping as her mouth took him to the very edge of his control. He fought the change, fought to keep from being too violent, too wild, but the feel of her mouth was killing him. He could feel his balls tightening, his cock growing in the hot slide of her mouth. He wanted more, both hands burying deep in her hair, holding her in place while his hips thrust and he threw back his head as he touched the back of her throat, brutal pleasure bursting through him like the sun.

She began to struggle, bringing him back to reality. "Relax." He tried to force his body to calm down, but he couldn't let her loose, couldn't bring himself to abandon the hot haven of her mouth. "Relax, honey. You can take me. Just relax."

She calmed a little under his soothing tone, forcing her throat muscles to relax as he pulled her head back more. He drove forward, murmuring encouragement, a hoarse cry escaping as her throat convulsed around him. He had to stop. He had to find control. If he didn't, he would be spilling his seed down her throat, and he needed to be inside her. He ripped his shirt off and flung the material aside, his skin burning hot.

"I can't wait, baby, not another minute. I'm sorry, I have to have you now. Later I'll take my time, I swear it, but not this time. I'll go out of my mind if I'm not inside you."

He pushed against her aggressively, gripping her shoulders, taking her backward to the floor. She sprawled out, her knees up, her hair spilling across the gleaming hardwood like silk, her breasts thrusting upward, heaving with her gasping breath. He towered above her like a conqueror, kicking aside his shoes, shedding his trousers before reaching down to rid her of her bra.

"Jake." There was uncertainty in her voice as she blinked up at him, a tinge of fear in her eyes. Her body was flushed, excited, and he scented her arousal, spurring the leopard to new heights of lust.

He knew he should slow down, reassure her, but the leopard wouldn't allow it, driving him now, past all sense, uncaring of anything but claiming her, tying her to him. He had waited forever, burning night after night, until he lived in a kind of hell.

He went to the floor, yanking her knees apart, jerking her body to him across the polished wood, and he lowered his head and stabbed his tongue deep into her hot, creamy center. Emma bucked, screamed, tried to writhe away, pushing at the floor with her heels in an effort to crawl out from under him. He growled again, his head jerking up, eyes burning at her, his fingers digging deep into her thighs, preventing her from moving an inch. She was so wet, so ready, her body already clenching, spasming, desperate for his.

"It's too much, slow down," Emma entreated, her hand fisting in his hair.

The pain in his scalp only spurred him on. He growled again, heightening the sensations with vibrations as he began to feast on her. Her taste was wildly exotic, and the blood rushed to his cock, straining his shaft to such unbearable fullness he thought he would burst. More cream spilled from her and he lapped at it like a starving cat as she moaned and writhed under his assault. Another hot, desperate growl rumbled deep in his throat as he devoured her. His teeth scraped at her clit. She drove her hips up and he caught her thighs, dragging them wider apart to give him better access. When he suckled on the small hard bud, she bucked wildly against his mouth, her cries turning to sobs of pleasure as he threw her into an intense orgasm.

"Jake . . . stop . . . I can't do this. I can't take any more. You have to stop." He was going to kill her with sheer pleasure. She needed to slow down, catch her breath. He was going to drive her insane. "Jake." She tried to gasp out *stop*, but it was already too late.

He didn't stop. Instead his reaction intensified. His tongue flicked the sensitive bud over and over, driving her higher, making her burn hotter, until the knot of nerve endings felt on fire against his tongue. She pushed at him, thrashing now, her own voice a hoarse sob as she tried to loosen his merciless grip on her thighs. Her ragged breath and bucking body drove his own lust higher. His leopard leapt and roared, clawing at his belly, demanding more of her addictive taste, wanting to mark her everywhere so she could never again attempt to deny who she belonged to.

His tongue stabbed and flicked, plunging deep, refusing to give her a moment to recover, deliberately controlling her. Her wild thrashing only fed his cat's need for dominance, and he slid his mouth from her, licked the slick wetness coating her mound several times and then settled his teeth on the inside of her thigh, once again marking her.

Her eyes went wide with shock as the pleasure-pain threw her into another orgasm and he immediately feasted, driving her back up until beads of perspiration dotted her body and her hair was damp.

Jake rose to his knees, staring down on his prey, fighting the ache in his jaw and the pain in his body. She looked beautiful. She was wild, her body an inferno. He could feel her heat as he pushed the broad, flat, so-sensitive head of his cock into her slick entrance. She closed around him, gripping him hard, so tight. He stayed still, showing her his power over her.

This was no quick lay. He meant to mate with her, to take her for all time as his own, to show her who she belonged to and leave his mark on her. She hissed at him, pinned to the floor by his larger, stronger body, her nails digging into wood, her breasts a temptation, her voice a pleading sob in spite of the fact that she struggled.

He stretched her, knew his entry skimmed the borders of burning pain, but it couldn't be helped. She was so tight and he was thick and long. She gasped, her eyes going wide.

"Mine." He growled the word, rocking forward just a little, watching the pleasure flare in her eyes. "Mine." Meaning it. Wanting her to know he meant it. There would be no going back after this. "Dare to tell me you're not. Deny it, Emma, if you can. Fucking try to tell me you want another man. Or admit the truth. Admit it's me you want and no other."

His eyes dared her to defy him. His hands gripped her legs tightly as he paused, lodged in the entrance of her hot, slick opening. Fear skated through the deep green of her eyes. Her sheath clenched tightly around him, grasping at him, trying to pull him deeper, and he fought not to give in, to slam himself home. Something wild and wickedly primitive in her wanted—even needed—his brutal possession; he could read that much. But she was afraid. She wouldn't just give herself to him, although every single cell in her body screamed for him, screamed for more. She just wasn't certain she could handle more.

Emma shook her head. "Yes," she hissed, "but not like this. You're too big. You're . . ."

"*Exactly* like this." He gave a small push with his hips and slid in another inch, watching her face, the pleasure rippling over her, the burning discomfort showing in the way her hips tried to pull back. "Any way. Every way. Say it, Emma. Say you're mine. Say you want this. Say you want *me.*"

He wasn't going to let her come back to him later and say she hadn't agreed. When she remained silent, staring up at him with that mixture of lust and fear, he pulled back just a little and felt her grasping at him. She cried out, her body following his.

Satisfaction settled the hard knots in his belly. "Fucking say it."

Her eyes locked with his. He could see the golden eyes of his cat staring back at him in the centers of her eyes. She licked her lips. Took a deep breath. Her body shuddered at her surrender. "I want this." Her voice trembled, came out in a soft rush.

He clenched his teeth, rewarding her with another inch. Her body clamped down on his, squeezing him tightly. He fought to keep from burying himself deep. "That's not good enough. Admit that you belong to me. Say you're mine. Out loud, Emma."

"Jake. Please." A sob escaped. "I do, I am. Whatever. Just please do something."

He slammed his body into hers, tearing through her

velvet folds, so slick and wet, fiery hot, tight as a fist, sheath-
ing himself until he bumped her cervix hard, taking it further, forcing her to accept all of him until he felt his balls
slap against her bottom. Her tight muscles stretched around
him, gripping him, clamping around his throbbing cock.
Fire streaked through him, mind-numbing pleasure. He
took her hard and fast, rough, the way his cat demanded,
pounding into her body with powerful, jackhammer strokes,
giving himself over completely to the sheer erotic heat of
her body.

He'd never experienced anything like this mating in his
life. His entire focus was on the center of his body, the
shaft slamming in and out of her, desperate for more, always more, driving himself deep, claiming her soul for his
own. And, damn, the heat raging in him now was nearly
unbearable. He swelled. She screamed and gripped his
shaft hard with her inner muscles, nearly strangling him,
the waves of pleasure pouring over him until he was damp
with sweat. Then her body pulsed. Once. Twice. Hot cream
bathed him and he poured himself into her, wanting his
seed deep, wanting it to take hold. She was his. Born for
him. In that moment he felt as primitive as his cat, and every bit as dominant.

Jake pulled out of her and flipped her over onto her
stomach. The sudden withdrawal caused another flash of
pain and she cried out. He hissed as his arm caught her
under her hips and yanked her up onto her knees, so she was
on all fours. He held her still, gripping her hard as he blanketed her, slamming his cock ferociously to penetrate deep
inside with no warning at all, driving through her tight
muscles until her already sensitive knot of nerves screamed
and spasmed again and again.

Emma had thought him spent—he should have been
spent—but he was wilder than ever. His body, pounding
hard into hers, robbed her of her breath. He went deeper

with each thrust, the way he held her giving him an even
better angle to possess her. She felt on fire, but at the same
time was shocked at her own behavior. She wanted him—
oh, so much; she doubted she'd ever get enough of him—
but never once had she envisioned or dreamt that it would
be like this.

His hands slid over her rib cage up to her breasts, where
he tugged at her nipples, sending streaks of fire to her inflamed sheath. His fingers felt like curved claws, teasing
and pulling, soft fur sliding over her aching breasts. His
face nuzzled at her shoulder, along her neck where she was
the most sensitive. He kissed her there, never once stopping the ferocious pounding. His tongue lapped at her skin
and then he bit down hard. Pain flashed through her and
something wild jumped inside of her, snarling and fighting
so that her hands curved into claws and she tried to buck
him off.

Jake snarled, the low growl reverberating around her. If
anything, her struggles provoked him into more dominant
display. He never took his teeth from her shoulder, holding
her still under him, while he pounded into her. One hand
curved around her breast, his fingers biting into flesh in
erotic warning; the other hand descended hard on her bottom. Heat flared, spread, her center pulsed and spilled
more hot cream onto his invading shaft.

She couldn't stand it. The tension in her built and built,
taking her closer to the edge of a deep abyss. She fought
off the gathering orgasm that welled up like a tidal wave,
threatening to destroy her, but he was relentless, driving
her higher and higher, so close to the edge now that she tee-
tered on the brink of pain, of darkness. She hung there a
moment, her breathing ragged, her breasts heaving, her body
tense. He slammed into her with another brutal drive and
she fell over the edge, screaming as the explosion ripped
through her.

Wave after wave, an endless, merciless series of orgasms rocked her body, leaving her weak and breathless. She writhed and bucked under him, unable to stop moving as the mind-numbing pleasure ripped through her body, her mouth opening wide, her vision blurring. Stars burst behind her eyes.

Jake felt her body clamp down on his, the wet heat gripping and squeezing, while her shattered cry of ecstasy drove him on, wanting everything for him, wanting her to feel the way she made him feel. Alive. So alive. So hot and wild and beyond any fantasy she could ever imagine. He wanted her tied to him, by *this*. Sex so perfect she'd never find it with anyone else. He wanted her limp in his arms, drained and exhausted and so sated she couldn't think of any other man ever touching her skin.

He gripped her hips, tilted her just that much more and slammed home again and again, while her body rippled and fought. She stiffened, shuddered, and he felt the grip of her, an intense bite of her muscles clamping down like a vise. His lungs burned for air, breathing so hard, the ragged gasps nearly hurt. The low growls rumbling in his chest were animalistic, but he couldn't stop them with his leopard so close and the pleasure pumping through him like a rush of adrenaline.

He lost every bit of sanity, every bit of reason, as her body clamped down around his, sending agonizing pleasure tearing through his body. He was so hot he thought he might burn up, turn to ashes, but he couldn't stop driving into her, seeking release, seeking the ultimate high. Then it came. He stilled. A heartbeat. A second. The rush was a roar of insanity, tearing through every muscle and sinew, every cell, his very bones, and for a moment he feared he wouldn't survive the explosive release rocketing through him.

The tidal wave started somewhere in his toes and ripped

up his body, through his thighs, and centered like a tsu-
nami in his groin. His release was harsh, erupting like a
volcano, exploding, tearing through him with such force
his body shuddered and strained as he emptied himself.
The roaring in his ears was like thunder, and even his vision changed.

Emma would have collapsed but he held her up with an
ease that shocked her. He was enormously strong as he
lowered them both to the floor. He rolled her to her side,
still buried deep in her body, his hands cupping her breasts
as they lay locked together on the floor. His breath came in
rough gasps as her body continued to pulse around his,
gripping, milking, relaxing and starting the cycle all over
again.

She tried to speak but no sound emerged, and she feared
that every brain cell was beyond repair and she was inca-
pable of thought, let alone speech.

Jake pushed the silky fall of hair aside and nuzzled her
neck, kissing the spot where his teeth had held her. He had
taken many women, been serviced by many more, but nothing had prepared him for the orgasm that had ripped
through him, exploding with such force. The hard ejacula-
tion had given him peace for the first time. He knew he had
a silly grin on his face, elation sweeping through him, and
he kissed the nape of her neck, moving just a little to feel
the joy as another spill of her slick heat washed over him.

Her body shuddered against his and she turned her
head slowly to look at him. Her eyes were glazed, her body
limp. He bent forward to kiss her mouth. She kissed him
back.

"Easy now, honey. This will hurt for a moment." His
leopard had been too close to the surface and he knew she
was going to feel his withdrawal. He fastened his mouth to
hers, thrusting his tongue along hers as he pulled his cock
from her body.

The pain flashed through her as his cock dragged over her sensitive wall, chafing her as he pulled free. He swallowed her soft cry, deepening the kiss. He moved first, rolling over and coming up on his knees. His cock was long and thick, even in his semi-hard state, one normal for him. He couldn't quite let go of her; not yet. He knew it was always going to be the same with him. She was an addiction, one he would need to have sated over and over.

Emma lay on the floor looking up at Jake as he knelt over her, his hand on his cock, absently sliding his palm along his shaft, watching her with hooded, glittering eyes. He was so male, so dark and intoxicating. Raw sexuality in its purest form. Her only sexual experience had been with Andrew, and he had been gentle, reverent even. With none of the explosive, raw power Jake had just showered upon her. Lately, with her body so restless and unsettled, she'd dreamt of violent, earth-shattering sex, but she hadn't really had an idea of what it was like.

Nothing had prepared her for the total invasion of her senses, Jake's enormous strength and terrible raw sexual hunger. She felt helpless in his arms, taken over, out of control. Her body was no longer her own, but seemed to belong to him, moving against his hand, her breasts swollen and aching, needing his hot mouth, needing his body buried deep in hers.

She couldn't even say the explosive sex between them had been all him. Something had taken her over until she craved him—desperately. Without her own identity. She would forever need Jake, need his stark, raw possession. *This.* An obsession. Not love. Never love. She would never be the same. Never want another man. And yet, not once had he been loving toward her. Even now, with his eyes commanding her, she wanted to obey, to lift her head and lap at him, taking every drop of him into her. She wasn't a sexual creature. She didn't understand what was happening to her, she only knew that she despised every woman who had ever come near him almost as much as she despised herself for not being in control.

His hot gaze drifted over her with absolute satisfaction. She looked down at her body. Her breasts were swollen and aching, nipples tight. Her skin was covered with the red marks of his possession. The sight of those marks should have angered her, but instead her body tightened again, her sheath clenching, already feeling empty and needing him.

"Can you get up?" He held out his hand.

The question was so mundane, as if nothing at all had happened, certainly not as if she lay naked, sprawled out on the floor with his seed running down her thighs. She forced her sore body into a sitting position, ignoring his hand. She hadn't known there were so many places she could ache.

"Emma? Are you all right?" This time there was demand in his voice.

She glared at him. "Do you have any idea what we've done?" She pressed a hand to her mouth, unable to stop the trembling, because she knew what *she'd* done. She'd had incredible sex, but there hadn't been a shred of love in there anywhere, not that she could feel.

"We're doing what we need to do," he said harshly, bending to take possession of her mouth again.

Emma moved her head back out of his reach. "This isn't right. This is too violent, Jake." She stared up at the harsh lines etched deeply in his face, his sensual mouth twisted cynically, a little cruel. His eyes were glittering brightly, burning hot with temper. "I'm not anything to you. You were angry and you wanted a woman, any woman."

He swore vulgarly, and his eyes went flat and cold. "That's a hell of a thing to say to me."

With calculated intent, he glided his hand up her leg, along the wetness of her inner thigh, over his mark of possession until his fingers found the hot wet core of her.

He slid two fingers deep into her, watching her gasp, watching the helpless pleasure on her face and the way her eyes glazed when he drew circles around her tight bud. She was still very sensitive, and when he tugged and twisted, her sheath clamped down hard, sending another orgasm ripping through her body. His seed and her cream coated his fingers when he pulled them free and held them up in front of her face.

"This isn't just me, Emma. This is also you needing a man." Deliberately he brought his fingers to his mouth, tasting her, his gaze burning deep, slashing at her with a controlled fury. "This is you needing *me*." He caught her hair in his fist and brought her face within inches of his fast-hardening shaft.

For a moment she stared defiantly, but that wild something in her refused to let her have dignity or escape her own needs. Her mouth watered.

"You think I can't see what you want? Or smell your arousal? This is us together, Emma, whether you like it or not. It may not be all neat and pretty and wrapped up with a little bow, but it's what we have."

She licked her lips, flicking her tongue out and swiping over the broad, flat head, unable to prevent herself from tasting him again. He shuddered visibly. Emma pulled back, ashamed of herself, fighting for dignity.

"We're violent, Jake. I'm not like this . . ." She trailed off, staring at temptation. He was so unashamed of his raw sexuality, of his need, standing up with his hand massaging his shaft with hypnotic strokes, so that it responded by growing thicker and longer and much harder. She shook with wanting him, her core liquid and empty. "It feels like a sin."

"You were made for sex and sin, Emma, whether you want to admit it or not. You were made for me. I refuse to be ashamed because I want you. I want you every minute of the day. When you walk by me in the house, I wish you were wearing a long skirt so I could just push it up out of the way and find you wet and eager for me. I want you in every possible way I can have you, and if you think I'm going to let you walk away from this—away from me— because you're afraid, think again."

He looked so masculine, the columns of his thighs strong. Emma gasped and leaned forward. There were scars, deep, long slashes fractions of an inch apart, up and down both thighs. She couldn't stop herself from running her palm over them and then holding her hand there as if she could make it better. Each mark had been deliberately made with a very sharp instrument. "What happened? Who did this to you?" She was outraged, that strange, primitive part of her rising fast and ferocious again. "What are these?"

"Victories."

The way he said it, with that soft little snicker, made her gaze jump to his face. He looked at her as if she were one of his victories. Self-disgust made her pull back, but his fingers only tightened in her hair to hold her still.

"Are you ashamed because you want me, Emma? Don't pretend you don't, because neither of us will buy that lie. I have your scratches, the marks of your nails, all over me. The taste of you is in my mouth, soaked into my pores, and the scent of you surrounds me."

He held her there, refusing to allow her to look away from him. "Be who you are."

She shook her head, uncaring that her scalp hurt, uncaring that her body pulsed and was wetter than ever at the way he was talking. Did she really want to be an object? A plaything for him to use and then toss away when he was done? Had she gone so far down the road of depravity with him that she couldn't go back?

"This isn't love, Jake. It isn't even a relationship."

He felt her words like a blow in the pit of his stomach. *She didn't love him.* No matter what he'd done, he couldn't make her love him. He could see the evidence of her arousal, every bit as strong as his own. He might not get her love, but by God, he could own her body. Shaken, hurt, anger rising to protect him, he stepped relentlessly closer, refusing to back away from what was between them. If the only way he could tie her to him was through sex, then so be it. He'd take whatever he could get.

"How would you know when all you've ever had was a few honeymoon months with that boy, Andrew? With your adolescent view of relationships I doubt you even know what's between a man and a woman. Men can be cruel and life can be messy and sex can be violent. It's all those things. But if this is what I get, you on your knees with your mouth on my cock and my marks all over your hot little body, then I'll take it."

She flinched visibly as he towered over her, straight and tall, his eyes antique gold, glittering with heat. His shaft was thicker than ever and his hand was a fist, gripping tightly, pushing his erection along her lips. She found the way he was so unashamed of his blatant sexuality both compelling and admirable—and erotic. Her body responded to his arousal no matter what her head said. His low, sexy voice, the way he talked, everything about him sent ripples of fire straight to her center until she wept with need—and wept for her own inability to resist him.

"I don't understand what we're doing, Jake," she said. "We could lose everything we have. You know how you are. Are you so willing to risk me? Don't I mean anything at all to you?" There were tears in her voice that she couldn't hide, didn't want to hide.

He had to understand the consequences of what they were doing. He used women and threw them away. He couldn't deny that. Leopards didn't change their spots. Wasn't that the old adage? He would use her and eventually he would grow tired of her. How could she possibly

keep a man like Jake happy? He had shredded her innocence, taken her far beyond her experience, and yet she
had somehow been every bit as wild and willing as he had
been. And then what? He'd throw her aside, move on to a
new woman, and she'd be left broken, ashamed and unable
to stay in a house without love. The children—everyone—
would lose.

Jake crouched down beside her, his hand sliding to the
back of her head. "I've never claimed another woman for
my own." His voice was gentle, compelling her to meet his
gaze.

There was a mixture of lust and something else she
couldn't name—tenderness, maybe. Possession. She was
too susceptible to him, her feelings too confused. She
wanted to fall into his arms and be held. Or rub herself up
and down his skin. Or slide her mouth over his tempting
shaft and lap at his cream like a starving cat.

Jake's fingertips rubbed her scalp in a hypnotic massage. "Not one woman, Emma. And I never will again.
You're mine. I don't let go of what is mine." His hand tightened in her hair, pulling her head back so he had access to
her mouth in another long, gentle kiss.

Emma felt herself melting. Jake, as a rule, wasn't gentle,
but his kiss, just for a moment, felt like love before his passion, his lust, took over and he was in a feeding frenzy
again, growing hotter and more wild. She opened her mouth
under the demand of his tongue and let him take her away,
let him carry her back into his carnal world of sin and sex.
His arms were enormously strong, circling her, sweeping
her into that vortex of mind-numbing pleasure.

He was so strong, his personality overwhelming. Everything about Jake was compelling and mesmerizing. Even
his aura of danger drew something inside of her straight
to him. His hands stroked her skin, soothing, tender—at
first—but when a moan escaped and her breath began to

come in ragged gasps, he took her to the next level, playing her body like the master he was. His fingers tugged at her nipples, twisting and pulling a little harder, his teeth scraping sensitive skin. His mouth found his marks on her breast and he lapped at them with his tongue so that it rasped over the sensitive nerve endings until she trembled anew.

She loved that roughness in him, that switch from tender to rough hunger, as if his need of her was so great he was on the edge of his control. And yet, even though she was so willing and wanting, there was a part of her that screamed: *No. No. Stop what you're doing. You're jeopardizing everything you have.*

Jake cupped her breasts in his hands. So firm. So tempting. How many times had he walked into the nursery and seen her breast-feeding Andraya? He didn't know about other men, but the sight always sent erotic pleasure streaking through him. He'd always wanted to drop to his knees and taste her. She was so beautiful, a sensual woman in her natural state.

He kissed her again, loving her mouth. He'd always loved her mouth, had dreamt of it so many times. She tasted even better than he'd imagined, all sweet and tangy and so Emma. He loved the heat of her body, the way she opened for him when his hands moved over her down to her thighs, already wet and needy and willing to accommodate him. Her body was his, even though she still wanted to deny it.

He watched her face as he applied pressure to the hard little point of her breast, saw her face flush as heat spread, watched the bite of pain blur with intense pleasure as he tugged. Her breath came in a ragged gasp and her eyes got that sexy glaze he loved. She was exquisite, even more so when aroused. He lowered his head and took one breast into his mouth. Licking, sucking, teeth tugging and nipping, he watched her every reaction, driving her higher and higher.

He moved down to lick at her abdomen, teasing her intriguing belly button, lapping up the drops from her fiery curls. Her breath came out in a long hiss as he flicked his tongue across her mound. He lowered his body, sliding down her, spreading her thighs, still watching her, loving the way her eyes lost focus and turned wholly emerald, nearly glowing at him with slumberous lust.

He took a long, slow, deliberate lick, his tongue swirling around her tight bud, and then flicked back and forth over it until she was gasping, fighting and writhing under him. Her nerve endings, already so sensitive, sizzled and burned. He made love to her in the only way he knew how—raw, sensual, driving her past all preconceived limits. Taking her as high as she thought she could go and then more, sucking, licking, stroking, using teeth, tongue and fingers. She might not think he was loving her, but it was the only expression of emotion he could give her. This was who he was. He took his time, kissing, paying attention to her slightest reaction before his mouth hungrily latched on to her hot, wet sheath to tip her over the edge.

She screamed, lifting her hips as he pushed his tongue into her with a slow, hard stroke. Her body was an inferno, so hot, so wet, a raging fire threatening to consume her. She sobbed for release. Jake sucked her clit into his mouth, flicking the tight bud with his tongue, raking with his teeth against it. She stiffened, sobbed again, her nails digging in his shoulders, and then her body melted, turned to liquid as the earth-shattering orgasm overtook her.

When she quieted, he was back standing above her, offering his pulsing shaft. She opened her thighs to accept him, but he reached down and urged her up to her knees, shaking his head, although he was desperate to be inside of her. "No," he said softly, his voice firm, demanding even. "Not this time. I need your mouth on me again, Emma. I need to see you wanting me, everything that I am." Because she had given him everything but what he needed and he was taking everything from her. She was *his*. And he was going to make her know it, whether she wanted to admit it or not. Withhold her love from him? She thought it wasn't love?

He did need her mouth, so hot and sexy, more than he could ever express or explain to her. She hadn't surrendered. Did she think he couldn't feel the conflict in her? Her body was his, but not her heart or mind, and he wouldn't settle for less than everything—total surrender. She had to know who she belonged to, who she'd been born for.

The leopard growled and paced, raked with claws, kept a relentless assault on his mind. *Take her. Take her. She belongs to me. She has to know she is mine.* The need thundered in his heart, in his body, a roar of absolute supremacy. The cat was wild, furious that she wouldn't submit totally to him.

"Emma." He said her name, no more. But it was a demand—a command—and Emma dropped her gaze to his pulsing erection.

She sucked in her breath, so aroused she would have done anything for him, so hungry for his body she needed him filling her mouth almost more than he did. She wanted the taste of him, the feel of him, scorching hot in the inferno of her mouth. It seemed so personal, the ultimate intimacy, a man's woman caressing him and worshiping him, bringing him exquisite pleasure. And there was his face, harsh with lust, eyes brooding, as if . . . as if he needed something from her, something only she could give him.

Mesmerized, she leaned forward and flicked her tongue over the broad, dripping head. His entire body shuddered. His growl was sheer animal, a guttural, harsh sound that sent another orgasm rocketing through her. "Son of a bitch, Emma, fucking do it before I explode."

He gripped her hair and yanked her head toward him. When she went to grip the base with her hand, to circle his shaft, he shook his head. "Put your hands on my hips and keep them there."

Her heart jumped. She looked up at him. His golden eyes had changed to cat's eyes, glowing with power, with lust, with need beyond anything she'd ever experienced. She felt the wildness in him and something in her leapt to meet it. She couldn't help licking at the drops of pearls before he gripped her hair tighter and pushed his shaft, steel-hard and scorching hot, into the haven of her mouth.

His hips jerked, he gasped, his jaw tightening and his growl growing harsher. Her tongue curled around him in a lazy slide that set his every nerve ending on fire. The feel of her wet, velvet mouth suckling him was shockingly erotic. He had taken her twice and he still was as hard as a rock, thrusting into her mouth, trying to be gentle, knowing she was exhausted. She started to lift her hands and he growled a warning, keeping the control, heightening his pleasure even more.

Her sharp nails dug into his thighs, but she didn't move her hands, didn't move away from him. He felt the pads of her fingers tracing his scars, sliding over them, rubbing, caressing, sending hot arousal straight to his cock. Her mouth was eager, her small little moans vibrating around him, driving him crazy until his lungs burned for air and his breath came in harsh, ragged gasps. Everything in him tightened, burned. Every muscle, every cell, every nerve ending. Heat boiled, fire scorched, burned as he neared his explosive orgasm.

The cat wanted his scent all over her, in her, wanted every man that came near her to know she belonged to him and only him. And God help him, Jake wanted the same thing. It was as if he was so merged with the beast he couldn't separate himself. He couldn't stop the dominating

thrusts, forcing her to take him deeper, the thrill and elation, the sheer pleasure rising like a tide at the sight of
her—his woman. *His.* He had to mark her as such, there
was no other way. Mark her with his scent, with his teeth,
with his seed. *His.*

He forced himself to give up the haven of her mouth,
dragging his cock free so that he could mark her, cover her
with his scent and seed. "You're mine, Emma. Only mine."
His harsh growl was one of brutal satisfaction as the hot
spray pulsed all over her.

"What the hell does that mean?" She tried to push past him, heading for the bathroom in the office suite. Jake calmly caught her arm. She was trembling. He brushed the pad of his thumb up and down her skin with stroking caresses, trying to soothe her.

She jerked herself away, her face stiff with pride. "It means go to hell." She stalked around him, slammed the bathroom door and locked it. Let him find another shower. She *hated* him. He had told her that another woman had blown him a couple of times and then he fucked her. Well, she felt well and truly fucked. He had called that woman a slut and then he'd deliberately made Emma feel like one. Damn him. Damn her for giving in to her own raging needs. Damn her for loving Jake so much she couldn't resist temptation. Just damn everything.

There wasn't a place on her body, inside or out, that wasn't sore. Her heart ached. Her soul wept. She'd given him everything and he'd totally humiliated her and had the gall to look satisfied. No wonder he thought the women he'd been with were sluts. He made them that way. *She'd* been that way—ready to do anything he wanted, anything to please him. She'd wanted desperately to please him.

She was sobbing as the hot water poured over her, great sobs that shook her entire body. She'd ruined her life. Ruined Andraya's and Kyle's lives. She had to leave, had to take her baby girl and leave Kyle behind. The adoption wasn't final yet. She had no rights to him. She couldn't believe how stupid, how selfish, she'd been, not thinking of her children, letting her hormones drive her. What kind of a mother was she?

Jake was so absolutely self-assured. The sheer power of his personality was hypnotizing, mesmerizing, and she had been far more susceptible than she'd realized. She slid down the wall of the shower, curling into a small ball, letting the hot water pour over her sore body. She was defi-

nitely leaving. She wouldn't be humiliated like that ever
again. How could she face him now? She'd seen the contempt on his face, heard it in his voice, when he spoke to
women on the phone, heard them begging and pleading to
see him. She would not become another one of his cast-
offs. And if she stayed, she would never be able to resist
his seduction. Her body throbbed just thinking about him,
and she was furious with him. What had she done? How
stupid.

She wanted to scream at herself. She'd always acted ra-
tionally. She was rarely even attracted to men, and certainly didn't feel the obsessive cravings she'd developed
for Jake. When had that even started? He wasn't her kind
of man. Greg Patterson was. Andrew. Her beloved Andrew, with his sweet smile, and gentle touch, asking permission before he even kissed her.

How had she gotten trapped in Jake's sexual web? She'd
even watched out for it. She'd felt his allure, the deep pull
of magnetism, but she'd warned herself from the beginning to see him as he really was, to not fall under his spell.
Here she was, lying on the shower floor, with his seed in
her and on her and her life crumbling around her.

Emma let herself cry until there were no tears left and
she knew she had to face what she'd done. She sat up and
slowly began to soap her body, feeling his possession with
every movement, trying to wash him away, to wash her
obsession with him away. She had to think carefully. Jake
was different from other men. She saw the scars on his
body—his thighs, his back, even his arms and belly. He
trusted no one. He had a particular dislike of women getting close to him. He never spoke to his parents or allowed
them near the children. The one time she'd met his mother
had been a nightmarish experience.

She loved Jake, but not in the same way she'd loved
Andrew. If she was truthful with herself, Andrew had been

her first love, a child's love, sweet and pure and perfect. Jake had never been a child. He didn't know what love or trust was. She had come to love Jake over the past two years, watching him struggle to learn to be a father. Watching him provide for the broken souls around him. Her feelings for him were not all just sexual, and that made it even harder to accept his lack of emotion toward her—but she'd known what he was like. He struggled with gentler emotions. She let herself become attached because he treated her differently than he did others, but she'd never given him power over her. His control over her had always been an illusion—at least, she'd thought it had been. Maybe she'd been the one seeing the illusion all along.

She'd known she was letting him take over her life when she'd made the move to Texas and settled into his home. She even knew he was counting on her to love Kyle. Jake seemed hard as a rock to everyone around him, but to her he felt vulnerable. In need. And she responded to his need. In some ways she let him down just as much as she'd let the children and herself down by letting her hormones rule her head.

She needed time. If she went to her room, she knew Jake would come and want to talk. She didn't have answers, and his personality—his pain—would overshadow all good sense. She needed time alone. He could deal with the children for once. She was going for a long drive, would maybe get a hotel room somewhere. She'd leave him a note and let him know she'd be back by the afternoon. She wasn't changing all their lives without first thinking long and hard about it.

JAKE laid his palm on the bathroom door, measuring Emma's height, dread filling him. He'd let the leopard control him and he'd pushed her too far. She may as well have been a virgin for all the experience she had, and the kind of sex he'd introduced her to had been too intense, too rough, too animalistic. Damn it. The last thing he'd wanted to do was destroy the trust he'd so carefully built up with her. Sometimes he'd even believed he'd changed enough to deserve her. But deep down, the beast always lurked, always snarled and demanded.

He smashed his fist into the door and stalked out, heading for the bathroom in his suite. He knew Emma, and he had to outthink her, had to figure out her next move and be one step ahead of her. She'd think about running. He saw the humiliation and self-loathing in her eyes. It hadn't been directed at him; she'd already excused his behavior. It was her own she took responsibility for. She wouldn't want to face him. She'd want to run.

He turned on the water as hot as he could stand it and stood under the scorching heat, wishing it would melt his skin off and burn the leopard, would let him feel what it was to hurt someone it— He caught himself abruptly. He didn't know how to love. Love wasn't even real. It was a word people used to trap one another. Emma thought love was important, but he knew better. Loyalty—that was what counted. He cared for Emma in his way. His body wanted hers, even needed hers. Sex was raw and elemental; sex was real. That was an emotion. He could give her loyalty and he could keep her body sated and happy. He had to find a way to convince her that the things that really mattered, like protection and devotion, he could do better than other men.

She didn't trust him. A part of him was furious that she didn't and the other part understood. She couldn't know that, thanks to his leopard, his body hurt every minute of the day, hard and desperate for relief. She couldn't know how so many women threw themselves at him. He'd never gone after a woman. Not ever, not before Emma. And he'd never taken an innocent. The women he'd been with had all wanted something other than his body—his money. They had no interest in his world or his children, only in the money and the pleasure his body could provide.

"Emma." He whispered her name aloud, craving her, the way she smiled, her scent, the sound of her voice, the laughter that always included him.

She had come to be his home. He actually looked forward to opening the kitchen door and finding his food carefully prepared. She paid attention to what his favorite dishes were. She arranged the house to suit him and helped him relate better to the children, and she did it all quietly, smoothly.

He hadn't even noticed the differences at first, but he remembered the moment it struck him, the total silence when he'd come home to a vacant house. The house was enormous, a mansion, a showpiece, as cold as hell and just as empty. He had never bothered to hire a cook because he didn't trust anyone. And then along came Emma, with her laughter and joy, and the house with filled with music and scents and the patter of feet.

The babies hugged him, their faces lighting up when he returned home—because of her. Emma. She taught them by her example. Where he was taking care of her, she was caring for him and teaching the children to do the same. Her face lit up when she saw him. There was that soft, welcoming note in her voice he'd come to rely on. When he was moody and edgy and being a complete bastard, instead of getting angry with him, she would smile at him and tell him she'd take the children upstairs so he could have some peace. Or she'd tease him, or rub his shoulders. But she never blamed him. Sometimes she'd even tease him and order him out, and he loved those times best. They made him feel part of something—loved.

Her bedroom was his favorite place. Her scent was all

over it, and when he lay on her bed and buried his face in her pillow, he could take her deep into his lungs. Before she had come, he'd spent most nights pacing off excess energy, both sexual and emotional. He had too many memories and he couldn't seem to shut them out in the night. But now he could lie in the dark with her body warm and soft beside him, talking for long hours into the night, and feel at peace. He'd never had that before, and if she left him, he would never have it again. He'd risked everything by being too primitive and forgetting her inexperience.

Jake pulled on a pair of jeans and a T-shirt and went to her room, padding on bare feet down the hall, careful to maintain silence, not wanting to alert her to his presence. Her door was ajar and he slipped inside. He knew instantly the room was empty. The faint scent of her lingered behind, but there was only silence and the white sheet of paper in the center of her still-made bed. He picked it up, eyes scanning it briefly, feeling the blow like a punch to his gut.

Damn her. She wasn't leaving the ranch. Not tonight. Not when she was upset with him and he hadn't had a chance to make his case. He was a businessman. He'd been in a thousand boardrooms. He could close a deal, but not if she got off the ranch. He picked up the phone, his jaw set, his expression savage.

EMMA stuck her head out the window and forced a smile at Jerico. "Open the gates."

To her astonishment, Jerico shook his head, a small grimace on his face. "I can't do that, Emma. Where would you be going this time of night?"

She scowled at him. "It isn't your business."

"I'm responsible," Jerico said. "I don't want to lose my job."

Emma let her breath out slowly, forcing her temper under control. It wasn't Jerico's fault. He had to follow rules just like everyone. "I'm going for a drive." It wasn't his fault that she was so upset. It was her own fault. *Hers.* She loathed herself, but she managed a small smile, hoping to charm him. "Please open the gate."

"I can't do that. I'm sorry. The boss said not to let you leave."

Emma's eyebrow went up. "Contrary to popular belief, Jerico, I don't work for Jake. He can't boss me around. Open the gate."

Jerico shook his head, although he did look remorseful. "You don't even have a bodyguard with you. He said you weren't to leave under any circumstances unless he specifically okayed it. If you're having trouble with the boss . . ."

Emma slid out of the Jeep and slammed the door. "Jake actually ordered you to keep me here, on the ranch? Like a prisoner? Open the gate now, Jerico. I want to leave. In case you haven't noticed, I'm a grown woman, not a child."

"Emma . . ."

"Is there a problem, Emma?" Drake came up behind her in his silent way.

Emma whirled to face him, caught in the headlights of her vehicle. His gaze dwelled on the marks on her neck—bright red and obvious—the bite mark on her shoulder. He inhaled and stiffened, his gaze shifting to Jerico and then looking warily around him. He even stepped back a few paces, putting distance between them as his sharp gaze studied the obvious signs of possession. He took another wary look around, scanning the night for something dangerous.

Emma felt herself blushing, but she stuck her chin in the air. "Jerico won't open the gates and I want to go for a drive." There was demand in her voice.

"You don't want Jerico to lose his job, Emma. If the

boss says no, what's the big deal? You have over a thousand square miles to drive on. Stay on the ranch."

Emma's hands closed into two tight fists. "I have the right to leave whenever I want to leave, Drake. I'm not arguing with you about this. Open the gate." She didn't want to be near anything Jake owned.

He shook his head, very calm. "Take it up with Jake, Emma. You and I both know how protective he can be. He's worried something may happen to you—"

"He's a control freak," she snapped, interrupting him. "And he's not controlling me."

She heard the truck but there were no lights as Jake drove up. Her heart began to pound and she tasted fear in her throat. He unhurriedly stepped out of the truck and tossed the keys to Drake before closing the door with a certain firmness that made her mouth go dry. She tried not to be intimidated by the width of his shoulders, the confident, fluid way he walked, or the roped muscles playing under his shirt with suggestive power. Was she afraid of him after all?

Her body betrayed her, going liquid, hot, melting, telling her she was more afraid of her own reactions than his. She had no will around him. No backbone. She hated that she wanted to wipe the pain from his eyes, the scars from his soul. She hated that she wanted him with every cell in her body. She couldn't put herself into the hands of a man capable of the kind of cruelty she knew Jake was capable of. He destroyed his enemies. She'd heard of his ruthless business tactics. He used and threw away women. He trusted no one. How could she ever respect herself again if she gave in to him?

"I'll take it from here. Thanks, Jerico, Drake," Jake said, his voice calm as he approached Emma with his long, confident strides. Everything about him was self-assured. He moved into her space as if he belonged there, moved close until she was under his shoulder and one hand casually rested on the small of her back.

Emma wanted to pull away, but there was something so compelling and assured about Jake, she found it impossible to move.

He bent his head to hers. "Come on, honey, I'll take you home." His hand pressed into the small of her back, down low, his fingers brushing her butt as if he had every right, guiding her around the hood of the Jeep to the passenger side. He gently handed her in and waited in silence until she'd snapped her seat belt in place.

Jake slid behind the wheel, lifted his hand in recognition to the two men and turned the Jeep around.

"I don't want to go back," Emma said in a low, mutinous tone. She glanced at his set jaw and then looked down at her hands. "I need time to think. You're everywhere in that house." His personality was too powerful, too overwhelming and dominating. She had decisions to make and she needed a clear head to make them.

He abruptly turned the wheel, spinning the Jeep in another direction, taking them away from the main ranch house and deeper into the property. "I know you're frightened of everything changing, Emma, but it isn't going to be changing that much."

"I couldn't get out through the gates, Jake. I'd say that things are already changing a lot."

His gaze swept over her, taking in the defiant set to her chin and her trembling mouth. "You shouldn't have been able to get through the gates without my knowing before, Emma. That was a mistake on Jerico's and Drake's part. They know better now. I have enemies and I'll be damned if something happens to you because of their carelessness."

She swept her hair up and started to clip it, more from nerves and the need to do something with her hands than anything else.

"Leave it down."

Her eyes widened. "See. Right there. You're already telling me what to do. I can't have you ordering me around all the time, controlling my every move. I can't breathe right now, Jake. I need space. I need to know what's happening to me. You just take people over. I've seen you do it, and now you're doing it with me. You humiliated me. Deliberately humiliated me." There was a catch in her voice and she turned her face away from him to stare out the window into the darkness.

"How? Why would I want to humiliate you?"

Emma glanced at him again, trying not to hear that hypnotic note in his voice that always had such an effect on her. "You know very well how. You could have come in my mouth." She blushed when she said it, avoiding his eyes, but he heard the hurt in her voice as if he'd rejected her. "Instead you came all over me. That was not making love. That was not respect. That was like some porn film and I was the receptacle."

"That was me making love, Emma. That was me showing more than respect. That was me claiming you for my own." He slammed on the brakes and brought the Jeep skidding to a halt. "Did you think you weren't pleasing me somehow? Fuck, Emma. I've never had a night like tonight in my life. I've never felt that way with anyone. Not anyone. I don't tell you lies."

She didn't know what to say to that, so she remained silent, hugging herself, rocking a little, trying not to feel so inexperienced and awkward. Something had possessed her when she'd been with Jake. She hadn't known how to do all those things. He'd taught her in minutes, and she'd wanted to please him so much she'd followed his every instruction.

"I know that with you I'm a demanding lover. I'd like to say it won't happen again, but it will. I'm primal, I have certain needs, and sex is intense with you. That's such an insipid word for what sex is with you."

The way he said it, with such stark honesty, would have sounded ridiculous with anyone else, but he was telling her the truth and she shivered, her body reacting to the sensual undertone.

"I won't be able to keep my hands off you, and I have every confidence that I can make you want me." He refused to look away from her, refused to let her look away. "I can be rough and animalistic and I know I'll be demanding things from you that may scare you, but, Emma, I would never harm you, or humiliate you or treat you without respect. If there is one person on the face of the earth that I respect above all others, it's you."

Her heart pounded so hard it hurt. He was no longer discussing what had happened between them; he was talking about a future together. She could see it in the lines of his face, the intensity only Jake had, the iron will and determination that made him relentless. He was in pursuit and she was his prey.

"I'm not comfortable with the kind of sex we had."

His hand slid over her hair, sweeping down the heavy, silken fall. "I know you're not, honey, but I also know you enjoyed it. I'll always make certain you'll enjoy it."

She couldn't deny she'd enjoyed sex with him. Jake made her feel as if he had to have her, that he couldn't wait another moment. He'd given her more pleasure than she'd ever experienced in her life.

"I don't do one-night stands or flings. Do you have any idea what's going to happen when we break up? We have children. This is my home. It's your home."

A muscle ticked in his jaw. His eyes went diamond-hard. "I have no intention of allowing us to break up."

"Women don't keep you satisfied for very long, Jake, and then you move on to the next one. Rough, exciting sex only goes so far, but what happens when the newness wears off and I'm old hat to you? Then what do we do? I'm not the type of woman you're used to. I don't share."

His hands tightened around the steering wheel until his knuckles turned white. "Then we find ways to spice things up between us, although I can't imagine we'd ever run into that problem. What the hell do other couples do? I don't want another woman in my life. I don't want you to have another man in yours."

Emma sighed and looked down at her hands. She still held the hair clip. She hadn't put her hair up. Why? She held the clip up. "Look at this. I did what you told me to do and I don't even know why." But she did, and it scared her. She wanted to please him. She wanted to be the one to take the pain from his eyes.

"What's wrong with doing something that matters to me when it doesn't matter so much to you?" He took the clip from her hand and tossed it onto the floor.

"The point is, I seem to lose myself in you and I can't afford to do that. I'll fall in love with you. I already am a little bit." *A lot.*

His gaze sharpened, almost as if he could read her mind.

"And you'll break my heart. You won't want to, you won't set out to do it, but you will."

He pushed down the satisfaction that welled up inside him. Emma was being brutally honest, putting herself on the line for him. If anyone was really capable of love, it was Emma. "I would never break your heart. I told you, you're safe with me."

"Not intentionally, but womanizers don't change, Jake," she said quietly, with regret. "You need sex all the time. What happens when you're in your downtown office and I'm on the ranch, or worse, when you're on a business trip?"

His smile was faint, no amusement, only a show of white teeth. "If I'm in my downtown office and I need you that bad, I'll send a limo for you. If I'm out of town and you can't go, I think I have enough restraint to last a few days. I don't indulge myself over every little thing I want. It's called discipline, and I have more than most people. If I give you my word, Emma, you can take it to the bank and you know that."

"What happens if I get pregnant and have to go on bed rest again and they tell us we can't have sex? That could happen, you know."

"Then I'll keep that talented little mouth of yours very busy, won't I?" he retaliated.

Her blush spread over her entire body. His gaze dropped to her mouth and his thumb slid over her bottom lip, to the corner, stroking caresses that sent little fingers of arousal tingling over her breasts and straight to her groin.

Emma drew in a ragged breath. "What are we talking about here, Jake? Where do you see this heading?"

"You. Me. Marriage. I want it all. We can negotiate whatever you want right here and now, and I'm not talking money. I know you don't care one way or the other but there will be no prenuptial because I'll warn you straight up—and hear me when I say this, because this is nonnegotiable. I do not believe in divorce. If you marry me, you'll stay with me. When you don't like something you'll trust me enough to come to me and tell me so I can fix it."

"Marriage?" The idea of being Jake's wife was terrifying. He was too intense for anyone to handle on a daily basis, yet, of course, it was exactly what she'd dreamt of, the fantasy of it, never the reality. "I couldn't keep up with you and you know it."

"I know you're afraid."

"Your parents, the people in your circle, would never accept me . . ."

"Fuck them. They aren't part of my life. You are. The kids are. Don't let fear stop you from doing something you know is right. I'll make it work, Emma. You know me. I'll help you. Tell me what you want."

"I don't know." She swept her hand through her hair in agitation. "I want you to care about me. I don't want to be just anyone to you."

Suddenly the Jeep was too confined. She couldn't breathe, couldn't think clearly. He was doing it again, keeping her off balance, overpowering her, not letting her work things out. She pulled off the seat belt and banged open the door, leaping out of the vehicle and walking out into the night. The cool air helped with the burning heat of her skin.

Jake slid out, stretching his muscles, his stomach settling a little. She was scared, more scared than he'd ever seen her, but she wasn't running from him. He believed he could make her happy and he was relentless when he wanted something. He wanted Emma more than he'd ever wanted anything in his life. He knew how to negotiate and come out on top; he'd been doing it all of his life. And he knew he was about to close the deal.

"Emma, you know damn well I care about you. You aren't blind. I've never in my life needed or wanted to mark a woman the way I marked you. I had a primitive urge to get my scent all over you so every man who came near you would know you were taken—that you belong to me. I'm thirty-five years old. I've never wanted to marry until now. I may not be gentle or romantic, but you know you'll have my unswerving loyalty and my absolute protection and care. And along with that, I'll make certain you're satisfied every day of your life."

He hadn't said love, but then, Jake wouldn't. He wouldn't have believed it of himself and he would have been lying if he'd used the word. He never even said he loved Kyle or Andraya, yet she'd seen evidence of it. Was she strong enough to take him the way he was? She didn't know. If she didn't love him, it wouldn't have been as hard. But she did. She couldn't look at him without wanting him happy. She knew herself, knew she'd give too much. She was an all-or-nothing woman. She loved Jake and she'd give him everything she was.

"Define loyalty. Does that mean you'll go out, have sex with other women and then always come back to me? Or does that mean a completely monogamous relationship?"

"I'd use my bare hands to break the neck of any man who dared to touch you, Emma. I don't expect less of my-self than I do of you. When I say loyalty, that's complete fidelity. I expect it of you, and if I cheated, I wouldn't be worth keeping, nor would you."

She took a deep breath. She had the feeling he was more than capable of breaking someone's neck, and that he would if provoked. There was a lot of violence in Jake. She suspected his past was one of abuse, but he'd never told her. She saw his scars. He referred to his parents as his enemies and he was never trusting, not at all.

"Let's dispense with some of your other concerns, honey. That might help. What are you thinking about right now? There's fear in your eyes."

Her gaze shifted from his and then jumped back to his face as if expecting him to be upset with her. "When you loom over me I feel threatened, physically threatened. You can be very frightening, Jake. Yell all you want, but no hit-ting. Ever."

He started to agree, then stopped. "We need to talk about this. If I ever hit you or the children in anger, Emma, I want you to take the children and go straight to Drake and Joshua. Tell them what happened and have them help you leave. And don't come back. Don't ever take me back. I want you to promise me you'll do that. Drake and Joshua will have orders to help you. They'll take you somewhere safe where I can't get to you."

She looked up at him, her gaze searching his. She nodded.

"But . . ." His smile turned sensual and her gaze turned wary. "There are things we can do in the bedroom that aren't done in anger. Things that can be very erotic."

She looked outraged and a little curious. "Hitting is not erotic under any circumstances."

"No, but a spanking can be. And there are other things. I don't want us to rule them out until you try them with me. If you don't like something, we won't do it again, but there will be no lying to me or to you. If you're finding pleasure but you're scared, we'll be continuing. When you tell me no, you make damn sure that hot little body of yours isn't wet."

"That's not fair, Jake," Emma protested. "You always make me wet, even when you terrify me." *Like now.* The words were unspoken but she blushed a dark crimson, afraid she might have said them aloud.

He framed her face with his hands and kissed her again, teasing at her reluctant mouth with tugging teeth and a dancing tongue until she opened for him. He was a phenomenal kisser, and she lost herself in him, giving herself up completely. He lifted his face first and traced her cheekbones with the pads of his fingertips.

"I like you wet for me. Don't ever be embarrassed because you want me." His hand dropped casually to the thick erection bulging in the front of his jeans. "I have the hardon from hell and I'm not embarrassed. Isn't it better that you're a little in lust with the man you're going to marry?"

"It doesn't seem normal," she confessed in a small voice. "We just . . ." Her voice trailed off and she made a face. "I'm still upset with you."

"There's no reason to be upset, Emma. You misread what I was doing. I can understand, after our earlier conversation, why you thought that, but never think it again.

You're mine, and I would never want you for my own if I didn't respect you."

He pulled a small box from his jeans. "This is for you. I had it made for you and if you put it on your finger, Emma, there's no taking it back."

He opened the box. The ring was unusual; brilliant golden diamonds shone up at her. They looked like a cat's eye, the way they were shaped.

She sucked in her breath and put both hands behind her back to keep from reaching for it. "Jake." She shook her head. "If I do this, you know you'll be worse. You control everything, you can't help yourself, and that's a serious red flag for me."

"I know I'm different, Emma," Jake said, his voice low. It held that same hypnotic note she found so sexy. He leaned toward her, cupping her chin in his hand and bringing her face around to look at him. "Is it so bad having me be in control?"

The question was so soft, so low, his voice moving through her body like a thick, molten lava. She felt her body's reaction and it frightened her—frightened her that she wanted to say no when she knew better.

"Have these last two years really been so difficult? Anytime you've come to me with a problem or a complaint, haven't I acted on it immediately?"

"What about the gate, Jake? I couldn't leave tonight. What about that?" She hated that she had a pleading note in her voice. She knew him. She knew he couldn't be any different, that control was a huge issue to him. Even if he promised her, how could he be anything but what he was?

"I should have explained to you, but I didn't want to scare you, Emma. That was wrong of me, but you've never wanted to leave the ranch before. When you did, you always told me well in advance and I could arrange for protection both for you and the children. I have enemies and they would hurt you and they'd take our children."

"What enemies? Are you certain you're just not being paranoid? You don't trust anyone at all, Jake."

"With good reason. No, I'm not paranoid. I wish I were. I've had to step up security over these last few months because evidence has come to my attention that someone plans to strike at me through you and the children."

She frowned. "Why would they try to use me to get to you?"

He sighed, his thumb rubbing across her lips as if to erase her frown. "You're the only person who would have to ask me that question. Aside from the children, Emma, who else do I care about? Everyone sees it but you."

"Jake." She looked at the ring. He just held it out there as if it were his heart. He looked so lonely. But . . .

"I need you far more than someone like Greg Patterson or even Andrew needs you. Look at me, Emma. I *need* you. I've never said that to another human being. It won't be easy. I have a high sex drive and I won't leave you alone. I'm protective and dominating—okay, controlling—and I don't have social skills. I can't promise you I won't be hell to live with, but I can promise you I'll do everything in my power to make you happy."

He took the ring out off the velvet and slipped the box back into his pocket. "Marry me. Spend your life with me. I'll spend my life making you happy."

He was putting the ring on her finger. She could feel the weight of it. He had been the one to take off Andrew's ring when she lay in bed and her hands were swelling and she was afraid they'd have to cut it off. He'd been careful and he'd wrapped it up and put it in her top drawer. He was just as gentle when he slipped his ring on her finger.

"Jake, are you certain this is what you want?" She

reached up to his face and pressed her fingers against his warm skin. It was cold outside, but, as always, he was hot. It was as if his core temperature was so much hotter than anybody else's.

Jake's wrapped his hand in the red silk of her hair and pulled her head back to bring his mouth down on hers. Savage triumph whipped through him. He'd done it. He'd finally done it. Emma was his. He pressed his tongue into her mouth, sliding over hers, dragging the sweet taste of her into his own mouth. His hands found her top and dragged it from her body, uncaring that the material ripped. He unsnapped her bra and tossed it away. "Your jeans. Get rid of your jeans." He was already dispensing with his clothes.

Emma looked around carefully. "We're out in the open, Jake. There aren't any trees. What if one of the men . . ."

He kicked his clothes aside and dragged hers from her hips. "I'd know if someone came near." His voice went harsh and guttural as he lifted her up by her arms and deposited her on the hood of the Jeep, pushing her legs over his shoulder and dipping his head to the hot, wet core of her. She tasted even sweeter than he remembered. She was addictive.

She moaned and pushed against his mouth, seeking more, her body melting for him. Even with her as responsive as she was, he felt the small shiver that ran through her body and noticed the gooseflesh on her skin.

"I'd spend all night here with you, honey, but you're cold and I need to get you home. I've never taken you in a bed before."

He lifted her again, positioning her over his thickened shaft. "Hold on, honey," he managed to growl and he dropped her hard right down on him. The large mushroom head drove through her tight folds as she encased him, and he threw back his head as pleasure streaked through him like fire. She was so tight. So hot. He felt as if she were strangling him, gripping with a silken fist whose center was a fiery inferno. He felt like he'd come home.

"Ride me. Arch your back and move, Emma. Yes, just like that. Slow and easy until you get the rhythm. You were made for this. We fit. I swear, baby, I feel like we've done this a million times and yet every time is the first."

Emma moved over Jake, choosing a leisurely rhythm, but when he caught her hips to urge her faster and harder, she shook her head and framed his face with her hands.

"Look at me, Jake," she said softly.

Jake's fingers bit into her hips, determined to take control. Her long waterfall of hair cloaked them, the breeze shifting the thick waves around their bodies like a living, silken cape. He could feel the soft strands sliding over his bare skin, adding to the erotic feel, heightening his pleasure, but the physical pleasure paled in comparison to the emotional, and he couldn't have that. He couldn't face that. He didn't want to know the truth about what she was doing to him. He couldn't give what she was taking from him. He had to distract her—had to distract himself so he was lost in the fire of their bodies, so their joining was the greatest sex and had nothing to do with making love.

Emma shook her head. "No, Jake. Look at me." Her voice was soft. Persuasive. Insistent.

The muscles of his stomach bunched into hard knots. He didn't dare look at her, because if he did, right at that moment, when he was buried deep inside her and his world was magical and pleasure ripped through him, he knew he wouldn't be able to hide the truth from either one of them. She would see. He would have to face it.

"Jake." She whispered his name and her voice slid over his skin like warm honey. This time there was a catch in her voice. A question.

He felt that soft little sound deep inside his chest, wrapping around his heart and squeezing like a vise. There was no resisting. There was no stopping the truth from pouring out of him. It rose up like a tidal wave. He raised his gaze slowly to hers. He saw her swift intake of breath. Felt her body relax into his, felt the giving of herself pouring into him, body and soul.

Tears burned behind his eyelids. *Love.* So this was what it felt like. Not just emotional, but physical too. Everything wrapped together until it was all in one bundle, one tight package, one woman. Until that one woman was *everything.* He stared into her eyes as eternity ticked by, letting her see, knowing that for the first time in his life he was truly vulnerable to another human being. She could destroy him, and now she *knew* that she could. He swallowed hard and buried his face in her neck.

Emma wrapped her arms tightly around Jake, holding him close, protectively, knowing how fragile he was. She had everything she needed to stay strong, to guide them through. Jake would be difficult and he'd fight hard to keep any control from her, but he'd given her everything in that one moment.

Where Andrew had been sweet and kind and reverent with her body, Jake was just the opposite. And he was right—he needed her more than a man like Andrew did. Jake's life was a storm of intensity. He used sex to control her, yet now, after she'd seen true reverence in his eyes, she knew the truth. He worshiped her. He looked at her with his heart in his eyes, as if she were the very air he breathed, the ground he walked on.

"You're safe with me," she whispered, and threw her head back as she felt the tightening of her inner muscles, felt pleasure streaking through her body like fire and heard roaring in her ears. She held him to her, giving him everything, letting him know in the only way he could understand—by her absolute surrender—that she was fully committed to him.

Jake dragged in his breath, fighting the waves of intense emotion that seemed to shake him every time he was near Emma. He couldn't ignore the truth anymore, or at least he couldn't hide it from himself. In trying to force her to love him, he had become tangled in his own web. She was wrapped around his heart, his soul, even his mind. She was so entangled inside of him, there was no way to get her out. He would have to find a way to live with it. Emma. She made him so vulnerable, he was terrified. Terrified she could destroy him. Terrified of losing her. Terrified of what she made him feel.

Shaken, he allowed her feet to drop to the ground, although he held her, feeling the tremors running through her, knowing she was still unsteady. The wind shifted. One moment he was surrounded by the scent of his woman, of their combined lovemaking, potent, heady, an aphrodisiac in itself, and the next he was smelling—rival. Enemy. Trouble.

Jake stiffened, lifted his head and took a long, slow look around, his arm holding her to him, his nose raised to sniff the air to get a better scent.

"What is it?" Emma turned in his arms to try to look around him, but his hands were hard on her shoulder, preventing her from getting out from under the shelter of his arms.

"Get your clothes and get into the Jeep. Close the door. You can dress inside."

There wasn't much left of her clothes, but Emma gathered them up and slid into the Jeep. Jake turned in a slow circle, still scenting the wind. If Emma hadn't been with him, he would have shifted to his leopard form, but he couldn't take the chance. He pulled on his jeans and drew the radio from where it was hooked to his belt.

"Drake, get Joshua. I'm sending my coordinates to you. I'm smelling a stray."

The radio crackled, then came to life. "Is it Conner? He went running tonight."

Jake tried for the elusive scent again. "I don't know. Maybe. I'm not that familiar with him. I'm with Emma. I'll get her back to the house and you and Joshua check things out. If there's trouble, let me know."

When Jake slid behind the wheel of the Jeep, Emma cleared her throat. "What was wrong?"

He knew she'd seen him radioing Drake. "I have horses running free on the range about five miles to the north of here, just a small experiment I'm conducting, but I thought I caught the glimpse of a mountain lion."

Her eyelashes fluttered and her hand came up to her throat. He remembered the story of the tracks around her parents' car. "Nothing to worry about, honey. Drake and Joshua will track it down if we have anything bothering the herd."

13

⟵

"Mommy."

Emma snuggled deeper against the warm, hard body lying so tight around her. He smelled of sex and spice, and she opened her eyes to see a golden gaze laughing down at her.

Jake leaned in to her to kiss her upturned mouth, his chest sliding over her naked breasts beneath the covers. "I think we've just been caught," he confided in a whisper, and turned his head to look at the intruders.

Emma followed his gaze to the open door of her bedroom. Kyle stood at the foot of the bed, his eyes, so like his father's, wide with shock, his smile big. Andraya stood in the doorway, her hand in Susan's, both looking surprised. Susan was biting her lip and trying not to blush.

"Good morning," Emma greeted, keeping her voice even, casual. She refused to acknowledge that Jake was curled around her, totally naked, his shaft, hot and thick, and already hard, pressed tightly against her buttocks.

"Mommy," Kyle said again. "Daddy's in *your* bed."

Emma took a deep breath, willing her color not to

change. It didn't help when Jake brought his hands slowly up her rib cage to cup her breasts beneath the covers, his thumbs teasing her nipples with velvet-soft strokes.

"Mommies and daddies usually sleep in the same bed together, Kyle," Jake said matter-of-factly. "Come here and kiss Mommy good morning." Wickedly he brushed kisses in the hollow of Emma's throat. "That's what I like to do. It starts off my day the right way."

He found himself smiling, realizing it was true. When he managed to get time in with Emma before he went to work, he felt better all day. Right now he wanted nothing more than to roll her over and bury his aching cock into the haven of her body, but somehow her soft laughter as she greeted the children, and her trust in him to keep the blankets up as she wrapped her arms around them, kissing upturned faces, was nearly as fulfilling.

He had to swallow a sudden lump in his throat as first Andraya and then Kyle climbed onto the bed and wrapped their arms around his neck and covered his face in kisses. He wanted to kiss them, but couldn't do it with Susan looking on, so he just held them tight, nuzzling their soft little necks and blowing raspberries while they squealed.

"What are your plans today?" He looked at Emma.

"We're taking Susan riding and showing her our favorite places, aren't we?" Emma asked the children. Kyle nodded solemnly and Andraya looked important as she climbed off the bed and took Susan's hand again. "As long as everything is all right?" She was asking about the cat he'd supposedly glimpsed.

"Drake and Joshua said they didn't even find tracks. It must have been my imagination." His leopard had been so close last night. "Everything's fine."

"Good. We'll go riding after breakfast then. We'll meet you downstairs, Susan," Emma said, fighting to control her blush.

Susan hadn't spoken a word, but there was no doubt that she saw the marks down Emma's throat, disappearing beneath the blankets. The girl inclined her head and, drawing both children out of the room, closed the door.

Emma covered her face with her hands. "I'm never going to be able to explain this. I went out on a date with one man and woke up with you in my bed."

He rolled on top of her, his knee pushing her legs apart.

"The door isn't locked, they could come back in," Emma protested, but it was too late, his hand had already gone between her legs to her find her warm welcome.

Jake plunged into her, pushing her knees up so he could bury himself deep. He closed his eyes, savoring the feel of her tight sheath surrounding him. Swallowing her gasp, Jake held very still, waiting for her body to adjust to his size. She was all fiery heat, an amazing silken fist, gripping him tightly. He kissed her over and over, long, drugging kisses, watching her eyes go slumberous and sexy. Hot need licked at his cock like hungry fire.

"Make certain you remember to lock it tonight because I'll be waking you up properly tomorrow morning." He licked the side of her mouth. "I crave the taste of you. All that sweet honey going to waste this morning when I could be feasting."

He loved the blush that stole up her skin, and his body began a slow, leisurely rhythm inside her. It was the first time in his life he luxuriated in the feel of a woman's body. He had never woken up in bed with a woman, and Emma was soft and warm and oh so tempting. He hadn't realized the pleasure of the simple act of going from sleep to awareness with a woman snuggled against his body. He had lain there beside her, curled around her, his skin wrapped around hers, his arms holding her and his face buried in her glorious hair.

The depth of his feeling for her terrified him, yet he

couldn't bring himself to give her up. He was taking her
for himself. His one weakness. His one failure. His one
absolute vulnerability. No one on earth had power over
him—until Emma. He had made certain of that. He had
the money and the brains to destroy anyone coming at him,
but somehow his experiment with Emma had turned out
all wrong. She was supposed to love and adore him, crave
him day and night. He would attend all her needs and take
care of her, but he had never considered that he would become emotionally involved with her. He didn't even know
how it had happened. He hadn't even thought himself capable.

He felt her hands in his hair, the tug of her fingers on his
scalp. He loved her little breathy moans and the way her
body rose to meet his. She was giving, receptive, as if she
craved him, wanted to please him. And no one had ever
done that for him either. He was leopard and he smelled
lies. He knew deception. There was none in Emma. Only
her sweet, giving body wrapped around his, open to him,
willing for him to use her however he chose. A gift without
a price—only there was. And she didn't realize how much
she was asking, how much he was willing to pay and how
difficult it was for him.

He caught her ankle and pushed her knee up farther
toward her chest, adjusting his angle, listening for the little
hitch in her voice, the one that told him he was sending
sweet agony surging through her body. Each time he moved
in her, he felt as if he were in another dimension, another
plane of existence. Although he didn't want to examine the
feeling too deeply, he felt almost spiritual as he thrust
deeper, wanting her crying out, wanting her pleasure above
all else.

Jake knew he was losing himself in her body, but right
at that moment, nothing mattered but the earth-shattering
pleasure roaring through him, her soft moan of complete

surrender, the sound of her shattered cry as she whispered his name, her purr of satisfaction and the intensity of his emotion welling up, pouring over him like a tidal wave every bit as strong as the soul-searing pleasure. He was amazed that he could no longer separate the two.

Love. He had detested that word, used for everything, meaning nothing. It had become a trivial word. And it meant nothing at all. *Nothing.* But lying there with his heart pounding, surrounded by her silken body and her heat, he knew there was more than sex. Far more than sex. He could no longer imagine his life without her in it. It terrified him to think that she might learn the way he felt inside.

He kissed the side of her mouth and slipped off her, not looking at her, afraid she'd see him—see too much.

EMMA poured Jake a second cup of coffee as he finished his breakfast. Susan had remained very silent throughout the meal. Emma wasn't certain if she was so intimidated by Jake that she couldn't speak, or if she was bursting with questions and was afraid one might slip out before she could stop herself.

Emma frowned at Jake and tossed her head toward Susan. He made a face at her, took a fortifying gulp of coffee and tried.

"How long are you staying with us, Susan?"

She dropped her fork and turned bright red. "Not very much longer."

Jake gave a long-suffering sigh. "I wasn't implying I wanted you to leave, I was merely trying to be pleasant."

Emma kicked him under the table—hard.

"Ow!" He jerked his injured shin out of reach and looked down at his immaculate shirt. He'd managed to keep his arm steady and no coffee had spilled. He let Emma see the promise of a later retaliation in his eyes. Okay, maybe his tone had been a little condescending, but he'd talked to the girl, hadn't he?

Emma leaned forward. "I forgot to tell you, Jake. Susan's father is sending her calculus tutor, Harold Givens, here this morning. Would you add him to the list at the gate for Jerico's men?"

"How long will he be here?" There was a bite in his voice he couldn't quite hide. He didn't like strangers in his home at all.

A regular security sweep was conducted once a week, varying the day and hour, but it didn't matter to him anymore, not after the small microchip was discovered. Anyone coming on the property was now suspect, particularly Harold Givens, as he'd been one of the two suspects they had. As a rule he had his employees sign an ironclad privacy contract before he hired them, insisting on complete silence during and after employment. He couldn't very well do that with unwanted visitors, as much as he would like to.

"I can ask him not to come," Susan said hastily, lowering her eyes.

Jake scowled at her. "Did I say I didn't want him here?"

That earned him another kick. He moved his legs out of harm's way once again, and this time reached under the table and put his hand on Emma's inner thigh. High. Her gaze flicked to him, but the warning in his eyes kept her from pulling away.

"He's just going to stay a few hours, Jake," Emma said. "We told Evan and Joshua to meet us at the stables at one. He'll be gone by then. And of course he has to come, Susan. I promised your father we'd make certain you continued with your studies."

"Maybe he should stay home and pay more attention to his daughter instead of pawning her off on other people and having them make certain she does her school work."

Susan burst into tears, jumped up, knocking her chair over, and rushed out of the room.

Jake swore.

Emma glared at him. "Of anyone, Jake, you should have empathy for that child. Do you have any idea how utterly alone and isolated she is? She has a father who is never home. Her mother's dead and she's turned over to strangers all the time. Strangers like Dana Anderson, who has no interest in her at all and does everything she can to make her feel small and miserable. She's highly intelligent and can't relate to other teens her age. She's too young to be taken seriously by adults."

"I get it, Emma." Jake stood up and picked up the chair. "I'm working here at home instead of at the downtown office today. When her tutor gets here, bring in Joshua and Drake." He felt like a fucking monster.

He knew what it was to be different, to spend his childhood alone—if one could call what he'd endured a childhood. He planted both hands on the table, caging Emma in as he leaned down. "I'll talk to her, honey, but I'll retaliate later for the reprimands." His gaze burned into hers, hot, sexy, a promise of things to come.

"You deserved them," she pointed out, looking a little wary, but her eyes clouded with desire.

"I know I did." He leaned closer to lick the corner of her mouth. "I need you to go into town later and pick up a dress for the Bingley thing."

She pulled back to stare up at him, wide-eyed. Distressed. "What Bingley thing?"

"It's an important party, Emma. I hate those things and this one will be particularly difficult, so I'll need you there."

She shook her head. "No way. Parties aren't my thing, especially in that circle. No way, Jake, not even for you."

She actually looked scared. Jake brushed his mouth against hers. Soft. Tender. Coaxing. "I need you, honey. The enemies will be there. I want someone I can trust with me, someone to watch my back."

Her first reaction was disbelief—he saw that in her eyes—but she kept staring up at him, her fingers plucking nervously at his sleeve.

"Do you mean that?"

"I want you there with me." He wasn't going to ask again.

She took a breath and his heart turned over at the capitulation he saw in her eyes. She squared her shoulders, overcoming her fear and revulsion of such an event. She knew they would try to embarrass and humiliate her, but she would put herself in that position for him. It was another victory—a big one. Another proof that she cared about him, was committed to him. How many times would she have to prove herself before he believed? How many ways?

"How dressy?"

"Wear something sophisticated but sexy for me. A cocktail dress. I'll have jewelry. High heels, Emma. I know you don't like them, but I'll love the way your legs will look in them. I've fantasized over that more often than I should have." He brushed several kisses over her soft, upturned lips before putting his lips against her ear. "Make it a little swingy and longer, just above the knee so you can just wear a garter belt and stockings and leave off your panties."

She went crimson, just as he knew she would. "I'm not leaving off my panties."

"We'll see," he said, deliberately wicked, tracing her ear with the tip of his tongue. "Are you wet for me?" he whispered. "If I buried my finger inside you, would I find you aching and hot for me?"

She pushed at the wall of his chest, laughing. Blushing. "Yes. Now go away."

Satisfaction swept through him as he sauntered out. Emma. No matter how outrageous, she would struggle to accommodate his needs, even when it was a little frightening to her. He had to be careful not to let his need for control and assurance push her too far. Those were two of his greatest failings. He would want—no, need—constant affirmation of her loyalty, of her complete commitment to him, because he wouldn't be able to fully believe and trust in her.

He made his way to the guest room where he knew Susan was staying. With his acute hearing, even through the solid oak door, he could hear her sniffling. His radio crackled.

"Mr. Bannaconni. The tutor's here and he's brought Miss Hindman's governess with him." The disembodied voice held a note of disgust. Drake obviously didn't like either of the strangers.

"Let them through, but don't leave the children or Emma alone with them. Conner can watch the two of them in the house." He slipped his radio back on his belt loop and resolutely knocked on Susan's door. He'd promised Emma. He smirked to himself. He'd promised her retaliation as well for the two hard kicks she'd given him—and he always kept his promises. There was silence, nose blowing, and then Susan timidly opened the door.

Jake smiled at her. "Come on out of there and talk to me for a minute, Susan." He held out his hand, his voice gentle but commanding. Susan hesitated, but she put her hand in his and followed him over to the long, wide stairway. He sank down and patted the step beside him, waiting until she sat. "I was careless this morning when I spoke to you. I spend so much time rushing through my work, I sometimes forget how to talk to people. I'm grateful that you're here to help Emma. She says you're great with our children and I really appreciate that."

Susan sniffed again but smiled shyly. "They're so sweet. And Emma's been so good to me. She talks to me . . ." She trailed off.

He nodded, pretending not to notice the tears welling up again. "She's like that. Did she show you the ring?"

Susan's eyes lit up. "I saw the ring on her finger but I was afraid to ask. You're getting married?"

"We have two children. I'd say it's about time. I want more, so we'd better make certain we're married before I get her pregnant again, don't you think?" At her nod, he stood up. "You'll have to come to the wedding." Jake held out his hand to her. When she put her hand in his, he drew her up. "I'm glad Emma has such a good friend in you, Susan. You're welcome here anytime and you can stay as long as you like. Hopefully, over time, you'll get used to how abrupt I can be."

"Thank you, Mr. Bannoconni."

"Jake," he corrected, keeping his voice gentle. He walked away from her but turned back at the door. "I really appreciate you speaking other languages to the children. We're trying to give them as much exposure as possible. You're very fluent."

She beamed, raised her hand until he was out of sight and ran back into the kitchen to find Emma. "Emma! Let me see the ring! Jake said—" She skidded to halt when she saw the company waiting for her, the joy fading from her face.

"Is that appropriate behavior for a young lady?" Dana, her governess, demanded with a little sniff. "You address the hired help with far more decorum, Susan, and less enthusiasm. And it's Mr. Bannaconni to you, miss."

Susan turned bright red, her gaze flicking to Joshua and Drake, who lounged idly against the sink. Andraya had her arms wound around Joshua's leg and Kyle stood slightly behind him, nearly hidden from their visitors. She almost didn't see the third man standing with his back to the door. He was so still he made her heart tremble.

Joshua snorted and winked at Susan. "That would be me, Susan, the hired help."

Emma's expression didn't change. "Your governess has come to check on you, Susan, along with your tutor." She glanced at Drake, uncertain how to handle their visitors and the clear attack on Susan. They made her uneasy and Susan looked close to tears. It was no wonder the senator had told her he was worried about his daughter.

She heard the soft click of the radio and a brief crackle as Drake or Joshua opened the line to Jake.

"You should have warned us ahead of time that you were accompanying Mr. Givens, Ms. Anderson," Drake said, his voice one of absolute authority. "Mr. Bannaconni doesn't like surprises, and he said to inform you that if you showed up again without an invitation or the courtesy of a call ahead of time, you would be refused entrance." He deliberately addressed Susan's governess, reprimanding her publicly as she had her charge.

Color whipped into the woman's cheekbones and her mouth tightened ominously. She looked down her nose at Drake, taking in his faded jeans, the T-shirt stretched across wide shoulders and thickly muscled chest, and with a little sniff of disdain, dismissed him as inconsequential.

"Please lead us to a room suitable to carry out Susan's studies," Dana snapped to Emma. "We don't wish to be kept waiting. Jim—Senator Hindman—requires promptness and expects his orders to be carried out. We can't have Susan falling behind *again*." Her coyness implied intimacy with the senator as she delivered her second strike at the girl.

"But, Dana," Susan protested, "I'm not behind at all. I tried to tell Dad, but you—"

"Do not contradict your elders." Dana glared at her. "It's important to know your place, Susan. Your father is a great man. You wouldn't want to embarrass him."

A rumbling sound, much like a growling cat, filled the room. The deep-chested growl raised hair on the back of people's necks, caused hearts to speed up, and everyone fell silent, froze, turning almost as one to see Jake's frame filling the doorway of the kitchen. He stood in the way he always did, utterly still, eyes fixed and focused, head at an angle like a stalking animal, a predatory hunter about to devour prey. Emma found herself holding her breath as silence fell, unable to tell if the harrowing sound actually emanated from Jake, but it chilled her to the bone nonetheless. She tried not to be afraid, but she knew Jake, and he was at his most dangerous.

Joshua and Drake shifted almost imperceptibly, shielding the babies with their bodies.

Jake's eyes had gone to savage, glittering gold. "Joshua, I would greatly appreciate it if you would take the children outside."

Without a word Joshua wrapped an arm around Kyle and Andraya and lifted them to his hips, striding for the door. Conner opened it for him and Joshua took the little ones outside.

"Susan?" Jake beckoned her with his finger. He waited until she crossed to his side and he dropped his arm protectively around her.

The silence stretched until Emma's nerves were raw. He didn't take his eyes from Dana's face. "I believe I have something of yours. My people are very good at tracing electronic equipment." He pulled a small plastic bag from his pocket. The microchip could clearly be seen. He tossed it toward Dana contemptuously, deliberately just out of reach, so the damning evidence fell at her feet for everyone to see.

Dana went stiff, her face very white and set, but she didn't speak, anger flaring in her eyes. Jake set Susan very gently behind him and stalked across the kitchen floor, moving in that silent, fluid way of his, roped muscles shifting powerfully, his eyes never leaving the woman's face. He inhaled, as if scenting her.

"You even smell like a traitor. You and your friend will be escorted off my property now. Don't ever make the mistake of coming back."

It was Harold Givens who bent down to pick up the microchip. Dana snapped her fingers. "Susan. Come with us now. This is an unsuitable place for you, not with this man and his little slut flaunting their bastard children to the world. My God, look at the hickeys all over her neck, like she's some whore."

Emma gasped, terrified of what Jake might do. Her hand crept up toward her neck, but Jake caught her wrist without looking at her and pulled her hand down to her side, holding it there. A long silence stretched, everyone's nerve endings taut.

Jake's smile was slow, humorless, utterly frightening, his white teeth gleaming, and he never took his eyes from his prey. "Susan will stay here. The senator will send your things to you. I doubt you'll be able to get a job anywhere unless it's with the Trents or Bannaconnis, who you obviously work for."

"I'll have you charged with kidnapping."

"Drake, remove this disgusting excuse of a human being from my sight immediately." Jake turned his back on the couple in dismissal, took Emma's elbow and waved Susan ahead of him, guiding them from the room.

Behind them, Dana sputtered, "Get your hands off me."

"I don't much care how we do this, sweetheart," Drake said. "As far as I'm concerned, you're garbage to be thrown out. I don't have to be nice."

Dana shrieked again. There was the sound of a scuffle. Harold grunted in pain. The door slammed and the sounds faded.

"Are you all right, Susan?" Jake asked.

Susan nodded. "But she'll tell my father lies. She always does."

Jake picked up the phone. "Not this time. Do you need a tutor? I can have one here in an hour."

She shook her head. "I know more about calculus than that man ever did. He's Dana's friend, but my father believes everything she says."

"Your father will listen to me," Jake assured, his voice certain. "Go riding with Emma and have fun. Don't worry about any of this. People like that try to make everyone around them feel small and useless. You're not. You're smarter than they are. And you're stronger, too strong to ever let someone like that make you feel bad about yourself."

"I'm a little afraid of her," Susan admitted.

"She wanted you to be afraid. That way you would never go to your father because you didn't want to know if he'd believe you or not. She destroyed your trust in him, that's what people like her do. There's no reason. I'll deal with her. Go change into your riding clothes." He reached out and caught Emma's wrist, preventing her from leaving the room while Susan headed for the door. "Susan." He stopped her, waited until she turned back toward him. "If you're ever put in a position you're uncomfortable with again—*any* situation, including when you go on a date— you call me. I'll give you my private number, which you won't give out to anyone at all. Understood?"

Susan's smile blossomed across her face. "Understood."

Jake waited until Susan's footsteps had faded down the hall and her door had closed before he swung Emma around in front of him and cupped her chin. His mouth was gentle, tender even, when he brushed his lips over hers. "Did she hurt you?"

"Calling me a slut? Or calling the kids bastards?"

"The children have a father. Me. My last name is on their birth certificates. And not just *a* slut—you're *my* slut. Let's remember the difference, Emma." He kissed her again, a teasing smile on his face. "You're my everything, so screw her."

"She didn't hurt me, Jake," Emma said, knowing it was true. "Do you think Senator Hindman will believe you? I think Dana will try to cause trouble for you—for Susan— maybe even for all of us."

"Don't you worry about that traitor," Jake said, his voice so low it terrified her. "She'll find out what it's like to lose everything and live on the streets, servicing anyone who can buy her for a nickel."

"Jake."

"She fucking called you a whore, Emma. She called my children bastards. She tried to spy on us. But worst of all, she abused her position of power over a sixteen-year-old kid. I'm going to take her down."

He kissed her again and she tasted his anger. He tasted wild, primitive and all male. She opened her mouth to try to soothe him, but he rained kisses all over her face.

"I'm more furious that I couldn't protect you from someone like her in our own house."

"What do you think she was after, planting the microchip?"

"I think my enemies want one or both of our children. I've locked down the house and you're a complete mystery to them. They needed a way to collect information."

Emma frowned up at him. "Do you think Senator Hindman is involved?"

"No." Jake picked up his phone. "The senator has a viper in his home. Trent and the Bannaconnis have been trying to find a way to blackmail him for years. He's never been controlled by them. They obviously planted Dana Anderson in his home."

Maybe it was obvious to Jake, but it wasn't so obvious to her. "I'm glad I don't have to be the one to figure out what's going on," she said.

Jake kissed her again. "Go have fun riding with the kids and Susan, and don't worry about anything."

He watched her turn away and then turn back toward him, shyness in her usually confident eyes. "What is it, honey?" he asked gently. He loved her like this, soft and so vulnerable to him.

"I just wanted to make certain you were all right. You're always so busy taking care of us, but did she hurt you with the things she said?"

He stepped close to her, to her warmth, drawing her slowly into his arms, pressing her soft body against his. He just held her, his chin on top of her head, his hand cupping the nape of her neck as he nuzzled the silky waterfall of red hair cascading down her back. Emma slid her arms around him and held him tightly, as if she were trying to comfort him.

Perhaps the memory of his childhood was too close, having witnessed Susan being made to feel so small and helpless, but he held Emma even closer, knowing this moment was another first for him—his first genuine offer of comfort from another human being. He wasn't in need of consoling, not because of the likes of Dana Anderson, but for all those lost childhood years, for all of his long, empty years isolated and alone as an adult.

She was tearing down his walls too fast, and he had to stop her before it was too late for him. His heart raced, adrenaline pouring in, flooding his veins. Hard knots formed in his belly. It was frightening to know a part of him wanted to strike at her, push her away, take back the control she didn't even know she had stolen from him. Already his fingers fisted in her hair, tight, close to her skull, deliberately pulling on her tender scalp as he forced her head back. He was breathing hard, great, ragged breaths, as he stared down into her face.

Emma felt the difference in him immediately. He went from Jake to a cornered beast, his eyes that slashing gold that indicated a fight for survival. She stayed pliant and unresisting, wanting to cry for him, for the feral animal trapped in those eyes. "I love you, Jake," she said softly, knowing it was true.

The eyes glittered at her, lips drew back in a snarl, baring white teeth as they snapped together. "Don't say that to me."

"I love you," she repeated, unafraid. His face was a mask of burning fury, but she felt his body shudder against hers in a kind of surrender.

The fingers tightened to the point of pain, bringing tears to her eyes. "Don't say it," he hissed, his heart already gone. Panic set in. She was so fragile. He could break her neck with one movement. He could tear out her heart. He could destroy her so easily, yet she looked at him without fear, her expression radiant. Absolute. "Like in the damned pictures," he whispered, and brought his mouth down on hers, afraid she would see—would know—about the burning in his eyes and the lump clogging his throat.

She gave her mouth to him, uncaring that he was savage, almost brutal, kissing him back, matching fire for fire until he calmed and couldn't stop the gentleness, the tenderness that she found in him, from emerging. "You're destroying me, Emma," he whispered, his forehead against hers. "You're fucking destroying me with every breath you take."

"I'm making you stronger," she answered. "You make me stronger. That's the way it works."

He hoped so. He hoped she knew what the hell she was talking about, because he was in virgin territory.

The kitchen door banged open. "Emma!" Joshua yelled at the top of his lungs. "The kids are losing their minds out here. If you don't move it, we're going to have a mini rebellion."

Joshua sounded harassed. Jake and Emma looked at each other and burst out laughing. She ran through the house. "I'm coming, sheesh. I had to take care of some business."

"I can see what kind of business you were taking care of," Joshua complained. He raised his voice so Jake could hear. "I'm not a babysitter."

"What a wimp," Emma teased. "A couple of little kids and you're whining like a baby." She caught up the reins Conner held out and swung up onto the little mare Jake had purchased for her. The horse had beautiful lines, but it was the training he'd paid for. She moved at the slightest request, her gait gentle and flowing.

Conner had Andraya sitting in front of him, her cheeks red with excitement, her pink riding helmet matching her beloved boots. Sometimes she refused to take off her boots, wanting to wear them to bed at night. Kyle was waiting impatiently for Joshua to remount behind him. He was all in black, matching his daddy's hat and boots, although he too wore a helmet.

"You're in so much trouble, Joshua," Emma warned. "You're not supposed to bring the horses up to the house. The gardener hates that. They trample his flowers and leave big messy surprises."

"It's your fault." Joshua still hadn't forgiven her. He knew the gardener would vent for hours, screaming in Italian at her and throwing rich, fertile dirt in the air in one of his frequent tantrums. Only Emma could soothe him when he was in a rage over the destruction of his beloved gardens.

Jake had sought out Taddio, his gardener, years earlier, after hearing several people first praise him as one of the top landscape artists in three states, then drop him after an accident had left him with one arm. He still had his genius, but none of them wanted to look at his "disgusting imperfection." He had been with Jake exclusively ever since, designing the landscaping around his buildings, the homes he bought and sold, and the ranch as well.

They rode in single file, Emma listening to the bantering between Joshua and Susan. The teenager sat with perfect form, shoulders straight, chin up, with a new confidence Emma hadn't seen in her before. Andraya and Kyle bounced and kicked and held the reins whenever Joshua and Conner allowed it, laughing in delight as they commanded the horses.

Emma had never really ridden a horse until a year earlier, when Jake had decided to teach her, along with putting Kyle on a horse for the first time. He'd been careful of her, but he'd pushed her to overcome her fears, until she'd finally realized there was freedom and joy in the power of the animal.

The riding trail was narrow as it wove through the trees to come to a small stream that the horses splashed across. This was the easiest trail, and one they used whenever they took Kyle and Andraya riding. No steep terrain, just flat land that stretched for miles. In the distance there were a few sloping hills. The wind had a bite to it and Emma was glad she'd insisted the children always have their jackets with them when they went riding.

In the distance, off to her right, as Emma topped a rise, she noticed dust rising, a large amount. She reined in to study the dust cloud, to determine what it might be. She glanced back and Joshua and Conner were talking to the children and helping them with the reins. She shifted her weight forward, lifting the reins slightly, and the little mare set off using her smooth, fast gait. Emma abandoned herself to the sheer joy of riding, feeling the wind in her hair and the breeze on her face. She urged the horse faster, using her knees to control the speed, just as Jake had said she could do. For just a few moments, she was alone, horse and rider charging across the land and her own laughter ringing in her ears.

She heard the sound of hoofs and turned her head to see Susan urging her horse up beside hers. They ran side by side, throwing grins back and forth, hair whipping in the wind, the horses running smoothly and confidently.

Emma's horse suddenly swerved, eyes rolling, head tossing. Emma pulled her reins just as Susan's horse began acting up. Emma lifted her head to try to catch the elusive scent, but her horse tried to bolt and she turned her attention to controlling the animal. She had to force its head around, circling. Susan's horse turned tail and made a dash back toward the ranch.

Thunder rolled ominously. The ground shook. She felt the vibrations travel up the horse's leg to her body, and she swung her head back to look in the direction of the dust cloud. It was nearly on top of her. The mare crow-hopped, letting out a terrified squeal. Emma kicked her hard in the ribs and bent low over her neck, racing back toward the relative safety of the treeline.

One moment she was riding alone, the next she was swept up in a sea of running horses. One broadsided her mare, crushing Emma's leg. For a heart-stopping moment the mare stumbled, her head lowered and she kicked out with her back legs, sending Emma flying to the ground. Hooves rained down on her. She rolled, curling into a ball, hands over her head to protect herself. The ground was soft from the rain and she wiggled into a depression against the side of a small boulder.

She heard the sound of gunfire and a man's shout. Joshua had shoved Kyle onto Conner's horse and had ridden right into the stampeding herd, in front of Emma, firing his weapon, shifting the flow of the herd. The horses thundered past, swerving away from her. When the sound died down and the earth quit shaking, she dropped her hands and rolled over to stare up at the stormy sky, tears blurring her vision. There didn't seem to be a place on her body that didn't hurt.

"Don't move, Emma," Joshua commanded. He didn't sound at all like the Joshua she knew, and when she looked at him, his eyes glowed, small red lights playing through them. "Drake will send the helicopter for you."

She meant to tell him that was silly, that she was perfectly all right, but for some reason, when she opened her mouth nothing came out. She heard Andraya screaming for her and lifted her hand to beckon Conner to bring the children to her so she could reassure them, but Joshua shook his head, crouching over her like a protective bulldog. When he even waved Susan off, she tried to move.

A groan escaped and everything went black.

14

"STOP moving around so much."

Emma let her breath out in a long hiss. "If one more person tells me that, I'm going to hit them over the head." She glared at Jake. "You especially. Don't you have work to do? I'm fine. I've been sitting in this den for two days doing nothing. You won't even let me pick up the kids. If you growl at Andraya one more time, she's going to think you've turned into a grumpy old bear." She pressed her lips together, aware she sounded bitchy, but she couldn't help it. She felt trapped, like the walls were closing in on her.

"Have you taken a look at yourself? You're covered in bruises." Jake stroked the pad of his finger gently down her left shoulder and arm, bruised from getting kicked by a horse. She'd been lucky her arm wasn't broken. She had bruises on her leg from a horse slamming into her and bruises on her hip from landing on the ground so hard.

"Can I just say you're overreacting?"

"I don't overreact," Jake denied.

"You were going to shoot every horse on the property, you maniac. I would call that overreacting, and keeping

me sitting here is definitely overreacting." When he just
remained looming over her like some Neanderthal man,
she sighed. "Jake. Come on. I'm going crazy." She winced
at the pathetic little whimper in her voice.

She was edgy and moody and wanted to rip and tear at
something. Jake had insisted she go to the hospital to be
checked out. He took the doctor's instructions seriously—
too seriously. When the doctor said he wanted her to be
quiet, Jake thought that meant completely immobile. He let
the children kiss her and talk to her, but only in short vis-
its. He'd slept in her bed, his arm around her waist, but that
had been all, no other touching. His kisses drove her wild,
and her body ached for his, but he insisted on handling her
as if she might break at any moment.

"Is your headache completely gone?"

"Absolutely. Totally." She started to stand and he dropped
a heavy hand on her shoulder, preventing movement.

"The doctor's coming today. If he says you're fine, then
we'll see."

"He will say I'm fine." Emma hesitated and plunged on
to the next subject. "Jake, right before my horse spooked, I
smelled something. It sounds silly, but I have a really acute
sense of smell and the wind shifted and for a minute it
smelled like a wildcat. Maybe a mountain lion. Could there
be a large cat in the vicinity?"

Jake went very still.

Emma dropped her eyes and shrugged. "I know it
sounds silly, but I can smell things others can't. I've always
been able to, and lately my sense of smell has been even
sharper. I can tell who has come into the house before they
get into the same room with me."

He caught her chin. "Don't do that. Don't be afraid of
saying anything to me. I'd never belittle you, Emma. You've
been thinking about this for two days now. I knew something was on your mind. I don't want you to keep things

from me. Not your fears, not your opinions, even when they differ from mine."

The pad of his thumb slid back and forth over her chin. "I know you think I've been a little crazy over this accident, but you're black and blue. You could have been killed. And if you tell me you smelled a wildcat, then I believe you. Drake and Conner have been looking for tracks. Something had to have spooked those horses. We let that herd run free on the property but they should have been miles away. The stallion keeps them to a territory about thirty miles from the house and he always stays on the same range."

Something in his voice caught at her. "Are you saying the horses were purposely herded or driven onto the trail we take the children riding on?"

"I don't know, honey, but I intend to find out. I just think it's best to keep the kids very close to the house. I'm beefing up the security when the children are outside."

Her heart slammed hard against her chest, and for a moment she couldn't breathe. "Do you think someone is trying to harm them? Tell me the truth, Jake. You've got to tell me what's going on. I don't like being kept in the dark like some child."

Jake sank into a high-backed chair opposite her, a sigh slipping out. "I don't want to scare you off."

"Jake, if anything was going to scare me off, it would be you. You're a very intimidating man, but do I look afraid of you?"

Faint humor lit his eyes. He smirked. "Sometimes."

She smiled at him. "Okay. Sometimes I am, but you don't sound remorseful."

"A little fear is good for you once in a while, otherwise you'd boss me around the way you do everyone else."

She refused to allow him to distract her. "I won't run. Tell me."

He pulled his chair close so their knees were touching. "The people who are my birth parents were involved in a bizarre experiment. What they were trying to do doesn't really matter. The point is, they wanted a child with certain talents, and when I was born, I wasn't what they had ordered. They have an alliance with the Trents, and I believe the Trents have been conducting the same sort of breeding experiments, rather like friendly rivals. Both families are very powerful, politically as well as socially. I'm sure you've read the papers and the suspicions surrounding both families. Nothing is ever proved, but Bannaconni and Trent both have been under suspicion in the disappearance of young women."

She noted that he referred to his father as Bannaconni, never as Dad or Father. Jake was always consistent in that. She tangled her fingers with his as he continued.

"Let's just say that not only do I believe Bannaconni and Trent are guilty in the women's disappearances, but that other disappearances have never been discovered. They've had women bring rape and torture charges against them in two separate incidences, but they were acquitted when, in fact, they were guilty. How do I know they were guilty? I know them and I saw them kill someone, a nanny of mine they blamed for their abuse of me. Their wives are every bit as depraved and cruel and bloodthirsty as they are. They are serial killers, yet they'll never be caught." He pulled his hands away from her, as if he couldn't have physical contact even when mentioning his childhood.

She went white, she knew she did. She could feel the color draining from her face. She believed him. She took a deep breath. "Did they try to kill you, Jake?"

"There were times I wished they had."

"All the scars?"

He nodded slowly. "Not necessarily all of them, but, yes, they liked to inflict pain. For the power and the rush.

It's all about power." He waited a heartbeat. Two. Wanting her to know the truth. Wanting her to know what she was getting into, or maybe he wanted her to prove that she really belonged to him. "I have the same genetic makeup. Their blood flows in my veins."

She tried not to see the understanding of his parents' deviant need for power in his eyes. That remote, cold look he often had on his face, the determination to destroy his enemies. The ruthless traits in him that made him a bitter, relentless enemy were stamped on his face. He took apart companies like others took out garbage. He reveled in his ability to scent weakness and he circled like a shark with the smell of blood before going in for the kill. His attacks were always swift, unexpected and ferocious. Emma moistened her suddenly dry lips and tried to breathe normally.

"Do you like to inflict pain, Jake? For the feeling of power? For the rush?"

His gaze jumped to hers, locked and held. "Yes." He wanted her to know the truth about him, about the monster living in him. Not buried deep, but close to the surface. She had to know. He hadn't started out thinking he would ever reveal the ugliness inside him to anyone, but she deserved the truth. He owed her that.

Emma's breath left her lungs in a rush, as if she'd been punched and couldn't catch air. He caught her hands again, locking them together, and she had to fight to keep from pulling away. She couldn't look away from his eyes, from the rejection there. He had bared his soul and expected rejection—maybe even was half hoping for it.

"Have you ever killed anyone? Done anything like your parents?"

"The enemies," he corrected.

She took a shallow breath. It was the best she could do. "The enemies, then. Have you ever physically harmed another human being?"

"Not like the enemies have, but I killed a man who meant to murder Drake. I felt I had no choice. Everything happened fast and there wasn't time to think."

Emma was silent, trying to wrap her mind around how the conversation had taken such an unexpected, shocking turn, yet she wasn't nearly as shocked as she should have been.

"Emma." Jake waited until she was wholly focused on him. "I had no choice."

He was telling the truth. She knew he was by his scent alone. "Have you ever been cruel to animals?"

"No, of course not. I would never do such a thing, nor have I ever wanted to."

"What about the children? Have you ever wanted to hurt them?" She held her breath, terrified of his answer. He never looked away from her, although it had to hurt him that she asked.

Jake felt his stomach turn. "*Never.* Never, Emma. Remember when I told you if I ever hit them—or you—that I wanted you to leave me and tell Drake? I meant it."

"What about me, Jake? Have you wanted to hurt me?"

There it was. The question he knew would come. The one he had hoped wouldn't come. He kept his gaze locked with hers. He couldn't have looked away from her even if he wanted to. He had to judge her reaction to his answer. He had to see the disgust and horror for himself. "Sometimes." His voice was barely a thread, barely whispered aloud.

She didn't flinch. She had courage, but he already knew that about her. She blinked up at him, digesting his answer, knowing he spoke the truth. She didn't look at him as if he were a monster, she didn't even pull her hands from his, but he felt her tremble.

"Why?"

It took every ounce of courage he had to look her in the

eye, to answer her, to let her see inside of him to the dark, ugly truth that he was exposing to her. "To make you prove your loyalty to me. To know you'll stay no matter what, that you want me enough to take whatever I dish out. Other times it's been because another man is too close to you and I need to show him you're mine."

Again she was silent, but she still hadn't turned away. Her gaze remained steady on his. "You've never hurt me," she pointed out.

"That doesn't mean I didn't want to, Emma. That means I choose not to be like the enemies. It's a conscious choice I make every single day. I choose my targets in business, people who have hurt others, and I don't take down those weaker than me. Or those who are honest. I made up my mind that if I had to be a monster, I would at least make certain it didn't control me."

"I'm not laying down for you, Jake. I'll *never* lay down for you."

"I know that."

"I can see you manipulating me at times and I allow it because whatever you want isn't a big deal to me, but if it ever was, if I wanted something, nothing would stop me." She leaned toward him. "You think about it long and hard before you ever decide to hurt me, Jake. If you hit me, I will walk away. I have too much respect for myself to put up with that kind of crap, no matter how much I love you. And I do love you. I know I do, whether you believe it or not."

"If I ever hit you, Emma, I would know it was time to pack it in. I wouldn't be worth much as a human being."

"And I would never, under any circumstances, tolerate another woman. If you decide to hurt me emotionally, know I will walk if you choose that as your test of what I will or won't do for you. I'm trying to be as honest with you as you're being with me."

She was killing him. Destroying him. Making him so vulnerable inside, he felt like paper in the wind. She turned him inside out. She should be loathing him, despising everything he was, but instead she looked at him with her soft eyes, her warm heart in them, and she *loved* him. It was there. That look. The one he'd been waiting for. She made no pretense of hiding it. She sat exposed, unafraid, courageous, letting him see inside of her. And she made him weak and scared. Not just afraid. *Terrorized.*

He dropped her hands and stood up, knocking the heavy chair backward, pacing like a caged animal. "What the fuck is wrong with you, Emma? You should be running screaming out of here. I just told you about my bloodline. I told you that sometimes I want to hurt you—test you—yet you're sitting there, all wide-eyed like some innocent virgin, thinking love conquers all. I don't even believe in love. You know that, right? You should be running, damn it. Do you really think you're going to be able to live with me? With the kinds of things I'll demand from you? Your idea of love . . ."

"Is adolescent?" She raised her eyebrow as she quoted him back. "Because I don't know about the kind of sex you want?" She didn't raise her voice at all.

She stood too, crossing the small distance he had put between them. His head was down, in stalking mode, his eyes fierce, focused, frightening in their intensity. She ignored the wall he was attempting to build and went right up to him, ignoring the danger signals, turning her face up to his, her heat surrounding him, her scent deliberately enveloping him. She kept her voice a low, intimate tone, but made certain she enunciated each word.

"I may not know about your adult sex. But I know about love, Jake, and you don't. You can teach me about your hard-core, kinky sex and I'll teach you about making love. Being in love—real love—the kind of love that endures.

The kind worth fighting for. The kind of love where when I look at you and you look at me, we can see each other all the way, deep down to everything hidden, and know we're where we're supposed to be. The good and the bad, strengths and weaknesses, everything we are and know. At the end of the day, we'll know we've been truly loved."

Emma put her palm on his chest, over his heart. "I'm not afraid of going where you lead. I believe in you. And I trust you with my life, but more importantly, with the lives of our children. I'm willing to put everything that I am into your hands because I trust you that much. I trust that you'll put me first and protect and care for me with everything that you are. I'm not afraid of what you came from, or the monster you think lives inside of you. You've learned a lot of things about life that are ugly, but that doesn't make me afraid either. Why? Because I know you. I see you. You aren't hiding from me. I've lived with you for two years and I know you."

She tilted her head to one side, studying his face. "Do you trust *me*? I think that's the real question here. Do you trust me enough to put *your* life in *my* hands and follow where I lead? Do you have the courage to let yourself love? That's the kind of man I want and need, Jake—a man with the courage to let himself learn from me. Because if there's one thing I do well, it's love." She stood on her toes and kissed the corner of his mouth. "You'll have to decide. Right now I'm going to go upstairs and get ready so the doctor can assure you I'm well enough to take my house back. And I'll buy the most beautiful cocktail dress you've ever seen so you can get all sorts of interesting ideas for later on. In case you didn't get it, I'm very proud of the man you've become." She turned to walk away and he caught her wrist.

"Emma, wait. We'll see about you going anywhere. Don't set your heart on it."

She made a face at him. "We won't see. Nurse Tell-Me-What-to-Do can leave and I can have my house back."

"We'll see," he repeated.

"If the doctor says I'm fine, then I want to go into the city and pick out a dress for the party." When he frowned, she glared at him. "Unless you've changed your mind," she said hopefully, "and decided I don't have to go with you." Although she was still going to get out of the house and off the ranch and just breathe for a while.

He massaged the nape of her neck. "You're not getting out of it. If I have to go, you have to go. I'm not suffering alone."

"Fine, I guess we're going. So I'll need a dress. I've never owned anything like what I'd need for this event."

He tapped a pen on the top of a side table, his frown lines not just around his face but also crinkling his forehead, giving her warning of what was to come. "You don't have to go out. We'll have dresses sent from some shops and you can choose."

She almost gritted her teeth. "I *want* to go out. Susan and I have been looking forward to going shopping. I'm sick of being cooped up."

"You've never felt cooped up before."

"Well, I do now. I want to go into the city and go shopping and get away from all this . . ." *Testosterone.* She felt overwhelmed by him sometimes, especially when he hovered so close when she was hurt. She felt like one of the children. She might as well be one of the children, lying next to him without him touching her. No, that was wrong—touching her without doing anything about it. She set her mouth mutinously. "I'm going shopping."

His eyebrow shot up. "Really. I doubt you'll go after Drake talks to you." He paused and called Drake on the intercom. "Emma would like to go into the city—shopping."

Jake heard Drake hiss and he folded his arms across his

chest and leaned his hip against the wall, waiting. There was plenty of satisfaction in knowing Drake was going to take the brunt of her anger, not him. Which was a good thing; she was getting edgy again and his experience with Emma was that if she felt pushed past a certain point, her sharp little claws would come out.

The security team was in place—her security team— and if Emma wanted to go dress shopping rather than have dresses sent to the ranch for her to try on, she was going to have to accept what Drake was saying to her. Things had changed significantly since he put that ring on her finger, although she wasn't going to like how. He sighed, wishing his life weren't so complicated. This would be one more added pressure, one more thing Emma would balk over.

Emma said nothing, dropping back into her chair, drawing out the silence until Drake arrived along with Joshua. Drake came in and took the chair opposite Emma. Joshua closed the door and stood by it.

Emma tilted her chin and shifted her gaze from Drake's stern face back to Jake. She didn't look as if she was going to be blaming anything on Drake.

"You want to go shopping today?" Drake asked.

"Yes." Her voice was firmer than ever. "If I don't get out of here, I swear I'm going to lose my mind and there will be bloodshed—preferably Jake's." Her skin crawled with a thousand little ants, and it took every ounce of self-control she had to remain seated and not fly at someone and rake them with claws until they just got out of her face. She had the waves of heat that seemed to rush over her, until she was so hot she needed to tear off her clothes and stand outside in the cool air. "I'm getting snappy with the children and more than once I've thought about clawing out someone's eyes." Again she looked at Jake.

Drake's eyebrow shot up and he flicked a quick glance at Joshua and then Jake.

Jake shrugged. "Just a minute ago she was being really sweet, Drake. I didn't do anything."

"If the doctor has okayed you leaving . . ."

"I swear, Drake, if one more person says that to me," Emma snapped, "I'm going to hit him over the head. I don't care what the stupid doctor says. I'm not staying in this room another minute. No one else is going to take care of my children. And everyone is going to stop telling me what to do." She was beginning to feel like a child herself, with parents standing over her telling her what she could and couldn't do. "And, Joshua, you can get away from the damned door before I throw something at you."

She could hear her voice swinging out of control, but she felt caged, the three men looming over her, intimidating her.

"Baby," Jake spoke quietly, "I'm your target, not him."

That made her ashamed. A reprimanded child throwing a tantrum. She just wanted . . . *out*. Away. Gone.

"Emma." Drake's voice was utterly low, but held that same commanding note Jake often got when he meant what he said. "You're engaged to Jake. That makes you a target. You don't have to like it, no one likes it, but it is reality. Jake doesn't leave the house without a bodyguard, and you can't either. If you want to go shopping, we'll go, but we have to make certain it's safe. I never want you to feel as if you're a prisoner here."

"I'm used to you going with me, Drake, and I've never objected. I know you have to be there if we're taking the children, but I thought Susan and I would go out together. If you want to come, I certainly haven't objected."

He shook his head. "Not Susan. It's too risky. She's a kid, unpredictable, and she's a senator's daughter. If Jake's enemies make a try for you, she'll be in the line of fire, and you wouldn't want that."

"This is silly." She pushed both hands through her hair.

"No one knows. Nothing's changed. I just want to get out of here." She wanted to cry. She felt like she could barely breathe, and now, if she insisted, she'd feel childish putting everyone to the trouble of protecting her. The whole thing was ridiculous. "I'll take off the ring."

"You'll keep the fucking ring on your finger, Emma," Jake snapped, his eyes glittering at her. He straightened, the lazy facade gone. "You can keep your ass home."

"Then I'm not going to the party," Emma said, pushing herself out of the chair.

Before Jake could say anything, Drake intervened, sending a warning glance to his friend. "Emma, I have no problem taking you shopping. Jake, I can handle it from here."

It was a dismissal, and one Jake wouldn't have taken from anyone but Drake. He knew the man was trying to help him, to save him from himself. Jake tried not to react to the thought of leaving Emma alone in the room with two male leopards in their prime.

He could feel his cat so close—too close. It leapt and clawed for freedom, raking at the inside of his belly. His hands ached, his fingers curling and knuckles hardening. He wanted her beneath him with every cell in his body. Domination? Or love? He had no idea, only that in her way, Emma was every bit as dangerous as he was.

She thought she knew him, thought she knew his secrets, but if she knew about his cat, hidden from her sight, raking at him to get at her, she wouldn't be so sure of herself—or of Jake—any more than he was. He knew, after her admission of seeing cat tracks near her parents' car, that she would never trust him once she knew the truth. Even if by some miracle she had a cat inside of her, she might wonder if he had something to do with her parents' deaths, if their meeting had been planned from the beginning. She knew he'd manipulated her into living with him. It wasn't that far of a step to take the conspiracy further.

He had tried to warn her, tried to show her the ugliness that was a part of him, and he couldn't help but admit that she might see some of it, but how could he ever show her the rest? Besides trying to live with him, she was going to have to live with the insanity of his world. He had personal protection. It was a way of life, and it would continue to be for her, for their children. He shook his head, knowing he was asking a lot of her. He needed to lose himself in his other form, to just run away from who and what he was.

"I'm heading out, then, I feel like going for a run." He looked Drake in the eye. Man to man. "I'm putting her in your hands." And it was the hardest thing he'd ever done, trusting another man with Emma, with his life, because he knew that was what he was doing.

Drake nodded, understanding. He watched Jake drop a kiss on the top of Emma's head, wondering if Jake knew just how far he'd come from their first meeting.

"Let's just get this over with, Drake," Emma said, looking close to tears. "I'll do whatever you want. Have the shops send the dresses here."

He shook his head. "No, we'll go. You want to go, we'll go. I'm not having you start your life with Jake thinking it's too much trouble for you to leave the ranch. We're just going to go over the rules. I want you to listen to me very carefully, Emma. When we're off the ranch, I'm the one in charge. Always. When I say stop, you stop. When I say move, you move. When I say get down, you don't hesitate, you don't question me, you just do it. If you have any questions, now is the time to ask them. I want you to be comfortable with your security, not afraid of it and certainly not fighting it."

She nodded. "I understand. That doesn't sound too complicated." Her fingers twisted together in her lap, and more than once, she slid her finger over the ring as if it were uncomfortable on her hand.

"You will never, under any circumstances, skip out on me or the team. That's an absolute. We don't want any more risk to you or to the team than necessary."

"Of course, Drake, but why do you keep saying 'team'? We're getting a dress."

"We're going to be high profile, Emma, because the threat to you is very real. Your engagement to Jake was announced in the papers. We'll have a driver staying with the car. I'll walk in front of you, Joshua behind you, and Evan and Sean will be on either side of you. We'll all stay together when we're moving and you will stay in the center at all times on the street. We'll go with the flow of traffic but try not to stop. We don't have a female and Jake should start thinking about getting one."

She stirred, her gaze flicking over him, the sudden thought of a female around Jake all the time irrationally irritating her. "I don't think that's necessary."

"It's necessary if we're out and you need to go to the ladies' room. You won't be too happy when we go with you and clear it. The same with the dressing room."

BY the time the doctor had come and gone, giving her permission to resume normal activities, Emma was sorry she had ever decided to go shopping. She was even more edgy and emotional, close to tears at times. She hadn't realized how much she'd come to regard Joshua and Drake as her friends, and now, thanks to the ring on her finger, she was something else to them, someone they would have to guard wherever she went. She sat in the large SUV, a black Cadillac, and twisted the ring back and forth, feeling alone.

This was supposed to be a fun outing, a way to get away from the children and from Jake's overwhelming personality, but instead she felt like a burden, and worse, was very embarrassed that she would have to walk in public with men so obviously guarding her. Ordinarily she was quite happy at home, but all of a sudden, as she feared, things were changing and Jake was taking over more of her life. Sitting alone in the car surrounded—not by friends she laughed and joked and shared her life with, but by bodyguards, men she had to obey—she felt very isolated.

The driver parked in the lot and Drake slipped out of the vehicle first. She watched him scan the area, his gaze touching pedestrians and a van parked in a corner slot with the engine running. He waited for it to pull away and turn out of the lot before he opened her door for her.

"Come on, Emma, let's just do this the first time and you'll see it's not so bad."

Standing in the center of the diamond formation the team made around her, following Drake, with Joshua behind her and the two other men on either side, she walked with them, keeping to their pace, her head down, not looking at those around her. She was aware of the traffic in the street and the people on the sidewalk. This was going to be her life. Worse, it was going to be how her children had to live.

Jake. She sighed, thinking about him, about how his life had to have been so difficult, yet for the past two years she'd never once had to think about it.

"Stop taking your ring off," Joshua hissed from behind her as they waited for Drake to check the first shop on their list.

She glanced at him over his shoulder. "I didn't realize I was."

"We don't want to have to crawl around on our hands and knees to look for the thing if you lose it."

He had a teasing note in his voice, but her stomach knotted. Did she want to lose it? Maybe she did subconsciously. She really was upset, more than she'd realized. Drake waved her into the shop and she stepped inside to browse, very aware of heads turning as Joshua and Drake entered with her. There was nothing inconspicuous about them; they weren't even trying to be. They looked like body-guards, nothing less. She knew Evan was at the rear entrance and Sean at the front outside.

She couldn't concentrate to really look at the clothes and barely moved through the racks. She wanted to go home. "I don't think I'm going to find anything here, maybe I'm just not in the mood."

"You've got a couple more stores, Emma," Drake said and led the way out. He spoke into his Bluetooth, presumably to call in Evan.

As they went past two stores and moved toward the small dress shop she'd heard about, she caught a glimpse of a pair of shoes. Forgetting, she stopped to turn back. Joshua put a hand on her back, moving her with the team.

"Emma wants to look in that shop," Joshua said.

It wasn't on their schedule. Drake had explained about that and how they didn't like to deviate. She shook her head, flushing bright red. "It's all right. I just really need a dress right now." She hated this. How did anyone get used to it?

The next shop yielded nothing and the third shop was closed, which meant they had to cross the street to the little French boutique where Jake had first taken her after Andraya had been born, which was perhaps part of the allure. The designers displayed there were some of her favorites. She found a black, very sophisticated dress with a low V-neck falling into a close-fitting skirt and a daringly bare back cut all the way past the waist, making it impossible to wear a bra. She held it up, hesitating to try it on. It seemed too much trouble.

Drake said nothing to her but walked to the dressing room, looked inside and indicated for her to go in. She didn't look at the clerk, but followed his unspoken signal and slid into the soft material. It clung to her as if made for her. Fortunately the shop carried other accessories, so it wasn't difficult to find a lacy black garter belt and high-topped stockings. The shop next door had perfect matching heels, and before she could take the purchases, Drake stepped forward and arranged for a courier to deliver the boxes to the ranch.

Emma fell into step behind Drake, with Sean and Evan on either side of her and Joshua right behind. "It's sort of like a parade," she said, glancing around her.

The men were looking out away from her, watching traffic and people, even buildings. She sighed as they approached the stoplight and were forced to halt and wait for the light to turn. She could feel the curious stares, and her fingers slipped to the ring, rolling it around on her finger. She wasn't cut out for this kind of life. She felt absolutely ridiculous and embarrassed. She was going to have to talk to Jake and make him understand that security was fine for the children and for him, but definitely not for her—not like this. Taking one bodyguard should be enough.

They stepped off the curb and started across the street with the pedestrians flowing around them. They were like a little moving island, she thought. The sound of a motorcycle barely registered when she felt Drake's hand on her arm, yanking her forward and away from her two side guards. The bike slid straight at Sean's legs, the helmeted driver leaping off as he laid the bike down in an effort to take out both Sean and Evan like bowling pins. Joshua dragged Evan clear and Sean tried to leap out of the way just as a Mini Cooper bounced over the grass and curb to slide sideways, doors open. A second motorcycle roared through the scattering crowd, heading straight for Emma, the driver stretching out his hand to catch her shoulder, presumably to shove her into the waiting Mini Cooper.

"Down, Emma," Drake yelled, whirling around to face the new threat.

She dropped and the hand stretching for her missed. Drake was already reaching out, snagging the driver and ripping him off the bike with one hand, spinning him around, using his cat's strength and shoving the knife he'd pulled deep. Blood sprayed across the ground, including across Emma. He drew his gun, his body crouched over hers, one arm out to cover as much of her as he could as he took aim at the driver of the Mini Cooper. The driver spun the small car in a tight circle, right into the crowd. Drake squeezed the trigger and the windshield spiderwebbed. The Mini Cooper fishtailed down the street, bumped onto a sidewalk and over the grass before coming to a halt.

Chaos erupted around them, people screaming and running, but the team performed as one unit, Joshua drawing and firing, taking out the first driver as their own Cadillac screeched to a halt, blocking the intersection. Evan yanked open the door and Drake all but threw Emma inside, jumping in after her while Evan took the front seat and Sean hobbled to the driver's-side back seat. They drove off fast, leaving Joshua to deal with the police.

Drake called the incident in, explaining to the dispatcher and then informing Jake they were coming in fast.

"Are you all right, Emma?" Drake asked, his voice gentle.

She nodded her head, but there were tears in her eyes and she refused to look at him. "I don't understand what happened." She was shaking, and when he touched her, she jerked away from him. She didn't know if she wanted to go home anymore. What had been safe and comforting for so long now seemed alien. The men who had been her friends, men she admired and cared for, weren't at all who she'd thought. "What did they want with me?"

"You're the only Achilles' heel Jake has. They've never

found a way to get to him. And now they have the means to destroy him."

"Did you kill those men back there?"

"Yes," he answered curtly. "We don't miss."

She swallowed hard and looked up at Sean. "Are you all right?"

"A few bruises, nothing to worry about," he assured.

Emma pulled her knees up to her chin and sat rocking back and forth, holding herself tightly. Drake put a gentle hand on her shoulder a second time. "I know violence can be shocking, Emma, when you aren't used to it."

"It's crazy," she answered. "This is so crazy and I don't even understand why." She lifted her head and looked at Drake, her eyes swimming with tears. "Do you have any idea how crazy this will make him? Jake will lose his mind over this. He will, Drake, you know him. He isn't going to wrap his arms around me and say he'll make it all go away." A sob escaped and she pressed her face against her knees, shaking her head.

"When a man goes his entire life with nothing, Emma, and then he finds a woman who is his entire world, who is everything to him, he'll do anything to protect her," Drake said. "Even if you took that ring off, the one you keep pulling off your finger, it wouldn't make a difference in how he feels about you. They would still be able to get to him through you."

"I'm not taking off the ring." She looked up at him, her gaze fierce. "You just don't let anything happen to him. I know this party is important and he's going to insist on going and he'll tell you that I'm to be your first priority, but you don't let anything happen to him, Drake. He'll risk everything for me, I know he will. You don't have to tell me. That doesn't make any of this easier to live with, but I'm not walking away from him. I love him. Now they've made me angry too." She rubbed her chin on the tops of her knees, her fists clenched, tears still falling. "Don't you let anything happen to him."

Jake was waiting, pacing back and forth, as the Cadillac pulled up to the house. "What the fuck happened, Drake?"

"Jake," Emma interrupted before Drake could answer, "you're supposed to put your arms around me and comfort me. That's what fiancés do when someone tries to kidnap their betrothed. Drake did his job, I'm fine, three men are dead, and in case you're interested, Sean's hurt."

Jake let himself look at her. For one moment time seemed to stop. She was alive. She was safe. Tears streaked her face and there was blood on her. His gaze quickly jumped to Drake.

"Not hers," Drake confirmed.

Jake's knees actually felt weak and he could only stand there, trying to stop the roaring in his head and the hammering of his heart. He reached for her, needing to touch her, to feel her warmth and know she was safe. The moment his arms closed around her and he drew her from the seat of the SUV, he felt complete.

"Thank you, Drake." His voice was gruff with emotion, and he turned away from them, burying his face in the silk of her hair, carrying her into his house. "I'm sorry, Emma. I shouldn't have put the announcement in the paper."

"It wouldn't have made a difference, Jake," Drake said. "At least we know someone's watching the ranch. How else would they have known we were on the move with her? And they didn't have a professional crew coming at us. It was amateur hour."

"The police are on the way," Jake said tersely. "I've got the lawyers waiting. I want your report. Tell them everything and do whatever they say when the police come." He kissed the top of Emma's head again. "They're going to want to talk to you, Emma. You'll need to talk to the lawyers as well, and don't answer anything the police ask until the lawyers okay it."

She nodded, looking a little frightened, and Jake kissed her, his mouth coaxing, feeling her tremble against him.

The process with the lawyers and police took long, exhausting hours. Emma eventually fell asleep, curled in a chair. The questions had been endless, but truthfully, everything had happened so fast she couldn't tell them much, only how scared she'd been. Jake draped a blanket over her while he and Drake and the lawyer talked with the police and she'd finally just drifted off.

After everyone left and the house was quiet and dark, Jake stood over Emma for a long time, just watching her sleep. His lungs burned with the effort just to breathe. His vision blurred as he picked her up, cradling her close to him, sheltering her against his heart. She murmured softly, frowning and burrowing against him.

"I'm just taking you upstairs," he said, his heart aching. If this was love, it hurt like hell.

15

"YOU look beautiful, Emma," Jake said, "absolutely beautiful."

She was grateful he didn't say anything about her hair being up. He preferred it down, but it didn't go with the sophisticated look she was trying to pull off. She was actually a great deal more nervous than she thought she'd be. She cared nothing for these people, but she wanted to be an asset to Jake.

Knots of gold were on her ears and gleamed in a collared necklace at her throat. More golden knots formed a chain around her wrist. The pieces were spectacular, one of a kind, yet very simple in their design.

She put her hand in his as he helped her from the car. She tried not to tremble, not to allow him to see her sudden nerves. After all, she was there to support him. But Jake saw everything about her, and she wasn't surprised when his fingers came under her chin to tip her face up to his. His eyes were sharp, focused, intent. "We'll be fine, honey. Remember the rules and stay very close to me. Trust no one here. No one at all. Drake and Joshua will be inside; they're coming as our guests and they'll stay close."

She pressed a hand to her churning stomach. "I'm pretty nervous, Jake. I can't imagine that I'll be making a lot of new friends tonight."

"You told me that you could smell a lie. Trust that tonight. Use all of your senses."

She slipped her hand into his. "I'll be fine. Let's get this over with."

He brought her hand to his mouth. "They'll be here tonight."

"Whatever you need here must be important," Emma said.

"I have to find out what they're after. I know they think I'll give them one of the children. They have to have something big to think I'd give up a child to them."

Emma stiffened. "I don't understand what that means. Have they threatened you? Us? Are they blackmailing you? Do you think they were behind the kidnap attempt on me?"

Jake shook his head. "Yes, but I don't know why. They've been working very hard, thinking they're under the radar, and I don't have a clue what they're up to, why they're trying to take over my company, the one that owns all the various tracks of land with the potential for natural gas or oil on them. They don't have a prayer. Even after buying off my man, it's locked up tight. I'm not that stupid as a businessman. They know something I don't, and I have to find it out. Knowledge can be the most deadly weapon of all."

"Do they think you'd give up a child for money? Or give them money for me?"

He would give up his life for her—or for the children. And maybe that was their ultimate goal. He couldn't see what the enemies were after, and that worried him more than anything else. "They would give up a child in an instant, so they might judge me accordingly. It's possible you'll find out more than I will. They'll be more inclined to think they can talk in front of you. They like innuendoes and think they're very clever with their barbed comments." His hand slid up her arm until he reached her shoulder and pulled her to him. "Be careful, Emma, and if it gets to be too much, signal me and we'll leave."

He was worried. Really worried. And that was very unlike Jake. There was something going on behind the scenes that she didn't understand, but for him to be this worried over a party, her nerves turned to full-fledged stomach flips as they walked toward the entrance, hand in hand.

"If we get separated—and we will, they'll see to that— take the opportunity to sit down in any chair in the center of the room. I'll keep an eye on you. Don't accept drinks from anyone else, and when you do get a drink from the bar, don't put it down and pick it up again."

Emma nodded, unsure whether he was just being paranoid or if he had information he wasn't sharing with her. Either way, she was very nervous as they walked toward the elaborate mansion. The noise hit her first, hurting her sensitive ears. She felt hot, as if she had a fever, her core body temperature rising until she felt beads of perspiration between her breasts. Her body burned in heightened awareness. She could only put it down to Jake's close proximity. She was becoming as bad as he was, needing sexual relief often or her body seemed to just burn all the time.

Jake glanced down at her. Her scent was alluring, her body nearly glowing. He could feel the heat radiating off her, stirring his shaft until it was engorged and hard, aching for relief. She could do that so easily to him, and he realized no other woman would sate him. It was her body he craved, and she was driving him close to the edge of his control without doing anything more than dressing up for an event he had asked her to attend with him.

As they headed toward the entrance, he let his hand slide down her back and over her round, firm bottom, seeking the line of her underwear. She had worn garters and heels just as he'd asked, but he could just make out the outline of very thin panties clinging to the shape of her. It amazed him, with so much at stake, the cat in him still needed the reassurance of her commitment to him, her absolute loyalty. He had to know at all times that *he* was her choice, that she belonged to him.

What the hell was wrong with him? Where was his control and discipline? He was shaky at best, had been for the last hour or two, and it was slowly getting worse. The longer he was in her company, the worse the sensations grew. If this party weren't so important he would have turned around and taken them home and out of harm's way, but his businesses were under attack. Employees had been bribed. Even one of his secretaries, who had been with him for years, had reported that she'd been approached by Trent's lawyer to feed them information. And now his family had been threatened. For what?

It hadn't surprised him to learn that Susan Hindman's governess was related to Trent and she'd been acting on his orders. She reeked of cat. A shifter who couldn't shift. He had put private detectives on her and learned she was one of Trent's nieces who regularly slept with him. She would do anything for him, including sleep with the senator to cement political connections for Trent. It still didn't explain why she had been ordered to bug his house phone. Trent would have known he'd never talk business on his house phone. What were they looking for? What information did they have that Jake didn't?

He leaned down to press his mouth against Emma's ear, not certain whether he needed the contact or she did. "Are you ready, honey?"

She looked up at him and smiled. His stomach knotted. She managed to look serene in spite of her nerves. "Let's get it over with so we can be alone. I dressed for you tonight, not for them."

A small smile formed and the knots in his gut slowly unraveled. "You left your panties on."

"True, but I can take them off when we leave."

He knew she was giving him something else to think about—a secret shared. His heart did a funny little flip. "I like your thinking." He let his hand slip along her bare back and high up around to slip inside the material and stroke the side of her breast. "I'm going to have a hard-on all night now just thinking about you taking off your panties and handing them to me."

"Just think how good you're going to feel when I actually do it," she teased.

Jake didn't have to knock on the door; it was opened as they approached and Joshua, Conner and Drake fell into step with them. His hand was back in place, at the small of her back, guiding her inside. The moment he stepped inside, the scent of male cat was heavy in the room. Even the fragrance of perfume couldn't drown out the smell. Jake's cat slammed hard against his skin, leaping and raking, snarling to get out, to remove Emma from the close proximity of any other male. He was going to have a difficult time tonight. She smelled alluring, her body hot as he moved her through the room, his hand on her back, a warning growl rumbling in his chest.

They had brought in male leopards! Rivals. They must have done it on purpose. They had to know about the madness, then, and wanted him to lose control. This was going to be an ordeal of wills, of nerves, a clash that would be win or lose everything. How many enemies were in the room? The Bingleys weren't leopard. Only the Bannaconnis and Trents were, but Drake and Joshua had told him there were some leopards willing to be employed by anyone paying top dollar for their services.

Drake jerked his head, indicating two men lounging in the corner, watching them enter. He obviously recognized them.

The room was crowded and Jake was greeted immediately as they wove their way through the throng and toward the bar. He spotted Cathy and Ryan Bannaconni and Josiah Trent talking together in the far corner. He knew they'd be there. He'd braced himself for seeing them. "In the corner, the enemies, and even worse than them, Josiah Trent," he said to Emma. "Do not make the mistake of being alone with them. Stay in the middle of the room, out in public."

So many people crowded around them, eager to meet Emma, as he'd known they would be. He kept her close as they moved around throughout the evening, talking briefly to as many people as he could, trying to get a feel for what the undercurrents were. Conspiracy. He smelled it. Tasted it. Inevitably, as the night wore on, he heard the soft whisper of it and satisfaction slid through him.

"I think I've found what I was looking for, Emma. I'm going to join the group of men over by the window and lead them into talking about real estate. Sooner or later they'll ask me if I'm willing to sell my company. You'd be a major distraction to all of us, me especially. I need to concentrate on nuances. I'll get you a glass of wine and I want you to sit on the couch in the middle of the room. People will come up and talk to you, probably even the enemies, so if you can't handle it, give me a signal and I'll get you out of the situation."

"But you need time."

"As much time as you can buy me."

"So, really, I'm the distraction to keep your enemies away from you."

He nodded. "I hate having to use you like this, but no one is going to talk if Trent or Cathy and Ryan are in on the conversation. The moment you sit down and I leave you, the three of them will be unable to resist and they'll swarm around you like bees to honey."

"Which is why you didn't want me leaving your side. You wanted to control when they approached me."

Jake studied her upturned face. It was difficult to read Emma at times. She seemed to be such an open book, yet right now, he had no idea what she was thinking. He caught her chin. "Are you upset with me?"

"No, I know this is important, Jake." She rolled her engagement ring back and forth on her finger. "But if we're going to be partners, you're going to have to start trusting me enough to talk to me about what's going on."

"I don't want trouble touching you."

She swept her hand around the room. "But it's already touching me. And maybe the children. I want to be a partner to you, not another burden." She stood on her toes and pressed a kiss to his chin. "Get me my wine. The sooner this is done, the better off we'll be."

He squeezed her fingers, tucked her hand behind him and made his way through the crowd. People parted for him, opening a path to the bar. There were several bartenders. One was free, but Jake didn't move forward. Another lifted his head to indicate he was ready but Jake ignored him. A third, Evan, served two people and Jake simply stood back, something out of character for him. Emma knew he expected—and got—instant service.

"Red wine," he ordered softly. "Something good."

Evan reached under the bar, ignoring the bottles already opened, and poured two glasses, handing them to Jake, not acknowledging Emma. The bottle disappeared back under the bar.

Emma took the glass, letting him lead her to the leather

sofa, which was occupied by several people. Jake stared at them until they moved. He sat her down and brushed a kiss on the top of her head. "Wait right here for me."

Emma nodded and took a cautious sip of the wine. It *was* good, and she wasn't that much of a wine connoisseur. She watched Jake walk away from her. There was something so fluid and confident about the way he moved, like water flowing over rock, nothing getting in his way. He was a formidable opponent, and it occurred to her, not for the first time, that she was in way over her head.

"Ms. Reynolds?"

Emma felt her stomach tighten. She forced a smile up at Cathy Bannaconni.

"My dear, may I call you Emma? I feel so bad about our unfortunate first meeting and was hoping for an opportunity to apologize and maybe explain?" The older woman held out her hand, smiling bravely.

Emma automatically took the woman's hand. Cathy patted her hand and then pulled away. As she did so, her sharp, bloodred nail raked across Emma's inner wrist.

Emma's hand jerked, although she managed not to spill her wine. A long, angry scratch beaded blood along her wrist.

Cathy gasped. "Oh no! I'm so sorry. How clumsy of me. Let me get you a napkin." She hurried away before Emma could protest, returning with a linen cloth dipped in cold water. "I really shouldn't wear my nails so long. It's just a weird little habit of mine."

Emma wrapped the cloth along the stinging scratch, holding the cool, soothing wetness against the angry slice. "I'm fine. It's really nothing."

"You're so sweet to be so understanding." Cathy gave a long-suffering sigh. "I'm certain my son has told you all sorts of stories about me. Now I've probably added to my terrible image after our disastrous first meeting."

"Jake doesn't talk about you," Emma said.

Cathy's eyes narrowed. She inhaled sharply. A slow, humorless smile curved her mouth. "That's good, dear. I know we got off on the wrong foot, but I was so concerned about my grandson. Jake can be quite cruel." Her gaze dwelt on the fading bruises still evident on Emma's skin. "But having lived with him these past two years, I'm sure you're already very aware of that."

Emma's murmur was noncommittal. She glanced up as Jake turned to check on her. He raised an eyebrow and she shook her head, indicating she could handle the conversation with his mother. There had to be a reason Cathy Bannaconni had sought her out, and she was going to find out what the reason was.

"I have something you might like, dear," Cathy said. "Now that you'll be my daughter-in-law. I read the announcement in the papers. There was quite a write-up, although they said very little about your family and their connections. I thought that strange, didn't you?"

Emma stiffened, going still inside. She took a sip of the wine Jake had brought to her. He had been very specific not to accept a drink or allow it to leave her hand, even for a moment. When Cathy scratched her, she'd retained possession of the fine, long-stemmed glass, and when she was forced to put it down, to lay the cooling cloth across the scratch, she'd watched her drink carefully. What did Cathy know about her?

"Aren't you even curious what I have? It belonged to your father."

She waited a heartbeat. Two. She needed the time to keep her voice normal. "How would you have something that belonged to my father?"

"Miss? Would you care for something to eat?" A young waiter presented a tray first to Emma and, when she shook her head, to Cathy. Emma barely concealed a smile as she recognized Sean. She felt much safer and her stomach settled a little.

Impatiently Cathy waved him off. "Your father was a dear friend of mine."

The words were tainted with untruth.

A shadow fell across her as a large, extremely handsome man loomed over her. He must have been in his sixties, but he looked younger. There was that same sensual stamp on his face, that mark of dangerously alluring cruelty to his mouth that Jake had, although he looked nothing at all like Jake. She stared up at his eyes. He looked vaguely familiar, although she was certain she'd never seen him before. She inhaled deeply and scented depravity.

"This is Josiah, dear. Josiah Trent. Josiah, this is Jake's delightful fiancée. Josiah is your father's uncle, dear."

For a moment she couldn't breathe. She actually felt dizzy, the room spinning alarmingly. She looked around, her vision blurring a little. Sean, instead of circulating around the room, was hovering just a few feet away, and that steadied her a little. Two men, just beyond the couch, were watching her intently, eyes narrowed and focused, and she sensed evil in the pair. Drake was just to the right of her, leaning one hip against the wall, talking, but she knew he was watching her every move. Joshua wasn't in her line of vision, which meant he was somewhere behind her. Jake was across the room, within shouting distance, although the music and conversations seemed abnormally loud all of a sudden. Emma let out her breath, forcing herself to remain calm. She was safe as long as she was out in the open.

"My father's uncle? *You're* my father's uncle?"

Trent enveloped her hand with his, patting as if to soothe her. One finger slid over the cloth on her wrist, pressing it deeper against the scratch on her arm so that it burned and she jerked her arm away. "You have no idea how long we've been searching for you. After my nephew's death, we lost track of you. It seems Jake managed to find and . . ." He hesitated, choosing his words carefully. "Win you for himself."

Emma extracted her hand and took another sip of wine. Her gaze met Sean's. Immediately he shifted off the wall and hurried over, bending down with the tray. It gave her a few moments to think as she chose a small bacon-wrapped quiche.

"Thank you. These are delicious." She knew she sounded grateful, which would only give Cathy and Trent an advantage. They would know they were getting to her.

"You're supposed to circulate," Cathy hissed to the waiter. She made an odd noise deep in her throat, somewhere between a growl and a rumble that was menacingly soft. Her eyes glowed ruby red in the dim light.

"Yes, ma'am," he said and moved away.

Emma felt like she'd lost an ally but she was determined not to signal Jake. She had to trust Drake and his team. Jake stood tall and straight, very distinctive, even in a room filled with many powerful men. Whatever revelations Cathy was going to tell would not come with Jake close. She took a breath and made herself smile blandly up at the two hovering over her. Their eyes were hard, calculating, and she knew they were every bit the predator that Jake was.

Her breath caught in her lungs. She had the urge to run while she could. This was a society she didn't want to understand or want to be part of. "You were looking for me?" she murmured softly, an encouragement to tell her more.

Trent shifted position just enough to block her view of Jake—or to block Jake's view of her. The movement was subtle, but with Emma's heightened awareness, she caught it.

"Long before you were born, Bradley, your father, was

quite the ladies' man. He was very good-looking and charming, and few women could resist him. We wanted a particular woman in our family. One . . ." He smiled, baring his
teeth as a shiver went through her. "One of a breeding and
bloodline befitting our family. I paid Bradley a great deal
of money to find and bring this woman to me."

"We have the contract he signed, dear," Cathy said, leaning close. "Perhaps you would like to see it? It has some
particular significance to you."

Emma felt trapped, caged in, and something inside of
her shifted, going from fear to survival mode. Very carefully she set the wineglass on the table next to her and
looked up at Cathy. "Why would a contract my father
signed before I was born have any significance to me?"

Trent's body swayed slightly, his head moving but his
eyes still. "He owes me still."

Emma's eyebrow shot up. "What does he owe you? And
as he's dead, how can that in any way impact me?"

"You're what he owes me." Trent smiled and leaned
down slightly, running his hand over her cloth-covered arm
again.

Her eyebrow shot up again. "My father owes you his
child?"

"His wife, actually. I financed his trip to the rain forest
and he was to bring me a suitable young woman. Instead,
he betrayed us and married her. He took the money and
went on the run with her. He *stole* from me, both the woman
and the money."

Emma knew, with the strange sixth sense she had, that
he was telling her the truth. Her childhood had been spent
on the run, never staying in one place long, never permanently buying a home and going to school like other children. There were weeks in a place, then abruptly they left
with no explanation. And perhaps, a little chilling voice
rose up, it explained why someone had tortured her father.

Someone looking for her? Or perhaps someone punishing him. Was she looking at the man who had murdered her parents?

"I see." What could she say? The revelation that she was related to Josiah Trent sickened her. She now knew a little of how Jake must feel with tainted blood flowing in his veins. And her beloved father had gone to the rain forest and seduced her mother with the intent of *selling* her to Trent. To say that she was shocked at her father was an understatement.

"Jake is the same ruthless type of man. I feel responsible for you," Trent said, his voice softening, almost hypnotic. "He's very dangerous. We've tried to minimize the damage he does to others, but I'm sure you've seen him in action. Very few can stand up to him. He knew about you and your parents after finding the contract and he decided to have you for himself. After he dumped my . . ." Trent's throat tightened, he choked, his voice coming out clogged and grief-stricken. "My daughter, she never recovered, turning to alcohol to drown her sorrows."

Cathy laid her hand on Trent's arm to comfort him.

It was all very plausible, but Emma had every sense alert, and the part of her that ferreted out lies was heightened to the point of screaming at her. Neither Trent nor Cathy cared in the least about Shaina's death. She shifted position slightly, with every intention of getting up. Her head spun and her mind refused to react. Her heart began to pound as she realized she'd definitely been drugged. Either the wine or . . . She tore the cloth from the open scratch and dropped it onto the floor.

"He's my son," Cathy said, one hand fluttering to her throat. "But he was born with a streak of cruelty. He has plans for you. I only want to protect you."

Emma's gaze fixed on the long, sharpened nails as each pressed again and again against Cathy's bare throat. The movement fascinated her, mesmerized her, so that she couldn't look around, her arms feeling tired, hanging heavy at her sides. Had she poisoned Emma with those long nails? Was that possible?

"I don't need protection," she murmured. Her voice was nearly as fuzzy as her brain.

Josiah smirked at her, his teeth bared like a wild animal about to enjoy a meal. "Don't be so certain of that." He picked up her hand and let it drop.

Her arm felt like lead. She couldn't control the movement. A part of her went into panic mode and she struggled to call out to Jake. Her throat closed. She hadn't tasted a drug. The wine couldn't have been drugged. Evan had poured the glass himself and Jake had given it to her. It had to be the scratch or the cloth Cathy had put on the scratch. Something introduced directly into her bloodstream.

She forced her head up in an effort to look for Jake. There was a wealth of people between them, blocking her view. The two men just across from the couch had moved forward fast, their speed nearly a blur, their eyes glowing. Fear skittered down her spine as she tried to find Drake or Joshua.

Trent had her on her feet, an arm around her waist, Cathy on the other side of her. It took four steps and they were in another room, hastily locking the door to drop her on the couch. It wasn't either of them she feared the most; it was the man who followed them into the room while another stood just inside the door watching with hungry eyes.

Cathy put her hand on Emma's body, down low near her ovaries. "She's close to her first heat, Josiah. I don't know if she's ready yet, but we have to try."

She looked at the man approaching them. Low, warning growls emanated from his chest. His head moved back and forth, but his heated gaze never left Emma.

Trent and Cathy hastily pushed Emma down onto the floor and stepped away from her, continuing to back up as the man approached and circled her limp body.

"Rory, you must get your scent all over her for this to work," Trent advised. "She's in heat and it will drive Jake into the madness. Once he smells you all over her, if he doesn't kill her, he'll throw her out or scare her so badly she'll run from him. Loyalty is everything to him. Without his protection, nothing will stand in our way. We'll be able to get her. She'll disappear and no one will be the wiser."

Emma opened her mouth to scream for Jake, but nothing came out. The one they called Rory snarled, his lips drawn back to reveal a mouthful of menacing teeth as he got closer to her.

The man guarding the door snarled too, suddenly moving forward in a challenging manner. "Why him? I'm bigger. Stronger. She should be mine."

Trent held up his hand, moving around Emma's body in a circular pattern as well. "I will dispense with both of your services. I'll take her myself."

"No!" Cathy leapt forward and caught at his arm. "We need a cub. They're shifters. They can't take a chance."

Trent slapped her hard, driving her away from him. Cathy turned in the air, landing in a crouch. "Don't you see? You're every bit as affected as they are." She spun to face the other man coming from where he'd been standing by the door. "Clayton, get back. We're paying you to guard the room, not to screw her."

To Emma's horror, Rory leapt on top of her, blanketing her body with his, tearing at his clothes to rub his skin over her dress, his tongue licking at her face, his glands marking her in his scent. He rolled her over, uncaring of her limp body, doing the same along her back and buttocks.

Cathy caught up a camera. "We can sell the pictures to one of the rag magazines."

Emma summoned every ounce of will she possessed, calling on the wild part of her that usually lay so dormant but now seemed closer to the surface. She slammed backward, catching Rory's face with the back of her head and rolling fast to get out from under him when he reared up. She pulled her knees to her chest, although she felt as if she were moving in slow motion. There was a roaring in her ears, but she refused to give in to the fog in her brain.

JAKE turned his head to find a solid wall of people cutting off his line of sight to Emma just as Conner reported, "I've lost sight of her."

Drake snapped, "Joshua, do you have her in sight?" He was already on the move, shoving people out of his way to get to the sofa.

Jake spoke into the small Bluetooth. "Evan, do you have Emma in your sight?"

The bartender shook his head. "Trent and Bannaconni are also gone. So are the two thugs they hired for the evening."

Jake swore. "Drake, Joshua, call them in. Call them in now." He was already pushing through the crowd. He was a big man, enormously strong and not afraid of hurting anyone. The sea of people parted, but there was no Emma on the couch. He swore, furious at her because she hadn't listened.

He was already close to the edge of his control, realizing that if Emma was in fact one of his species, she had to be close to her first true heat. He had experienced the maddening thrall once before and he could feel the temper and dominance of his kind raking at his belly and churning with a black rage. His body was hard and hurting, and every bone and muscle ached with the effort to hold back the change. Now she was gone and the scent of male cat was strong.

His men converged from all sides, Drake, Conner and Joshua bursting through the crowd. Evan leapt over the bar and Sean tossed his tray aside and rushed toward them. Jake pointed to a door just a few feet from the couch where Emma had been sitting. "Her scent is strong this way."

The door was locked, but he expected that. He was enormously strong, and when he called on his cat, that added to his physical strength. They took down the door in seconds, splintering the hard wood. Emma was on the floor, on her knees, her face so pale she looked like a ghost. Her stockings were torn and her clothing disheveled. A man was reaching for her, but he stopped abruptly as Jake and his men poured into the room. The man's face was bloody. It looked as if his nose might have been broken.

Already Jake's body was contorting, his clothes ripping.

"Take her," Drake snapped as Conner and Joshua moved between Jake and Emma. "Get her out of here."

Jake looked around the room. "You're dead," he said quietly, and reached for Emma.

She had trouble getting her legs under her and standing, so he simply swept her up, cradling her body close, and turned and went out, Sean leading the way with Evan flanking them. Drake, Joshua and Conner held back the two leopard mercenaries with warning growls of their own. Jake strode through the curious partygoers, paying no attention to the gasps and questions. The men closed ranks, the others catching up as they exited the house.

Jake put Emma in his Ferrari, slammed the door harder than necessary and started the engine. "Put your seat belt on."

When she fumbled with it, he swore and did it himself. Looking straight ahead, he pulled the car onto the deserted street, following the vehicle carrying two of the body-guards. Behind them, another vehicle followed close.

"What the hell were you thinking, going off alone into a room with them?" Inside the close proximity of the vehicle, the other man's stench was overpowering. She reeked of something half man, half leopard. He could smell the other cat and it drove his leopard into absolute madness. He could barely control the car, his fingers contorting and curling, curved claws pushing against the ends of his fingers.

Emma moistened her lips, trying to get past the cotton in her mouth. Her brain was still fuzzy, refusing to work properly. She knew Jake's fury with her was building, but she seemed unable to find a way to answer him. Her arms remained heavy, the drug in her system clinging in spite of her best efforts to shake it off.

She was close to tears. Rory had come close to raping her. That had been his intention, with Trent, Cathy Bannaconni and the other man, Clayton, looking on. If Clayton and Trent hadn't wanted in on the action, in those few moments, Rory might have succeeded, while Cathy documented the entire assault. She didn't know if their plan to make Jake throw her out would have been successful, or if it had without the assault. He was nearly out of control, low, menacing growls rumbling constantly in his throat.

She needed comfort, not tantrums, and Jake was close to a violent tantrum.

"I told you to stay in plain sight. What did you think was happening? After what happened yesterday, did you think this was some kind of game?" His vision was changing, and he saw heated bands of color. The lights of the cars hurt his eyes. His jaw ached. He breathed hard through his nose, trying to hold back the change. His cat was in a fury, the stench of the other male driving him mad.

She didn't respond, and in truth, Jake was grateful she

didn't make excuses, knowing it would have infuriated him even more. He drove in silence until they were on his property and the security peeled off, leaving them alone. Instead of heading for the house, he chose to drive out toward the back part of the property, taking them away from the children and his security team now that they were on his ranch. He didn't trust himself. His intention was to get out, to tell her to drive back without him, and then he would run until the cat was exhausted. He no longer trusted himself in his present state.

He slammed on the brakes and brought the car sliding to a halt, shoving open his door and nearly falling out, his cat pushing hard against his skin. He tore off his jacket, tossing it on the hood of the car, and ripped at his shirt, popping buttons so that they fell to the ground, scattering everywhere.

Breathing hard, he went around to the passenger side and yanked her door open with every intention of having her get into the driver's seat. The stench of the other male filled his lungs and he scented . . . *leopard*. She had another male's mark all over her. Without even being aware of his actions, he jerked her out of the car. Emma tried to pull away, falling back against the car, fighting to shake off the lethargy the drug had produced.

Her resistance triggered the leopard in him. Snarling, he ripped at the offending dress, raking down it with sharpened claws, tearing it off her in strips. The material went everywhere as the wind blew across the sky, carrying ribbons of black satin into the trees. Emma didn't move, holding perfectly still, watching him with her wary gaze. Her eyes were greener. Her skin softer. Her body nearly glowing and so hot it was all he could do not to throw her onto the hood of the car and bury his body in hers.

The change had him in its grip now, his body contorting, bones, sinew and tendons popping and cracking. He couldn't stop it. He screamed silently, terrified for her. "Get in the car. Get out of here." He tried to speak, to save her from the cat's jealous fury, but his voice was already gone, coming out a growl instead of words. His knuckles turned, claws bursting from his fingertips. He tried to tear off his shirt. Already his body was bending, going to the ground. His shoes hurt, the seams bursting as he fell.

Emma should have been running screaming from him, but she went to the ground with him, pulling at his shoes, dragging the shirt from him. The leopard, more prominent than the man, scented the drug in her system. Despair spread like lightning. She'd been drugged—almost raped– and he'd been like an animal, clawing and raking at her instead of pulling her into his arms and holding her, comforting her. He'd been at fault, failing in his protection of her. Now his leopard was bursting free in front of her, his teeth sharp, his temper ferocious.

Please. Emma. Honey. For God's sake. Get in the car. He tried to tell her, tried to shove her away from him, but his vocal cords weren't working.

He didn't know if he could fight the leopard for her. He'd hurt Drake, raking him with his claws, tearing open his chest. Drake had never said a word of recrimination, but Jake would never forget the sight of his friend with the mark of the leopard striped across his chest.

Emma tore at his trousers, dragging them down his legs so he could kick them aside. He breathed deeply, holding off as long as he could, trying to give her time. His claws raked long strips of dirt from the ground. He felt fur rippling over his skin and groaned with the effort to hold back. It was too late, far too late.

Emma! He cried out her name in his mind, pleading with the leopard to get away from her.

Emma sat on the ground, her back to the tire of the car, exhausted, Jake's clothes scattered all around her. A few remnants of her dress lay on the ground. She was clothed in only her panties, garter and torn stockings. She'd lost her shoes when Jake had pulled her out of the car. Her nipples were tight buds due to the cold air, her breasts bare. She watched him change, the large man in the throes of shifting, his bones re-forming, his muzzle lengthening and filling with teeth, his eyes glowing and wild, fixed on her.

The leopard, fully formed, stepped forward, thrusting its face into hers, its breath hot on her skin, one huge paw on her shoulder, claws digging into her. The huge cat snarled, scenting the other male. He rasped his tongue over Emma's face and rubbed along her body with his cheeks and his scent glands to warn the other male off. She pulled back to look him in the eye, her green eyes glittering, his golden gaze furious. They stared at each other until she buried her fingers into the lush fur coat and pushed him away from her.

"Go away, Jake. I'm really upset with you right now." Her voice sounded odd, far away. She clutched the fur tighter, but her fingers slipped. The ground tilted. She slid down the wheel of the car and found herself staring up at the leopard's fur-lined belly. Her lashes fluttered, her lids too heavy to keep up.

The leopard nuzzled her as she closed her eyes and gave in to the drug.

16

EMMA woke slowly, her mouth dry, jackhammers drilling through her temples. She burrowed into the warmth surrounding her before she realized Jake was rocking her in the large chair he'd brought to her room a year earlier when Andraya was born. He liked to sit in the chair and rock Kyle, feeding him his bottle while she fed Andraya.

"I don't like you very much," she murmured, keeping her eyes closed. The room was dark, the house silent. His chest was bare beneath her cheek.

"I know you don't," he answered softly. "Go back to sleep. The doctor said you'd have a headache and would probably feel like a truck ran you over."

Mostly she felt exhausted. It shocked her a little that he'd brought in a doctor and she hadn't even roused from the drug enough to know. "You should have been thinking about me, Jake, not yourself. That was a terrifying experience. That man would have raped me. Maybe all of them."

He nuzzled the top of her head. "I wasn't thinking like a man, Emma. That's no excuse, but it is the truth."

"My mother was leopard, Jake. There was no difference

between her and her leopard, and there shouldn't be with you either. You use your leopard as an excuse."

He smiled at the little bite in her voice and briefly buried his face in her hair again. "You should have told me about your mother."

"Why? How? It isn't exactly normal. You didn't tell me." Emma passed a hand over her face. Her arm still felt like lead.

"You weren't afraid or even shocked when I shifted."

"I lived with you for two years, Jake. Did you think I wouldn't see the claw marks on the floors and walls, especially in your office? Did you think I wouldn't know what you were doing the nights you went running and came back with your clothes shredded? Or the time your mother—the enemy," she corrected herself, "came and you left fresh marks on the floor in the nursery and punctured your own palms? I lived with my mother for nineteen years. It's not like I couldn't read the signs or smell the cat. If you didn't want to tell me, I wasn't going to bring it up."

"And your family had been hunted. You didn't entirely trust me—or anyone else," Jake prompted, knowing it was the truth.

She shrugged and lifted her head up, for the first time opening her eyes. His eyes were still a cat's eyes, glowing red in the dark. "You have to admit, it was a big coincidence, my mother being a leopard, our family hunted and eventually killed, and then you bringing me here. Drake. Joshua. Conner. Aside from my mother, I'd never met a single leopard until I met you. I had to know what you wanted."

At least she hadn't run from him. She'd had the courage to stay, giving him a chance to prove himself even though she had to know there was a possibility he had ulterior motives. "And Trent and the enemy told you, no doubt." His voice held a note of bitterness. He knew they wouldn't resist planting seeds of doubt in her mind.

"They told me what they wanted me to believe. And I know what they wanted, that was made very clear. Me. A cub from me. They think I might be a shifter, or at least be able to produce one for them. They think one will give them an advantage in the oil fields, but I doubt if all shifters can scent oil in the ground or they'd be doing it already. They want me to believe that's the only thing you want from me as well, that and to prevent them from having me." She looked at him. "I thought it strange that they didn't even realize what a sense of entitlement they have, believing they have the right to buy people, that somehow they are superior to the rest of us."

"All this time, it was a game to me, the enemies, pitting themselves against me," Jake admitted. "I thought they were after an unknown oil field or natural gas reserve. I knew they wanted a shifter of their own to control, but even though I was certain you had the bloodline, it didn't occur to me you were what they were after all along. The real estate offer was to throw me, make me look in other directions, and I fell for it."

"Then you did know about me?" Her voice held a hint of wariness.

"Not until recently, until you began to . . . blossom. The female development is difficult to pinpoint. No one knows what brings out their leopard, or their first heat."

"I'm not a shifter. I have the blood and can feel things, smell things, but I don't have a leopard." She sounded regretful.

"Maybe it just hasn't come out yet," he said, brushing his mouth over the top of her head. Jake smoothed back her silky hair with gentle fingers.

"The thing is, Jake, you're nothing like them, no matter what you think of yourself. I've lived with you too long for you to hide that from me. You aren't anything at all like those people." Her eyes locked with his. "Whatever you think about the blood running in your veins, believe me, I have firsthand knowledge, and you're nothing like them."

"I used you as bait," he said, hating himself.

"We needed to see what they were after, to protect our family—the children. I go into things with my eyes open, Jake."

His heart contracted. "Well, close them now. Go back to sleep, honey. We can talk in the morning."

Emma snuggled deeper into his arms, surprised how safe she felt. She let herself drift, aware of his strength, his even breathing, the gentle motion of the rocking chair. When next she woke, they were on her bed, the covers over them, his body wrapped tightly around hers. She could feel the pads of his fingers stroking along her ribs, gently, back and forth.

"Jake?" She said his name in inquiry. It seemed so much easier to face him in the dark. "Thanks for rescuing me."

He kissed her bare shoulder. "You did a pretty good job of rescuing yourself."

"They told me that my father is Trent's nephew and that he took a great deal of money from Trent to bring back a female shifter. He lured my mother back to the States. They said he planned to sell her to Trent, that he'd already taken their money."

"He married her and kept her safe."

"But I think they were telling the truth, Jake," she said, her heart beating too fast. "I think he was bringing her back with the intention of handing her over to them, but changed his mind. What does that say about him? That he would consider selling a woman to his uncle?"

"Honey, you can't let them taint your memories of your parents. You said they loved each other. That they loved you. Whatever mistakes your father made as a young man, growing up in that family with the kind of upbringing he would have had, he overcame it. Trent was worse than the enemies. I know he was. Your father must have been punished in the same way I was for not being what they wanted."

She was silent for a long time. "Jake? When I woke up, you looked very scary. What were you thinking about?"

He groaned and rolled over. "Why do you have to ask me questions like that when I don't want to tell you the answer?"

Emma smiled in the darkness. His body wasn't in its normal hard-as-a-rock state. He was upset; she could feel that his introspection distressed him. "Just tell me."

"I always look my worst in front of you." His voice sounded strained. "I don't think I can really afford to look any worse than I already do. Let it go this time."

She rolled over to look at him. She had excellent night vision and he looked strained, ravaged. She pressed her fingertips to his face, tracing the lines there. "Tell me anyway. So far I haven't run from you."

He caught her fingers and kissed them, holding them to his mouth. "But you should have, Emma. You were right, you know, about last night. I thought a lot about what you said. I *was* thinking only of me. Of my cat's rage and the scent of another man on your skin. I didn't hold you, or comfort you, or even check to see if they had hurt you. I didn't give you a chance to talk to me. I don't understand how you can even look at me."

"You have a fast learning curve, Jake. How can you expect to know how to react to something when you've never been shown the right way? Not everything is instinct."

"My cat's reaction is instinctive."

She smiled at him. "You are your cat. Your cat is protective, and so are you. He's strong. So are you. Whatever is inside of you is inside your cat. You aren't separate, Jake. You're one and the same."

He was silent for a long time, his teeth scraping back

and forth on the tips of her fingers. "What you're really saying is that my leopard is a convenience for me to blame all my worst traits on."

"Possibly. I know what my mother was like. Yes, she had a temper and she could be jealous and possessive, but she didn't let it rule her. Your leopard is still you. If you aren't separate, you have to accept that part of you."

"You sound like Drake now." He rolled onto his back, taking her hand with him. "There are so many animal traits not to like, Emma. I don't like that possibility."

"But there are so many to like," she pointed out.

"I was lying here watching you sleep and planning to kill them—the enemies. I should have killed them a long time ago. Is that normal? Is that something people do? How they think? Is that me, or my leopard?"

"You and your leopard are one in the same. You're more aggressive than the average man, but that just means you need to have stronger control. Of course you want to eliminate any threat to your family. Some people might think about killing someone, but they don't actually do it. That's one of those unacceptable things you don't ever do if it's possible to avoid it."

"No one else is going to stop them. They'll keep coming at us." His hand slid over her hair. "I don't honestly know what I'd do if something happened to you."

"You'd take care of our children." She propped herself up on her elbows and pushed back the dark fall of hair spilling across his forehead. "That's what you'd do, Jake."

His hand came up to the nape of her neck. She could feel his body trembling as he pulled her head down to his so he could find her mouth. His kiss tasted of tears. Of love. Of everything he couldn't say aloud. He was tender, incredibly gentle.

"You're so beautiful, Emma. And I don't mean physically, although you're that too. I don't know where you came from, but it wasn't anywhere here on this earth."

She laid her head on his chest, listening to his heart. "I've got leopard blood running in my veins, Jake. Believe me, I have the same bad temper and jealous streak that you do."

"I feel lost tonight," he whispered, holding her to him there in the dark.

"It's all right," she said softly. "I'm here and I won't let anything happen to you." She closed her eyes and let herself relax against his body.

"Mommy?" Both turned their heads toward the door, where Kyle stood uncertainly. "I'm afraid."

They both held out a hand simultaneously. "Come here, son," Jake encouraged. Kyle climbed onto the bed and Jake tucked him between them. "There's nothing to be afraid of. You're safe."

"Daddy?" Andraya took her brother's place in the doorway. She'd either seen Kyle coming out of his room, or he'd awakened her to accompany him, which was more likely.

Jake uttered a soft groan and beckoned her, his smile widening when he looked at Emma. Andraya crawled over her father and, ignoring Kyle, wedged herself in the middle, wiggling until she found a comfortable position. Jake put his arm around all of them—his family—and lay back, his fingers tangling with Emma's, remembering that it wasn't that long ago that he was completely alone in his house. Now, they could barely fit in the bed.

"We'll have to have another one to fill this space over here on my side," Jake said, patting the only bare spot he could find.

Emma's fingers tightened around his. "We'll have to get a bigger bed."

Jake fell asleep first and Emma watched him, sleeping

like their children. He didn't look younger, only more relaxed. Her heart ached for him. He was struggling to become the man she knew he wanted to be, but he fought it
every step of the way, terrified of being vulnerable. She
could have told him it was already too late, that he was already there, but she knew he had to come to that realization on his own—not just in a moment in the middle of the
night when it was dark and he didn't have to look her in the
eye. He had to accept that he knew how to love all of them.
Her. The children. Their life together.

She drifted off, dreaming of her mother and the way
Emma had always wanted to run with her. She loved it
when her mother would assume her animal form and she
could lie next to her, fingers tangled in her fur, feeling the
extraordinary pleasure of being so close to something wild
and powerful. Her father wasn't a shifter, and the odds
were against her ever being like her mother. At least she had
Jake and she could rub her face in his fur and get her fix that
way.

Emma woke to the sound of laughter and several whispering voices. Conspiracy hung heavy in the air. She turned
her head and saw them all lined up. The ones she loved.
Jake, between Kyle and Andraya. He held a tray and they
each carried a flower. She sat up. Jake grinned at her as the
sheet slipped, revealing the curve of her breast, and she was
forced to yank it up quickly. He set the tray down and
handed her a shirt from her closet. It was a button-down,
and she hastily put it on, doing up the buttons under his
amused gaze.

"We made breakfast, Mommy," Kyle announced.

Andraya nodded. "Breakfast," she echoed.

"It looks great," Emma said. "Thank you so much."
Jake set the tray on her lap and she tried not to look dis-
mayed at the strange mixture that looked like it might have
eggs in it. "Did you two cook?"

Kyle nodded solemnly. "Daddy helped."

"And he let you choose what you wanted to put in Mommy's eggs?" Emma watched Jake's face. He'd had fun. He'd learned to have fun, spending the morning with his children, letting them mix the ingredients into her eggs. She could see the lines of strain had eased and imagined him with the children on chairs, hunched over a mixing bowl, and Jake laughing to himself.

"They were very certain of what goes into a breakfast scramble," Jake said, trying to look innocent. He failed miserably.

Emma's heart melted at the mischievous joy in his eyes. He had never learned the art of teasing, yet here he was, two little chubby hands clutching his, all three faces beaming at her.

"Aren't you hungry?" Kyle asked anxiously.

"I was just thinking Daddy should share this with Mommy," Emma said, holding out a spoonful of the egg mixture.

Both children looked at Jake expectantly. He stared at the gooey mess like it might bite him. "Daddy ate, remember?"

"You're always hungry and the children did such a good job," Emma countered.

"You have a mean streak in you," Jake observed, perching on the edge of the bed. "I'm going to retaliate, you know." Reluctantly he took the spoon from her.

"I think I'm pretty safe," Emma said, knowing his retaliations tended to be sexual. She smirked at him as the children watched him reluctantly put the spoon into his mouth.

She held out the glass of orange juice as he swallowed so he could wash it down. Jake choked a little, smiled at the children and raised his voice. "Susan. Could you see if the nurse is here to watch the children while Emma showers?"

He had that black velvet voice that insinuated all sorts of erotic things. Susan came running and caught each child by a hand. "I'll take them downstairs." She blushed to the roots of her hair, obviously thinking Jake wanted to be alone with Emma.

"You can't eat this stuff," Jake said as soon as Andraya and Kyle were gone. "You'll be sick for a week." He took the tray from Emma and set it aside.

She started to get out of bed but he stopped her, taking her hand. "I want to get married."

Emma looked up at him startled. "We just got engaged."

"I'm aware of that, Emma, but we have two children. Let's just get it done. I can get us a license immediately and we can get a judge here and just do it. By the way, I have the papers for you to sign for the adoption."

Emma pulled her hand away and shoved the covers back, rolling away from him to the other side of the bed where she had a robe. She couldn't think straight being nearly naked with him fully dressed. There was something too erotic about the way his eyes brushed over her skin and heated her body. Her brain just refused to function. She wasn't going to say yes just because she wanted sex—and she did want sex. Just looking at him filled her with love.

He was so lost. He'd admitted it to her. He fought himself over the growing feelings he had for her. She knew he wanted to keep his emotions in check and regard her and the children the way he did his possessions. His. He cared for them, protected them, provided the best for them, but he didn't invest his heart. The problem was, Jake didn't know himself very well. He cared for the people working for him. He cared for Drake and Joshua and every other lame duck he'd brought home. And he loved Andraya and Kyle. In his eyes, when he held her, in his voice when he talked to her in the middle of the night, Emma saw and heard that he loved her. He might not recognize it, but she did.

"Emma, stop stalling. How hard can it be just to say yes? Why wouldn't we?"

"You're like a gazillionaire, Jake. You need a prenuptial to protect you. That takes time to put in place, especially when you have the money and property and companies you have."

His eyebrow shot up. "Did Stillman contact you?" he asked suspiciously.

Emma shrugged, trying to look casual. "I contacted him."

He stood up, towering over her, looking incredibly intimidating. Emma refused to step back, looking up at him, refusing to be sorry for doing what she felt was right.

"You did what?"

"It was important to me to protect you," Emma said quietly.

"No."

Emma swept past him, heading for the bathroom, her nerve breaking at the muscle ticking in his jaw. Jake caught her arm, abruptly halting her.

"I'm not discussing this with you, Jake," she said, pressing her lips tightly together.

"No, I'll be discussing this with Stillman. I don't want a prenuptial. It's going to be difficult enough without you thinking we're not on equal footing. Whatever I have is yours. I meant what I said when we first talked marriage. I don't believe in divorce. This is it for us. We do it, and we find a way to live with it."

Her heart jumped. "Jake, try being just a little romantic about marriage instead of being ruthless. You sound like you're threatening me instead of proposing."

He caught her chin and tipped up her face. "I've tried never to lie to you, about what I am inside or how difficult I can be. I have every confidence that I'll do my best for you, but I'm also very aware I'll want everything my way.

You're sweet and kind, Emma, and I'm likely to take advantage of that and walk all over you if you let me. I want the playing field leveled so you never feel as if I have the advantages all on my side."

She shook her head. "Your logic is so elusive, Jake."

"I plan on having a half dozen more kids with you. Why? To keep you right here, on this ranch, so there's no place you can run to. That's my kind of logic, Emma."

"You're supposed to have children because you want them, Jake," she pointed out, exasperated. "Not to keep me occupied so I won't run away."

"I want them because you're going to love them. I want to watch you love them. I want to watch that look come over your face whenever you look at them. I want to hear the sound of your voice, that special note you have reserved just for them. I could live forever listening to you talk to the children." He couldn't tell her what it did to him inside. Made him soft. Happy. Stupidly happy. She scared the hell out of him the way she made him happy.

"Jake, someday you have to realize I'm staying with you because I want to stay with you. You only think you manipulated me. I knew what you were doing all along. I stay because I love you . . ."

"*If* there's such a thing as love, Emma, and I'm not saying there is, I trapped you into loving me."

She burst out laughing, threw her arms around him and hugged him tight, lifting her mouth to his and kissing him in a long, leisurely kiss.

As he held her to him, his heart did that curious melting thing that always alarmed him. He couldn't have this. He couldn't be like this with her. She was taking him over and making him so vulnerable he could barely breathe with the way he felt about her. He had to find a way to establish his dominance and take the control back.

He set her firmly aside, trying not to show his breathing was ragged and forced. "No prenuptial, Emma. Let's just get the thing done."

"The thing? Meaning our wedding? You're such a romantic, Jake. Go away. You're annoying me again and I was just feeling all loving toward you."

It was obvious to her that Jake, along with having the doctor check her, had scrubbed her skin in an effort to remove the scent of the other man. She couldn't blame him; as a leopard he was highly sensitive to what he would regard as the stench of another male. But now her skin felt raw in a few places.

Of course he didn't leave because she'd told him to do so. He watched her dress, heaving a sigh when she put on a bra.

"Why do you have to wear that?"

"Because I don't want my body to break down as I get older. And I'm not a sex object for you to drool over all day. I've got work to do."

"What's wrong with being both? I like the idea of you being a sex object while you work." His voice held sensual speculation and a little too much interest.

Emma frowned at him and hastily finished, clipping her hair up out of the way.

"You know I like your hair down."

"Which is why I don't cut it. Be happy with that. You try having hair down to your butt, getting in your way while you're taking care of children." She scooted past him. "I'm giving you an assignment today, Jake. Look up the meaning of the word *romance*."

"I'm romantic." He followed her down the stairs. "Ask Susan. She'll tell you."

Emma paused by the window in the small breakfast nook where she'd left her day watch. She'd taken it off when she was dressing for the party the night before. "Susan is sixteen and her hormones are running amok. She thinks you're hot."

"I am hot. You should listen to her more."

The window was open and the faint smell of skunk made her wrinkle her nose. "Isn't this the wrong time of year for skunks to be hanging around under the house? It smells like one sprayed outside." She closed the window to shut out the odor. "I think I'll put some potpourri in here."

"Too much information for me," Jake said with a small laugh. "It's your house, honey. Do whatever you want to do with it. I'm going to be working all day in my office, hopefully without the smell of skunk or potpourri, but I might need you later." Jake gave her a wicked smile, his golden eyes sensual as he patted her on the butt.

"Anytime," Emma agreed, her body growing hot at the thought as she slapped at his hand. There was something about him that could turn up her temperature in a matter of minutes.

"Susan." Jake beckoned the teen to follow him as the girl came around the corner. "I wanted to show you the library."

"I didn't know you had a library," Susan said, fascinated. She followed him down the long hall, past the closed doors that led to the wing of his private offices. "I've never even come into this part of the house. I stay upstairs or in the rooms with Emma."

Jake opened the double doors to the huge room. Behind him, Susan gasped as she took in the floor-to-ceiling bookcases, and the ladder on rollers that ran along all four walls on a track. "You're welcome to use this anytime. You're extremely intelligent and you can be anything you choose to be. It doesn't matter if your father is home a lot or not. You're welcome here. I've got a tutor coming for you and a self-defense instructor. If you need anything else, let me know. But this . . ." His hand swept around in a semicircle to encompass the entire room. "This is my sanctuary. This is where I learned to survive."

"I love books," Susan said.

"I keep the library up-to-date. If you need anything on any subject and you can't find it in here, don't hesitate to ask me. Everything is cataloged. And there are computers for you to use as well. I have a library of videos as well."

"Jake. I can't believe this. Thank you." Susan stepped inside and did a little hop and skip, rushing to one side of the room to examine the book titles in the history section.

"Don't neglect any subject. It's amazing what knowledge can do for you."

She pulled out a large book and opened it, her gaze scanning the pages. "I love books," she repeated. "I had no idea you had this library."

"Susan." Jake went back to the door and paused until she looked up at him. "Never let anyone make you think you're less than you are. Very few people have your gift for languages. You have a quick mind and a sweet nature. People may want to make you feel small or put you down to build themselves up. That's their problem, not yours."

Susan nodded her head, clasping the book to her chest.

"And I want you to learn self-defense. Emma can join you for the lessons. You may need them someday."

Susan nodded again, her eyes sparkling. "Thanks, Jake."

"I'm heading for my office. If you need anything, use the intercom."

Susan waited until he had disappeared before running down the hall to find Emma to tell her everything.

"Self-defense lessons? A tutor? Does he think he gets to keep you?"

Susan hugged herself. "He made me feel like part of the family." She blinked rapidly to keep back tears. "I haven't felt like that since my mother died. Dad is always gone and I am so lonely. I don't go to a regular school and I don't really have anyone at home. Dad hires different people, but it isn't the same."

Emma hugged her. "Well, you know Jake. If he claims you, he watches over you. You won't be so grateful when you want to start dating."

"Maybe I could date some of your bodyguards. I really like them."

"Maybe you could just forget about that," Emma said. "I promised the kids they could play on the swings. You want to go with us?" She activated the small radio transmitter she had set into her watch so that she could alert Drake that she was leaving the house with the children.

"If you really don't mind, I want to look around the library. It's enormous," Susan said.

Emma didn't blame her. Pushing two demanding children on the swings wasn't a teenager's idea of a dream afternoon. She called Kyle and Andraya to her and they hurried out to follow the path to the side of the house where the elaborate play yard Jake had built for them was located.

The air was cool, the wind blowing, but the play yard was protected and Emma had them bundled in their sweaters. Kyle ran to the slide and Andraya reached up her arms to be put into the baby swing. Emma carefully snapped the safety belt around her and pushed her while she squealed with delight. Kyle called out to her over and over, making certain he was getting his share of attention.

Emma was surprised their constant bodyguard didn't show up immediately. They were usually very prompt, but both children were being good so she didn't radio a second time, not wanting anyone to get into trouble for not moving fast enough.

"Mommy, look!" Kyle pointed to the corner of the house where the gardener had planted tall, grassy plants. She especially liked the varieties there and Kyle and Andraya loved to play in the mini-jungle.

"What, baby?" she asked, not seeing anything but the waves of grass as the wind played through the plants.

Kyle gave her a stern look. "I not a baby. I'm Kyle," he announced firmly.

Emma looked contrite. "Yes, of course you're Kyle." His identity meant a lot to him.

He went down the slide again, watching the grass intently. Emma did her best to see what interested him, but it was impossible to tell whether it was the play of the wind, the tall variegated grasses of various colors or some shiny rock on the ground.

Andraya kicked her feet and yelled again. "More. More."

Emma pushed her higher. Andraya wiggled around in her seat, laughing out loud. Emma looked back over at Kyle to find he had slipped off the slide and was just entering the tall field of grasses.

"Wait, Kyle," she called and pushed the radio button again. She hurried after him.

Of course he didn't wait, disappearing into the thick, tall plants. Emma glanced back at Andraya and ran after Kyle, calling his name as she hurried after him. She caught a glimpse of his shirt as he wove his way through the grass. Kyle crouched low, following something.

"Kyle, I mean it. Stop. What are you following?"

The wind shifted slightly and for a moment she thought she smelled cat. Her heart stuttered. Her breath caught in her lungs. Terror shifted through her. The scent filling her nostrils was the same as that of the man who had assaulted her the night before—Rory. She would never forget his smell.

"Kyle!" She began to run. The wind picked up, blowing directly in her face. The scent of skunk hit her hard, obliterating the stench of her assailant. "Don't touch anything. Come back here now."

As she ran she stabbed at the radio again. Where the

hell was everyone? "Evan! Drake!" There was a note of hysteria in her voice. She caught another glimpse of Kyle and she put on a burst of speed. He didn't even look up at the sound of her voice. Just ahead of him, sliding into the jungle of grasses, was a small furry animal. As her fingers skimmed the back of his shirt, Andraya screamed, a long, high-pitched shriek that sent goose bumps rising on her flesh.

She snagged Kyle's shirt and jerked him to an abrupt halt, ignoring his wails of protest. Scooping him up into her arms, Emma turned back on the run, afraid of leaving Andraya out of her sight even for a short moment. Kyle fought, squirming, going boneless, determined to get back to the little creature he was so interested in.

As she burst from the grass she saw Evan running toward Andraya. Tears streamed down the little girl's face. She held out her hands to Evan and he pulled her from the swing, forgetting, in his haste, to undo the seat belt so that he had to unsnap it while he held the sobbing child to him. "Why the hell didn't you radio us that you were coming out of the house?"

She glared at him as she skidded to a halt beside him, still wrestling Kyle. "I did call you, several times. You didn't come." Her heart still thundered in her ears. The smell of the cat had long since been drowned in the skunk's odor, but she couldn't get it out of her mind. Her stomach churned. "Call Drake and Joshua. And Jake. Call Jake."

She couldn't stop shaking. Evan regarded her with a puzzled look, but he obediently radioed the others before holding out his hand for her watch. "Let me take a look. Something must be wrong."

Emma didn't move, just stood there, frozen to the spot, until Jake came out, striding toward her, looking invincible, a tower of safety. She handed Kyle off to Joshua as he arrived and flung herself into Jake's arms, bursting into tears.

Jake looked to his men for an explanation and all of them shook their heads. "Joshua, take the children inside. The nurse will be showing up soon. Stay in the playroom until she arrives and then watch over them until we're back to normal. Kyle! Go with Joshua and behave yourself or you'll be in your room on time-out."

Kyle ceased struggling immediately and went with Joshua. Andraya stopped crying the minute Jake sounded stern. Both children wrapped their arms around Joshua's neck as he carried them back up to the house.

Jake brought both hands up to Emma's back and rubbed soothingly. "You've got to tell us what's going on."

"Her radio didn't work," Evan offered. "I heard Andraya scream and came running. I didn't see Emma or Kyle until she came bursting out of the grass. She told me she'd radioed for me, but I never got the call."

"He was here, Jake." Emma looked up at him. "I know he was. The one from last night. I smelled him, but then Kyle was chasing a skunk and I could only smell the skunk, but I'm sure . . ." Now she wasn't so sure. Maybe she was paranoid. Maybe the trauma and the aftereffects of the drug were playing tricks on her.

"We'll check," Drake assured. "I'll call Conner. He can track anything."

Jake took a careful look around, then escorted Emma back to the kitchen, putting her into a chair and making her a cup of tea while they waited. He sat across from her, holding her hand, his thumb gently sliding back and forth over her wrist.

The radio crackled. "No leopard tracks, Jake. Skunk tracks. Conner found the den, but the skunk is gone. No odor of a cat anywhere, Jake."

Emma hung her head, wrapping her hands tightly around the teacup. "I must be paranoid. I'm sorry, Jake."

"Don't be sorry, Emma. You've been through hell and you have every right to be upset."

"Even without the stupid leopard man prowling around, the skunk could have sprayed Kyle, or worse, what if it had rabies? I should have been more careful."

Jake wrapped his arm around her. "Nothing happened, Emma. Kyle's fine, and so is Andraya. You're just shaken after last night. The nurse is here today and can help inside the house and they'll play in the playroom where you know they're both safe."

"Stop calling her the nurse. She has a name. Brenda. And I can't believe you've gotten her to come here when she isn't even a pediatric nurse. You're so spoiled, Jake." The minute the words escaped she covered her mouth, horrified at the bite in her voice, horrified that she sounded so bitchy with him.

"I don't like strangers in my home. She's been around a couple of years now and she knows how we do things around here. She likes the kids and she's good company for you."

"I know, I'm sorry. I'm not myself this morning. I need . . . I don't know what I need. Anything could have happened to Kyle. He could have gone down to the stables, Jake. One of the horses could have kicked him."

"But nothing happened. You grabbed him before he got too far. Parents have scares all the time. I've been reading about it in one of the parenting books I have."

She looked up at him, startled. "You're reading a parenting book?"

He looked sheepish. "How else am I ever going to figure this out? Things keep changing as they get older. It used to be I could just pick them up and hold them and they were happy. Now I have to do things. I don't have a clue what makes a kid happy."

Emma pressed her lips to his chin. "You're awesome sometimes."

He leaned toward her, his gaze holding hers. "You know you could be shifter like your mother, right? Have you thought about that? You're giving off the scent, very potent, of a woman in her first heat."

She wrinkled her nose. "That doesn't sound good. Are you saying I stink?"

He rubbed his shadowed jaw. "I wish. The scent is very alluring to males. *All* leopard males, whether they can shift or not. Drake, Joshua and Conner have a difficult time being close to you now. And I'm ready to lose my mind over it."

"Really?" She knew she didn't sound as upset as she should. Sometimes she felt something wild inside, and she often hoped there was the presence of a cat, but she doubted it. On the other hand, she didn't mind in the least being alluring to Jake.

"I'm going back to work," he said, frowning at her. "I can see you're not a bit sorry for making me as hard as a rock."

"Not really, no." She smiled up at him.

"You're going to be taking care of it," he warned.

She nodded her head. "I'll be looking forward to this evening."

17

<hr/>

THE ache in his body invaded his mind for the millionth time. He couldn't concentrate. There was just no way. He dropped his hand to his lap and rubbed in an effort to alleviate the burning tightness. If he grew any thicker, he was going to burst right out of his skin. He'd been fantasizing more than working, wishing Emma was in his office with him instead of just outside his door, somewhere in the house with the kids.

Was she thinking about him? Did she hurt the way he did? He could only hope that she was. He wanted to occupy most of her thoughts and found himself a little jealous of her spending so much time with everyone else. He rarely had her to himself, and when he did, his emotions got in the way. He tapped his pencil idly on the desktop. There had to be a way to seal her to him. Yes, he could keep her pregnant, but that didn't mean her loyalty would be to him. He had to find another means.

Again his hand fell to the thick, throbbing length of him. He was so engorged he was afraid he might split his trousers, and he sure as hell wasn't going to make it until the evening. He had many women and none sated him the way she did. He didn't crave their soft skin, or want their bodies wrapped around his. It was as if his body knew hers, remembered hers from another life. Maybe all the nonsense Drake told him was more truth than legend, but whatever the reason, his body was tied to Emma's body.

He knew a million sexual tricks, ways to make any woman want more, crave more, become obsessed. If he could get her to go along with him while he trained her body, she'd always need him. She'd be bound to him completely.

He rubbed his jaw for a long moment and then dropped his face into his hands. He didn't know what was right anymore. He only knew that he couldn't live without her and he couldn't live with being so emotionally vulnerable to her. Somehow, some way, he had to get the upper hand. He had to take it back, return their relationship to a footing he could deal with.

EMMA took several different types of lettuce from the refrigerator, trying to ignore the building tension in her body. Her body temperature was going up; she could feel the heat radiating off her, coming from her very core. She was hot and aching and needy, and getting moodier by the moment. She was slick and inflamed, the dampness between her legs keeping her on edge. She'd snapped at Brenda when she brought the children in for a snack. They sat in their high chairs eating, as she began to make the preparations for dinner.

There wouldn't be any eating for her. She was tempted to try a cold shower.

"Emma." Jake's voice was quiet on the intercom.

She glanced up automatically, although it was just his voice and not his body. A note in his voice. Soft. Sexy.

Commanding. Her body tightened even more in instant response, flooding with more heat. She was going to have to ask him to install fans throughout the house. "Yes?" He was up to something, she was certain of it.

"Get Brenda to handle the kids for two hours and come into my office. Ten minutes."

She hesitated but he had already clicked off. She could instantly feel the difference in her body, arousal teasing along her thighs and centering deep so that she pulsed with need. Just from his voice. He scared her sometimes, the way he controlled her body. Just his voice changing had such an effect on her nerve endings.

She looked around the kitchen at the preparations she'd begun for dinner. Ten minutes. She couldn't get things done in ten minutes. She radioed Joshua, alerting him that she would not be with the children and he needed to come in and be present in the house with Brenda. She put everything away, but she was finished long before he arrived. Andraya and Kyle stayed in their chairs, eating their snacks while she worked. It took a few minutes to get them settled down with Brenda and Joshua before she felt she could safely leave them.

She knocked on the door of the office and stepped inside. Jake was working at his desk. The office was spacious, the entire wing soundproofed so that once she closed the door, she could no longer hear the sound of the children. Her painting hung on the wall opposite his desk. Jake didn't look up.

"You're late."

"Two minutes, Jake. It isn't all that easy to settle children down."

He still didn't look up, studying the papers before him. "I didn't ask you to settle them down, I asked you to come into my office in ten minutes. Joshua is capable of settling them down."

He was going to be difficult. She stayed silent, waiting, refusing to make any more excuses or rise to the bait. Minutes ticked by. When he looked up, his eyes had that glitter to them, somewhere between menace and pure lust. A fireball hit the pit of her stomach.

"Lock the door and take off your clothes, fold them and put them on the chair by the fireplace."

Excitement spread through her, but she didn't allow it to show. She studied his face. The lines etched there. The set of his jaw. The dark lust and intensity of his focus. She kept him waiting a full minute before she kicked off her house sandals and slowly began to unbutton her blouse. When the material parted, she shrugged it off and took her time folding it. Carefully she set it on the chair, reaching behind her to unhook her bra.

"Turn around and face me." Now there was a harsh rasp to the velvet of his voice.

Emma turned and looked at him, waiting a few heartbeats before she complied, then slowly slid the straps of her bra down to allow the cups to fall into her waiting hands. Her breasts were so much fuller after she'd had the baby. She heard his swift intake of breath and saw his eyes narrow, become hooded. His gaze burned over her, brushing her nipples into hard peaks, arousing her further.

Deep inside, she felt that something primitive that always seemed to rise when Jake was like this. She inhaled, the action lifting her breasts as she dragged the scent of his arousal into her lungs. Wildness unfurled, clawing at her, until she wanted, even needed, to bring up her hands and cup her own breasts as an offering, to allow her fingers to drift below to the slick, wet center of her where she throbbed and pulsed with emptiness.

"Slide off your skirt and panties and fold them too."

The material hurt her skin anyway. Something moved just below the surface like a wave of desire, itching, moving fast through her body to collect between her legs, scorching hot and aching. She took her time, wanting to entice him, to bring him to the edge of his control, when he was so sure of himself and so sure of her.

Deliberately she turned her back to him, giving him a good view of her backside as she padded across the hardwood floor to the chair and added her skirt and underwear to the pile of clothes there. She turned slowly, her hair swinging around her, cascading down her back to the curve of her hip, feeling silky and sensuous against her bare skin.

"Come here and undress me." His voice rasped even more.

He was already barefoot in anticipation of carrying out his fantasy, and she couldn't fail to see the thick, hard length in the front of his slacks.

Emma walked over to him, her breasts swinging gently, and reached up to unbutton his shirt, pushing it off his shoulders to neatly fold it and take it to the chair without being told.

"Kneel this time."

She returned to the position in front of him and dropped to her knees, reaching for his belt buckle, knowing the picture she made, knowing she was making him harder each time she complied with his orders. The experience was making her more moist than ever, more ready for him. Her knuckles deliberately brushed over his thickened shaft several times, while she opened his trousers and pulled them and his underwear from his hips. At eye level, his erection was intimidating, thick and long and angry looking as it burst free from the confines of his clothing.

Emma folded his trousers and took them to the chair.

"Get up on my desk, Emma, on your hands and knees."

"Jake . . ." Emma glanced at the door, a faint frown on her face.

"On the desk. Don't look at the door. Look at me."

Her gaze locked with his and immediately was held captive. She moistened her lips and slowly climbed onto his desk, ending up on all fours. There was something very sensual about kneeling on top of his desk, her body on display for him as he walked around, looking at her from every angle, inspecting her as if she were his prized possession.

"Knees apart for me." She had the most beautiful ass. Round. Firm. Her skin rose-petal soft. "Farther, Emma." His voice went husky. He caressed her bottom with his palm, rubbing her satin skin. "You're so beautiful. I could look at you all day."

Jake continued to walk slowly around his desk, his breath coming in a ragged rush at the sight she made. She was beautiful, like a sleek cat. She reminded him of one, her movements graceful, sensuous, fluid even, the muscles sliding under her silky soft skin. Her hair hung down in a heavy fall of red waves. Her breasts were beautiful, the nipples erect, begging for his attention. And her bottom. He couldn't stop his hand from stroking her smooth buttocks, the heart-stopping shape that drew his gaze like a magnet.

He rubbed for a moment, enjoying the feel of her skin, smooth as silk, soft as a rose petal. Deliberately he brought his hand down hard on the smooth skin and then rubbed the reddening spot with tender caresses before repeating the action a second time. "That's two, Emma, for the two minutes you were late getting here."

She hissed, an animalistic sound of hostility, turning her head to glare at him. "Is this supposed to be the sensual spanking you were telling me about? Because I don't think it's working for me."

He slid his fingers into her channel. The air escaped her in a heated rush. "I'd say you were finding it sensual." He showed her his fingers, slick, coated with her cream.

She wanted to deny it, but there was something so sensual about the way Jake moved around her, pacing like an animal, his gaze so intent, so focused, a soft, mesmerizing sound rumbling in his chest. The golden eyes were hypnotic. He licked his fingers and she nearly came on the spot.

Emma tossed her head, aware she was burning inside, a hot furnace of need. And the way he was looking at her, possessively, as if she were *his*, her body belonging to him, was making her even wetter for him.

Intellectually she found her reaction interesting. There was no doubt that her body wanted to submit to his. Her hips pushed back against his hand, wanting more of the erotic massage. She yelped when he brought his hand down once more and then rubbed again. It hadn't hurt, but it did make her body glow, the furnace burning hotter.

"What was that for?"

"Deliberately making me wait before you took your clothes off."

"Is this going to be one of the times you teach me all about adult sex?" Emma asked weakly. "The sex I know nothing about?" She was beginning to think there might be something to his lessons, even though she was trying to be a smart mouth. Her body was on fire, every nerve ending focused on him, every sense heightened.

"Yes. So behave. You're being sarcastic."

"Jake." He was massaging her buttocks, alternating between soft caressing strokes and rougher, deep-tissue massage. The combination made her weak with need.

"Yes?"

"Are you going to make me wait a long time before you take me? Because I'm quite willing now." She was very aware he'd said two hours of her time. Two hours was going to be endless if he didn't pick up the pace and take care of her very needy body.

He laughed softly. "A very long time."

"What if I'm not so receptive a long time from now?"

"You aren't supposed to talk unless I ask you a question."

She tossed her head again, her eyes gleaming at him. "Really? I thought I was being educated. How can I learn if you don't let me ask questions?"

"Emma."

She turned her head to look over her shoulder at him, trying not to laugh. "Yes?"

"Remember that sensual spanking I told you about? You're about to go over my knee."

She hid her smile and tried to look submissive. Her body was so aware of him she could feel his breath on her skin, the warmth of him radiating out when he wasn't even touching her.

"Lie down for me, honey, on your back. Just drape yourself over my desk, keep your ass right on the edge." He guided her to the very edge and then spread her legs apart, taking one foot and tucking it over to the side and pulling her other leg to curl around the other side, so she was stretched out like a feast. Her foot slipped and flayed about, kicking the highly polished wood.

"This is crazy," Emma said. "I can't stay in this position. And you'd better have all the doors locked."

He swirled his tongue in her belly button. "You don't want someone to come in and find me devouring you whole?" His palm slid down her leg and found her foot, guiding it to the small loop of leather he'd attached to his desk. He did the same with her other foot, so she didn't have to hold the pose herself.

Her breasts looked so enticing, jutting up at him, he couldn't resist cupping them in his palms. The soft weight felt like warm silk. He rubbed his thumbs over her nipples as he buried his face in the side of her neck, instinctively biting down in the way of the leopard.

She gasped, shivering, and he licked at the teeth marks. That untamed self inside her leapt toward him, craving more, needing his touch, even his domination. She felt so hot, so unlike her, yet right—exactly right—as if she'd been born for him, to please him.

He pinched and tugged at her nipples and massaged her breasts, and then his mouth covered one soft mound, suckling, a hot, moist furnace that was pure torture. Her womb clenched and her inner muscles clamped down hard, needing. She heard her own soft cry, and it didn't sound anything at all like her.

Jake lifted his head, eyes gleaming with sheer male satisfaction, and then caught her hand and slid it into the loop he had waiting. "Hold that. Don't let loose." He placed her fingers around the loop attached to the other side of his desk.

"You've been thinking about this for hours, haven't you?" she asked, gripping the leather tightly. "Bondage, Jake? Is this my lesson for the week?"

"Hours?" His eyebrow shot up. "Weeks. Months."

He bent his head and licked at her nipples again, first one and then the other, his mouth hot as he suckled at her, tugging with his teeth, laving with his tongue while she arched her back to push herself closer into his mouth. Her hips bucked and she writhed, trying to rub her body against his, to get at his leg or his shaft, anything to relieve the building pressure. But her thighs were spread too far apart, and if she stayed where he put her, she was helpless.

"You aren't ready for bondage yet, honey. You can get out if you start to panic or feel uncomfortable. I never want you to be afraid of anything we do. I just want to drive you crazy until you can't think about anything but me being inside you and when I'll let you have your next orgasm." His smile was a little wicked smirk. "Until you beg me. Begging would be appropriate."

She touched her tongue to her upper lip, panting, trying to remain calm when all she wanted to do was jerk her hands free and grab him. She tried a little snort of derision, but she was already hot enough to start the begging process. "Now what are you going to do?"

"With my new desk ornament?" He licked her belly down to her mound. "I'm going to work. You're an inspiration for me."

Naked, he sank back down into his chair and awakened his laptop. Pulling up a report, he slid his hand up the inside of her thigh, fingers massaging while he read. Emma gasped as every nerve ending went into a frenzy. She hadn't realized how waiting could be so erotic, or how it would feel to be spread across his desk, her body open, completely on display for him, while he frowned at his work, his fingers sliding almost absently over her silky smooth skin, climbing higher and higher until—

He dropped his hand away to do something on the keyboard. Emma released her breath in a little rush of disappointment. He hadn't really touched her, and yet she'd never been wetter or more ready for him. Every point in her body strained for his touch. Her breasts ached, her throat felt stretched and needy, her mouth dry, wanting him to fill it. Her sheath was on fire. She wouldn't be surprised if the desk burst into flames underneath her, and Jake was barely paying attention to her.

She closed her eyes, determined not to let him get to her. The pads of his fingers were back again, stroking her thigh, moving higher. His thumb traced along her wet slit, made absent circles around her hard nub until she moaned and her thighs jumped in reaction. He dropped his hand away from her and continued to read.

A few minutes later, his tormenting fingers were back, this time traveling the same route, making the circles on her inner thighs, stroking and caressing, and then his fingers plunged into her. She cried out as his fingers retreated and returned, over and over, stretching and teasing, dancing inside her, flicking at her hard little bud, sending streaks of fire racing through her body, but never giving her relief. He just built the tension higher and higher until she was stretched on a rack of pleasure so intense she was nearly crying for release.

Close, so close, she reached for the edge, but abruptly he withdrew his hand and sat at his desk, absently licking his fingers while he continued to read.

"The word 'bastard' comes to mind," Emma hissed.

"I was having trouble concentrating all day, thanks to you. I think you deserve a little sensual torture."

"Jake . . ." Emma couldn't stop the faint pleading note from creeping into her voice. Demands weren't going to work with him, but, honestly, she was going to go up in flames. He'd said she had to beg him. Well, that wasn't going to happen.

Jake pressed a button and music flooded the room. He ignored her again and she closed her eyes, listening to the weeping notes, feeling every one of them vibrating through her throbbing channel. She considered allowing her hand to pull free of the leather and drift down to relieve the ache that built and built, but that would be cheating, and she wasn't about to cheat.

His hands circled her thigh and she felt the rub of his shadowed jaw on her sensitive skin. Her eyes flew open. His head nuzzled between her legs, his tongue licking at the insides of her thighs. His teeth scraped, making her muscles tighten. Waves of pleasure wracked her entire body and her sheath was flooded with liquid desire. His hair slid over her skin, teasing the insides of her thighs, her mound and her exposed, hardened nub.

His tongue flicked and she cried out as every muscle tensed and a streak of fire raced through her. His smile was wicked, his eyes molten gold, hooded, heavy with lust. He dipped his head low and stabbed his tongue deep. Her hips bucked. A sob escaped as she writhed under his assault, trying to push herself onto him. He kept his hands on her thighs, holding her pinned to the desk while he feasted on her. He was careful to avoid her engorged clit, careful to keep her teetering on the edge. Every now and then he'd flick the hard bud and scrape against it with his teeth so that she cried out and squirmed.

"Jake." Her voice was a wail now. "I really can't take it."

He pressed kisses into her soft, moist heat. "What do you want, honey?"

"You. Inside me. Just let me—" She bucked again when his tongue made lazy circles around and over her. Her entire body shuddered. So close . . . Just out of reach. If he touched her just one more time, she'd go spinning off into subspace.

He stood up abruptly, leaving her gasping.

"Jake. What are you doing?" She lifted her head slightly to try to watch him walk around the desk again. "Get back here and do something before I spontaneously combust."

"I don't think so. You're not being very good." His hand slid up her belly to tug at her nipples, making her breath hiss out between her teeth. "I think you need to wait."

"Don't I get a safe word? Because I think this is torture."

He laughed softly and tugged on her head until she slid just a couple of inches, straining her arms and legs just a little and allowing her head to hang over the side of the desk. She had no hands, no leverage, leaving her completely at his mercy. "I think we're going to use that mouth of yours for something other than trying to torment me." He cupped her face and kissed her, a long, leisurely, hungry kiss.

He moved behind her head, his impressive erection over her face. Her heart beat faster, her thigh muscles twitched

with arousal and her mouth watered at the sight of him
standing there, long and thick and so on fire for her. She
knew what he was doing. Claiming her. Showing her who
she belonged to. Feeling in control.

She had gone from simply going along with his silly
domination routine to wanting his pleasure above all else,
even above her own. Whatever he needed, she wanted to
provide. Without her hands, Emma realized she had to
really work at understanding how to please him—to pleasure him. And she never wanted him to forget this moment—
or her, and what she could do to him. When he moved into
position above her, she rubbed her face against him, all
over him, almost purring like a cat. She saw his start of
surprise and he stopped trying to take control from her,
allowing her to nuzzle him.

Jake was shocked at the sensations exploding through
him just at the feeling of her face rubbing along his shaft,
at the sensuality of the act itself. He was shocked at how
she loved him, never pulling away, never turning her face
from him. Her eyes went soft, almost glazed, as if by giving him pleasure, she was enjoying herself, even delighting
in her sensual play. His breath nearly stopped when she
took him in her mouth, not deep, just enough to apply slow,
wet heat and soft suction. Just enough for her tongue to
curl and tease around and under the mushroomed head
where he was most sensitive.

She made him soft inside—like mush—when his body
was rock-hard. He looked down at her face, her eyes half
closed, long lashes like two thick crescents fluttering against
her skin, her mouth worshiping him. *Worshiping.* He had
been with a lot of women and none had ever looked like
that. Enthralled with giving him pleasure. Caring that she
took him to another place. Other women had fallen under
his domination and submitted to his will, wanting their
reward—wanting *him* to pleasure *them.* Thinking they

would come away with a ring on their finger and a fat bank account at their disposal.

She kissed the broad, flat head and then along his shaft before sliding her mouth over him again in a slow, loving movement that nearly had him on his knees. She sucked gently, the feel of her tight mouth sizzling along every nerve ending he had. Her mouth left him again so she could give the same treatment to his balls. He was already tight, boiling hot, and she nuzzled, kissed and licked him with that same purring vibration that nearly drove him wild.

He was melting, damn it, turning inside out. She was taking control of him again, making love to him. He felt the emotion wrapping around him like living silk, squeezing him, milking him, tightening around his heart the way her mouth tightened around his cock—strangling him until he couldn't breathe for the pleasure.

He caught her long hair, wrapping it around his fists, startling her. His heart beat too fast, nearly exploding in his chest. His lungs burned for lack of air. He took back control the only way he knew how, taking over, forcing her compliance when she would have given it to him freely, because if he didn't—if he didn't—he would be lost for all time. Her mouth was tight as he slid deeper. Jake thrust his hips closer, his head thrown back in ecstasy.

"Come on, honey, you can do it. Breathe. Take me farther. I love the feel of your mouth and throat squeezing me like this. You want this as much as I do. This is one of those lessons that is very important. Relax your throat for me." He didn't want her to ever know that she had cut him off at the knees with her lovemaking. He couldn't let that happen.

Emma wasn't certain what happened. One moment she was thoroughly enjoying herself, loving him, feeling his response, and the next he was treating her objectively, as if her only reason for living was to service him. Was that his only way of receiving pleasure? She tried to please him, struggling to take his thickness, feeling the need in him, the pleasure bursting through him. Her throat was sore from his size and he controlled every move, which was just a little frightening, but also vaguely exciting to her. His fists were tight on either side of her head, as he slid in and out of her mouth, holding himself deep for a few moments and then pulling back just enough so she could breathe.

The phone rang and Emma froze. Jake released one hand from her hair and hit the speaker phone before gripping her hair again and thrusting more gently this time, urging Emma to continue.

"Yes?" His voice was gruff.

Emma smiled, relieved he wasn't as casual and unaffected as he acted. Deliberately she swirled her tongue around the flared head, teasing the underside. If he could try to keep his mind on his business while she lay naked, sprawled out on his desk with his shaft sliding erotically down her throat, she was going to make certain it wasn't going to be easy for him.

"They've come back with a counteroffer, Mr. Bannaconni, one I think is really exciting as well as advisable to take." Dean Hopkins, the manager of his real estate business, once again called to persuade him to sell. "I took the liberty of beginning to draw up the papers so you would just have to sign them."

"No." The word was clipped, harsh. Jake threw back his head and moved his hips, so close to ecstasy his ears were ringing.

"But, Mr. Bannaconni, we're losing money every month. It's pouring out of here, covering the mortgages on all the property you've bought up, and nothing is coming in. We're not going to get another offer like this."

"No." His voice was hoarse.

Emma flattened her tongue and stroked, humming softly as Jake slid deeper, increasing the vibration, going back to her way of making love to him. He gave a soft sigh of pleasure and she relaxed, focusing completely on his erection, making it her entire world, a playground of sensual pleasure where nothing else mattered to her. She used her lips and tongue and the gentle edge of her teeth, used her throat and her mouth, pouring her love into, around him, so that the world surrounding her receded and even the sound of his voice drifted far away.

She reached her head back farther and the position caused her to be aware of the stretch of her arms and legs, of her neck, and she moaned. She knew he felt it from his reaction. She felt him swell more.

"We're done, Hopkins," Jake hissed and abruptly leaned over to punch the button on the phone again, disconnecting. The action caused her muscles to squeeze him tightly. She didn't fight, although it must have hurt, must have been frightening, the loss of breath and complete control. He hadn't meant to do it. He withdrew, hardly able to breathe himself, let alone walk with his body full and hard and pulsing with desperate need. Her eyes watched him, sparkling emerald jewels, just watched and waited, never condemning, never hating, her body lying open and ready and willing to do anything for him. Not for money. Not for her pleasure. Simply because she loved him.

"Damn you, Emma," he said softly, moving around to position himself between her spread thighs. "You're killing me slowly."

"Maybe I should give *you* a safe word, Jake," she answered, her voice soft.

"What would it be?" He caught her foot and tugged it out of the loop, wrapping her leg around his waist and then repeating the action with the other one.

"Love." She smiled at him, that slow, gentle smile that

left him weak. "I know you won't use it and we can go on like this forever. I want you to be inside me forever."

"What the hell am I going to do with you?" There was soft despair in his voice, a strangled note of love that rasped over his skin like the caress of her fingers.

He thrust into her body, driving through her soft folds, needing to be deep within her, to feel her surround him, skin to skin, the hot flames licking up his legs to his thighs, centering in his shaft as he welded them together. "Stay with me, honey. Right with me." He kept his pace slow, savoring the heat of her, the way he moved inside of her, the way he felt in that moment, almost as if their souls slid against each other. "Give me your hands."

He bent his body over hers, and when she held up her hands, he wove his fingers tightly through hers and stretched her arms over her head, holding her beneath him, covering her, blanketing her, his body driving deeper, wanting to touch her inside as deeply as she touched him.

Her hips picked up his rhythm as he rode her, rising to meet each hard thrust. He was big and he could feel himself bumping against her cervix, pushing deeper, insisting she take all of him. And she did. No matter how much he asked of her, she gave him more. This time he was the one who needed to see into her soul.

"Look at me." He had to know it was there, real or not. He didn't even give a damn anymore, he had to see her looking back at him with love in her eyes.

Her gaze met his and he was lost again. Drowning. Whatever he had been before her was gone and only this man—both man and cat; he didn't know anymore—looked back at him.

"Who am I, Emma?" he challenged softly. "Who's inside of you so deep I'm part of you. Who am I?"

He surged forward again, plunging through the tight muscles, feeling the fire spread up over his belly, threatening to consume him. Her breath hissed out between her teeth and her eyes glazed, but she didn't look away. She kept her gaze locked with his.

"Jake. You're Jake. The man I love with every breath in my body."

"Can you really love who I am, Emma?" He took another dizzying stroke, watching her eyes go opaque.

"Yes." Her hips rose to meet him.

"The man and the cat? The rage? The domination? Can you live with that?" He slammed into her hard. Aggressively. Tearing through her silken sheath to bump hard against her cervix.

She didn't even wince. Instead, she smiled that slow, gentle smile that turned his heart inside out.

"I love everything about you, Jake. *Everything.* But can you live with me—with this? With me loving you? With you loving me back?"

His eyes burned and his throat closed. He held her pinned beneath him, his body thrusting in and out of hers, while his blood sang and the fire ran up from his belly to his chest, burning over his lungs and heart to consume him. He heard his hoarse shout. Her name. Emma. His life. His world. Emma. That was all. That was everything.

Her muscles clamped down on him, raw silk, alive with heat and fire and something much, much more. He didn't know what she did to him, only that when he was deep inside her she took him all the way in, to someplace far beyond what he'd ever known or imagined. He heard her soft cries, knew there would be no holding back, and he let himself go, giving himself up to the sheer ecstasy her body provided. He emptied himself into her, feeling the earth-shattering orgasm ripping through her body, through his, so that for that never-ending moment stolen in time, they were one body, one soul.

Jake stayed draped over her, still deep inside her, spent,

fighting for air, his body sated and limber, stretched out across hers, his arms caging in her head while he buried his face in the softest part of her neck. His eyes burned, his body shuddering. He held her tight to him, his lips pressed against her pulse while she wept for him. If this was love, whatever was between them, he had no intention of ever losing it.

"Jake." Emma untangled her fingers from him. His face was wet against her neck. She stroked caresses over his head, not wanting to make him move, but barely able to breathe with his weight pressing her into the wood of the desk. "Are you all right?"

He lifted his head, his hands framing her face. He looked stricken and his eyes seemed wet, but she couldn't tell if there were tears.

"I swear, Emma, every time I'm in you, the fucking earth moves." He lowered his head and kissed her. Not one of his usual demanding, take-charge kisses, but a long, lingering, tender kiss that left her weak and shaken.

Jake carefully slid his body from hers, helping her to sit on the edge of his desk. His hands steadied her as she swayed a little. "Can you stand up, Emma?"

"Jake?" Emma wrapped her arms around his neck and used him to pull herself into a standing position. She stood, swaying against him, afraid her legs wouldn't hold her. "Next time, I want a bed. I mean it. No floors, no outdoors, no desks—an actual bed."

He laughed softly and hugged her to him. "That's a promise."

She lifted her face for another kiss. "Sex with you is an adventure, but I'm thinking I might be getting too old for it. Give me a mattress and I'll be a happy woman." She looked at the bathroom door. It seemed miles away. "You're going to have to carry me."

"What makes you think my legs are working?" he demanded, cautiously straightening to his full height. His golden eyes searched her face. "I didn't hurt you, did I?"

She smoothed the lines of anxiety from his face. "I'll let you know when you've hurt me, Jake." She slid her arms around his neck and held him to her. "I'm not going anywhere."

"You should, Emma." He buried his face in the fall of silken red hair. She smelled of sex and essentially Emma. She smelled like *his*. "Why don't you want to marry me immediately?"

Emma sighed, savoring the feeling of his body against hers. "Because you still think you have to trap me into staying, Jake. How are you going to believe I love you and accept who you are if you can't trust in me? If you can't accept who you are and believe you're worth loving?"

He swung her into his arms, cradling her against his chest. "You don't have their blood running in your veins like I do. It's hard to trust myself when two monsters made me."

She tilted her chin at him. "Yes, I do have bad blood running in my veins. My father was Trent's nephew. He went to the rain forest to find a woman, seduce her, bring her back to the States and sell her. I don't really think my bloodline is all that much better than yours. And as Trent was very willing to rape me that night, and watch someone else rape me, I'm thinking he's right up there with your enemies."

She smoothed his hair and leaned into him to brush kisses along his jaw and the corner of his mouth. "You made something of yourself, Jake, because you had a code and you've always lived by it. You're strong and you're good and so is that part of you that is your cat. The traits you don't like in yourself will always be there, and like the rest of us who have undesirable traits, you'll have to find a way to overcome them on a daily basis. That's what the rest of the world does."

"You make life seem good, Emma, and it really isn't. You need me to protect you from yourself, otherwise people like Trent—like me—would eat you alive." He set her down in the large, tiled shower.

"As long as it's you," she agreed and went back into his arms.

18

KYLE was officially her son! Emma danced around the kitchen before flinging herself into Jake's arms, nearly knocking him over as he stood smiling at her. A courier had delivered the papers from the lawyer's office in the late afternoon and Emma had burst into tears when she saw the official record.

"I can't believe you managed to do this so fast, Jake. You're a miracle worker. I just signed the papers a couple of days ago."

"I knew it was important to you, honey, and there was no reason to delay it. Fortunately the judge saw it the same way." Jake held her in his arms, using his fingertips to brush the tears from her eyes. He kissed the tip of her nose. "I'd like to stay and celebrate with you, but I have to fire Hopkins and make certain he hasn't done any permanent damage to my real estate business. I've had my secretaries, Ida and Clara, going through the paperwork for me. Ida, in particular, is really good at spotting inconsistencies. Basically Hopkins was used to distract me from the primary target, which we now know was you. But in going over to the other side, he was dumb enough to try a little creative bookkeeping since we were already losing money. He can be prosecuted."

She hid her smile against his shoulder. Jake with his unconventional employees. Ida was nearing eighty years old but was as sharp as a tack. He'd found her in the back office of a small accounting firm some twelve years ago. Her husband had left her years earlier, forcing her back into the work force, and despite being brilliant at what she did, no one treated her with the respect—or wages—Jake thought her due. No one wanted to hire her because of her age, and the small firm had kept her working for minimum wage, so he'd had no qualms about stealing her away from them.

Clara was another misfit. Her husband left her when their fourth child was born autistic. She'd married him right out of high school and had no work experience whatsoever. With her children young and Clara often having trouble getting a sitter, especially for her youngest, she'd been desperate, homeless and trying to acquire skills in order to keep her family together by going to school when she could. Jake had spotted the children in the beat-up car and, furious, had confronted her. He'd hired her on the spot. Found her a place to live and put a small day-care center into one of his office buildings.

Emma had no doubt that the two women would be meticulous in going over every single document, and if Dean Hopkins was stealing from Jake as he suspected, they would find the evidence. She kissed him again, just because he was Jake and never suspected the goodness in himself. He would have said he'd hired Ida and Clara because they were brilliant and loyal, not realizing he had created their loyalty through his own actions.

"The news said the storm is going to be very bad," she reminded. "There's going to be widespread flooding. If you can't beat it home, stay in town so I'll know you're safe."

Jake pressed her tighter against him, hearing that note in her voice, the one that conveyed worry and love, the one he listened for now. Going to his office to confront Hopkins wasn't nearly as much fun as he had anticipated. He'd much rather stay home with Emma and the children now, but he'd put the confrontation off for too long.

"I'll be fine, honey. I'll call you if I think the roads are too bad."

Emma pressed the papers against her heart again. "I love seeing my name on his birth certificate. Thank you, Jake, this means the world to me."

"I'm the one who's thankful to have you as Kyle's mother, Emma." He kissed her again and picked up his briefcase. "If you need anything at all, let Drake know."

"Storms don't scare me," she assured.

Emma watched him leave. Although it was still only late afternoon, the sky had already darkened and the winds had picked up. She wasn't frightened of storms, usually she really enjoyed them, but she did feel uneasy. Knots developed in the very pit of her stomach. Andraya ran into the room, chased after by Susan.

"Mommy." The little chubby arms went up.

Emma bent down to pick up Andraya, and as she settled her against her hip, the little girl brushed against her breast. It hurt. Really hurt. So much so that she immediately put her daughter back on the floor, inhaling sharply. Her muscles ached. She didn't want to come down with the flu and have the children get it.

As the afternoon wore on, her symptoms increased. She developed a sensitivity to sound. The light bothered her eyes. At times her eyes would abruptly change vision, so that bands of color appeared before her eyes. Her joints hurt, cracking and popping with every movement she made.

But more than the physical pain, the soreness invading her body was something much, much worse, something insidious and frightening.

She was very aware of her body. Every curve. Every square inch of skin. The heat building inside of her. The tension stretching along nerve endings. She rubbed at her arms as an itch spread, not over the top of her skin, but *under*, as if something long dormant was rising and trying to get out.

Emma tried to play with the children, but as evening approached she found herself watching the clock, her teeth set grimly, hoping the time would pass faster so she could put them to bed. Her emotions swung out of control in either direction. One moment she was close to tears and the next she was snapping at everyone. Several times Susan asked her what was wrong, and she caught the girl looking at her strangely, as if even her appearance was different.

By dinner time, Emma was certain she was going insane. Her body ached with need. If Jake hadn't gone to his office she would have been begging him to make love to her. Her breasts ached beyond belief, her nipples hard, brushing against her bra with every step she took until she wanted desperately to rip her clothes off to get some relief. It felt as if a million ants were crawling over her skin, soft, tiny brush strokes feathering up and down every nerve ending. Deep inside, she burned, empty and desperate to be filled. She was hotter than she'd ever been, her temperature rising by several degrees, and not even an ice pack on her neck alleviated the heat.

The brewing storm added to her growing discomfort and unrest. Twice she picked up the phone, and then dropped it back down. She couldn't let fear put Jake in danger. The weather forecasters had been sending nonstop warnings about possible flooding, and already the rain had started.

With the wind picking up, the rain was being blown sideways. She didn't want Jake out in danger because she was uneasy and becoming afraid.

Emma put together a nice dinner, trying to do something positive with the restless energy building up inside of her, but she was ready to crawl out of her skin. It hurt to wear clothes. The sexual need came in waves, each one stronger than the last, so that her skin flushed and she wanted to tear her clothes off and rub her body against anything to relief the terrible pressure.

"Susan, after the children finish and while I do the dishes, do you want to give them a bath for me? They like to play in the tub and it might keep them occupied for a few minutes until I can finish up and read to them." And get everyone out of the way so she could find out just what was happening to her.

"Sure. They're good in the bathtub. I know where all their toys are."

Emma didn't trust her voice. She wanted—no, needed—to strip, to get the weight of her clothes off her too-sensitive skin. She couldn't stop moving. Her body was undulating with need now. The heat was building, the pressure on her most sensitive bundle of nerves causing her hips to seek relief. She wanted to cry with the ache between her legs.

Emma kissed Kyle and Andraya on top of their heads and gratefully sent them upstairs. Hanging on to the sink, she hung her head, taking huge, deep breaths. She could barely walk, her feet aching, the knuckles on her hands burning along with her fingertips. She kicked off her shoes and dropped to the kitchen floor, crawling toward the intercom, terrified now, desperately needing Jake.

Her body moved with a sensuous slide, her bottom lifting, her arms pushing back, as if her body was separate from her mind and she could no longer control it. She had the urge to touch herself, to trace the curves of her body, to find her burning center and alleviate the ache. Her mind screamed for Jake. She needed Jake.

Outside the rain lashed at the windows and her pulse beat in time to the wild rhythm of the whistling wind. The fever built in her blood. Images of Jake filled her mind, naked, his body muscular, demanding, conquering hers. Not the lovemaking she craved from him, but something altogether different. Her pulse pounded deep inside as blood pooled and demanded. Her mind turned chaotic and her hands—oh, her hands—curling, bending, raking at the floor in frustration.

Sobbing, she hit the intercom button. "Drake." Her voice was different. Her throat ached. Was raw with burning need. There wasn't a place on her body that didn't ache. If the lacy material of her bra brushed against her nipples one more time, she might go insane.

"What's up, Emma?" Drake's voice was tense.

She knew he was working to secure the ranch for the storm. Everybody would be. She coughed, felt her hands sliding over her breasts, trying to ease the terrible ache and quickly pulled her hands down. "You have to come here. The kitchen." And God help her if anyone else came. She had to have Drake tell her what was happening. She knew he was the one with all the knowledge of their species. She knew he talked to Jake. Her mother had never said a word about the change, but something terrifying was happening and it had to be her leopard.

Minutes. Hours. Each wave of sexual hunger was worse than the last one. She was nearly sobbing when she heard the door open.

"Emma?"

"Drake." Relief poured into her voice. She hadn't realized just how much she was counting on him to help her. Once she understood, she should be able to manage the intensity of the need burning through her. If this was the way Jake felt all the time, she could understand his need for continual relief.

"Emma, are you all right?" Drake entered the kitchen, took several steps in when the scent hit him hard. He halted abruptly, his fingers curling into tight fists. Deep inside, his leopard leapt and roared, raking at him, clawing deeply in an effort to get out.

"Drake, you have to tell me about what happens to a woman when she goes into heat. Jake started to tell me about it, but I was so certain I didn't have a leopard. You have to help me."

He studied her body from across the room, gripping the back of a chair, nearly crushing the wood, clearing his throat before replying, "You need Jake."

"I know I need Jake. He isn't here, obviously, so you have to help me. Tell me what to do. I can't stand this."

He grit his teeth, fighting down the urge to leap over the table and take her. "None of the men can come in here, Emma, including me. It's too dangerous. Get the kids down for the night and lock yourself in your room. Don't let Susan near you. Everyone of the men, leopard or human, is going to be affected by you right now. You have to stay away from them."

"You're not helping me."

"Damn it, Emma. I'm a male whether I can shift or not. I can't be here." His nails dug into the kitchen chair.

When she peered around the table at him, her breath caught in her throat. His eyes had gone molten, fixed and staring like that of a predator. His head moved from side to side, but his stare never wavered. His body changed, muscular, compact, so strong. She felt the emptiness pulsing between her thighs as she stared at each breath he took.

Drake backed away from her, almost to the door, as she crawled forward. "I have to get out of here, Emma. Your leopard wants out. She's in heat and you're going to feel everything that she feels. It's intense and difficult, and you'll need Jake."

She didn't want to hear that again. She laid her head on the floor and wept, terrified of being selfish enough to call Jake back in the midst of one of the worst storms of the season. She had to control herself. That was all there was to it. She heard the kitchen door close and she stayed there, right on the floor, as the tide of feeling ebbed, leaving her drained. She slept and dreamt of Jake, of a forest, hot and humid, and the two of them rolling together on the ground, consumed with the need to be as close as possible.

"Emma." Susan's voice called to her. A hand touched her shoulder, gently shook her. "Are you sick? Should I call Drake?"

Emma reluctantly opened her eyes, blinking rapidly. The room was dark. Outside, the wind was howling. She could hear the occasional scrape of a tree branch against the house. Her mouth tasted like cotton. Experimentally, she ran her tongue along her teeth.

"Emma." Susan's hands were gentle as she tried to help Emma sit up. "You're burning up. You're running a temperature."

The touch on her sensitive skin burned, and Emma forced herself not to pull away. "The flu, maybe, nothing serious." It felt serious. Her body ached, every joint, every muscle. She took a deep breath and pushed herself to her feet, using the table to help drag herself up.

Susan rushed to the refrigerator to get her a glass of ice-cold water. "The children are ready for bed. I could try to put them down for you, but they're sort of scared of the storm."

Emma took a long, cool drink. The water felt good on her throat. The symptoms in her body had eased, leaving her with a sore and achy feeling, but at least she could manage it. "I'll tuck them in and read them a story. Thanks, Susan."

As she went up the stairs, she glanced at the windows, wishing she was outside where raw nature was elemental and alive. She felt trapped, caged in. Her skin so tight over her bones she was afraid she'd burst.

Kyle ran to her, throwing his arms around her legs, and Andraya, as usual, followed his lead. Both looked up at her with fear in their eyes.

"It's just a little storm," she soothed. "Come on. I'm going to tell you one of my stories of the two magical children. Let's get in Kyle's bed."

She took their hands and led them into his room. They climbed up onto the bed with her. The storm hit full force just as she began the story. Lightning zigzagged across the sky, sizzling and cracking like great whips, lighting up the roiling black clouds. The force of the wind drove the rain against the windows. The children burst into tears, frightened as thunder boomed loudly just overhead, rattling the windows.

Emma pulled Andraya and Kyle into her arms and looked up as Susan came running into Kyle's room, looking a little shaken as well.

"I want Daddy," Andraya sobbed.

"He's at the office, baby," Emma said, kissing the top of the little girl's head. "He'll be home soon." She hoped he wouldn't, that he'd have the good sense to ride the storm out safe in his office rather than trying to drive a car in the downpour. She patted Kyle's bed. "I was just going to tell the kids a story, Susan. Come join us."

Susan quickly sank on top of the bed, dragging Andraya into her lap and rocking her gently back and forth while Emma rocked Kyle.

"Emma?" Drake's voice called out. "You okay in there?"

She knew he didn't want to come up the stairs and be

close to her. Her leopard was too close, and the heat in her had spread, nearly consuming her. It was all she could do to sit with the children and settle them into bed.

"We're fine, Drake, thanks." Every part of her body was sensitive, and the storm wasn't helping her at all. She could feel every beat of wind and rain, wild and untamed, lashing at her, wanting her to break free, like the storm itself.

Another flash of lightning lit up the room and Andraya burrowed into Susan as thunder roared like a freight train. Far off, a horse screamed. The sound froze Emma's blood. It wasn't the cry of a frightened animal, but the sound of terror and agony rolled into one. She leapt to her feet. Then other horses began screaming, the sound horrifying.

"Drake!"

"Stay in the house, Emma," he called from the stairs. "I'm locking down the house."

An automatic lockdown meant that every window and door closed and locked and an alarm activated. For the first time, Drake didn't post bodyguards in the house, afraid for Emma's safety and ultimately the safety of any of the men who might be foolish enough to touch her in the throes of the madness. Jake would kill anyone who laid a finger on her.

Kyle and Andraya clapped their hands over their ears to drown out the sound of the screaming horses.

"Is there a fire?" Susan asked. "I'm scared, Emma."

"Drake will handle it," Emma said calmly. She tucked Kyle beneath the blankets and began to tell them the story of the magical children.

The loudest horse abruptly ceased screaming, but the sounds of distress continued from the stables. The wind increased in fury and the lights flickered. Once. Twice. The house was plunged into darkness. Both children wailed loudly. Susan's swift intake of breath told Emma her nerves were rattled as well.

"The generator will come on in a few seconds," she said confidently, careful not to betray that fact that her stomach had knotted and nerves fluttered over her heart. She counted in her head. It seemed to take an extraordinary amount of time. The lights flickered. Went off. Came back on, dim, and then the house was once more plunged into darkness.

Emma hit the intercom button. Nothing happened.

Her uneasiness exploded into full-blown fear. "Okay, kids," she said, keeping her voice even and calm. "We're going to go on a little adventure. I'm going to show you a secret place and you'll stay there with Susan until Daddy comes home. We can even sleep there. Susan, get their favorite blankets."

"I can't see in the dark," Susan said, her voice trembling.

Emma could see very well, although her eyesight was more in bands of heat. Information poured over her as if she had antennae, telling her where all the objects in the room were and where the kids and Susan were. She gathered up the blankets, caught up the pillows and pushed them into Susan's arms. "Everyone hold hands. This is a great adventure."

"Don't wanna," Andraya said. "I want Daddy."

"He's coming," Emma said, uncertain whether it was true, but the fear was now giving way to something else altogether. She raised her head and sniffed the air and scented—*cat. Him.* The leopard who had attacked her at the Bingley party. He was in her house, stalking her children.

Her own leopard leapt and slammed hard against her skin and bones. "We have to hurry," she said urgently. She didn't trust herself to be locked in the safe room with her children. She didn't know enough about her leopard, but it was wild to be free, pacing, roaring, furious that something threatened her children.

She caught up both toddlers and ran from Kyle's room down the hall to Jake's suite, Susan hurrying to keep up. He would hear and he would scent them, but once she had them inside, he wouldn't be able to get to them, not without a blowtorch. She tore open the door to the walk-in closet and pushed his clothes out of the way to get to the secret room.

"Get inside, Susan. There's plenty of room. There's a lantern. Get the kids settled on the mattresses. Lock the door and don't come out for any reason. No one can get to you. There's water and food."

"But you have to stay with us."

Emma pushed her gently inside, reached in and turned on the lantern. The babies clung to her but she quickly pulled them off and gave them to Susan. "We're trusting you with the children, Susan. They're everything to us. Keep them safe."

She shut the door herself, and immediately the sound-proofed door cut off the sound of the children's sobs.

Emma turned slowly, flexing her muscles, her fingers, listening to the popping and crackling of her bones. She was close now. Her leopard. Her other half. "He wants to take our children," she whispered softly, no longer afraid.

Her feet were already bare as she padded across Jake's floor, taking comfort in the scent of him surrounding her. She knew exactly where the other male was, in his leopard form, creeping toward the stairs, thinking himself unknown to her and able to do as he wished. He was strong, as all the males of her species would be, but she was a mother defending her young. She slipped each button from its hole and let her blouse slide from her shoulders to the floor, unhooked her bra and tossed it toward Jake's bed, all the while walking toward the open door.

In the hall she shed her skirt and panties, feeling the cool air with relief on her sensitive skin. She stretched again, resolve filling her. He might kill her, but she would take him with her. He would not get to her children. She padded down the hall on bare feet, silent, her vision superb, her muscles loose and accommodating. She caught the railing with one hand and leapt over it, touching down lightly in a crouch on the first landing above the flight of stairs.

The leopard had one huge paw on the stair, his eyes gleaming in the dark at her. He pulled back, startled as she went to all fours. She flung her head back, her long hair falling around her like a cloak.

The man's face contorted, his chest and hands shifted, so that he was standing on cat legs, facing her, half man, half leopard. Rory, the man who had been paid to impregnate her, to rape and use her against her will, stared at her with vicious, calculating eyes. "You belong to me. You were promised to me."

The heat was nearly unbearable, her body temperature soaring. She should have been embarrassed to be naked in front of him, but the cat in her had already merged so deeply she didn't care. "Get out of my house."

Lightning flashed across the sky, lighting up the landing where she crouched. Tiny beads of sweat clung to her flushed skin. She knew her sex was swollen and moist, her scent calling to him. Her breasts ached, her nipples hard, her breath coming in ragged gasps.

"Look at you. You're in heat. You need me." There was satisfaction in his voice. "Soon your cat will take over and you'll crouch in front of me and I'll have you, both the leopard and the woman. You'll be mine and none of them will be able to do a damn thing about it." His voice was hoarse with sexual tension.

"I won't accept you."

He smirked at her. "You don't have a choice. In case you haven't noticed, I'm quite a bit larger than you."

"Drake will come."

"Drake can't even shift," Rory sneered. "He's useless to you."

"He'll come and he'll bring the other men with him."

"The men are down at the stables where a wild leopard has wreaked havoc with the horses. They'll be a while trying to save Bannaconni's precious horses."

"Your partner."

"That's right. And he can't get in here. You locked the place down, only I was already inside. Your precious Drake didn't scent me."

"You cover yourself with other scents."

"Like skunk." He sounded pleased with himself for outsmarting the other leopards.

"Jake will hunt you down and kill you."

"He'll never find us. I'm from the forest, and once we're back there, he'll be on my turf."

Emma's hands curved, knotted, her muscles extending. She reached for her leopard, called it to her, unafraid. Accepting. They were intelligent together. They were strong. She had need of her other half.

The Han Vol Don was upon her and she embraced it rather than fought it. It didn't matter that her skull felt too big for her head and pain pounded through her temples. She reached for the change—wanted it.

Another flash of lightning illuminated the room and he saw her muscles contort. As soon as he saw her body shifting, he took his other form, prepared to fight for her, fully prepared to make his claim on the female leopard. He was fascinated by her aquamarine eyes and held her stare, refusing to look away, showing her he was the male who would conquer her.

Emma ran her tongue over sharpening teeth, all the while holding the male's gaze. She knew she was alluring to him and she used her sensual state to mesmerize him, as the rippling under her skin ran from her belly to her arms.

Adrenaline flooded her body, and with it strength—the strength she would need to defeat the much larger, heavier male. A wave of reddish golden fur broke through her skin, decorated with dark rosettes. Rather than finding the change repulsive, she found the half-transformed state sensuous, deliberately stretching her body again, allowing him to scent her readiness.

Her senses heightened even more and the wildness burst through her. She turned her head as her muzzle formed and fur rippled over the rest of her body. The female leopard came to her four feet, fluid, graceful, sleek. Emma had expected to find herself in the background, but she was there, only now her intelligence was twofold, now her determination and will were backed by the aggressive animal that was her other half.

In the throes of her sexual heat, the female leopard rubbed the length of her body along the banister, spreading her tantalizing scent everywhere, broadcasting to her mate. The male stared with his yellow-green eyes, fixed and focused. His nose wrinkled and he curled his upper lip, grimacing with an open mouth and wide yawn in the response of male leopard claiming a female.

Emma displayed her teeth and snapped at him, warning him to stay away from her, even as she slid her body low to the ground, enticing him by bringing up her bottom. She crouched low, but the moment he took a step toward her, she hissed and curled her lip at him, driving him back away from her as if she were too skittish to accept him.

If she could buy time, lure him away from the stairs and the chamber where the children were hidden, Drake would come to check on them. He wouldn't like that the generator wasn't running as it should be. Even if the horses were in a terrible state, the fact that they'd been attacked by a leopard would send Drake running back to her and he would bring the others. She needed time. If nothing else, she could pull the leopard into the great room where the huge windows were. And if all else failed, she could leap, break the glass and set off the alarm. That would draw all the men to the house.

Her wary gaze focused on the male, she took a step down, continuing to rub her body along the spokes in the banister. The male locked eyes with her, watching her just as warily. She extended her claws and hissed, clearly telling him to back off, that she wasn't ready. The male took a step away from the stairs, cautiously, as expected. No self-respecting male leopard would attempt to force a female until she was receptive to him, not unless he had a death wish.

Emma knew from extensive reading that a courtship between leopards was noisy, but the sounds the female was emitting shocked her. To the male, the vocalization seemed quite alluring. She hissed another rebuff and he retreated further, giving her more room. She continued rubbing her fur along every object she came in contact with. When she reached the floor at the bottom of the stairs, she rolled seductively and stretched.

The male approached, chuffing softly, trying to entice her, and she immediately leapt to her feet, delivering a swipe toward him with her outstretched claws. The male circled her as she continued to tease and play in the seductive manner of the leopard during courtship. She could smell him, a blend of cat, sex and man, all rolled together.

She rolled again, trying to ease her way from the stairs, leading the male toward the great room where the windows were larger and much more abundant. Every few steps she crouched, nearly offering herself to him, but when he tried to come in close to rub his body along hers, she swung her head, hissing, raking with claws, forcing him to leap away from her.

His circles became tighter as they passed the marbled

foyer that opened into the enormous great room. As lightning whipped across the sky, the floor gleamed for a brief moment, white with small threads of gold running through it. Propelled by the fury of the storm and the enticing scent she was giving off, the male rushed her, broadsiding her without warning.

Emma staggered, using her flexible spine to turn even as she went down. The male was on her in an instant, gripping her neck with his teeth, biting down hard enough to draw blood as he blanketed her, using his superior weight to crush her body beneath his and hold down. Emma slashed with her claws, trying to rake his belly or sides, going for his legs, but the teeth drove deeper, trying to force her to submit.

She fought with everything in her, continually attempting to rear up like a horse on her hind legs to throw him off, using the powerful ropes and bands of muscles to aid her. Blood ran down the back of her neck and seeped into her fur, the smell of it overpowering in the room. The male leapt away to keep from killing her as she thrashed and raked at him. He knocked her back with a heavy paw, the claws raking her side again, the blow hard enough to knock the female sideways. She rolled and came up on her feet, head down, sides heaving.

Emma knew another battle was imminent and she would lose. She had to find a way to kill him. She hadn't expected his superior strength. In her leopard form she felt so powerful and strong, and she had thought she could match him in battle. He had lived most of his life in the rain forest, and he'd been shifting for years. She was new to it and had no real experience fighting.

She turned her head slowly and looked into his eyes. Her heart slammed hard in her chest. She felt her leopard pull back as well. The yellow-green eyes held triumph, gleamed at her with evil satisfaction. He was wearing her down, exhausting her, and then he would have his way. He was fully leopard now, even his cunning intelligence defeated by the maddening thrall that was on him.

The male began circling again, vocalizing his interest, his eyes staring directly into hers. She hissed, warning him off, turning with him to prevent him leaping onto her back again. Behind her, she heard the roar of another male. Rory spun, his accordion spine giving him the ability to nearly fold in half. He had recognized the sound before she did and had already launched himself at the intruding male.

Emma caught Drake's scent before she registered the sound of his voice and she flung her body at Rory, slamming into his side in an effort to keep him from getting to Drake, who had only partially shifted. His back legs refused to shift and he was at a severe disadvantage. He'd left the doors to the house open and the other leopards couldn't fail to hear the noisy battle.

Rory turned his fury on Emma, delivering a powerful cuff that staggered her, and then he leapt on her back and drove his teeth into her throat in a suffocation grip. Instantly she went still beneath him, recognizing his ability to kill her. Drake shifted to his human form and stopped Conner and Joshua as they burst into the house.

"Let her go, Rory," Drake said, recognizing the man from the rain forest. A traitor who had thrown out the code their people lived by and had chosen to use his unique abilities as a mercenary, to hire himself out to the one who would pay him the most.

Joshua and Conner, in leopard form, closed in from either side of the male leopard, each roaring a full-throated challenge.

Emma felt the larger male press tight against her, urging her to move toward the entrance Drake guarded. She took a step, then a second, before her legs went out from under her. The teeth raked her throat, caught and bit down again. Rory sunk his claws deep into either shoulder, dragging her back to her feet. Her coat was streaked with blood, dark now with stains. Her sides heaving, Emma struggled to keep moving toward the door.

"Damn it, Rory, let her go," Drake entreated. He stepped aside, but just enough to allow the two leopards to slip through.

Rory took a firmer grip on Emma, half dragging her past Drake. At the last moment he dropped her, whirled and slashed across Drake's thigh with a powerful blow, ripping muscle and tendon down to the bone and dropping the man like a stone. Blood sprayed across the floor and up the walls.

Emma sank her teeth into Rory's leg from where she lay behind him. Even as Joshua and Conner sprang forward, the male leopard had her by the throat, gripping hard, furious now, ready to kill. Conner shifted back in order to save Drake as blood pumped from the massive wound.

Drake shoved at him. "Not me. Save her. If he takes her out of here, he'll kill her out of spite or take her with him."

"Sorry, man," Conner said as he pulled Drake's belt from his jeans and wrapped it around the wounded thigh. "That's Joshua's job now. He can take down the son of a bitch."

Emma heard Drake and her heart sank. She was not going to allow Rory to take her off the ranch. If his partner waited somewhere in the night to help him, they might defeat Joshua, and she refused to allow Joshua to die on her behalf. But she wasn't going with Rory. She moved with him down the wide hallway and through the kitchen toward the open back door. Joshua followed, warnings rumbling in his throat.

Emma gathered her strength, her resolve. Once outside the door, she would force Rory to kill her, or he would drop her. If she struggled, Joshua would leap on Rory and if she was still alive she could aid him, but she couldn't be taken far from the house. Who knew where his partner waited?

The male leopard felt the female tense and knew she was about to resist again, so he opened his jaws and shut them instantaneously, sinking his teeth deeper for a better hold. Warm blood filled his mouth as the night air hit his face. The wind whipped through his fur and the rain slashed at him. The female gasped, her sides heaving, her lungs struggling for air. He was very aware of the male following him, his rival, and knew he had to drag her away from the others in order to give himself fighting room.

The blow hit him from the side, tremendously powerful, enormously strong, as a third male entered the fray with no warning. Even the wind had betrayed him, masking the presence of the huge, fit male with golden, savage eyes that held killing fury. Rory lost his grip on Emma as something inside of him broke and his cat screamed, twisting in the air to come down in a crouch, prepared to fight to the death.

Drake's frantic call to Jake earlier had put him on the road immediately, uncaring of the ferocity of the storm. He had arrived to find the scent of male leopards overpowering and Emma's female screaming in pain. Then he heard Drake's hoarse shout and knew he'd gone down as well. He shed his clothes as fast as he could, summoning the change, racing to intercept Emma's assailant. He hit him with full strength, catching him off guard as Rory emerged from the house, holding Emma by her throat.

Jake swung around in a half circle, changing his direction in midair to follow where his opponent went, arching his supple spine, sweeping out with a lateral sideswipe to catch Rory again, ripping through the thick fur, past muscles and sinew, down to the bone. With the scent of Emma's blood filling his nostrils, Jake nearly went mad, leaping onto Rory's back, digging his claws in and raking at the soft underbelly while he struggled for a death grip on the throat.

Rory fought back ferociously, the two cats twisting and rolling in a fight to the death. Emma staggered to her feet and turned toward the males, took a step in an effort to join with her mate in defeating their enemy, but she went down again. Rory, spun around and rushed her, his one hope of escape.

In that split second, Jake knew he had one recourse—to trust his leopard. He gave himself up to the snarling male, relinquishing control, allowing the leopard to merge fully into his mind. His leopard was on Rory in a second, faster than Jake thought possible, taking him down like prey, sinking his teeth for the suffocating kill and holding him utterly still, dominant, a male leopard in his prime completely unleashed.

19

RORY thrashed and clawed at the earth, but Jake held on relentlessly. He had embraced his leopard, given it full and free rein, and found that he was in as much control as ever. He was just as much a part of the leopard's form as he was in his own form. The leopard was no crueler than he was, no less dominant yet no more so. No matter the form, he was still Jake with good and bad traits, and just as much control.

He held the other male until the breath left the lungs and the heart ceased beating. And he waited still as the dead weight slumped to the ground, holding on to ensure there was no mistake and the man who would have killed or taken Emma was truly dead. Jake released him and padded over to Emma's leopard form. She lay bleeding from her throat, neck, shoulder and sides. Joshua crouched beside her but moved out of his way as he approached.

Jake shifted, uncaring that the rain poured down on his naked form. He lifted Emma into his arms and carried her back into the house. Her leopard looked up at him, shaking her head weakly. He felt muscles contorting as she shifted in his arms. He was amazed at how she was able to do it, injured as she was. She gasped, her cries muffled against his chest as her body protested the additional strain of shifting.

"Where are the children, honey?" There was a note of urgency in his voice.

"Safe room," she croaked, her hand fluttering to her sore throat.

He relaxed until he stepped inside the hall. "What the hell." Jake stopped abruptly at the sight of Drake on the floor with Conner crouched naked beside him. "How bad?"

"He's losing too much blood. I've radioed the helicopter. The pilot says he thinks he can fly him in if the wind dies down a bit. He's meeting us at the helipad."

"The men?" Meaning his all-human hands.

Conner shrugged. "Most of the horses got loose and few were badly injured. They're out looking for them as well as trying to tend to the injuries. A leopard had a lot of fun with them trapped in the stable."

"Joshua," Jake called. "Get clothes for everyone, including Emma. I'll need towels and hot water. Who's the best man we have to guard the children and Susan?"

"Evan."

"Get him here. Let him see the dead leopard. We're going to need an explanation for all of this. Conner, hang in there until I get Emma situated. I need to see how bad her wounds are."

"I've got this under control," Conner assured.

"Fucking bastard," Jake muttered as he bent down, preparing to set Emma on the couch.

She gripped his neck. "I'm bleeding. We'll ruin it."

"Don't be silly. Who gives a damn about the couch? I need to look at you. Hold still, honey." His hands were gentle as they probed at the wounds marring her soft skin. There was no arterial blood. Most of the rake marks were deep enough to draw blood but not to leave scars. The bite marks on her neck and throat had a few punctures that worried him, but Rory had been careful to miss anything vital. He hadn't wanted to kill a female.

He tossed a blanket over her, heedless of her blood getting on it, and crouched beside Conner. "How long has that tourniquet been on? You don't want him to lose his leg."

"I already lost it a long time ago," Drake said tiredly. He closed his eyes. "My leopard can't hold on forever, Jake, and this isn't a bad way to go."

"Fuck that," Jake snapped. "I told you, we're fixing that leg. When you wake up, you'll be stronger. I'll have the surgeon I've been talking to about this problem of yours on standby."

Drake's eyes flew open. "You cannot talk to a non-species doctor about us."

"I'm well aware of that," Jake said. "Have a little faith." He tapped Conner's shoulder. "You'll be going with him?"

Conner nodded. "Leave him to me, Jake."

Joshua rushed in, clad only in his jeans, still barefoot. He tossed Jake a pair of jeans and another to Conner. "We've got to load him on a gurney and get him moving. We've got a short window, according to the pilot. Now or never. Evan's on the way up. He says it pretty bad at the stables." He placed lanterns in the two rooms and lit a few candles to help. "The generator's been tampered with. I'll have to fix it later."

"Go up and get the kids out of the room. Get some light up there first. They'll be scared. Tell Susan to put them both to bed together and to stay with them. Tell her Evan will be there in a couple of minutes, and Mommy and Daddy will be up to reassure them. Evan can let them know Drake was injured and that's the reason we can't come right away."

Joshua nodded and raced up the stairs to follow the

scent to Emma's room where he grabbed the first thing he
found, gathered towels, soaked washcloths and then called
down the stairs to Jake. "Here's Emma's robe and everything else."

Jake caught the robe and then the towels and wet cloth.
"We'll have to put antiseptic on, as well as treat you with
antibiotics so you don't get infected. Cat scratches and
bites can be lethal just from infection."

Emma nodded. "I'm fine, Jake, just take care of Drake."

"There's nothing we can do until we get him to the helicopter. I want to clean you up and put you in a robe so
we don't scare the kids any more than they already are."
He wanted to check out every single square inch of her
body to make absolutely certain that there were no serious
wounds.

He washed each slash, each puncture, poured fiery io-
dine into the wounds so that she came off the couch and
clawed him, and then he bandaged each one as best he
could before slipping her into the soft robe.

"We've got to go now, Jake," Joshua yelled. "The kids
are in bed, crying a lot, but safe, and Evan's here. We've got
to take Drake while the weather's calmer. The pilot says
move it." He crouched beside Conner, and the two men slid
a backboard under Drake before placing him on a gurney.

"Stay with the kids, Jake," Drake said.

"Shut the fuck up, Drake," Jake said, hating the lump in
his throat. "I'm taking you to the helipad and making certain you live whether you like it or not." If he had one man
he could call his friend, it was Drake. And after all he'd
done, Jake wasn't about to let someone else see to his care.

Jake ran ahead of them, trying not to hear the sobbing
of his children upstairs, but the sound stirred his leopard
just as it did him. Rage swept through him, shaking him
as they rushed through the rain with Drake toward the helipad.

Below the kitchen, in the large wine cellar, something moved in the dark, creeping up the stairs as the sounds of activities faded and the stench of male leopards receded. Silently the animal padded up the stairs and lifted one giant paw toward the doorknob. He had followed Drake from the stables, intending to kill him, but he'd caught the scent of the others as they shifted on the run, and knew he had to stay out of sight. It had been easy enough to slip through the open doors and secret himself in the wine cellar.

The scent of the female was a powerful aphrodisiac, and the leopard kept lifting his head and curling his lip, taking her into his lungs. The sound of crying children bothered him, but the overpowering scent of blood beckoned to everything wild in him. His priorities had been laid out. The adult female first. The infant female second. The male child was the last resort. His paw shifted, became fingers and settled around the knob. With great stealth, he turned it and opened the door a crack and crept out.

There was one bodyguard, the one called Evan, and Susan and Emma were left in the house with the two children. He crept through the darkened halls, avoiding the spills of dim light from the lanterns. The group was at the top of the stairs. The babies were sobbing and Emma tried to comfort them, pacing back and forth with both in her arms.

"Andraya, just wait. Daddy will be right back," Emma said. She spoke into the radio. "Say you're coming back, Jake, let her hear your voice."

Jake shoved his hand through his wet hair. Drops were in his eyes, cold against his skin. The helicopter was already on the pad warming up, blades rotating fast. Justin Right, his pilot, came running out to them.

"Please, Jake. They're so upset."

Emma was so upset. She needed a way to be back in control, to make things right for the children. Jake let his breath out, angry that he couldn't be in two places at one time. "Draya, be a brave girl for Mommy. I'll be right back." He hated this, Emma needing him, the children needing him, sending Drake to the hospital with Conner when Jake should be going with him. Love was a cruel thing, tearing a man's heart out.

"See, Andraya? Did you hear Daddy?" Emma had both children in her arms now, ignoring the way their small bodies rubbed against her many wounds. Their hands dug into the bite marks and puncture wounds around her neck and throat, but nothing mattered to her other than comforting them. Even Susan was crying. She'd held up, trying to be cheerful, alone in the safe room, but once Joshua had come, she'd broken down right along with the children.

Emma alternated kisses between Andraya and Kyle. "Come on, I'll make hot chocolate for everyone."

"Emma, the generator isn't fixed. You can't," Evan said.

She glared at him as the children cried more. "Cold chocolate then. It will be fun. We'll sit at the table, all together. Come on, Susan, come sit with us."

Andraya hiccupped and clasped Emma tighter around her neck. "Don't go."

"I'm not going anywhere, baby," she crooned softly. "We're all going together."

"Come on, Kyle, don't you want chocolate?" Evan asked.

Kyle nodded his head over and over, but didn't look up from her shoulder. Evan held out his hands to take him but neither child would leave Emma. Emma shrugged and carried them, one on each hip, praying her robe would stay on, as she went down the stairs to the long hall. She avoided the area where Drake's blood hadn't been cleaned up. The lanterns didn't throw off much light, so the two children saw very little, but Susan, who was following, gasped aloud.

Evan's hand on her shoulder steadied her and they went on through to the kitchen.

She bent to settle Kyle in his chair. The windows rattled and a howling shriek caused Andraya to bury her face against Emma's neck. Kyle screamed and threw himself at Evan, who immediately wrapped his arms around the little boy.

"The wind seems to be blowing harder," Emma said, uneasy. "Do you think the helicopter got off all right?"

"I'll check for you," Evan said and stepped to the window to look outside at the helipad. "The lights are gone, Emma, so Jake is on his way back."

"Thank God," she breathed and for the first time all day, she truly relaxed. She hadn't realized how much she really counted on Jake and his strong presence. There was just something invincible and powerful about him.

Kyle wiggled and turned boneless, trying to escape Evan to get back to Emma. Evan put him down so he could run to her.

Evan reached out his hand. "Come on, Kyle, give Mommy a break. I'll put you in your high chair. Emma, you look like you're going to fall down, and your neck is bleeding through the bandages."

Emma reached up to press her fingers against the bandages where the puncture wounds were and came away with smears of blood.

Susan gasped. "Here, Emma." She held out a small handkerchief.

Emma half turned toward her when she heard Evan grunt and she spun back around. She saw his large body stagger. Emma ran toward Kyle as Evan toppled to the ground, firing the gun in his hand at a large, snarling cat as it leapt toward Kyle. Emma's hand missed the back of Kyle's shirt as the leopard snatched him on the run and nearly slammed into the door, one hand shifting to open it. Evan rolled over and started to fire a second time, but Emma screamed, "No! You might hit Kyle."

The leopard flashed through the door with her son, leapt over the flowers and the low garden wall to disappear into the night.

Susan screamed. Andraya became hysterical. Emma caught Susan by the shoulders. "Lock down the house and do your best to help Evan. Tell Jake what happened. I'm going after them."

"You can't," Susan protested. "Wait for Jake. You'll be killed."

Evan tried to catch her leg as she ran past him, but he missed, cursing. He tried to get to his feet, but his ribs were broken and it was difficult to draw a breath. Susan crouched beside him, looking warily into the night.

"I can't see her anymore."

"Don't worry. Jake and the others will come running. They had to have heard the shot." He couldn't get to his feet, so he dragged himself to the door in an effort to close it.

Jake, Conner and Joshua burst out of the darkness as if the wild wind had driven them, howling at their heels every step of the way. They were soaked, barefoot and shirtless, running flat-out, yet hardly winded. Susan screamed again and backed away as Jake towered over Evan, his face a mask of fury.

Crouching low, he nearly jerked Evan off the floor, his fists twisted in the front of Evan's shirt, death in his slashing gaze. "Where is she?" He bit out each word distinctly, his teeth sharper, his canines longer in the dim lighting.

"She went after the leopard." Evan had to gasp out every word. "He took Kyle. I couldn't stop her, Jake."

Jake swore, and let go of the man. "Lock the fucking door, Susan." He pressed Evan's fingers around the gun. "Shoot to kill next time."

Jake spun around and ran into the night, Conner and Joshua following close behind. They found Emma's robe just outside the flower beds and they picked up their pace, peeling off their jeans, shedding them just beyond the yard and shifting as they ran.

The scent of blood was strong in a couple of places, along with that of the male leopard. This, then, was Clayton, the other man hired by the enemies and Trent. He was flat-out running, holding Kyle in his mouth. It couldn't have been easy; the boy had to be squirming and fighting, although he might have been so scared he had gone limp.

Jake ran with his heart in his throat and the taste of terror in his mouth. His son. Kyle. He had held the boy in the palm of his hand. Changed his diapers. Fed him. Looked into his eyes—eyes so like his own. He'd told himself he didn't love anyone or anything, yet his son had managed to wrap himself tightly around Jake's heart and refused to let go. Just because Jake hadn't acknowledged the way he felt out loud—or even to himself—didn't mean it hadn't happened. He couldn't live without the boy, without that trust in his eyes and the love and eagerness shining on his face every morning.

He told himself they would have killed him outright if they'd wanted that. No, this was a kidnapping to secure a leopard, or an attempt to exert control over Jake. And they'd have it. He'd do anything to get Kyle back—anything at all. If he had to trade his life for the boy's, he would do it without regret.

Jake couldn't let himself think about how Kyle's little heart would be beating so fast, the feel of the sharp teeth and hot breath on his skin. Bile rose, and he forced his mind away from his son in order to preserve his sanity while he covered the trail.

The direction Clayton took was odd, not toward one of the open areas, where he could leave Jake's land, but deeper into the interior. Twice they came across drag marks where Kyle's heels had forged twin trails in the mud. There were small spots of blood where the skin had been torn off. None of the men looked at each other; they kept running.

Moving as leopards gave them extreme velocity, as their muscles enabled them to run so fast they could actually lift all four feet off the ground and go aerial over long distances. But the leopard form also burned up energy fast. Knowing Clayton was carrying a two-year-old, and would have to readjust his grip often to keep from killing the child, meant that he would be much slower.

Jake's heart slammed hard in his chest as he realized that meant Emma would catch up with the kidnapper before Jake could reach her. She was smaller, requiring her to move her legs more often to cover the same distance, using more energy, but she had no burdens and he knew her, knew her nature. She would be tenacious and she would give herself over to her cat in order to recover their son.

How much of a head start did Clayton and Emma actually have? Not much. Jake and his men had run back to the house the moment they'd heard the sound of the gun, and they'd already been working their way back from the helipad.

The wind whipped through the trees, nearly bending the trunks double. He heard ominous cracking sounds as branches broke under the assault. The full fury of the storm was back, but it only suited his mood, the rage that had been with him since childhood welling up like bubbling lava, hot and thick and tasting of death. His large paws plunged into the swollen stream without hesitation, wincing a little as he thought of his son in the cold water. Had his face gone under? Had Clayton protected him at all?

Jake clawed his way up the embankment and picked up the trail on the other side, hardly aware of the other two leopards running with him. He now understood what Drake had been silently trying to tell him—to show him. A man did what he had to do. He took care of those who were his, protected them and his friends and his community, just did what he thought was right. All the rest of it, all the temper and day-to-day irritations, didn't matter. Just this. This merging of his two halves so that he ran as one, thought as one, enjoyed life and faced danger as one. His behavior was his choice.

The leopard was every bit as concerned for Kyle and Emma as Jake was. It ran, plowing through the mud and puddles, never hesitating to plunge into swollen streams or to leap down treacherous embankments with the danger of flash flooding imminent.

Once he found a place where the male leopard had put Kyle down and his son had tried to run away. There was no blood and no more spots, as if the male might have tried to care for the boy before resuming his run. He saw Emma's smaller tracks inside the big male's. She was gaining on him fast. Jake increased his speed, pushing the others to keep up with him.

EMMA could hear the sound of the male leopard's paw splashing through the mud as they neared a clearing. He knew she was behind him and made no attempt to throw her off the chase, or to drop Kyle and backtrack to fight her. That meant he had a specific destination and wherever it was, he would have the advantage.

She was so afraid for Kyle her heart felt like it was bursting. She could hear him crying occasionally, sometimes loud and screaming, other times his voice dwindling down to a piteous moan. The leopard's muzzle was wet from both the constant rain and her tears, but she never faltered, even when her vision blurred, relying on the radar whiskers to tell her what everything around her was.

The wind was blowing toward her and she could smell the humans now—the enemies—waiting in their expensive trucks to steal her child from her. Cathy and Ryan Bannaconni and the despicable Trent, probably ready to fight over her baby, unless the plan had been for Rory to return with Andraya so they would have two.

She bared her teeth and without hesitation followed the big male leopard and Kyle into the clearing. Emma's leopard skidded to a halt some distance from the group. They were very aware of her, Trent holding a rifle on her, while Ryan Bannaconni lifted Kyle into the air, ignoring the boy's struggles. Cathy smirked, although her fascinated gaze kept shifting toward Clayton as the leopard's body contorted and writhed on the ground for a moment before the man stood, totally naked, all roped muscles and heavy genitals. He stood uncaring of his bare state, inspecting his shoulder where the bullet had kissed him.

As she broke into the clearing and halted, Clayton turned his hungry eyes on her. Emma paid him no attention. Kyle was the only person who mattered to her. She shifted, not quite as fast or as eloquently as the male, but she stood in her human form, naked, only her long hair cloaking her body.

Cathy gasped. Ryan lowered Kyle to the ground, still holding him prisoner.

Trent looked into the trees, shook his head and dropped the rifle to his side, barrel down, a smirk on his face. "I knew it. I knew I was right about her." He looked at Cathy. "You said she couldn't shift. The genes were strong, but she couldn't shift. My family did produce a shape-shifter after all, and a female at that. She belongs to me."

"I don't think so, Trent," Ryan said. "I'm the one with the bargaining chip." He tightened his grip on Kyle and the boy cried out.

"Give me the child," Emma said very calmly. "You're

scaring him." She refused to cover herself up, standing as tall and as confidently as she could. Jake would come. The knowledge was her shield. He would come and no matter what, he would keep Kyle safe from these terrible monsters.

"Come to me and I'll let him go," Ryan answered, holding Kyle by his hair. "A fully grown female is worth far more to us than this little runt." He actually lifted Kyle by his hair a couple of inches from the ground and shook him.

Kyle screamed, kicking out with his feet toward Ryan, his eyes glazed with fear.

Cathy laughed. "He's not quite as stoic as Jake, is he, darling? He probably isn't even a leopard. Jake never made a sound, no matter what we did to him." She tilted her head at Emma. "How stoic are you, dear? When you feel the lash or the cane, are you going to scream like this worthless baby or be silent like Jake?"

Emma refused to be intimidated. She let the other woman see death in her eyes. If she had to die this night, Cathy Bannaconni was dying with her. She would not leave her son in the hands of a madwoman. "You're insane. You know that, don't you?"

Cathy continued to smile, but her eyes went bright and hard, a flicker of cruelty giving her away before she kicked Kyle hard in the stomach. The boy doubled over and would have fallen but for Ryan's grip in his hair.

A low, warning growl rumbled in Emma's throat. She felt her muscles contort and her hands curl. A wave of itching ran beneath her skin and she breathed hard to stave off the change. She forced a smile. "I wonder how you'll scream when I tear out your heart and show it to you," Emma said, very calmly, her voice low, meaning every word.

Cathy went pale and glanced quickly toward Clayton, as if for reassurance that he could stop the smaller leopard should it be necessary. She actually took a couple of steps toward the man but he looked her up and down with contempt. It was obvious she wasn't getting protection from that direction.

"I own her," Trent said. "It was my money my nephew took to bring back her mother."

Emma glanced at Clayton, sensing his barely concealed disdain for the others. They carried the leopard blood, but they weren't shifters, and although Clayton had sold his services to them, he didn't respect or like them. And with her so close to heat, his leopard was reacting whether he wanted it or not. She sent him a small smile of camaraderie, even an alluring one, moving her body in a slightly sinuous manner, as if her leopard needed to get out, hoping for an ally when the fighting came. She wasn't going to be able to take them all.

Emma turned back to the enemies, not waiting to see Clayton's reaction. "No one owns our kind, Trent. You haven't really learned much after all the years you've had to study our species. You're so arrogant, thinking that thin blood running in your veins makes you special. Clayton *allowed* you to buy his services. Jake *allowed* you to torment him as a child. He could have crept into your room any night and killed you both. Have you ever thought about that even once? Probably not because you're not really very intelligent, are you?

"We have retractable claws, and they're sharp, Cathy, sharper than any other mammalian claws. Did you know that? They're rather like stiletto switchblades. We have five on the forefeet and four on the back. A good number to take you out at the breakfast table with, don't you think? And then there are our teeth. We can shear through muscle like knife blades. I'll bet Clayton has more than once considered killing you just to shut your insulting mouth. Jake certainly did. A lot of times. Leopards are silent and cunning and you'd never have seen it coming. We don't do anything we don't choose to do."

Cathy took a step toward her, her eyes flat and cold, teeth set. They were nearly pointed, as if she wanted to shift, her fingers curling into claws tipped with bloodred nails. "Really? You wanted those men all over you the other night?" She tossed her head, her sophisticated style long gone in the pouring rain, making Emma think of a drowned rat. "Are you going to want my nails raking down your oh-so-pretty face? Tearing it off?"

Emma looked down at her own hands, held them out and willed the change, admiring the way her thick fur rippled down her arms and over her hands, how the knuckles curled and long, sharp claws burst from the tips of her fingers. She turned them over and showed them to Cathy. "Your pathetic little nails can hardly compare with the real thing. You're nothing to me, certainly no threat."

Clayton snickered. Trent laughed. Even Ryan gave a snort of derision.

Cathy's face rippled with fury. A shrill shriek escaped and she ripped Kyle from Ryan's hands, slapping the child's face repeatedly. Kyle screamed. Ryan swore. Clayton moved then, coming to life, his speed incredible, just as Emma did the same. Clayton reached Cathy a split second before Emma, shifting as he did so, his giant paw slicing into Cathy's skull, knocking her into Ryan so they both fell. He sank his teeth into Cathy's throat and held in the death grip.

Emma dragged Kyle into her arms as Trent lifted the rifle. She ran for the treeline just as a large male leopard with fiery golden eyes emerged, running at full speed past her, straight at Trent. Two more large leopards flanked him. The sound of the rifle was loud in the night despite the howling wind and rain. She heard Clayton roar and then the night erupted into the horrible sound of growls and screams of agony.

Emma didn't look back. She ran with Kyle in her arms, heading back toward the house. The boy was sobbing and clinging to her, half limp, half mad with fear and pain. "She can't hurt you now. She can't hurt you now," she soothed over and over, stumbling over the uneven ground, trying to shelter him with her body. Her hair was plastered to her skull and face, hanging in dripping tails down her back.

The wind shrieked, carrying the horrifying sounds of the battle. With it came the scent of blood and flesh and wet cat. And the scent of something else. The merest sound like the scrape of a boot against bark. Emma covered Kyle's mouth with her hand, her body going still. She hissed at him to be silent, remembering Trent as she'd shifted to human form. They hadn't been expecting her. They hadn't thought she could shift. They had expected Jake to be following Kyle and they hadn't been in a hurry to run.

Kyle's body went still, as if he knew the urgency and understood the need for silence. His eyes looked into hers, too old, frightened, but determined. She kissed him and hugged him closer as her heart began to hammer loudly in her chest. The leopard had brought Kyle to the clearing on purpose, to draw Jake there. She put Kyle down and put her fingers to her lips, signaling him to remain silent. He was so frightened, she was certain he was nearly frozen to the spot. She crouched beside him.

"Mommy has to help Daddy, baby. You can't move. I know you're scared, but I need you to promise me you'll stay right here and not move, or make a sound." She pressed his little body into the deeper grass.

He looked up at her with his eyes, so like Jake's, eyes that seemed to have more intelligence than possible for his age. He took a deep breath and nodded his head slowly. Emma covered him with nearby branches and twigs and swept up the grass around him, taking only seconds as she hid him.

Then she ran toward the scent, shifting as she went, her body going down to the ground, on all fours, fur sliding over her skin, muzzle rounding and expanding to accommodate the teeth bursting through. The experience was becoming less painful, and faster, and she was getting used to the roped muscles and sinewy body that allowed for much easier travel.

She circled to come at him from behind. There. In the tree, he was easing his weight along a thick tree branch, to try to get a better shot. She could imagine the chaos he was viewing through his scope. Four leopards, three humans fighting to the death in a rolling, clawing, tooth-filled battle. He set the rifle to his shoulder and his eye to the scope, settling his finger on the trigger. She came up behind him silently, stealthily, her gaze fixed and focused, hunting the hunter.

"I see you, you big son of a bitch," the man said softly, satisfaction in his voice.

She leapt, making the jump easily into the tree, landing on his back, her weight slamming him down hard against the knotted branch. He grunted, maintaining his hold on his gun as she bent her head and bit down on his shoulder, easily tearing through the thin skin and muscle, puncturing deep. Blood filled her mouth and she recoiled, horrified.

Emma pulled back and the man rolled, falling from the tree to the ground, discharging the rifle. She felt the bullet burn through her fur and she launched herself again, her weight hitting him full in the chest. He tried to bring the rifle up, and when he couldn't, he used it as a club, slamming it into her shoulder to drive her backward. The leopard raked her claws down his belly and gripped his throat, biting hard more out of fear than aggression.

Emma held on to his neck grimly, tears running down her face. She wanted to throw up, the bile rising. She was so distressed, she had to fight her body to keep from shifting back to her human form. The man struggled, slamming the sides of the leopard with his gun, trying to get it around to fire off a shot. Just when she was certain she couldn't make herself hold him another moment, Jake came rushing at them.

He was on the man in seconds, and Emma fell back, exhausted, sick, disgusted and horrified all at once. She staggered, fell and began to crawl, dragging the leopard's body through the mud away from the scene of death. She didn't want to see or hear any more killing. Once away from the terrible struggle, she shifted, sobbing, bending over to relieve her stomach of all contents in protest of the night's activities.

She could still taste blood in her mouth and she was desperate to rid herself of it. She turned her face up to the sky, allowing the rain to pour over her, wanting it to cleanse her. She wasn't sorry, but she hated that she'd had to make a life-and-death choice for another human being. She tried to scrub the blood off her body, shivering continually, although she didn't know if it was from the cold or from deep revulsion.

"Emma." Jake called her name softly.

She turned to face him. He looked like a warrior, with his glittering eyes and smears of blood decorating him, along with deep scratches, but he appeared to have come out of the battle unscathed for the most part.

"Where's our son?"

She could see the fear in his eyes. His hands trembled as they reached for her. She pointed toward the grassy slope where she'd hidden Kyle. He took her hand and ran, setting a fast pace. In her exhaustion, Emma could barely keep up, stumbling over the uneven ground until he wrapped his arm around her waist and nearly lifted her off her feet, taking them over the last few feet of muddy terrain before he came to a halt, staring down at the little mound. His chest heaved, breath exploded out of his lungs and he sank to his knees.

"Kyle!" Jake tore through the camouflage Emma had covered him with. He dragged the toddler to him, his hands running over his son, brushing the tears from the boys face, unaware of his own as he saw for himself Kyle was alive. "You have bruises all over you. This was never supposed to happen. I'm sorry, Kyle. I should have . . ." He shook his head and pulled the boy tight to his chest, holding him against his heart. "You're safe now, son." He kissed the top of Kyle's head and nuzzled the thick hair with his chin, murmuring soothing nonsense, almost unbelieving that he had his son safe in his arms.

Kyle flung his arms around his father's neck and buried his face against his throat. Jake reached out and swept Emma beneath his arm as well, and they all knelt in the grass and clung to one another, weeping. It was Emma who finally lifted her head and tried to be practical.

"We have to get Kyle out of the storm, Jake. How are we getting home?"

Jake rubbed his face over Kyle's hair one more time, inhaling him, just thankful he was alive. He sighed and made his mind focus on the plan already in place. "We stash clothes in various places. Conner is gathering some for us while Joshua runs back to the ranch to get a truck. He'll be here as soon as he can to take us home."

"The ranch hands will be edgy," Emma said, anxious for Joshua's safety. "If they spot a leopard, they'll shoot him."

"No one will spot Joshua," Jake assured her. "Not until he wants to be seen."

"What are we going to tell the police?" Emma didn't have to ask what had happened to the enemies or Trent. "They're powerful people. They can't just disappear."

"Leopards attacked the horses. They must have come from a private collector or a ranch illegally raising wild animals for hunters and somehow they escaped. The storm must have made them a little crazy."

"I read that things like that can happen—that wild animals are very affected by storms," Emma agreed. "And certainly everyone knows of those awful breeding programs."

Jake nodded. "We do get edgy." He managed a small grin. "And moody. You and Drake rushed to save the horses, along with the grandparents and our good friend Trent who was visiting at the time along with their bodyguard. The leopards attacked you and Drake. Drake's injuries were so severe we called in our pilot in the midst of a terrible storm."

"Which we did have to do," Emma said. "That can be proved and our wounds are consistent with a leopard attack. Do you think Drake will be all right?"

"I had an orthopedic surgeon in place already to check out his leg. I found one who has a history with the leopard species. He thinks he can fix Drake's leg so he can shift again. The wound forced the surgery forward, and maybe complicated it, but at least we already had the right doctor. Winston was meeting him at the hospital. I paid him enough money to continue his research for some time in order to make certain he takes very good care of Drake. The amount of money a success with Drake generates will be more than enough incentive to ensure that Drake not only lives, but that his leg will be one hundred percent."

Emma closed her eyes briefly in relief. "I've been so worried for him I was afraid to even think about him."

"The rest of the story will be that Kyle was attacked in our absence and the grandparents, along with Trent and the bodyguard, hunted the leopards. Kyle has bruises and puncture wounds, as well as skinned heels from being dragged." Jake rocked Kyle gently, soothing himself more than the boy, wanting to hold his son forever, never to let him out of his sight. The boy's soft weeping had stopped and he appeared to have gone to sleep, exhausted by his ordeal. "By the time we arrived, the leopards had mauled and killed them and we shot the leopards. We did burn the leopard carcasses, of course. All wounds will be consistent with leopard attacks."

"Do you honestly think they'll buy it?"

"What else could have happened? We have wounded and dead horses. We have Drake in surgery and you and Kyle alive with very evident wounds, and four dead human bodies, three killed together and one off by itself, dragged from a tree by a leopard from behind, all with wounds consistent with a leopard attack. They'll believe it. They won't be so happy we burned the leopard carcasses, but they'll be very understanding with a man who just lost his parents. Every hand on the ranch will back up the story because they already believe it."

"I just want to go home, Jake," Emma said. "I'm exhausted and still upset and I want to see Andraya. Susan's father should be called and she'll need reassurance too."

He reached around his son and framed her face. "I'm sorry, Emma. I should never have gotten you involved in this."

She turned her face so her cheek rubbed along his palm and she brushed her lips over the pad of his thumb. "He's my son too. You're mine. I'm not letting someone take either of you from me. And that was my choice, Jake."

His heart contracted as he leaned in to kiss her and then

20

JAKE hung up the phone and took a long, thoughtful look at the stairway. Emma wasn't feeling good—again. The news on Drake was very good. All of them should have been elated, but Emma had only given Drake a few encouraging words and handed off the phone to Jake—very unlike her.

The police had come and gone, their investigation seemingly over after a few days of intense scrutiny. Hopkins had already pleaded guilty to embezzlement, hoping for leniency. The children had settled back down. Even Susan had gone back home to see her father. Things should have begun to slip back into normalcy, but his Emma wasn't the same. Twice he'd caught her in tears, although she'd said nothing was wrong. She stayed close to the children, almost as if she was afraid something might happen to them. She hadn't objected when he tightened security and asked Brenda to work more days for a while, which was totally unlike Emma—she never wanted anyone else in her home doing her job.

She was moody and edgy and snapped at him more

than once today. He sighed and walked to the stairs, rubbing the hand rail back and forth as he started up the stairs. The children were in bed—she'd read stories to them until they both fell asleep—and there was no longer a barrier between them, preventing them from talking, but she still refused to come to him and tell him what was wrong.

He took a breath and let it out, all too aware of his heart pounding with dread. She must have been so frightened. And they could have lost both children. He hadn't warned her of his parents, not really. He'd never shared his childhood with her. He never trusted her enough to give that part of him to her, yet he'd expected her to live with him and with the danger surrounding him. He sank down onto the bottom stair and covered his face with his hands.

He couldn't lose her—not now. Not when he knew she was his world. He had gone from a man selfish enough to maneuver her into his life for all the wrong reasons, pretending to love his son, to loving his son because of her. Emma had shown him how to love. She brought joy into his life. Tenderness. Laughter. He looked forward to every evening, to waking up in the morning. He looked forward to life.

She couldn't leave him. She just couldn't. He had to find a way to let her know what she meant to him. He wasn't certain he could take that step yet. He could at least admit it to himself, but was he already too late? It couldn't be. He lifted his head, determination sweeping through him. She was so close in her leopard's cycle and yet she seemed to be fighting it every step of the way, so much so that she was keeping Jake at a distance.

Could that be the problem? She had told him to accept his cat, to merge and become one, but had she become frightened of her own leopard? How the hell did men ever understand women and their moods?

He stalked up the stairs, determined to force her to talk

to him. Emma sat in her favorite chair in her room, the lights off, only moonlight spilling through the window illuminating her face as she stared out into the night. Jake closed the door and locked it, drawing her immediate attention.

"What's wrong, Emma?" he asked quietly.

Her mouth tightened. She took a breath, pushed a hand through her disheveled hair. "Nothing. I'm just enjoying the solitude."

A clear order to leave her alone. He tilted his head, his gaze drifting over her body. She had the allure that females got when they were in need of their mates. When he inhaled and pulled her scent into his lungs, he felt his body stir. She was definitely in her cycle and more than ready, yet she was resisting, sitting stiff, fingers twisting together.

Emma glared up at him. "Quit staring at me, Jake. I'm not in the mood."

"You're in the mood, all right, you just don't want to admit it." His voice purred at her. "If you want me, honey, all you have to do is say so. There's no need to get all moody on me."

Her gaze jumped to his face. "*She's* in the mood. *She's* the one edgy, not me. She's insane right now and I'm not letting her out. She was like a sex kitten, rubbing herself all over everything, and I swear in another few moments she might have let that horrible man mount her. She was that bad."

Now he knew. Her leopard had led the male away from the children, seducing him with her every movement. Emma was ashamed of that. Her scent had been all over the banister and she couldn't help but smell it. She'd scrubbed and polished the stairs three times.

"She's you," he reminded gently. "She wouldn't have allowed any other male to mount her any more than you would."

"I *detest* feeling like this." And she did. Hot. Moody. Out of control. Able to only think of attacking him and having him deep inside her. Was this going to be her life? Sex without love? Was that all there was for her? She didn't want it. Someone else could have it.

Jake slowly unbuttoned his shirt and dropped it to the floor beside her chair. Emma's fascinated gaze jumped to his broad chest in spite of her intention to stay in control. He was all roped muscle, his chest broad, his nipples hard, and she felt her body tighten in anticipation as she took in his tapered waist and the expanse of muscle covering his flat belly.

Emma wanted to groan aloud. Her mind protested, but her body caught fire, was already on fire with need. He was just throwing fuel onto the flames. She didn't want this—mindless, without love, just hot sex the only thing that mattered. Yet how could she stop her own body from betraying her? "What do you want, Jake?" Her voice went husky, every nerve ending on alert.

"You, Emma."

She just stared at him, shocked that his voice could reduce her to raw sexual desire.

His eyebrow went up as he dropped his hands to the opening of his jeans. "If your clothes are particular favorites, you might want to get the hell out of them."

She hated that her body reacted to his order, to the velvet seduction in the crude order, her feminine core going completely liquid. Heat rushed through her body and spread like wildfire. With one hand he unsnapped his jeans and his long, thick, very-aroused cock burst free, drawing her mesmerized gaze. Her womb did that now-familiar clenching and fingers of arousal teased her thighs.

"I'm not doing this. Sex rules everything around here and I'm not going to be like that. I'm not, Jake, so just put that thing away."

She might have done better if she'd managed to stop staring with hunger in her eyes, stark and raw, but she knew it was in her expression, in her mind. Consuming her just like it did every moment these days until she could barely think with wanting him inside of her. Not the gentle lovemaking she craved from him, but rough and wild, and God help her, she didn't want to be that person. She wanted to feel love when he touched her, not madness, not a frenzy that was an obsessive craving.

Never taking his golden gaze from her face, Jake shoved the jeans past his narrow hips, and down his legs to kick the material away from him. "Do you think I don't know what you need, Emma?" He looked utterly confident, supremely male.

"I don't care." She swept her hand through her hair. "I don't, Jake. Do you have any idea what it's like for me to find myself rubbing my body all over the bed like I'm a cat in heat? Do you know what I felt like when I . . ." She pressed her lips tightly together and looked away from him.

"Yeah, honey. I do. You walk through the house and I want to flip up your skirt and take you right there in the middle of the kitchen or on the floor. So, yeah, I know what it's like." He stepped closer. "But I also know it's about you now, not any other woman. I know I'm like this because I'm responding to *you*. Emma. Not just any woman."

She held up his hand to stop him. "I have to get some control."

"No, you don't. You have to let me take care of you."

She leapt from her chair, using her leopard's agility, backing away from him to put the chair between them. He could see and smell the effect he was having on her treacherous body. Her nipples were hard, her breasts swollen and aching. Her panties were damp and useless as any kind of barrier beneath her long skirt.

"It's obsession, Jake."

Jake kept coming, his shaft swaying against his belly with every step he took, a lethal weapon, thick and strong and already leaking small, pearly drops. His scent was an aphrodisiac she didn't need. Her mouth refused to stop watering. She wanted to be like Jake and blame her leopard, but she knew better. She and her leopard were one and the same. She just wanted him. Desperately. She craved his body like some terrible secret addiction that would never go away.

"I don't much care what you want to call it, Emma."

She groaned as his hand surrounded his staff and he stroked it hard, unashamed. Waves of arousal surged through her bloodstream, making her feel lightheaded and dizzy with need. She was grateful she was no longer sitting down or her skirt would have been soaked right along with her panties. She was so hot she was afraid she might spontaneously combust.

She looked so lost. His Emma. Fighting her arousal. For the first time fighting her cat and fighting herself. She needed and he provided. The way of the jungle. The way of their people. His way. "Stop running from me, honey. You're not going to get away."

Jake leapt onto the chair, landing in a crouch, startling her with his sudden aggression. She backpedaled rapidly until she hit the wall and couldn't go any farther. He followed, landing right in front of her, close, so close the pearly drops leaked onto her shirt, his body caging her in, deliberately dominating, triggering her fight reflex. His fingers bit hard into her upper arms as he dragged her even closer, bringing her up onto her toes so he could fasten his mouth to hers in a rough, almost brutal kiss, knowing exactly what she needed.

She kissed him back just as brutally, her teeth sinking into his lower lip, biting down, her nails raking down his back in long streaks, drawing blood.

He groaned, somewhere between passion and pain. "Yeah, honey, that's it," he encouraged. "Put your brand on me." His shaft hardened even more and his hooded eyes filled with lust. "Make them deeper. Brand me as your mate. I want it, Emma. I need it and so do you. Put your fucking brand all over me."

The low growl rumbling in his chest made her womb spasm again. She hated that he was right, that she had to rake his skin and bite at his neck and chest, that she couldn't seem to control the terrible impulses to be rough and crazy and so out of control. She tried to pull back, to find her center but he fastened his mouth on hers again, taking everything she was with his mouth alone. He deliberately branded her, biting down, taking and conquering, overwhelming her with his scent and taste and his very hunger for her.

A tidal wave of lust rose up to meet him and Emma tried to rub her body along his, desperate to feel him inside of her. He ran his hands down her spine to her bottom and lifted her, pushing her mound against his cock, rubbing like a cat in heat. She caught at his shoulders, crying out as sweet pleasure coursed through her body.

He bit out an expletive and tossed her onto the bed, his golden eyes glowing savagely, his leopard and the man rising over her together, one and same, merged so strongly she could see them both stamped into the lust-filled lines in his face. So hungry for her. Ravenous. And she felt the same, her cat rising to edge the surface, moving sensuously along the silk sheets, calling to her mate with every line and curve of her body.

Jake licked at the blood smeared on his lip and her breathing roughened. His tongue flicked out again, tasting the thin trickle, and he reached out, caught the front of her blouse and yanked. The suddenness of his violence sent another wave of arousal pounding through her body. The material parted easily and he swept it aside. Her bra followed, as he easily tore the lace and pulled the scraps away from her arms, leaving her breasts bared for his pleasure.

He tore at her skirt and panties, ripping them from her so that her entire body shuddered with scorching need. She writhed on the bed, her skin so sensitive the sheets sent darts of pleasure sizzling through her veins.

Jake dropped over the top of her, pinning her beneath his hard muscular frame, his mouth crushing hers, driving her lips into her teeth as his tongue speared her mouth. Their tongues tangled as he forced his way in, his mouth bruising, his teeth grazing, over and over as they fed on each other. Her keening noises only drove him wilder, his hand yanking her thighs apart to settle his hips in between, all while his mouth continued to feed at hers.

Emma felt the broad, flared head pushing against her tight entrance and she moaned, bringing her heels onto the sheets and pulling her knees up to give him better access. She was panting now, her body undulating under his, desperate for him to fill her.

His mouth left hers and licked the corner of her lips, her chin, sucked on her neck just below her ear and then bit her earlobe, his hot breath sending another shudder through her body. He marked her throat, licking at the wounds still evident there, leaving his marks covering them. He kissed and sucked his way down her throat to the swell of her breasts as he brought one hand up to cup one creamy mound. He rolled the nipple between his finger and thumb as his mouth nuzzled her other breast and then settled there, his teeth and tongue wickedly nipping and lapping.

Emma cried out, her hands going to his head, yanking him closer by his hair, holding him to her while he bit and sucked and she moaned and writhed under him, arching her body to push her heated flesh into his mouth. All the while his fingers were busy at her other breast, tormenting her nipple, teasing and tugging, even pinching until she was nearly sobbing, wild for him to take her. She spread her thighs wider, pushed with her hips, bucking to force the broad head of his shaft into her hot, moist entrance.

Emma had never felt so aroused, so desperate for him as his teeth scraped at her breasts, sharp, stinging bites that only enflamed her more. She could feel the warm liquid pooling inside her, gushing to engulf the head of his shaft in enticement. She squeezed her inner muscles, making every effort to drag him inside, to force him to fill her and relieve her of the terrible ache that just built and built and yet never eased.

"Please, Jake. *Please*." She felt frantic, afraid she couldn't wait a moment longer. She was stretched over a rack of desire, of hunger, that seemed insatiable. Building, always building, with no relief. "Jake." His name came out in a sob, a plea.

He reared up on his knees and flipped her over onto her stomach in one lightning-fast move. His arm hooked under her hips and yanked her onto her knees, slamming his shaft deep into her without mercy. She was hot and slick and so tight his breath hissed out between his teeth. Pleasure washed over and through him, her tight muscles strangling him with fire, a scorching inferno that felt like a silken fist clamping around him. He drove through her sheath, not waiting for her to adjust to his size, burying himself deep, withdrawing, listening to her ragged breathing as he poised both of them on the edge of absolute ecstasy. So close. He slammed home again, deeper this time, dragging her hips back to him as he thrust forward.

Emma screamed. He was too big for her this way, in spite of her slickness, burning and stinging as he drove through her tight folds. "I can't take all of you," she protested, head down, panting, although even now she was helplessly pushing back against him, desperate for him.

"You're too big." He was. He really was. But she couldn't stop her body from following his as he withdrew and hammered himself deep again.

Her breath rushed out in a ragged cry. "Jake. It's too much." Flames seemed to engulf her from the inside out. Every part of her body was aroused beyond imagining.

He pulled back, giving her a moment of relief and then slammed inside her again, harder and deeper than the first time. "This is . . ." He pulled back and drove home again, her cries of pain turning to sobs of pleasure. He clenched his teeth and tightened his fingers on her hips. "What we . . ." He pulled her to him as he slammed forward. "Need."

He was right. Every single nerve ending in her body was on fire, the pleasure agonizing, taking her outside herself to another realm. He showed no mercy, pounding into her, driving her higher so that her body clamped down on his, and every breath in her was poised, waiting—waiting, but she couldn't go over the edge. It just wouldn't happen. It was agony, her climax hovering just out of her reach.

"Jake, I can't. I can't." She was sobbing now. "I can't get there and my body's on fire. What's wrong with me? I wanted this so much, I thought and I feel like I'm going insane. I can't . . ."

He loosened his tight grip on her hips and pulled out. Emma cried in protest, but he flipped her back over and dragged her thighs apart, lifting her legs over his arms and slamming deep, harder than ever. He filled her completely, more than filled her, so hot and thick, so deep she swore he was part of her body. But even though he set a merciless pace, each stroke sending streaks of fire through her, she only wound tighter.

"I can't," she said again.

Jake reached for her hands, joined their fingers together and pulled her arms over her head. "Look at me, honey. Open your eyes and look at me."

She whipped her head back and forth on the sheets, her fingers clinging to his, her hips feeling his body as he moved in and out of her, desperate for release.

"Emma, honey, open your eyes and look at me. See me." His voice slid over her like a soothing balm, caressing her sensitive skin with strokes of velvet—with tenderness. "We left something out and you need it. I need it."

"I'm going crazy, Jake. I am. She's driving me insane." She wailed it, pushing her hips tight into him, grinding, trying to get release when her body refused to give it to her.

"Emma," Jake said softly. "Love me. I want you to love me." His voice was husky and tender. "You think you're separate from your cat because she did something you found abhorrent, but she saved our child. She saved me. She's you, Emma. And you love me. Every time you touch me, you love me. Look at me and let me see you loving me."

Hot tears burned her eyes, but she forced her lashes up and looked at Jake. There was love etched into every line of his face. It was there in his eyes. He leaned forward and kissed her trembling mouth, his fingers pressing her wrists into the sheets. "I love you, Emma. And thank God you love me."

He continued to thrust hard, pounding deep, yanking her legs to him and drawing up her hips to the angle he wanted, his gaze holding hers so she couldn't fail to see the love there.

Her eyes went wide, glazed over as her orgasm ripped through her, destroying everything she was, shattering her with exquisite pleasure, making her wholly his. She cried as every bone in her body seemed to melt into him, as they shared the same skin, the same body, the same soul.

Jake emptied himself into her, pleasure ripping through his body beyond anything he'd ever known. He collapsed, holding her tight as her body rippled and rocked around his. He buried his face, hot with his own tears, against her throat, which was marked with wounds gotten from defending their son. She stroked his thigh, her fingers running caresses over each scar.

"I love you, Emma. I can't live without you and I don't want to. We can't separate love from sex. You taught me that. No matter if we're feeling like the cats, rough and hard, or more like my Emma, tender and gentle—we're making love. We're showing each other love. It's the same. You saved our lives with your courage. And you gave me the courage to love you."

He lifted his head, framing her face with his hands, his voice filled with emotion. "Do you have any idea what you've given me? I love my son and my daughter because of you. I *feel* love for them. I have friends. Most of all, I have you. I love how you love me, Emma. You take everything I give you and make it into something special. That's what I want to do for you."

He wiped at her tears with his fingertips. "Emma, I'll never be easy. I won't. I'm not going to pretend your life will be a bed of roses, but I can tell you that no man will ever need you more, want you more, or love you more than I will."

She stared up at his beloved face through the tears swimming in her eyes. "We just seem so crazy sometimes, Jake. It isn't normal."

"Why do we have to be normal, honey? This is normal for us. The children are happy. I swear I'll make you happy. You certainly make me that way. Let this be our normal."

She squeezed her eyes closed tight. "She killed that man. I tasted his blood." She began to cry all over again, this time burying her face in his neck. "There's nothing normal about that."

He held her tightly, reaching down with one hand to press her hips tighter against his. "Honey, my cat—me—I killed him. Without you there to protect me, I would have been dead. If not me, Joshua or Conner. You did what you had to do by stopping him. We don't have to like harming others or ending life, but we had no choice if we wanted to survive."

"I didn't know that was a part of me, that I could be like that." She lifted her head and looked at him. "It is a part of me, isn't it?"

"Yes. And I'm grateful. I saw it in you the day Cathy came to try to take Kyle. I know you can protect the children if you have to. And I know you love me enough to do something that abhorrent to you. No one has ever loved me, Emma. No one. Believe me, more than any other person on the face of this earth, I know what a gift that is. Spend the rest of your life loving me, Emma, and I swear you'll never be sorry."

"I said yes."

"Say it again and say we can arrange it immediately."

"You're so relentless when you want your way."

His white teeth gleamed at her and his golden eyes went molten as his hips began to move again in hers. "Always," he agreed, unrepentant.

Emma laughed and rose up to meet him. "Yes, a million times over."

Turn the page for a sneak peek at

HIDDEN CURRENTS

the next novel in the Drake Sisters series
by Christine Feehan

Available in July 2009 from Jove Books!

"HAVING fun, Sheena?" Stavros Gratsos rubbed his palms up and down Elle Drake's bare arms to warm her as he stood behind her at the railing of his large yacht.

All around them the sound of laughter and snatches of conversation drifted past her out to the shimmering Mediterranean Sea.

Sheena MacKenzie, Elle's undercover name—and her alter ego. Sheena could sit at any dinner table and rule, her polish and sophistication and air of mystery guaranteeing she'd get attention. Devoid of makeup and with her hair in a ponytail, Elle Drake could slide into the shadows and disappear. They made a nearly unbeatable combination, and Sheena had done exactly what Elle needed her to do— she'd lured Stavros and kept him interested long enough for Elle to poke around in his glamorous life and see what she could turn up, which so far was . . . *nothing*.

Elle couldn't read Stavros's thoughts and emotions the way she did others when they touched her, and that amazed her. Elle's psychic ability to read thoughts was disturbing most of the time, but there were a very few who seemed to have natural barriers, and she had to purposely "invade" if she wanted to see what they were thinking. Elle rarely intruded, even when she was using her undercover persona, Sheena MacKenzie. But she would have made an exception in Stavros's case. She had been investigating him for months and had found nothing either to clear him or to point toward his guilt.

She glanced over her shoulder at Stavros. "It's been wonderful. Amazing. But I think everything you do is like this and you know it." Stavros always put on the best parties and his yacht was bigger than most people's homes. He served the best food, had the best music, surrounded himself with intelligent, fun people.

In all the months she'd been watching him, she had yet to discover even a hint of criminal activity. Stavros had been kind and generous, giving millions to charities, supporting art and working out deals with his employees in a hands-on discussion that avoided laying off an entire group of workers. She had come to respect the man in spite of earlier suspicions, and she was ready to go back to Dane Phelps, her boss, and write a very strongly worded report that the rumors concerning Stavros were wrong—except that his aura indicated danger and a strong penchant for violence. Of course, some of the men her sisters had chosen as their mates had that same vivid color swirling around them.

"I held this party in your honor, Sheena," Stavros admitted. "My elusive butterfly." He tugged on her arm to turn her around so that her back was against the rail and she was caged in by his body. "I want you to come to my island with me, to see my private home."

Her heart jumped. According to rumor, Stavros never took any woman to his island. He had homes all over the world, but the island was his private retreat. Any undercover operative would have relished the opportunity to enter

Stavros's private sanctum, but her boss had been adamant that she not go if the opportunity presented itself. There was no way to communicate from that island.

Stavros took her hand and carried her knuckles to his mouth. "Come with me, Sheena."

She tried not to wince. Sheena. She was such a fraud. This was the man she should fall in love with, not the worm—he who could never be named, who had broken her heart. Here was Stavros, handsome, intelligent, wealthy; a man who solved problems and seemed to care for many of the same causes she did. Why couldn't *he* be the man she fell madly in love with?

"I can't," she said gently. "Really, Stavros. I want to, but I can't."

His eyes darkened, became stormy. Stavros liked his way and was definitely used to getting it. "You mean you won't."

"I mean I can't. You want things from me I can't give you. I told you from the beginning we could be friends—not lovers."

"You're not married."

"You know I'm not." But she should have been. She should have been settled in her family home with the man destiny had provided for her, but he had rejected her. Her stomach churned at the thought. She'd put an ocean between them and still he tried to reach her, his voice a faint buzz in her head, trying to persuade her to return—to what? To a man who didn't want children, or a legacy of magic. He didn't understand that was who she was—*what* she was. In rejecting her legacy, he rejected her. And she needed a man who would help her, who would understand how difficult it was for her to face her future. She needed someone to lean on, not someone she had to coax or take care of.

"Come home with me," he repeated.

Elle shook her head. "I can't, Stavros. You know what would happen if I did and we can't go there."

His white teeth flashed at her. "So at least you've thought about it."

Elle tipped her head back and looked up at him. "You know how charming you are. What woman wouldn't be tempted by you?" And she was. It would be so easy. He was so sweet to her, always attentive, wanting to give her the world. She reached up and touched his face regretfully. "You're a good man, Stavros."

She was ashamed she'd suspected him of the heinous things she had—human trafficking among the worst. Yes, he'd started out smuggling guns in his freighters, years earlier when he had nothing. But he seemed to have more than made up for all of his mistakes, and as far as she could ascertain, he was truly legitimate. At least she could clear his name with Interpol and the other agencies around the world where his file kept coming up. That would make her feel better about spending these last months working to befriend him and earn his trust.

"I'm hearing a 'but' in there, Sheena," Stavros said.

Elle spread her arms wide, taking in the yacht and the shimmering sea. "All this. This is your world and I can step into it occasionally, but I could never live in it comfortably. I've looked at your track record, Stavros, and you don't believe in permanency. And no, I'm not holding out for marriage with you. I just know myself. I get attached to people, and breaking up is terribly painful."

"Who says we have to break up?" Stavros said. "Come home with me." His voice was soft, persuasive, and for a moment she wanted to give in, wanted to take what he was offering. He made her feel like a beautiful, desirable woman when no one else had. But in the end she wasn't glamorous, sophisticated Sheena; she was really Elle Drake, and she carried her baggage with her everywhere she went.

"I can't tell you how much I want to go with you, Stavros," she said sincerely, "but I really can't."

Swift impatience crossed his handsome face and he blinked, his dark eyes growing a little frosty. "The boats are beginning to take some of our guests back to shore. I need to speak with a few of them. Stay here and wait for me."

Elle nodded. Where was the harm in that? After tonight, Sheena MacKenzie was going to disappear and Stavros would never see her again. Maybe he already knew she was saying good-bye. She couldn't blame him for being upset. She'd tried to stay within boundaries and not lead him on, yet gain his trust enough to get into his inner circles. She'd attended his charities and his parties, and never once had she heard the whisper of illegal activity. If he was the criminal her boss suspected, he was amazingly adept at hiding it, and she no longer believed it was possible.

So why couldn't she fall in love with him? What was wrong with her? Certainly the worm—he who could not be named ever again—was not worth holding out hope for. Was she stupid enough to do that? Hope that he would come after her? That would never happen. He didn't want her. He didn't want her legacy, or her name, or her house—and he certainly didn't want the seven daughters that would come along with her.

No, she had stopped hoping Jackson Deveau would ever come to love or even want her.

Now she just had to stop hurting.

Elle used to envision a life of laughter and happiness with her soul mate. That was before she'd met him. He was a morose, silent, brooding, very dominant male. She knew he could bring stillness and peace to her, or turn her veins to liquid fire with one smoldering look. But he refused to accept who she was—refused to love her as she was. And if he didn't, she feared no other man ever would—or could. Not the real Elle Drake, at least.

Movement caught her eye and she shifted her gaze to see the captain approach Stavros and whisper something in his ear. She was adept at reading lips but she couldn't see his mouth clearly. Stavros frowned and shook his head, glanced at his watch and then over at Elle. She kept her face still and turned her gaze back to the sea. Stavros's bodyguard, Sid, said something as well. He was facing her and she caught his words distinctly.

"It will be dangerous to have her on the island, sir. Think about this. Take her off the boat now and we'll give the driver orders to take her to your villa. They can hold her there until the meeting is over."

Elle's stomach tightened. The bodyguard was talking about her. Stavros shook his head and said something she couldn't catch, but the bodyguard and captain both looked toward her again and neither looked happy.

That built-in alarm, which had saved her numerous times on countless assignments, shrieked at her and she didn't hesitate. She moved quickly through the thinning crowd toward the side of the yacht where the boats were coming in to pick up the guests and return them to shore. Though her purse and overnight bag were still in the cabin down below, Elle was careful never to carry anything in her purse or her belongings that could betray her. She would leave the yacht, and if Dane wanted her to return, she could use the retrieval of her things as an excuse to contact Stavros again.

She made herself small, trying to blend in with the other guests. As Elle she could disappear easily into the shadows, but Sheena stood out. Her heart sped up and a sense of urgency rode her as she wound her way to the departing boats. It wouldn't do to look back and check to see if she was being hunted; she already knew she was. She had one chance to step onto the departing boat as it was taking off. She had to time it perfectly.

Elle slid through the last of the guests waiting for the next boat and stepped onto the platform, holding out her hand to the young man pushing off the departing boat. He grinned and guided the boat back into position so she could step into it. Just as his fingers slid around her hand, she felt another hand catch her upper arm in a firm grip, pulling her back.

"Mr. Gratsos would like the pleasure of Ms. MacKenzie's company a while longer," Sid said smoothly, drawing her much smaller frame against him.

Elle inhaled sharply, feeling the burst of emotion spilling from Stavros's bodyguard. He almost wished he hadn't caught her—in fact he'd considered just missing her, but knew Stavros would have stopped the other boat. She allowed herself to be pulled back without a struggle. The bodyguard was bigger and much stronger than she was, and even if she could have caught him by surprise, what would be the point? None of Stavros's men were going to let her leave the yacht against his orders. She smiled graciously at the driver and looked up at the bodyguard. He wasn't Greek; she wasn't certain exactly where he was from. He spoke with a Greek accent, but there was something off about him.

"You're hurting me." She kept her tone low, very low, her gaze on his face.

He let her go immediately, so fast as if her skin burned him. "I'm sorry, Ms. MacKenzie. Mr. Gratsos asked me to bring you back to him and I was afraid you'd fall into the sea if I didn't keep hold of you. I didn't realize how hard I was gripping you."

He's been afraid she'd make a scene, but strangely, that was all she could get from him. Why was that? How was the bodyguard protected from her psychic abilities in the same way Stavros was? It couldn't be coincidence that two people who worked together had strong natural barriers, and yet Sid's barrier was as strong as or stronger than Stavros's, although it felt different.

Elle flashed him a quick, forgiving smile, very much in keeping with Sheena's sweet personality. "I certainly wouldn't want to fall into the sea with this dress on."

He stepped back and indicated for her to make her way through the small knot of guests. Elle hesitated. "Sid, this is the last boat for shore and they're already boarding. I have to get off." Deliberately she glanced at her slim, diamond watch. "I have an appointment this afternoon."

"Mr. Gratsos will get you to your appointment in time," Sid assured.

That was a lie. He didn't like lying to her. Whatever protection he had built on or had been provided with, his more intense emotions slipped through—unless he'd allowed it, which was possible. She could do that. Sid was worried about her, and if he was worried, she needed to be worried too. She stayed very still, measuring the distance to the boat. She was fast, but she doubted the boat would take her against Stavros's orders.

Sid shook his head. "Don't try it, Ms. MacKenzie. If Mr. Gratsos wants you here, you'll stay."

It was a warning. A clear warning. And had he read her mind? She didn't think she'd given away her thoughts on her face. He looked at her directly, his dark eyes meeting hers. Her heart jumped at the caution, her mouth going dry. "Let me go now."

For a moment regret showed in his eyes, but she knew he wasn't going to cross his boss. "You'll have to take that up with him."

Elle nodded and made her way back toward the shipping magnate, very aware of Sid following directly behind her.

Stavros held out his hand to her, closing his fingers

around hers to draw her to his side. "I thought you were trying to leave me."

"I told you I couldn't stay," Elle reminded him. "I want to, Stavros, but I've already been gone long enough." She was careful to keep her tone light and regretful even as she deliberately opened her senses and tried to psychically read him.

Stavros was very used to getting his way, and trying to force her to comply with his will would be something he might do without thinking it was wrong. It was her first real reprimand, gentle as she could make it when she really wanted to spit fire at him. He seemed to have a natural barrier in place that prevented her from sliding into his mind the way she did everyone else.

His eyes darkened to a stormy color. "I asked you to stay with me. To go to my home with me. I told you, Sheena, I've never brought a woman there."

She took a deep breath. He was taking her to his island and she would be cut off from all aid. Did he suspect her? And if he did, did that mean he had something to hide? Already the engines were starting to rumble and she could feel the deck vibrating beneath her feet. "Stavros, maybe I should meet you there later, tomorrow or the day after."

Stavros patted her hand and led her across the deck to seat her in a plush chair. "We need time together, Sheena. I want to spend a week together, just the two of us, and perhaps you'll change your mind about me."

"I don't have enough clothes for a week," Elle said, trying to be practical.

"I'll send for them."

"I'm not sleeping with you, Stavros. I told you I can't be in a relationship right now, I'm not ready."

"You told me this man broke your heart, Sheena. Who is he?"

She shrugged, suddenly concerned by the steel in his eyes. She had the uneasy feeling that if she named anyone, he might turn up dead. Which was silly, since up until now she'd been very certain that Stavros was no criminal. But then why were all her internal radars screaming at her?

"He's of no consequence."

"He must be, if you won't consider another relationship." Stavros drummed his fingers on the table. She'd seen him do that when he was deep in thought or very agitated. "Did you live with him? How long were you with him?"

"That isn't your business," Elle said firmly.

His eyes narrowed. "I can hire someone to find out these answers for me."

Her heart jumped. He'd had her investigated. Dane had told her to be prepared for that. They had meticulously built her life and provided everything down to college pictures and records as well as a detailed past, but would it stand up to the kind of investigation a man like Stavros Gratsos would demand? Was this the reason he was taking her to his island? Because he'd discovered that she was undercover?

"Why are you pushing me?"

Stavros leaned toward her, his gaze locking with hers. "I want you. I have never wanted a woman the way I want you."

Was that the simple truth? She doubted it. Sheena was beautiful and a woman of mystery and intelligence, the type that would attract and intrigue Stavros. But he wasn't known for falling for women. He escorted them, spent time with them, but he inevitably walked away. Why was he so determined to claim Sheena for his own?

Elle sighed. "You're going to have to get over it, Stavros. I'll be as honest as possible with you. Birth control won't work on me. I have this anomaly that runs in my family. No form of birth control works. Even if you used a condom, chances are still very high that I can get pregnant. I'm not doing that to you. Or to me, for that matter."

His eyes darkened even more as he searched her face for the truth. She actually felt his mind reach out to hers and she pulled back, afraid for the first time that he might be able to read her as she did others. She allowed only the truth of her statement in her mind where he might catch her thoughts. Not only did he look intrigued, he looked pleased.

"You speak the truth."

She nodded. "I have no reason to lie. I really can't take the chance, and since I want children someday, I can't take care of the problem permanently."

"So you didn't sleep with the man who broke your heart?"

She shook her head and looked out toward sea. The shore was fading as the yacht picked up speed, heading toward his private island.

Stavros let out his breath, drawing her attention back to him. "Then I will be your first. Your only." There was deep satisfaction in his purring voice.

"I told you I can get pregnant. No, not can, Stavros. I *will* get pregnant."

"I want children," he said. "I have no problem with you getting pregnant."

Her heart jumped. There it was. Stavros was handsome, charming, wealthy, and he wanted children. She was certain he was psychic. Why couldn't the Drake house choose him? Maybe there was more than one man who would fit with her, and fate had intervened to give her another choice. Stavros Gratsos who was forcing her to accompany him home.

"Stavros," she said gently, "you are the sweetest man, but you're way out of my league. Half your guests wonder what you're doing with me."

"Let them wonder."

Sid approached in his silent way and leaned down to whisper in Stavros's ear. Stavros immediately patted her hand. "We'll be home soon. I have to take this call." He dropped a kiss on top of her head as if they had already settled everything and walked away.

Elle stayed by herself as they moved across the water, but either Sid or one of the other bodyguards hovered close to her, as if Stavros was afraid she might fling herself over-board. She fought with herself, trying to figure out whether she should try to reach out to Jackson. She knew it would take a trauma to reach her sisters across the distance, but Jackson—the worm—could find her just about anywhere. And why was that? Why did it have to be him when he didn't want her? They weren't that far from their destination—Stavros's island was only a few miles off the mainland—and they were rapidly getting closer.

Elle took a breath and let it out. As the yacht approached the island, she could feel a faint buzzing in her head. At first it was annoying, but it began to swell in volume al-most to the point of pain. Pressing her fingers to her tem-ples in an effort to relieve the ache, she caught Stavros watching her. There was a gleam of satisfaction in his eyes, as if he knew of the pressure in her head. She glanced at Sid. Whatever she was feeling, so was he, but he hid it bet-ter. He kept walking with Stavros, his face turned away from his boss, but she knew that same pressure was in his head as well.

She closed her eyes. She needed to reach her sisters and let them know where she was, but the distance was too great. They were back in the United States, and unless the psychic link between them was shattered, they wouldn't feel her. But . . . There was the worm. Jackson Deveau. His psychic connection to her was strong, and if she reached out to him, she might be able to connect and let him know she where she was being taken. Did pride count when one's life might be in danger? Was she really that stupid?

Elle took a deep breath and let it out. The island was getting closer, and the pressure in her head increasing. It was now or never. She closed her eyes and blocked out everything but Jackson. The way he looked. Remote. Broad shoulders. Scars. Thick chest. Piercing eyes filled with shadows. *Jackson*. She whispered his name in her mind, sent it out into the universe.

There was a brief moment of silence, as if the world around her held its breath. A dolphin leapt from the sea and somersaulted back under the glassy waves. Elle nearly screamed when Stavros jerked her from her seat. She hadn't even sensed him coming up behind her.

"What are you doing?" he bit out, his white teeth snapping together. Fury etched the lines in his face.

He knew. Elle glanced toward his bodyguard. Sid knew too. They not only had natural barriers, but they were sensitive to telepathy. *Both of them*. She was in way over her head.

"Sheena! Answer me."

"Let go of me." Elle jerked her body away from him. "I don't understand why you're behaving this way." Even Sheena, as calm and collected as she was, wouldn't put up with being manhandled. Elle glared at him. "I've had enough, Stavros. I want to go home."

She was never going home again. The thought came unbidden but settled into her churning stomach. Once she set foot on that island, her life as she knew it would be over.

Elle? Where are you? Stay alive, baby, any way you have to. Stay alive for me. I'll come to you. I'll find you. Do whatever you have to do.

Jackson's voice was warm, a soft, intimate slide into her mind—into her body. He felt like home. Like comfort. She wanted to fling herself inside him and shelter there. He must have heard or felt the despair in her—the fear.

Stavros caught both of her arms and yanked her against him, giving her a little shake as he brought her up onto her toes. "You will stop this moment unless you wish Sid to put you to sleep. I know what you're doing."

Elle. Answer me. There was a hard command in his voice, almost a compulsion to answer. She gasped when Stavros's fingers tightened hard on her upper arms.

"Don't!" he warned.

Had he heard? She doubted it. But he'd felt the energy vibrating and knew she'd received a response.

Damn it, baby. Just fucking stay alive. Whatever it takes.

Elle glanced at Sid. He held a syringe in his hand. She forced her body to relax, not wanting to go to his island unconscious. "You know about me." She kept her voice even. Very calm.

"That you are telepathic? Yes, of course. I felt it immediately."

"Well, at least I don't have to try to explain that to you," Elle said, spilling relief into her voice. "I hate hiding who I am from the world, but people think I'm crazy."

His fingers relaxed their hold on her, although she knew she'd have bruises. "You don't ever have to hide from me Sheena. I'm very much like you are."

Elle studied his face. Stavros was just a little too okay with kidnapping her to be as clean as she'd first believed him.

"We'll talk at my home," Stavros said, effectively stopping her questions.

Elle remained silent, determined not to allow him to see that she was afraid. She let Sid help her from the yacht to the pier and then into the waiting car. The island was beautiful, lush and green under the late morning sun. She noted the way as they drove along the road up toward the villa.

Once there, Elle turned gracefully on the rich leather seats of the chauffeur-driven car and extended her high-heeled foot out the door, allowing the slit along her glittering gown to slip open and reveal her shapely leg just for a brief flash as she exited the vehicle. Beside her, Stavros tucked her hand into the crook of his arm and guided her up the walkway to the enormous house that overlooked the sea. He stroked her fingers and she glanced up at him, sending him a faint smile before turning her attention to his masterpiece of a house.

The structure was long and sprawling with multiple levels, nearly all of which appeared to have glass walls so the views could be seen from any direction. Since it was reachable only by small plane, helicopter or boat, the island afforded Stavros as much privacy as he wanted. She knew he was trying to impress her, that she had intrigued him, because so far nothing of his world had impressed her. He was used to women throwing themselves at him, and she was different enough to be a challenge. Well . . . that and he somehow had a built-in radar when it came to psychic abilities. It must have been how he'd found his bodyguard and why he had been so drawn to her.

At least she knew why he was so interested in her now, or it might have been difficult not to be flattered by his attentions. Stavros was a handsome, intelligent man, and he knew how to pull out every stop to seduce a woman. He was charming about it, but there was an aura of danger surrounding him, and she never discounted reading auras. He wasn't going to let her go, his black eyes piercing and cunning, a predator unsheathing his claws. She was in trouble and she knew it. Stavros didn't like taking no for an answer.

Her heart beat a little too fast, and she took a couple of

deep breaths to calm the flood of adrenaline. She knew she would be out of range of communication here, completely cut off from all help, especially with that bothersome pain growing stronger in her head. The current felt electrical, interfering with her ability to reach out psychically. There had to be a transmission of some kind to block psychic energy. She wasn't certain it was even possible, but the moment she was alone, she was going to test her theory.

"Sheena?" Stavros rubbed the back of her hand again. "I wanted you to see my home." His voice purred. "Say you're not you upset with me for kidnapping you and bringing you home with me," He paused on the intricate walkway leading to his magnificent home, tipping up her face to stare intently into her eyes.

Elle could imagine that his intent look would make most women feel a little faint. She just felt sick. Whatever Stavros's intentions were, he didn't much care if she agreed or not.

"Does telepathy run in your family?" She wanted him to think only of that ability and no other. She kept herself strictly under control, not giving in to fear when she wanted to raise her arms to the wind and use the force of it to gain freedom.

"Don't talk about that in front of anyone," he hissed, still smiling. "This is for us alone.

Another bid to join them together. She recognized manipulation when she saw it. At least he was still trying to be charming to gain compliance rather than forcing it. She nodded her head, unwilling to try to fight a losing battle. She'd much rather wait and see what Stavros wanted from her. Maybe she could collect information that Dane would find helpful—if she managed to make it out alive.

The door was opened by a matronly woman who managed to look right through Elle as if she wasn't there. "This is Drusilla. She's our housekeeper," Stavros introduced. "Without her we'd all be lost."

Drusilla beamed and smiled a welcome to Stavros while she nodded a little warily at Elle. Elle stepped inside the enormous multilevel glass-walled room. "This is beautiful, Stavros."

"I'm glad you like it, as it will be your home."

Elle heard Drusilla's swift intake of breath and Stavros immediately sent her a glaring reprimand. Elle forced herself to step farther into the room, looking around her. The view was breathtaking, the most incredible she'd ever seen. The bedroom was enormous, with the bed on a platform close to the glass wall overlooking the sea. Several steps down took her to a sitting area with plush, comfortable chairs and a table off to the side, but she noticed that there seemed to a pulley system of some sort overhead. Her heart began to pound. It was an amazing silken cage, a prison beyond her wildest dreams.

She allowed Stavros to lead her through the long, starkly beautiful room and up the wide staircase to a large bedroom. He pushed open the door and gestured toward the four-poster bed. "This will be your room. Mine is just down the hall."

Someone had already placed Elle's small overnight bag on the bed. It looked ridiculous in the rich opulence of the room.

"Stavros, wait." Elle caught his arm. "I really can't stay. I have an appointment this afternoon and I can't be late."

"You're going to stay, Sheena, and you're going to have my babies. I've been looking for a woman like you for years. I'm not about to let you slip away now." He pushed her farther into the room and glanced at his watch. "You are to stay here in this room until I come for you. The door will be locked, Sheena, and you are to stay."

There was no missing the iron in his voice, or the warning. Elle stood very still in the center of the room. He was showing his hand now, blatantly letting her know that not only had he kidnapped her, but that he expected total cooperation. She said nothing as he closed the door, waited to move until she heard the lock snick into place.

Elle opened her bag only to find it empty. Someone had already unpacked her things and put them away. After a brief search, she found her clothes neatly hanging in the spacious, walk-in closet. Elle stripped off her gown and changed into a pair of slim cotton pants and a snug cotton tee. She only took minutes to braid her waist-length hair and pull on her climbing shoes before going to the window.

Below her room, large boulders and rocks formed the cliffs that led to the dazzling sea. Ordinarily the sight would have soothed her, but the way the house hung out over the ocean made climbing dangerous. The window was wired for security, which was interesting to her. She could open the window but an alarm would trigger if she so much as stuck her arm out. With the way the house was built, it was nearly impossible for anyone to break in. So was he keeping women prisoner here at his whim? Had he brought others here?

Elle studied the room carefully, gliding her palm over the walls and bed, seeking psychic energy left behind by any others. She felt nothing at all but that faint, annoying buzzing in her head. As far as she could tell, only the housekeeper had been in her room. Now that she was alone, she needed to send a message home and let them know where she was.

She opened the window and inhaled the sea and salt. The moment the salty mist touched her face she felt better, lighter, more hopeful. Elle lifted her arms and called the wind. Pain crashed through her head. She barely managed to suppress the cry welling up as stars burst behind her eyes and everything around her swirled black. She bent, retching, gagging, staggering toward the bed, pressing both hands to her pounding head.

Stavros was psychic and he had somehow managed to deploy some kind of energy field to prevent psychic energy from being used. Feeling weak, she slid her back down the wall and put her head between her legs, breathing deep to keep from fainting. She wasn't going to be able to summon help until she was off the island or could find the source of the energy field.

Once she could breathe again, she rose unsteadily and dealt with the security, a small beam she redirected so she could slip through the window and cling like a spider to the side of the glass villa. And spiders were much better at clinging to glass than she was. She had to find tiny indentations on each panel with fingers and toes, much like climbing the seemingly sheer cliff faces she often practiced on.

Elle clung to the edge, reaching with her toes, wishing she was at least another inch taller as she tried to gain the roof. For several heart-stopping moments she found herself staring down at the rocks and sea a good hundred feet below her, afraid she couldn't reach and would fall. She studied the distance above her. She would have to lever her body up, using the power of her legs to catch the edge. One chance. That was all she'd have—and she was going to take it.

ALSO BY #1 *NEW YORK TIMES*
BESTSELLING AUTHOR

Christine Feehan

Wild Rain

"Readers...will be seduced
by this erotic adventure."
—*Publishers Weekly*

To escape an assassin, Rachael finds
sanctuary in the rain forest, where the most
exotic of all creatures walks: Rio. But when
he unleashes his secret animal instincts,
Rachael fears that her isolated haven could
become an inescapable hell...

M388T1208

#1 *New York Times* Bestselling Author

Christine Feehan's

Drake Sisters

novels are

"Exhilarating...sultry."
—*Publishers Weekly*

"Enchanting."
—*Romance Reviews Today*

"Spine-tingling."
—*A Romance Review*

OCEANS OF FIRE

DANGEROUS TIDES

SAFE HARBOR

TURBULENT SEA

penguin.com

Also from #1 *New York Times* bestselling author

Christine Feehan

———•———

DARK CURSE
A Carpathian Novel

———•———

Born into a world of ice, slave to her evil father, Lara Calladine knew only paralyzing fear as a child. Only by escaping with her mysterious gifts unbroken would she survive to claim her great Carpathian heritage as a Dragonseeker...

penguin.com